Critical Praise For *Silent Letter*

Winner of French WIZO Prize for Literature, 2014

"A remarkable mature literary work...[about] a mother whose personality pervades the book...The author's impulse is to tell the story the way that it happened, and to memorialize a remarkable mother...But through her, [the book] also illuminates the uniqueness of the author...[the narrative] has a breathtaking flow."

-- Hillel Weiss, Professor Emeritus of Literature at Bar Ilan University, Tel Aviv, *Makor Rishon*

"Read this book and tell others about it: it is a quality book."

-- *Tribune Juive*

"Warmly recommended. Rosie Mayer will be branded in your memory."

-- Raya Frenkel, *Pnai Plus*

"A book like this has never been written...unique. This is an almost breathless stream of consciousness , in which facts, memories, dream fragments, and thoughts are woven together into a single delicate, sensitive tapestry, with latent suspense... The rare beauty of the prose...The author recreates a conflicted and intense feminine awareness...in a marvelous manner, and penetrates the heroine's tender and tortuous thoughts...Thrilling and out of the ordinary."

-- Shmuel Faust, *Makor Rishon*

D1190597

Continued Critical Praise For *Silent Letter*

"Yitzchak Mayer's story is not only more important, but is better than many others. More important because he presents us...with a reality that this and coming generations are incapable of even imagining...The woman must succeed at something which many men would not be able to survive...Not only important, but also a good book...that penetrates the heroine's inner world...A great love story...[and] an appealing read...with an element of a detective novel."

-- Dov Landau, *Ma'amakim*

"The memories of Yitzchak Mayer, a man gifted with a discerning eye, eloquence and courage, a compassionate heart, restraint, responsibility, and deep wisdom. His clever and inspired writing... brightly illuminates the dark in which unseen chapters of Jewish existence occurred in the modern world, before the State of Israel was established. This superb storyteller creates a whole world and skillfully relates the painful chronicle of his family from a totally surprising perspective and a complex dialogue with various worlds...Unreservedly recommended to anyone interested in the endless complexity of the Jewish family, and in engrossing documentation of the days of the Second World War."

-- Rachel Elior, *Blogspot*

"The Mother's restrained monologue has the musicality of a subdued flame...The son's point of view as he looks through his mother's eyes...imbues terrible human scenes with sober, sarcastic tone... This is the essence of the Holocaust, and, perhaps as the human condition taken to an extreme, this is the life itself, replete with contradictions and painful to the point of horror or absurdity...."

-- Chayutta Deutsch, *Mariv NRG*

SILENT LETTER

Library and Archives Canada Cataloguing in Publication

Me'ir, Yitsḥaḳ
[Isha achat. English]
    Silent letter / Yitzchak Mayer.

Translated by Binyamin Shalom.
Translation of: Isha achat.

Issued in print and electronic formats.
ISBN 978-1-77161-243-2 (softcover).--ISBN 978-1-77161-244-9 (HTML).--
ISBN 978-1-77161-245-6 (PDF).--ISBN 978-1-77161-278-4 (Kindle)

 I. Shalom, Binyamin, translator II. Title. III. Title: Isha achat.
English.
-PJ5054.M35453S55 2017   892.43'6   C2017-901269-X
                                                C2017-901270-3

Published by Mosaic Press

Published by arrangement with the Institute for the Translation of Hebrew
Literature (ITHL).
Printed and Bound in Canada
Designed by Courtney Blok

We acknowledge the Ontario Arts Council
for their support of our publishing program
We acknowledge the Ontario Media Development Corporation
for their support of our publishing program

Funded by the   Financé par le   Canada
Government   gouvernement
of Canada   du Canada

MOSAIC PRESS
1252 Speers Road, Units 1 & 2
Oakville, Ontario L6L 5N9
phone: (905) 825-2130

info@mosaic-press.com

SILENT LETTER

YITZCHAK MAYER

TRANSLATED FROM HEBREW BY
BINYAMIN SHALOM

PART ONE

So I am writing, at last, but I have no idea where this will all end up. You are in the North; the South. You are in a basement; in the city; in a tent in a camp; in a prison cell. In France; in Germany; in Poland. You are everywhere and nowhere all at once; off in a forest, running away. I know you are far from a post office. You would write me if you only could, you would send me some sign of life. But you are alive, it can't be any other way. And you'll be back, I know you will. Somehow, you'll suddenly show up, show up wherever it is that I'll be when you finally return, in a place of whose existence I am not aware. Even if the very heavens themselves never recover from the madness and no longer know how to fulfil what their God commanded concerning you and me and the children and everything - in the end, even if there isn't a single soul left in the world who knows whether or not you've returned, no witnesses who might testify as to whether you could even possibly return - you will return. I want you to, so badly. And then, once you return… you'll read what I've written.

I'm not going to write about every day that went by without you. That is simply impossible. I wouldn't even know how to write such facts. What goes on every day without you is beyond my powers of description. I want you to read about the every-now-and-then that keeps life moving from place to place, and then moving on once more to some new, unknown destination. But just the facts, without my presence altogether, the facts that you need to be aware of now - and if that's too much for now, then at least at some point in the future, you will need to be aware of them. I will leave you every page that I write - I do not know where, but when you return, you'll find them, and read them, and then you'll know everything, and, at the same time, you'll know absolutely nothing.

We boarded the train on a Sunday night. We didn't take anything with us, just our winter clothes. I had the big block of laundry soap that you had prepared in my bag. You had sliced it lengthwise with a string, dug a little well out of the two halves and hid the few diamonds that we had left and then put the halves back together, moistening them carefully so that no one would have the slightest idea what lay hidden inside. You had prepared it for me, 'just in case', as you put it, and I needed it. I took along a box of bleach as well, so that if they asked, as you said, I would just tell them I was on my way to do a load of laundry for myself and the boys. There was nothing else, just our clothing and the winter coats with some Swiss francs hidden in the folds. How much? It doesn't matter. It doesn't matter at all anymore. I never asked you how you managed to get a hold of Swiss francs, you just did, the same way you did everything. That's just the way you were.

For a few months, we lived in an apartment on Rue Aix-les-Bains, but we knew none of our neighbors and none of the neighbors knew us. We lived on the top floor and we certainly ran into a few of them, but not one of them ever greeted me with a "Bonjour Madame Mayer" and I never offered a single "Bonjour Monsieur Boulanger" or "Madame Charpentier." As it was, other than 'bonjour' I didn't know a single word of French, and no resident started anything resembling a conversation during the course of which I would have stumbled miserably before we even had a chance to get off the ground.

But what is certain is that someone somewhere turned us in.

Was it the people coming up the stairs as we descended or coming down as we made our way upstairs? Not a single one of them, or so it seems. Perhaps it was the concierge, who never once said hello to me and only ever spoke to the boys, telling them to be quiet as they flew down the stairs in their hobnailed shoes. There wasn't a single nail in them, but she said 'hobnailed' all the same and demanded, in strict, angry tones, that they never laugh even as they competed to see who would descend the curving stairwell first. She would rebuke them for merely breathing. She was wicked. They became accustomed to going up and down the stairs in absolute silence, but she would still tell them 'no audible laughter.' And then they would apologize. They apologized every single time. They didn't laugh once, neither audibly nor otherwise, and they were constantly apologizing. I didn't make them do it. They just picked that up on their own - life itself had taught them. I like to refer collectively to these life lessons and all the other life lessons that followed as 'the concierge.'

You were very respectful towards her, addressing her as though she were some sort of aristocrat of noble descent. I thought you were overdoing it a bit. You were a ragman posing as a scion of the upper class who had fallen on hard times and was living, as the result of some accident or other, in a hovel, when, by right, you should have really been living in a mansion. Was that just some sort of a justification, a mere excuse? You said it suited a researcher, a man of science, someone who worked in a laboratory somewhere. You wanted to camouflage the truth with the closest possible thing to the truth itself. You altered your identity by showing off just a little part of it. You didn't even change the name you brought with you from Romania, that country of origin that left no mark on you whatsoever. You were Romanian by a simple twist of fate and posed as a gentile as a matter of taste, or simply because you had no other choice. It's all the same in the end. And so we too became what you at once both were and were not. You thought it was a rather clever solution - lying by telling a bit of the truth, if not the whole truth. You were always in the habit of innocently dreaming your many dreams at the same time that you employed every bit of cunning at your disposal to interpret them.

Not a single Sunday went by that you didn't give her a flower. And you always accompanied the flower with a quotation from some poem, with an accent befitting any native poet born and raised in France. You liked all that, incurable romantic that you always were. You were generous. You seized every opportunity, real or imagined, to slip her a few francs.

And still someone turned us in.

If I had told you it was she you would have said that you couldn't stand unfounded accusations. So I won't tell you it was her, or anyone else for that matter. I'll just say that someone did it. You know that someone turned you in. I know that the true identity of that someone doesn't concern you anymore. If you could, you would tell me that this sort of information would not undo what was done, would not bring you back to me, to us.

But they turned you in.

You knew it right away. When the scoundrels in the black raincoats stood before you in our narrow room, and the kids emerged in shock from their own tiny bed room and stared at you without saying a word - because that was what their life had taught them, which consisted then of one fear after another in an end-less concatenation, and which forced even a child who had not yet turned six, seven, or eight, to be wise beyond his years. They stared at the men, these men who ad-dressed you with their exaggeratedly benevolent tones, "Monsieur Mayer, would you be so kind as to come with us? Please, Mrs. Mayer, there's no reason to worry, he'll only be an hour or two, just a minor matter that needs to be cleared up with the police, a mere trifle, go to sleep and when you wake up he will be by your side once more." What language, what breeding! And the kids heard what was said and stared at the men and I could see in their eyes that they would never forgive these men in their black raincoats for as long as they lived. You knew this then and you know it now, and the same goes for that anonymous somebody who was to play the most pro-found role in the story of your life, and mine, and that of the boys, that somebody who turned you in - we do not know who that person was and we do not know their name and we have no real proof, we have nothing at all, we just know that it was somebody, no more than somebody! And the concierge said, "they were giggling again."

You did not say a word. You were about to leave with them in nothing more than your house clothes. One of the men then said, "A coat, Monsieur Mayer, it's January, the nights are cold even in Marseille." And you smiled. You wrapped yourself in your worn overcoat and stood still for a moment. It was a farewell stance. You said nothing, hugged no one, kissed no one. You deceived your self and us too into believing that you would only be away for an hour or two. I stood there rooted to the ground, as did the children. The front door, which had remained open the entire time, was shut behind the last scoundrel who walked you out. And then there was silence, a silence so profound that it tore through my very eardrums. Afterwards we just sat there, the children and I, sat on the faded couch until dawn and said not a word, not a word, not a single, solitary word.

They took you away on a Tuesday. Wednesday morning - in a city that came to life as though men in black raincoats had not disturbed its rest during the night - we began to look for you. First we went to the police station right near Rue Aix. But you weren't there. They told us that we should perhaps have a look somewhere else, so I went with the children close to my side so that we wouldn't be separated from each other for even a moment. And so we roamed into the night and the entire next day as well, until an officer whispered to us, in a barely audible voice, that the prisoners from the 26th of January had been taken to the Gestapo building to be interrogated. He said when we go there, that we should never tell them who revealed this secret to us. When the war is over I am going to go look for him, that frightened officer who gathered the courage to whisper to a woman all alone with her children who were swallowed up behind the counter... I will find him and I will greet him with a kiss on the cheek.

We walked over to the Gestapo building utterly exhausted and with our nerves well-frayed. I was convinced that in the entire city no one but me knew the secret address that the officer had whispered to me in a moment of kindness. But there in the doorway stood literally hundreds of people - some men, but mostly women and children standing around with their mothers. They all knew the address. Perhaps the entire city knew it. Well-armed German soldiers in their helmets stood there and maintained order.

A few hours later it was our turn to enter. A man in uniform with his hair carefully combed and his outfit rather well-pressed received us. suit sat at a nearby desk and her long fingers, with their manicured nails, tapped away at a big, black typewriter. Next to the typewriter there was a tray filled with documents that seemed to have been arranged by the hand of some exacting artiste. From time to time she raised her head and listened for a moment to the many things that the uniformed man was saying. Her hair was pulled back and a golden braid rolled off her shoulders, fastened there with a long, black pin just above her neck. She gave off the scent of a perfume that filled the room with a sweet smell that was completely out of place. There were quite a few such well-ordered desks scattered around the room, and at each desk there was a soldier in a well-pressed uniform and a woman typing away with her hair pulled back and her perfume ever-present, and before each one of the soldiers sat people just like me and my children, wearing rumpled clothing and smelling like they hadn't slept all night, people who came alone or two by two, in groups of three, to ask where their loved ones had disappeared to after they were taken from their homes in the night.

All the people posed their questions in near silence. The answers were delivered almost soundlessly. Even those who wept were careful not to weep beyond what their shoulders could bear, or revealed the many of tears they held back. Everything unfolded as though in some temple where those who entered were all warned to worship in shock and sorrow, but with the restraint appropriate to an assembly of the faithful. I was convinced at the time that you were in the bowels of the building with who knows how many other people, in the infamous cells that hid behind this large, long, silent, perfumed room. You could not possibly have imagined what this hell looked like as it prepared to receive those who came along to inquire as to the whereabouts of their lost loved ones.

Erwin spoke up. But even he spoke softly, in his exaggerated politeness. He projected tremendous pain across his small, pale features. His words were well-chosen, his sentences measured, restrained. There was not a stitch of supplication. He said that the men in the raincoats had only mentioned a minor investigation. They had said that our father would be back in no time, and now, two, three days had passed already and he hadn't returned - where was he? The soldier listened patiently and replied that, indeed, it was no more than a simple investigation. Our father would certainly return in no time at all, and our concerns - the concerns of a wife and mother, and beloved sons - were only natural and certainly understandable, but it was also unnecessary and as such, without a doubt, excessive. It would be best for us to go home and wait there. That would be a much wiser approach. The woman next to him raised her head above the typewriter. Her weightless fingers kept tapping away as the hint of a benevolent smile formed across her painted lips. She went back to her typewriter once again. The tapping sound her fingers made joined the tapping sounds of the typewriters going simultaneously. The sounds filled the room like tiny drums that seemed to tirelessly announce and repeatedly proclaim that, in this place, one would do well to give up all hope.

We got up and left. Outside there were many more people standing around, some of them in well-ordered lines as we did before entering, while others were scattered around the square. Somebody told us that we had come in vain because just the day before a number of buses and trucks had departed filled with the prisoners who had been seized in the night between Tuesday and Wednesday,. The entire city already knew of the transit and there was nothing to be gained by waiting around or searching anymore. As soon as we heard the news a number of other people gathered around us and repeated the same thing we had already heard from the first group.

One woman told us that with her own eyes she had seen her husband in the window of one of the buses and that he had waved to her from behind the glass. Another woman refused to believe this even though she swore she had really seen him. There was another man who listened to everything the woman said and nodded his head. He said that someone had thrown a note from the window of one of the buses in which they had been taken away. Immediately the entire crowd tried to seize the note, but it was trampled underfoot after it torn to pieces and covered in mud. It was lost beyond all recognition. Every member of the crowd was certain in their heart that the note had been sent to them alone and they clambered and climbed over one another, but little by little in absolute silence they all gave up finding what it was they were looking for and retreated, one by one making way for all the others. The man who was describing the scene said that somebody came back after a little while and tried to look once more for the note that was gone forever. Maybe he was still there, or he might be back tomorrow or he may well never stop looking for it as long as he lives. Some notes are just like that.

We listened to everything that was said and we stared at all the speakers and believed each and every one of them. Erwin asked the people standing in line if they knew that they were standing there in vain. "They've been told to," the people all replied, each one of them pronouncing the words with their own particular emphasis. An old woman dressed elegantly in black, as though she had been to some ball the previous evening, stared off into the city above the heads of all the people around her and said, as though speaking to herself, "They're standing there because waiting around with no purpose is a sort of prayer that has no answer, and even so the people keep offering up that same prayer since time immemorial." "I never heard such useless talk," some man or woman said, and added "They're standing there because they wouldn't be able to forgive themselves if they didn't stand there, and some of them are standing in line because it is the only thing that they can do for someone whose destiny has already taken them away to that place of no return."

One man, who I guess never quite managed to understand what was going on, said, "It's all very clever. They're standing there because the Germans want them to. It gives hope to all the others to come and ask where their relatives have disappeared to. Then they write their names down and the next day they're going to come round and give them the answers in their homes." "So why are you standing around?" somebody challenged him. "Because I have no home," he replied. "And besides, the Germans are getting one over on me too and they play with me, the same way you knead and roll out a lump of dough. In the end, there's no escape, I'm doing exactly what they want me to do. And so are all of you. So is the entire sorry country of France, just like the rest of the world and all its inhabitants, and even our very Father in heaven, along with His son and the Holy Ghost, and even if they won't admit to it in any church anywhere in the world, they're all just doing what the Germans tell them to do, openly, secretly, or in silence. Either way, the earth below and the heavens above only ever hear the hum of hearts humbled by the occupation." He said his piece and disappeared and went wherever it was he went and was gone.

I hurried home to prepare for our departure with no intention of returning ever again.

The next day, when the sun came up, I sent the boys out by themselves as though they were heading off to school so that we would not be seen emerging together from the building and arouse any suspicions. About an hour later I walked out myself, locked it behind me as usual and headed down the stairs so that if anyone ran into me they would have no idea that I would be never coming back again. I didn't take a suitcase with me, just a handbag. The block of soap was stuffed deep down inside. The hand bag, covered by all sorts of needles and thread. The children had their clothing in their own bags. As I left the concierge spotted me. I didn't see her but I could feel her eyes upon me, as she considered whether I intended to return, or was heading out without any intention of ever coming back. Even a concierge who knows nothing at all knows everything there is to know, all the more so in the case of our concierge who we always treated with such respect and decency. I was extremely cautious, like a person who had been bitten by a snake behaves when they spot a coil of rope. I wanted to avoid someone who could report me to someone else, which would result in the authorities waiting for me when I reached the train station where they would then stop me and ask, "Where are you headed, Madame Mayer?"

The French passport that you had prepared for us in the rooftop apartment was among all the various passports and official documents that you had prepared for the Resistance. It sat inside my handbag along with the boys' French passports, as well. I had already burned the Romanian passports with the names of Madame Mayer and the Mayer children which you had also prepared and then flushed the ashes down the toilet in the communal bathroom on our floor in the building. You were Romanian in every sense of the word, but where are you? I saw no sense in pretending to be Romanian as it clearly had not helped you at all. So I became a Frenchwoman. With my own name. And the children became French too, with their own names. At first you had recommended alternate names, something like DuChenne, or LaChenne, or maybe Chendelle. For some reason I just couldn't get used to being a complete fake. What was wrong with Mayer, I asked you? So you said you'd prepare one with Mayer, too. DuChenne or LaChenne or Chendelle had all gone up in smoke along with that Romanian Mayer. And with that, we were on our way.

We gradually made our way to the station on foot on the last day of the month of January, on a Sunday. Along the way I stopped at a store and bought myself a little suitcase. Then we headed over to another store where I bought another little suitcase for the boys, as well. There was no way that we could leave our building with suitcases in hand but it would also have seemed strange to board a train with absolutely no bags at all. We spent the rest of the daylight hours walking around. The children didn't ask any questions whatsoever. They understood everything. How do children know all that they do? We were lucky, at any rate, and it did not rain. It was cold, but we were wearing everything that a single person could possibly wear. I was sweating. I was alright and my body weighed me down, like any woman about to enter her seventh month of pregnancy. In the evening the streets were almost completely empty. The three of us, the boys and I, looked like any other little family hurrying to get home before the rain started. I told myself that we were in fact a little family hurrying to get as far away from home as possible. I imagined that instead of a few drops, we had already been drenched by the very flood itself. But I realized that the image wasn't mine. I had never been blessed with an intense imagination. Yet three days after you failed to return I started thinking the very way you thought. Dear God, how strong your presence felt, even in your absence.

We boarded the train headed for Saint-Claude, a little town in the mountains not far from the Swiss border. You and I had discussed this in the event that something happened to you and we weren't able to survive the war in Marseille. You yourself had said that in wartime even the most clever invention can suddenly seem colossally stupid, and so we had to prepare our escape route by relying on our own cleverness. Your friends had recommended Saint-Claude. They had contacts there. The place was literally crawling with smugglers and poor souls who might either die or be saved and who had paid for their courage and cunning in cold, hard cash. Your friends, who died for nothing other than liberty and country - or so you believed - recommended them. The poor souls paid and the smugglers collected. It wasn't some elementary school operation rife with youthful innocence that ripened into this mercenary exchange, nor an academy of ethics set in stone either. It was an open-air survival market teeming with the amateurish cunning, riddled with money-hungry rogues and traitors. Still and all, if someone were to ask me whether these smugglers should be cast into the fiery furnaces of hell or welcomed through the pearly gates of heaven - if such things still exist or ever existed at all for that matter - I would recommend that they be allowed into heaven, even though common sense might dictate that I really ought to decide otherwise. But common sense had no place in Saint-Claude in January 1943.

You had sent my sister there, a few months earlier, after the Gestapo - or their Vichy minions, it was one and the same - arrested her husband Jacques. She was to await the first possible opportunity to steal across the border into neighboring Switzerland. She was in the first months of her own pregnancy at the time. You had no idea. She got held up in Saint-Claude of her own free will because she was afraid to cross the border before giving birth. She was sure that Jacques was dead, or as good as dead. "I am carrying an orphan inside me," she wrote me, "I owe it to him to be as careful as possible." And now I was headed there as well, carrying your third child inside me, along with our two boys, in order to await our first possible opportunity to steal across the final border. As far as I could see I only had one chance, there would be no second chance, not for me, not for the boys, and not for your unborn child.

The train platform was almost completely empty. Here and there a few German soldiers stood around with their rifles on their shoulders and satchels strapped to their backs, wearing helmets, of course, along with French policeman wearing mere dark hats and raincoats cinched tight at the waist. There was no mistaking them. All the passengers were already sitting in their respective cars. I planned to arrive at the last possible moment. I was afraid of everything that might happen before the train left the station, even though I knew there was no way to get around going up to the counter to purchase the tickets and getting asked, "Where to?" and "One-way or round-trip?" Erwin was the only one who could handle the task, our son who in just three days had matured beyond anything you could have imagined and had become an independent adult, a manchild. I also knew that there was no way other to display our documents as we boarded the train. I had stopped by the station the day before to check out all the possibilities. I saw that a French police-man accompanied by a German soldier stood there asking people for the documents, one by one, but without paying any particular attention to them or demonstrating any persistent suspicions. I had no choice but to rely on what I had seen. It was time itself that I feared most. It was a fear I had never known before I had become a single mother caring for her children - the two holding my hands and the one still stirring inside me. My sole desire was that they should all survive - the two living and the one yet on its way. Suddenly there was no greater threat or enemy than time itself, because all the horrible things that might God forbid occur would certainly come to pass if there was enough time.

Erwin bought the tickets and nothing extraordinary happened. The German and the Frenchman glanced a moment or two at our documents and then handed them right back to us the same way that they handed back the documents to everyone else who had come before us. I did not dare breathe until we had boarded the train. The papers you had forged for us had passed the test. You had done a masterful job.

I had hoped to find three seats together for the boys and me but there were none. Somebody noticed my swollen belly and asked the others to move over and make room for me. The boys stood out in the corridor of the narrow car, rocking back and forth as the train rattled along, staring through the glass of the windows into the night without any illumination. At the first few stations a number of the people got off the train and I was able to sit a bit more comfortably. Even the boys found seats, and while they weren't next to each other, people made room and were kind enough to change places so that a mother and her sons could sit together. War, which wrecks everything, had somehow not managed to ruin this minor bit of humanity, which suddenly seemed rather major, once all sense of proportion had been lost.

Jackie fell asleep but not Erwin. He kept his eye on me. I wanted to tell him, "Go to sleep and I will too," but I held my tongue.

We did not make a sound. That was what we had decided, the boys and I, even before we left Marseille. It was not part of the preparations that you had gone through with me. To this day, I cannot under-stand how a man who had thought of everything had failed to think of what might happen to a supposed Frenchwoman, whose passport attested to her being a full-fledged citizen, if she were asked a question in a language she completely failed to understand. It is not all that unusual to think of everything and yet fail to consider this minor point. And you were so very intelligent. I did not for a moment consider blaming you. On the contrary, I was certain that there would be so much more yet to come which had been impossible to foresee. It was actually imperative that there be this oversight on your part, because it prepared me and the boys to face whatever trials we might have to overcome in order to survive, even without you.

I was afraid to fall asleep. I waited for the authorities to come around and check our documents. I had no way of knowing how they checked these things once you were on the train. I gradually became anxious as I considered what might happen if the papers that you had forged for us would suddenly fail to make the grade. I had no doubt that they would appear quite valid even to some. But I lacked the strength to be absolutely certain. That is what fear does, it confounds logic to the point that everything that could possibly happen seems to be happening retroactively and drives one insane. My eyes came to rest from time to time on the boys. Erwin could read the fear in my face, I am convinced of that. He would stare at me, and when the fear had invaded every single inch of my lungs, he would suddenly look away, as though he had seen my very blood run cold in my veins. What a fool. "You are a foolish woman," I said to myself. "The child does not see a thing. He can not possibly see it. Who ever said that I was afraid? Who said that the thing that I feel is actually fear?" Jackie's head rested in his hands where they were joined on the back of his seat. His eyelids fluttered from time to time. What was he dreaming? I stared at him through my own fears.

When we ran for our lives from Antwerp, the very first day after the war broke out, he was only four years old.

The war had erupted on a Friday, and within just a few short hours you already knew that we would be travelling by train, and you knew the hour of our departure, and that we would arrive first in Spain and then Portugal and would then get on a boat headed for America. You did not ask anyone for advice - not you - not from me, at any rate. The things that you decided in consultation with yourself in the mad moment when we were being uprooted from our home and being asked 'Where to?' and forced to offer very specific, detailed responses, tripped off your tongue almost by chance, in carefully measured doses, in clipped sentences that added up in my ears to nothing more than what was minimally necessary to ensure that I went along with you without raising any objections. You were only at home for a few moments at a time. I do not know where you ran to, other than over to see your brother Zollie, who, on his own, was never able to decide even the most basic things, like where to shop for food and such. Gizzy, his wife, was the wily absolute ruler in their home - a woman who, if she had been so evilly inclined, could have gone to war with the entire world around her - but she was a good woman, and stood naked, of necessity, before the innocence of her beloved Zollie. It seems that the two of you had apparently arranged and planned the entire trip by train, including how to handle the children, the what, where, and why, and, at any rate. The next morning as we stood jostling on the train platform with all the other thousands of people who were trying to board and could not, her little kids were right there alongside our children, and she was there with Zollie. We were all ready and weighed down beneath more suitcases than we could possibly carry, and all in vain, as you now know, completely in vain, each with our train ticket in our hands.

You had hung little cardboard squares around the children's necks to which you had taped strips of paper and on which you listed their names and the names of their father and mother - our names, that is. Erwin, your pride and joy, because you had managed to teach him what no other child of five or six had yet learned and he already was able to read. He turned the sign hanging from his chest around to look at it and asked you, "What is this?" The bombs had started to fall that Friday, but somehow you found a little pocket of patience in the midst of the chaos. You got down on your knees and explained to him that if the train were to suffer a direct hit and the passengers panicked and started to run every which way so that nobody knew who belonged to whom and who was headed where, they would at least know the name of every child and the names of that child's father and mother, and find some authority who could then return the child to his parents. "But you did not write an address," Erwin said to you. "We do not have an address anymore, my son," you responded, and you got up and kissed Jackie on the cheek, you kissed him but you did not kiss Erwin, because Erwin only needed an explanation, whereas Jackie needed your affection. For all I know, to this very day you never really understood Jackie. You may never have asked yourself what dreams he dreamt during those three awful years that passed between that train ride we all took together, and this trip I was now taking on my own with the boys, as we ran once more for our lives. Most of the time during those three years you were not at home, and you failed to see how your kids were growing up. When you did stop by from time to time you would take a moment to talk to Erwin and embrace Jackie with a love that looked no further for any signs of an intellect which you seemed to think you had bequeathed to Erwin alone. How wrong you were.

My thoughts were all confused. They shifted from that first day, May 12th when we boarded the train with Antwerp, and hurtled forward to the beginning of September. But what was so special about the first day? The train dropped us off in some place called Bondigoux, a godforsaken village in the south of France. We had spent the summer months there, June, July and August, and then suddenly the Vichy 'folks' showed up and led us to the little Municipal Building in Bondigoux. And we did not know why. You carried Jackie in your arms and Erwin walked on his own by your side as I trailed along behind. Erwin was not yet six years old but in your eyes he was already independent and could stand on his own two feet while you still considered Jackie a baby who needed support. Erwin could bear it, but Jackie needed support.

Bondigoux consisted of no more than a few dozen farmers but the Municipal Building, which also doubled as a day school, was filled with a few hundred people, most of whom I am sure were Jews. I was suddenly unable to figure out where they had all been living during the many weeks that they had been waiting for someone to come along and help them make their way across the border into Spain. Where had they found a home? I was completely confused by the fact that I did not recognize most of them even though we had all been cast off in this unlikely place to wait for someone who did not seem to be able to make it.

Zollie and Gizzy were pressed together with us in a single space-the two of them, the two of us, along with all our children. It seemed that we had not developed any connection with the rest of the people who shared our same destiny. In those days since we were only living in order to survive and we had no strength left over to bother trying to experience anything that did not concern us alone. The boys were joined by Marion, Gizzy's oldest, a girl about the same age as Erwin, and they never stopped running around during those awful weeks in Bondigoux, from the barns and the pig pens to the fields, and all sorts of other places between that I can not imagine. When they were not busy running around the little urchins cuddled and dandled Gizzy's little girls and infants. The war had uprooted us from our homes and forced us to find shelter in abandoned granaries, without bathrooms or running water or almost any change of clothing or towels and the like. All those things that we had heaped into our suitcases and which got lost along the way from Antwerp during a trip that lasted eight days and nights aboard a train that was bombed and lost numerous cars, and we moved from our own cars into whatever other cars were left over. This cursed war was the furthest thing from the children's minds, as though it was nothing more than a mere word. They passed their time as though they had fallen into some wonderful summer camp in which the missing home where they had all grown up was just one more unexpected benefit.

War runs wild in one place in the form of bombs and blood and flames, but at the same time it wreaks havoc all over the rest of the world in false silence, making our daily routines seem no more than an illusion laid bare by reality. That was how it seemed when I later spotted the coffee houses down by the old port in Marseille, filled with men and women sipping lemonade and sampling chilled ice cream while they read papers that portrayed military fronts and victories and whatnot. That was the effect on me of those French beauties promenading arm in arm with the Germans along the Canebière on New Year's Eve as they celebrated the arrival of 1943. It was the same thing with the people all lined up outside the movie theaters where the Americans Laurel and Hardy made the French roll with laughter in the aisles, or *The Rebel Son* with Harry Baur playing Taras Bulba, which we saw together before the war broke out at the movie theater in Antwerp, and you thought that he was the greatest actor in the world. But that was exactly what Bondigoux was for our children, and it all came to an end one Sunday in September, all of a sudden, inside the Municipal Building. We were all exiled from Bondigoux - our two families along with all the others who were with us in the camp at Brens.

At night Erwin slept like any child should, but Jackie would wake up in a panic and then fall back asleep, then begin mumbling something and wake up once again. He sensed something - I know that now and I am now telling you that his life is filled with something very, very deep, much more than just a wonderful summer camp. He is a child of unfathomed understanding and feeling. He was not to be misled by his dreams. Perhaps Erwin also glimpsed the truth during the nights, but Erwin talked, whereas Jackie simply absorbed it all in silence. I looked at him now on the train as he slept and I thought of all the things that had happened just a few days ago and it already seemed so distant. I thought of you - you who had been with us but who was now gone - and I asked myself if you really knew Jackie the way that I do, if you had ever really recognized him the way that he truly is, or if you had just let the image that you already had of him determine your perception and prevent you from ever seeing him the way that you actually should have. I never talked to you about all this. I had somehow wanted to protect the little boy. I sanctified the privacy of his world to the point that I held myself back from delving deeply with the things that I just said, or even merely allowed myself to think. I even refrained from even raising the possibility with you. What a mistake that was… perhaps.

I suddenly stiffened and switched to high alert. Jackie stirred for no obvious reason whatsoever, curled up against me, wrapped his two little arms around my neck and gazed on two men who stood there facing us like phantoms who had suddenly risen out of thin air, one in a raincoat and the other dressed in the uniform of a German soldier. Erwin stared at them without moving a muscle. He was silent and focused, his features fixed immovably. "Papers!" said the one in the rain-coat. Erwin got up, went over to my bag, pulled out our documents and showed them to the inspectors. The one in the raincoat read through the documents languidly, handed them over for a moment to the German who clearly did not know how to read French, then took them back and returned them to me, not to Erwin, saying, "*Merci*, Madame", in the polite tones of a bureaucratic functionary. He then turned to the person sitting next to me. I did not dare breathe until the two of them had moved on up the train. Jackie kissed me on the cheek and lay his head on my shoulder and did not return to his previous spot. Erwin checked my bag to make sure that the documents were put back properly in their place. I can not recall if he said anything before settling down once more in his seat. I imagined you, drawn up to your full height with the fine features of your face in profile, present before my eyes. I imagined a faint smile stretched thin across your lips, just the hint of a smile, a vague gesture that, as ever, was impossible to properly decipher. Sage irony, satisfaction, inspired confidence. The documents had once more passed the test. Who knows where they might have taken us if you had not done such a perfect job on the documents.

At that point I thought that I might finally allow myself to fall asleep for a bit. I closed my eyes in order to try and hint to Erwin that the time had at last come for him to close his eyes as well and sleep. I could not say a thing to him. Through the slits of my eyes that I barely opened so that he would not sense that I was still awake and observing him, I saw that he was not asleep. He would look at me from time to time to check if I was resting and relaxed. The child was not yet even eight and a half and he was already an adult. Even you would not have believed how he could identify the space that you had vacated and which he was now trying to fill fearlessly without ever being concerned that he might get lost inside the vacuum you had left behind. I wish I could have been impressed. That is all that I wanted to feel. But I was unable to. I was afraid, not for myself, but for his sake.

The train began to slow down, hitting the brakes in fragmented, screeching intervals. After a few moments it came to a complete stop. Through the window there was nothing to see other than night - not a house in sight, not a single tree, no blinking lights in the distance, just the night; night like an abyss with no edge and no bottom. The people sitting next to us did not say a word, asked no questions, and barely stirred in their seats. Gazes that stared straight ahead without batting an eyelash were now and then turned toward the window only to return vacantly once more to the silent space inside the car. Like me, they wanted to know what had happened - where were we, why had the train stopped? Who boards a train as it stands still along the tracks in the middle of nowhere? Who gets off, and where do they go? You do not ask questions at all during wartime. When you do not know if you should run, or if you even can run for that matter altogether, and you can do no more than just sit there without moving until it seems like you've been bound and gagged;

and the winds rush through your mind stirring all the thoughts and images of worst-case scenarios... then you do not ask any questions.

Even the most practiced mind-reader does not reveal any evidence of the absolute terror that has him in its grip, does not move a muscle and tells himself whatever will be will be. We waited and waited and, to my knowledge, nothing happened whatsoever. Life was governed in those days by mysteries whose codes we had not yet cracked. After about an hour the train once more began to move, slowly at first, then picking up speed to the point that it seemed to be hurtling for-ward beyond its very physical capacity and began to rattle as though bursting with the blood throbbing through its iron veins. Then the pace slackened once more ever so slightly.

The vague outline of houses began to appear in the darkness. First one, then another. Eventually the outlines became somewhat crowded and began to jostle up against one another until they formed the outline of a city. Here and there some scant light shone through a window, and suddenly we found ourselves entering the station, and signs for the city of Lyon flew by before our eyes, one after the other. Long flags decorated with swastikas hung down all along the platform. German soldiers stood in an orderly row with their helmets, backpacks and rifles, the canine units' handlers each held a German Shepherd on a leash, and the officers' boots had been buffed until the lights of the station were reflected in their sheen. "The Dark Lord's Circus," I thought to myself. These are midnight's polished soldiers at attention in the face of the foe hidden away aboard the arriving train - the travellers, a woman like me, young children, farmers with their worn straw hats and dull berets, women in their winter coats who seemed, as such, even wider than they truly were. Someone who had gone absolutely insane had been crowned master of Lyon and hung these threatening red flags with their circles of white with the pitch-black crooked crosses seemed even blacker than black, and then sent along their idiot soldiers to stand there facing our train as it lurched into a station that was not of this world.

The car trembled, the wheels shrieked, and the train came to a halt. The soldiers started to move towards us with their measured steps, along with the canine units, the handlers and their dogs. One row remained standing in place, like mummified sentries in their dark-green uniforms. A loudspeaker blared as its echo rebounded, doubled and tripled to the point that it was impossible to make out just what was being announced in French that seemed completely out of place among the empty platforms, soldiers, and the pendant banners. "No one may leave the train until further notice." That much I understood. I was struck by terror which stuck in my throat like a moist, nauseating knot that quickly dried up everything inside me until it hurt just to swallow. Jackie clung to me. Erwin did not move as he stood there rooted to the floor. His face was pale and his eyes were sharp and cold. The loudspeaker once more drove its echo through the air. A row of soldiers that had already boarded the train passed us in the narrow corridor without looking our way. An almost tangible silence had fallen over all - thick, dense and grave. I had never before been touched by a silence like that. The minutes ticked by interminably. Every minute seemed like an hour and every hour seemed an eternity. Suddenly the sound of hobnailed boots began to smack against the platform and a row of soldiers with their canine units, handlers and dogs, approached the others who had still not moved, leading a group of six men and one woman. The soldiers moved as one, in lockstep, left-right, left-right, while the prisoners each straggled along at their own pace. There were no handcuffs, their arms had not been tied behind their backs. But there was no mistaking them. They had been bound forever.

Bits of information and events came together and began to make sense to me at a dizzying clip. Someone had turned in the people who had just been taken off the train - members of the underground, or smugglers suspected of being members. Someone had ratted them out. The soldiers were waiting for them. While the train was stopped outside the city, I now understood, plainclothes officers had boarded the train unnoticed and seated themselves right beside the suspects without them ever suspecting a thing or realizing that they now were trapped. Lyon was waiting for them when they reached the station and whisked them off the train and led them down into those unlit cellars. No one ever confirmed for me if I had put together all the pieces properly and whether the little story that I had fleshed out on my own had actually taken place or not.

The soldiers who owed no explanation to anyone anywhere vanished with their prisoners. But the other soldiers who had not boarded the train and had stood rooted in place the entire time remained standing there just as they were. One German Shepherd would not stop straining at the leash, but was held firmly in its master's hands, then lay down at his feet and was abruptly yanked to a standing position with a short, sharp jerk of the leash that, even from afar, seemed violent and painful. I should have shaken my head in sorrow and sympathy for those poor souls, the six men and single woman, who had disappeared with the column of soldiers that had just left the station. But there was no space for sorrow inside me. I thanked whatever God manages the accounts of pity and compassion in His particular fashion during a time of war. The soldiers who had boarded the train were not looking for me and my sons, but was only interested in those sorry souls who had now disappeared. It was as though my children and I had been saved as some sort of reward for the ones they took away. If not for them, they would have come for me. In my mind I knew that I was thinking foolish thoughts but my heart knew other-wise. And I was embarrassed and terribly ashamed and could not stop offering up my thanks and asking Heaven to forgive me - if there was still any pardon to be found up there, the way things once used to be pardoned when everything was still so different for these tainted thoughts that just would not leave me be.

People began to descend from the train and hurried off to wherever it was that they were headed without looking up at the soldiers who eyed them the entire time. What did these mute folks think of the passengers - who had made the same long trip right in their midst - and their relative destinies? Maybe nothing at all. Perhaps it is impossible to maintain your sanity during wartime if you stop to think about someone other than yourself. Maybe they thought to themselves that they were innocent because, after all, if the others, the prisoners, had not sinned then they would not have been arrested. They had chosen their own fate and whatever happened to them from here on was their concern alone. Or maybe these folks were seized by thoughts similar to mine. Perhaps, like me, they were ashamed. A bunch of people all travel together and for some of them the trip was now over, while for others there seemed to be absolutely no end in sight.

The locomotive suddenly let out a shrill whistle and the train began to move once more. It rolled out of the station as the soldiers who were no longer needed remained standing there. From afar, they looked to me like little tin soldiers, tiny toys their true height at last, and it was as if Lyon had never even existed. But I was unable to calm down. The shame would not let me be. At last I fell asleep even though I had tried not to doze off. I slept for about an hour, or maybe it was just a brief moment. I could not tell.

All that I remember is that I woke up to the sound of "Your papers, Madame!," I was immediately on edge like the flash of a razor blade, and, with an added sense of urgency, I knew that I had to stay silent, I had to look up helplessly at the men standing there before me in the doorway of the train compartment. No German soldier accompanied them, for a change. The French were no less diligent than their German counterparts after all, and did their job just as faithfully all by themselves. But it was strange. Jackie quickly beat Erwin to the punch and reached out his hand to open the bag with our documents inside. Erwin refrained from pushing him aside - not a word, not a single gesture - but all the same it was he who actually took out the documents with a firm, fast grip and gave them over to the officers. Jackie retreated as though he had never even intended to get involved in the first place. It all took place in the blink of an eye, instantly I understood that Jackie no longer wanted to play the role of the little child clinging to my neck. He too had undergone instant maturation and wanted to play his part in the war whose rules he seemed to fathom better than I had ever figured he could. Erwin did not relinquish his position as the eldest but at the same time he refrained from definitively returning his brother to his former place. It was that decisive moment in which the two brothers became partners in a world where children, if they wish to survive, are weaned from their own childhood and the protective bosom of their mothers.

The officers seemed to be paying particular attention to the documents this time. They read for a bit, then raised their eyes to look at me and the boys, then read some more and once more raised their heads to examine our faces. It seemed as though their eyes were trying to pierce my breast and probe inside the inner recesses of my heart to find the secrets and deception that I had hidden there. I was terrified even beyond the ordinary terror to which I had already grown accustomed. But in the same way that they were examining us, the boys, in their turn, examined the officers. Nobody had yet said a word. The two officers passed the documents to a third man, who I guess must have been the senior and commanding officer, and after he had given the documents no more than a quick once-over, he turned to me and said, with a civility that absolutely crushed me, "Madame…" Erwin immediately got to his feet and before the man could get a single word out of his mouth said, "Mother is mute. Tell me what you want to know and I can communicate it to her." I stared at Erwin as though I had forever been this helpless woman, as if he had always been my interpreter, as if my only sin was travelling alone with my two boys without a man to accompany me, either on the way there, or on the way back.

The civil senior officer curled his lips into something resembling surprise and said "Ah!", in ridicule. He looked over the boy standing before him and said, "If so, my young man," with deliberate derision, "tell me where you are headed."

"Saint-Claude," Erwin replied. We had trained ourselves to tell as much of the truth as possible within the lies where we now had to hide. That was indeed where we were headed and so that was precisely what Erwin gave as our destination.

"Where in Saint-Claude?"

"To visit our aunt."

"And what is 'our aunt's' name?"

"Resnick." That was in fact her name. She had changed it but we still said 'Resnick.'

"That is not a French name, my young man."

"It is Romanian. Her husband is Romanian." That was not true. Jacques was Czech, but it was okay to be Romanian whereas it was forbidden to be Czech, and Erwin knew from the many conversations that we had had around the table when you were still with us, and so he said 'Romanian' as naturally as could be.

"And what is 'our aunt Resnick's' first name?"

"Marie." This was also not true. Her name was Manya. But Erwin knew that Marie sounded better than Manya. We had discussed this as well. I nodded my head as though to affirm everything that my boy was saying in general, without actually having heard any of the details. I could sense and was certain that I had a sort of stupid smile stretched from cheek to cheek that stayed there till it hurt, and it was not because I was playing dumb but it was just that this was the only way for me to over-come the fear that flitted and flew from the soles of my feet to my scalp on through. Jackie's eyes were fixed on the man the entire time, without blinking. He sat there, immobile, but it was as though he were on trial right next to his older brother. It is something that no stranger could ever manage to understand.

"I assume that you are not on your way to go skiing in Saint-Claude."

"No, sir. My aunt is expecting. My mother is on her way to help her through the birth and we are just along for the trip." This was another partial truth. A baby was indeed on the way, but I was not headed there to be with her and help her through it. We were running away, running for the border to try to seize the only chance that we had left to survive and stay alive.

"I assume that she has no husband, young man - 'our aunt', that is - and yet she seems to have a child on the way..." The junior officers who were with the man realized that this was the point in the proceedings that called for laughter, so they chuckled a bit.

But the senior officer did not laugh. He looked at me as he pronounced these words, and it was as though his eyes lay bare my belly where it was hidden beneath my coat and clothes, as though he was not in charge of interrogating passengers who were trying to steal across borders or travel for free, but was there to weed out pregnant women who lived in the mountains and travelled by train with no husbands or fathers anywhere in the world for the babies that they carried around inside their abandoned wombs.

"Her husband died, sir, he died about a half a year ago, sir, and she is alone, sir, she is a woman living all alone."

I had no idea if Jacques was actually alive or dead at this point. He had suddenly disappeared - left the house one day and never came back - they had snatched him off the street, but Erwin - even without our ever having discussed it previously - knew enough to say that he had died during the early months of Manya's pregnancy. What else do the children of war know that we did not yet know when we were their age?

"Young man, is your father's name Maurice or Moritz?"

"Maurice, sir."

"And I assume that he also died about a half a year ago, or maybe it was just a month or two ago, is that it?" The man did not take his eyes off me.

"We do not know where he is, sir."

"Ah!" the man said snidely, as he fixed his eyes on my belly where it rose like a mountain beneath my winter coat.

"He did not die a half a year ago, he did not die in an accident about a half a year ago as well?"

"We do not know, sir. He went on a trip and never came back."

"He went to Saint-Claude, I assume?"

"No. He went from one place in Marseille to another and never came back. That is just the way he is."

"This is not the first time?"

"No, sir. He will be back. He always comes back."

"Very interesting," the man said, as he waited for Erwin to add something else, to respond, to give in to temptation and continue talking once it was absolutely imperative to stop. But Erwin remained silent. His eyes did not leave the face of the officer. There was no fear in them, no expectation, no supplication, no ire whatsoever, just a cold, calculating glance that had no place in a child's world, a child who was waging a war all by himself as foot soldier and commander in one, and was asking himself whether he had been defeated by the awful man who stood before him or if he had been victorious and managed to save his mother and brother and save himself along with them. Jackie's eyes were just like Erwin's, as he too stared fixedly at the man holding our papers. God does not make children like that - this cursed war does.

"A propos," the man suddenly said. "This train does not go to Saint-Claude. You will have to get off and change trains. But you know that already, don't you, young man?" Erwin nodded and did not say a thing. I suppose that he had simply forgotten the name of the station where we had to get off and change trains for Saint-Claude. The senior officer did not ask. He clicked his tongue with repulsive contempt, and without taking his murky eyes off me, licked his upper lip as though it were dry and clicked his tongue once more. With an almost imperceptible nod of his head he motioned to the two lackeys who were with him. One of them went over and clapped another one of the passengers in our compartment on the shoulder and then repeated the gesture with a woman seated there and then proceeded to the shoulder of a third passenger. Nothing was actually asked of these people, there was neither the hint of a command nor an outright order, but the passengers who had been singled out knew that they had to stand up. While the interrogation was underway these people did not look up for even a moment into the faces of the officers who had just finished investigating me and investigating Erwin, as they had all the while pretended as if they were unable to hear a single solitary word. They just stared straight ahead without batting an eyelash with a sort of extended diligence that seemed to be sub-merged in its very self. It was as though some glass wall separated them from us and allowed no contact whatsoever between their world and ours, and the distance delineated between us was immeasurably greater than the imaginary proximity that ordinarily unites people seated together in the selfsame compartment aboard a train. Throughout the entire trip we did not speak, neither the children nor I said a single word, so it was impossible for the other passengers to know whether I was truly mute or had just turned silent by choice and of necessity. But I knew that they knew the truth. They were connected to everything that we had tried to hide through the absolute estrangement from us that they had adopted. They had shut themselves off from everything that was not related to their own destiny and they appeared to be no more than some sort of human icebergs in our midst, but the panic had penetrated their very innards at the certain realization that they had just witnessed our definitive deployment of deceit and it shook them to the very frozen core beneath their skin. Although it was impossible to actually see them trembling I could nevertheless make out the tremors in all their terrible force. They rose from their seats as though they had no life left in them and exited the compartment to head off wherever it was they went. The senior officer and one of his assistants sat down among us in the compartment, while the other assistant remained standing in the doorway, where his considerable height absorbed the rattling motion of the train, as it made its way through the tunnels of the night that seemed to have been constructed expressly for us.

Erwin did not speak. Jackie remained silent. They knew that we had become prisoners. In my heart I envisioned how my life would unfold up to the point when the train would come to a halt, up to that moment when they would lead the children and me all along the length of the platform with its plaintive echo and then separate us from each other to lead the children off to where it is so very unnatural to ever take children at all. I imagined that they would bring me to some basement of peeling plaster and scarred stucco, with a single light bulb dangling naked from the ceiling. I could see it tossed on the gusting wind and throwing shadows over the damp space with its acrid smell. Some sinister officer sits facing me and makes a note, for the thousandth time, of the death of yet another woman, in a notebook that has no sense of the number of its own leaves and pages, and none of us will ever know - not me, not my children, and not those pages themselves - if we passed away just before dying, or if, even after we were dead, we did not stop dying over and over again. And I was ever so still as I imagined all these scenes in my mind's eye, and no rebellion rose up within me, it was as though I had made some peace with the end that I was contemplating and it would brook no transgression whatsoever. Our children were also extremely still, as were the senior officer and his assistant who sat with us in the compartment, and the third man who rocked back and forth in the doorway as though he were locked with a demon in some nauseating dance. You really get to see just what hell looks like when you are not the only one trapped inside it and you get to travel through it all the way as it rides right beside you.

At that very moment, aboard the train, the children and I were heading for a place that was in every way identical to the one I had already visited, just two days earlier, in Marseille, when I sat in a waiting room that I suppose was no more than a hallway, a corridor, an anteroom - where now my children and I were headed for the very belly of the beast. And yet the urge to rebel refused to rise inside me and the terror was like a captive that had no idea how to break out. Where were you?

The train continued on for a while, stopping now and then for a few moments in the middle of nowhere where there was nothing out there but the night. There are things that no man knows which take place in wartime all along the train tracks, and no one knows the key to the code that governs them, buried there in the darkness, dictating unseen stations that do not appear on any schedule whatsoever. Perhaps the trains are held up by spirits and demons. Do not shake your head at me when I say such things - you who would be filled with something verging on fury when anyone would merely hint at the fact that they were willing to entertain the thought that supernatural forces existed beyond our comprehension and had their way with the world. I suppose that when peace reigns supreme there are no spirits and demons, but during a time of war, which knows nothing of either the natural or the comprehensible, who knows if such things do not indeed exist and if it is in fact spirits and demons who hold sway over nature and the intellect, cities and small villages, wagons rolling over dusty paths, horses and rumbling trains. Vain thoughts like these also made their way through my mind as I sat riding alongside the boys with our end in sight.

The officers did not speak. The seated assistant dozed off for a moment and his head sank to his chest, but the senior officer immediately slapped the former's thigh and woke him without saying a word and the assistant straightened up in his seat and began shaking his head as though trying to shake loose the sleep that seemed to have settled down inside his skull. I thought about the fact that the three of them were French and I wondered how they worked things out in their own foul tongue - who decides what the Germans handle and what is to be handled by the French, who is serving whom, and who had been dressed in these black raincoats and who had donned one of his own accord, who was fitted with a helmet, handed a rifle and sent off to kill and who went off to do all these things of his own free will, who was taking us down into the basement and who would examine us when we got there, who was going to be our judge and jury and who would be our executioner - the Germans, the French, the whole lot of them - who?

And which of these thoughts was also going through the minds of Erwin and Jackie as they each sat there all alone while the final station approached - albeit intermittently - with every passing moment? I did not ask them, certainly at the time I did not, and afterwards I never asked them either. There is no way to talk about such things, not with children and not with adult relatives either, no way to bring it up with our children or even with you, for that matter. The only reason that I am telling you these things is because I am writing them down, because you are not sitting in front of me and listening to me, because you are not here to see me now, to see them, to look inside our souls laid bare. We are stripped naked in the ears of our loved ones when we tell them of the terrible things to which we were subjected. I think that when you get back I am going to fall silent forever, before you and before the children. I am writing because you are not here to listen. Exposed like this, alone, I manage to remain concealed.

It may well be that Erwin and Jackie did not think anything at all. At the time the-re was no way for them to fathom that these little prisoners seated silently in the same compartment as their captors who kept an eye on them until they were to be handed over to their hidden masters - those who see all and remain unseen - these prisoners, as a concept, were something that did not even exist, even as they hurtled in-to being. It was something that you could not even think of because even as it was taking place it was not happening at all - it both was and was not - because no reality actually exists in which children should be forced to live out such a reality. Now I am confused. As I write this I am even more confused than I was then, or maybe the truth is that I was even more confused then than would appear from what I have now written. But I refuse to be ashamed. I want you to read it, one day, I want you to read it all.

A cold, clammy morning already clung to the window as the train creaking came to a halt at a station right in front of a large sign that said 'Annemasse'. I had never in my life heard of a place called Annemasse, and I had no idea if it was a village or a town, or even some large city, but here I was in Annemasse. We rose from our seats. The senior officer and his assistants helped us take down our worn suitcases from the overhead luggage rack. It seems that good manners manage to survive even among the hangmen. They did not say a word as they made their way along the narrow corridor to the door and we followed them. They got off the train and we followed them once more, walking, as they walked, right behind them. They spoke to three or four men who were waiting on the platform and we waited right beside them as though we were old hands at the role we had been given. After what could not have been more than a mere moment or two the senior officer turned to me and clicked his boot heels together, bowed ever so slightly and said, "Madame!" then immediately turned his back in the direction of the boys and said "Young man!," then turned on his heels like an overgrown marionette and headed off with his two assistants trailing along behind him as though they were attached to his back by some hidden strings.

Other than the scream that bursts forth spontaneously from the mouth of the child when it emerges into the world from its mother's womb, all of life is a well-staged ceremony, a show with clearly written rules upon arrival and timeworn traditions etched in stone at our departure, a show of song and a show of silence, a show of joy and a show of fear, a show for the saved and a show for the damned. Everything is an act and both the murderer and his victim are players, the former interpreting the role of the one spilling blood while the latter plays the part of the one having his blood spilled. There was no doubt in my mind that I was headed towards my death and my children were headed there along with me, and I stood there rooted to the platform waiting for the sentries with their hats that held a flourish of force in the brim, and the men in black raincoats belted black at the waist who looked so alike that it seemed some identical abyss had spat them all out - yes, I waited there for them to start walking so that we could walk along behind them to wherever it was that they had been ordered to take us.

When I think of it now, I am shocked and ashamed at the fact that I did not even consider in the slightest trying to run away while I stood there waiting for the end to come, that I did not try to discern some frail sliver of salvation in the face of the unavoidable fate that unfolded right before my very eyes. No, I do not have a sense of shame as I now recall my complete capitulation at the time. I am simply in a state of shocked amazement and vague regret. How is it that I was completely emptied of my will to freedom as though it had never once stirred in me to begin with, I who was so sure that this will filled my very essence till it overflowed? How? Was I alone in this? Were my children and I the only ones? Am I the only one who went through this or is there another person out there like me, another two or three people, quite a few people, a veritable horde of people, every single person, in fact, at the moment that he or she stands there like a blade of grass at the feet of those mammoth monsters who consume everything in their path?

We were led on foot through the streets of Annemasse. We were careful not to slip on the ice that stuck to the sidewalks. All the stores were closed. A large sign in one of the display windows announced 'Souvenirs' behind the locked iron grate. Very funny, I thought to myself. Who comes out of nowhere to purchase souvenirs in this empty town, and where do they go afterwards, and whom do they give their gifts to, where in the room would you want to situate such a souvenir and what does it bring to mind when you stare at it in its little corner? Does it make you think of me and my boys? Do you think of the sentries - and why do I refer to them as sentries, these silent plainclothes officers who have arrayed themselves around us in formation with one leading on in front, one on either side and one more behind us bringing up the rear, or the bicycle that passed us by in the opposite direction bearing a rider dressed all in black who did not even so much as look at us - neither out of curiosity nor compassion, just nothing at all.

Every so often we would stop to rest and put down the suitcases on the sidewalk. The sentries waited until it seemed like we had been given some sign to bend down and bear our burdens once more as we made our way in ever-measured, mincing steps to ensure we did not slip and fall. The men did not lend a hand. They were too strong for that. They restrained themselves mightily as they waited for us to recover in every stage of our journey. The snow on the roofs of the houses where the chimneys emitted thin trails of dark, wintry smoke seemed frail , though where the snow was piled in drifts between the street and the sidewalk it was filthy and filled with brown blotches and patches of rust. A chill like death shook through us beneath our winter coats. After what seemed like an interminable hour we reached a police station. We ascended the stairs that led from the sidewalk up to the front entrance of the station house, carrying out suitcases behind one of the sentries, who preceded us with catlike alacrity up the stairs and kept looking over his shoulder to ensure that we were indeed following along behind him. His companions slowly accompanied us from behind, step by step. A policeman who was dressed only in his shirtsleeves suddenly emerged from inside the station house and hurried over to help me carry my suitcases.

Inside it was rather hot, somewhat sweltering in fact. Boiling water whispered in the lobby atop some invisible stove somewhere. The officer in shirtsleeves sat back down behind the counter. The senior sentry placed a bundle of papers in his hands. The officer spread them out on the table before him and inspected them without touching them as he rubbed his hands together, rubbed one and then the other, to warm them up once more after they had caught cold in the brief moment when he had helped me carry my suitcases. He called aloud first one name and then another, names I do not remember and have no need to recall, and immediately two more officers and a woman emerged from some room at the far end of the lobby, and the woman looked at me as though her eyes were encircling my body and taking its measurements beneath my clothes. The head sentry left without a word from the officers, and his assistants left with him, following him out as though they were no more than the many shadows of their considerable commander.

The officer behind the counter began to study the documents

before him and from time to time, as though speaking to himself, he let the word 'voila' slip, each time with a different lilt. First it sounded like it was meant to confirm that which was clearly self-evident. Then it seemed to announce that he had deciphered some secret code, and then again it seemed to say that now he had all the information necessary to decide what was to be done with me and my children. After he seemed to have read through the documents once or twice he called over the other people standing in the room to have a look for themselves. They leaned over his shoulder to peer at the papers without touching them. While they read, the original officer looked us over and his gaze came to rest alternately on me, then on Erwin and Jackie, and he nodded his head as he emitted little couplets of 'voila, voila,' and it seemed as though the meaning of this barren word had been doubled, tripled, and quadrupled, and that its only purpose in being brought into the world was to allow the person who pronounced it to taste all the various different flavors of the myriad things he was capable of imagining, while the person hearing the word did not taste any-thing at all and had no idea if the word was even being addressed to him or simply being pronounced in his presence with no real purpose whatsoever. I felt like I was nothing more than an object sitting there being discussed rather than actually ad-dressed, like something whose fate was being decided in a purely random fashion, such as whether to toss a particular piece of wood onto the bonfire or rather wait until some other branch collapsed alongside it, burning brightly in the flames.

Throughout the entire endless train ride in the night I did not once think of the child that I was carrying inside me. I was just trying to survive, and I had faith that I would live, and that Erwin and Jackie would live too. At every moment I was terrified that I would make some sort of mistake from which neither my intelligence nor my cunning would suffice to save me, and I would become entangled in all sorts of suffering until my children and I would be rescued by some subtle deus ex machina, but I was not afraid to die and for that reason - perhaps, for that reason - my unborn baby and I still seemed to me to be a single being. But standing now as we were in the lobby of the police station, cut off entirely from life and the living, I knew that I was going to die alone and that the baby growing inside me would also die alone, and Erwin and Jackie would each die alone, and only you, you who were not there with us in that shabby final destination of ours in Annemasse, would outlive us, simply because it is impossible for death to destroy absolutely everything. Death seizes what it can but always leaves someone behind to suffer through the loss. That is the law. You who were missing would be the one who would remain when we were gone. There was no way you could have foreseen that unseen presence which was forever lying in wait. Death strikes you down and elsewhere inflicts pain. It freezes the eye of the dead and sears the surviving eyes of the living with the bitter flow of tears. You were not there; and so, you would live forever.

My unborn baby was suddenly very much alive because he was about to be put to death. I felt like I was biting my lip. I began to grow angry, filled with a sense of ire that rose and overflowed, to the point that my very veins felt as if they just could not take it anymore and were about to explode. Why were they going to take his life, just why exactly, why steal his cries in the crib, why rob him of his first smile and the first sounds of his laughter, why remove his little head as it rose above his pillow, why cancel his energetic crawl across the carpet in our room, why destroy his shaky stance as he first learned to stand holding on to a leg of the armchair or the edges of the coffee table in the living room, why erase his first wonderful steps that would arouse his own amazement and that of all who would have been there to watch him advance hesitatingly with his hands spread out before him to balance his body as it suddenly tottered forward atop his legs, why silence the first broken syllables that would try to trip off his tongue in all their often erroneous glory as they astonished his listeners with their winning, inadvertent exactitude that actually managed to exceed the words' original intent, why negate his youthful knees that would return each time from the park newly scarred by the sandy and pebble-strewn paths, why cancel all the innocence of those kindergarten holidays filled with the sounds of the good, old songs of youth, why remove the schoolbag from his back, why, oh why were they going to destroy his childhood, his adolescence, his life and all that it would have been filled with day after day, year after year, decade after decade, even before he ever had a chance to truly be?

I suddenly wanted to know what he looked like, wanted to embrace him, wanted to hold him close to my breast and nurse him and caress his calming little head. I suddenly wondered if the baby was a boy or a girl and I was angry with myself for automatically thinking of him in masculine terms when I after all had no idea if the baby was in fact a little girl - after all, dear God, now that the baby boy and I, or the baby girl, were right up against the end, oh how, my God, could I not know such a basic fact?

The officer in shirtsleeves began to speak. He stared at me with a look in his eyes that was neither good nor evil, it was just nothing at all. "Voila," he said - what else could he say? "We need to investigate a bit," he said. "Your papers are in order, Madame, they may well be in order, but you, Madame, you are not quite right, perhaps..." He looked me over for a brief moment and then added, "It is a strange world. Once upon a time papers and people were one and the same thing, but these days things are not so certain, life has become rather confused and each item must be examined on its own merit, the papers are now one thing and the people another. So what am I saying then, if that is the case? I am telling you that you are under arrest, prison and all that. I am very sorry Madame, but it is prison, in accordance with the law and proper protocol. The letter of the law, as always, you understand. There is no other way, no other possibility - prison. There is a need - and I am sure you understand this as well as anyone - for a minor investigation. A more fundamental examination of the facts. It is not a big deal. It requires just a day or two, or maybe three, or more, for that matter. There is no way to know at the outset. Are you mute, Madame? No need to answer, you can not answer after all. Perhaps you can not, that is. Are you concerned for the children's welfare? Do not be concerned Madame. We will take care of everything. We are locals, we know our business here."

As he spoke two nuns came in dressed in long, black capes, wearing starched, white bonnets on their heads. The palms of their bare hands - no gloves here - were clasped tightly across their chests. They both wore these small pairs of eyeglasses whose lenses immediately fogged up, and their faces were each flooded with a pallor that is rather particular to nuns, as they projected a love that swore to be never-ending, yet whose essence is something of which I am completely unaware, to the point that it terrified me so much more than common sense would have called for. The thin line of their lips was adorned with a smile that seems to be frozen in all seasons - winter, spring, summer and fall - a sort of eternal smile that only seems to begin there where it ceases to be seen.

"The children are not going to accompany you to prison, Madame, we do not do things that way in Annemasse, they will be held in a rather pleasant environment where the people know precisely how to take care of children and show them the proper affection." The officer in shirtsleeves continued speaking. I stared at him. Erwin translated in a sign language that he had invented on the spot. The two nuns took me in fully and their smiles sweetened beyond all measure, driving a fierce chill through my very veins. I still did not know if I should break the barrier of my silence, and so, I had no way of responding beyond a sort of slight nod of the head and a fleeting smile that seared my face. Erwin and Jackie stood right next to one another, and when the nuns' smiles came to rest on them in all their clinging transparency, Jackie placed his hand on his older brother's shoulder and huddled even closer to him, grabbing on to him and holding him close as though he were not just his brother but his shield. "These ladies, Sister Marie and Sister Yolanda (why did he have to call the nuns sisters? and why do I recall their names?) will accompany the boys to the convent and take care of them there.

You have no idea how much love they lavish upon the children there, even Jewish children, they love them as though the children were our very own. There is no greater testament to, no more fitting example of what love truly is. They will be fine, Madame, better off, I admit, than you, but, voila, you are a mother and what more does a mother's heart desire than that her children should have it better than she does, as good as things can possibly be these days, here in Annemasse and throughout France, or perhaps anywhere at all, for that matter."

I had not yet given the slightest indication that I heard or understood anything he was saying. His voice was not exactly mild but it was somewhat apologetic, mingled with a certain knowing precision that seemed to be well aware of just what behooved a person who was required to submit to the discipline of the authorities, of which he was in charge. In my heart I thought that there was absolutely no way for him to understand just what I was going through, or what my kids were going through, for that matter, and that his world did not extend at all beyond the perimeter of the obligations that were prescribed within his official manual, and this manual was open to the selfsame page in times of war as in times of peace, under foreign occupation just as in a time of complete autonomy, and he had a good heart - I think, at least, that he had a good heart - he could not, after all, be more than the narrow circumference of his minor life.

Erwin began to translate once more in his sign language but the officer suddenly signalled for him to stop, raised his voice and ordered, "Take her away." It would seem that he thought his soft words might have the effect of being taken for weakness and thus cause his underlings and the nuns - the representatives of the Lord - to forget that he was the absolute ruler here, and that it was his word that determined what would happen under the roof of his station house - that is, throughout the entire world. That brusk "Take her away" which tore me from my children was, in his eyes, no more than a matter of reclaiming the authority which had perhaps been lost. It did not occur to him for an instant that he was shouting in our children's ears the same thing that a foul beast screams in order to silence its prey. He had come out to meet me in his shirtsleeves in the cold morning air, had carried my suitcases for me, had addressed me with as much kindness as he could possibly muster, put forth the best of what his down-home goodness would allow, but at that very moment it became apparent to me that there was absolutely no way that any glimpse of humanity whatsoever should deceive the hunted animal into believing that the hunter who would root her out wherever she might hide was in fact human, and had, himself, a human heart. He is a hunting knife, always, polished steel plunged deep into your belly, splitting your womb, devouring your children, flaunting orphaned life like a banner overhead.

The female officer, who had been waiting until that moment to be assigned her single, solitary role, was called upon, approached me first and said to me, with her hand resting on my shoulder, "Come with me." The two other officers joined her and took up positions on either side of me, without saying a word. The officer in shirtsleeves did not stand up, adopted the air of one who was deeply involved in examining some document that was not even there and did not even emit his usual 'voila.' His job was done.

The two nuns approached Erwin and Jackie. One of them inclined her sanctimonious head in their direction and asked them what their names were, as they stood there frozen under her gaze and made no response - neither Erwin nor Jackie made a sound. "You'll tell me your names a bit later on," said the sanctimonious one, and the other nun added that, "When we get to the convent and sit down in the *refectoire* and we pour you some fresh mountain milk we will have a heart to heart conversation and you will have a chance to introduce yourselves." I could see that Erwin was immediately filled with hatred for this particular nun and that Jackie could sense Erwin's reaction in every limb of his body. They did not cry. They did not move a muscle in order to come over and throw themselves around my neck or grab hold of me so that we should not be separated from one another. They were like two little angels filled with this wonderfully suppressed indignation that no one throughout the seven heavens has any idea how to decipher and that I, for as long as I live, will never cease to acknowledge as a more faithful expression of inner ire than any cry, or scream, or tear that has ever been shed. It was a force that filled the interior of the station house entirely with a silence that was never-ending, throughout all the worlds, both above and below.

I, too, did not shed a tear, nor did I beg for my life. I, too, did not throw myself upon my children in order to sweep them up into my arms and hold them close to my breast until the predator that would tear my flesh from my bones tore me away from them as well. I stood there like an issued sentence, like some sealed-off sector. I had no idea where I was headed and I had no idea where my children were headed either. I had no idea if I would return and I had no idea if my children would return and one day come back to me. I had no idea if I would live or die. I had no idea what my boys would be put through and how long they were to be crucified with monastic compassion upon that awful cross of pity, had no idea if they would be there forever or if they would run away and come looking for me, come looking for you, their father, anywhere they could think of - whether they could actually find us there or not, and even if a place like that does not even exist in this world. I did not want to know what the boys were thinking for even the slightest instant. I refused to allow myself to even formulate the thought. The worst part of it all was that in this little rundown police station, with that single officer seated at his desk and these two other officers to either side of me, with one female officer standing next to me and the two nuns bent smiling over the tiny profiles of my children, I was like a lone traveller who had been surrounded by tens of thousands of enemies armed to the teeth, and I was weak and small and robbed of all my strength and I had no way of crying out, no way of striking out, no way of scratching and tearing and kicking away - I was still, paralyzed, and absolutely silenced.

You, if you had been there, if you had only been there, what would you have done? I know exactly what you would have done. You would have risen and drawn yourself up to your full, towering height and placed yourself between the officers and the nuns and the boys and would have declared into the empty space of the lobby - audibly or perhaps without even saying a word - 'Over my dead body' - and you would have drawn me close and shielded me and ordered them in the name of all the deities in the entire world to not dare send a pregnant woman off to prison nor separate her from her children. And they would have overpowered you, they would have begun to beat you down, they would have grabbed you by your hair and the ends of that wavy black mass atop your head would have fallen wildly across your high forehead where it rises over your eyebrows, and the fire would have flashed in your eyes of green as you were cast to the ground with your hands cuffed behind you, and as one of the officers held you down with a knee in your back you would have looked up from the floor where you had been thrown and seen them taking me away from you and taking the children away from me and you would have let out a heart-rending scream that would have brought God back to the vault of heaven from which you had banished Him - but all to no avail, to no avail at all, though your entire being would express this tremendous sense of wonderful rebellion which had nevertheless been put down, uttered some solemn, desperate oath that evil is above all, first and foremost, a terrible lie; but that evil would pay you no more mind than people pay the prey that lies trampled by the side of the road in some noisy city concerned solely with itself.

That was pretty much what happened at the camp in Berns where the Vichy folks had sent us off after rounding us up in Bondigoux. You and a few other men who had been molded by that indecipherable innocence of yours put together an ill-advised uprising over the fact that we were being fed split-pea soup infested with worms that they would serve us from tremendous pots with these huge ladles, poured into the tiny plates we held between our hands as we stood in line, all the while covering us in abuse as though we had been put on this earth to begin with as worthy of no more than worm-infested split-pea soup poured all over the palms of our hands, our coats, and our clothes.

You did not rebel because of the horribly overcrowded conditions in the shacks. You did not rebel over the weak that passed away each day all alone along the wooden planks of the bunks. You did not rebel because they led your wives in long lines beyond the confines of the camp to labor in the city's knitting factories and sweatshops only to return in the evening more exhausted than even seemed humanly possible, trapped inside a daily routine that uprooted a woman's very soul. You did not rebel over the children who all seemed to be no more than walking diseases on two feet, skinny and pallid, suspicious and slow, who nevertheless did not cease to entertain themselves with games that, at the same time, seemed to have had the wind knocked out of them. And you did not rebel because these children had no kindergarten, elementary, and high school teachers, no classes, no studies, nothing at all, growing up as they were like wild grass in parched forests filled with wretched people who had no expectations whatsoever.

You rebelled over the soup, the split peas, the worms, the godawful pots, the cruel ladles, the shame of being forced to live like no more than worms yourselves, over the fact that your whole world had been reduced to this rank soup in outsized pots placed before you like tin troughs before some farm animal. I cannot quite recall just how it all began. Nothing was organized, nothing had been planned or thought out in advance. There was no external sign that something was about to take place. What ripened into a rebellion had perhaps been born in some other time and place, along hidden alleyways of anger that suddenly all linked up to lead into the self-same square, and once they had arrived there, all the boundless anger that could not be contained poured forth and found release. The room where we were fed suddenly turned into a wild, riotous scene. Plates were tossed into the air and smashed to sorry bits of cheap clay, as the floor was suddenly covered with the greenish liquid of that cursed split pea soup as it spilled forth from the huge pots, and dippers and ladles lay like iron ruins amidst the mass of broken clay, where solitary peas floated on the floor like bubbles of green pus.

A few men burst into the kitchen and emerged pushing the scared, sorry workers before them, people who were in prison just like us but had been converted into cooks and dishwashers, and trash and garbage pickers, and they were forced to humiliate themselves and sit down in the filthy mess of spilled soup as if they themselves were no more than our sworn enemies and the enemy's henchmen. The French head chef, who seemed to me to actually be a Spanish exile, stood in the center of the circle of his workers seated on the floor and somebody sprayed him with the re-mains of the split-pea soup so that his face ran with the liquid until it seemed like these big, green tears were running down his cheeks and neck and apron. You, you were the only one that I saw out of all the men running around, wildly screaming in all their anger. You stood on a bench and shouted something that I could not make out until a few guards suddenly came out of nowhere, and the ones who did not slip and fall to rise like dummies, dripping sticky and wet, only to stagger and shuffle off who knows where, made their way to where you were and grabbed hold of you and hit you and dragged you off outside the dining hall and led you to some solitary cell, where they left you for two long weeks during which I did not know if you were dead or alive, if you were still in Brens or had been transferred to some other hellhole.

But what good did it do? Afterwards you said to me that it had made a difference. But what had changed? You actually admitted that nothing had in fact changed but that "You could not remain silent any longer without losing your very right to live." That was how you put it. "And what right is that? In whose eyes?" I asked you. Who grants these rights, who takes them away, who even cares about these imaginary rights over which you waged a lost war that had no chance of success against the absolute masters of our camp. "Me," you said, "I do!" And I thought you sounded like a child. "I care, you care, the children care." And when I replied by saying, "I don't know," you cried and hid your head in my breast and there was no way for me to comfort you or calm you down, until finally, after quite a while, you walked away and never talked to me again about that little uprising of yours that left no mark anywhere but in my mind when I thought of it and thought of you, and in your mind where you thought of it, and thought of humanity in general - including, perhaps, yourself.

These are the thoughts that went through my head when I told myself that you were not with me at the moment that they tore the children away from me.

Back then the boys had stood facing the uprising and the guards who came rushing forth from every direction to put it down and stared silently like stones scattered in the field, the same way they stood there now, almost three years later, facing the officers in Annemasse. The things that they had seen and the voices they had heard back then had left an indelible mark deep inside them, and not a muscle now moved in their faces, so that it would have been impossible for anyone to tell - even I who could decipher the secret meaning in every breath they ordinarily drew - what this overheated police station in the dead of winter with its officers and nuns and the sentences issued to lock me away and drag them off without me to the convent had etched and carved into the hidden walls of their little hearts. There was no escaping it. Everything that had rushed over them so rapidly in these few short years would apparently be seared in their minds forevermore, all crowded together and pressed into a single solid mass in the face of anyone who might one day come along and try to separate things out into their component parts.

Just a short while after the uprising you and your brother Zollie did not return to the camp when night fell, after a long day of forced labor that the men and women carried out separately just a few miles away from where we were being held, neither one of you returned. You - who else if not you - had some sort of a plan that you had come up with, but of course you had given me no indication whatsoever of its existence. Your brother Zollie had been sworn not to let slip even the slightest detail to his wife Gizzy, but he was incapable of bearing the burden of such a secret all by himself, and after a little while he had apparently told Gizzy everything, because she knew all about it.

When I got back from work I took off my coat, and when I pulled my arm out of the sleeve I felt something inside it get in the way. I turned the sleeve inside out and found a piece of paper attached to it with a safety pin, which I guess you had stuck inside my sleeve the night before you went off for work with no intention of ever returning. You had written in Hungarian something like, "My dear Rozhika, I have purchased my freedom in order to be able to purchase yours as well once I am out, that is the only reason I did this. You know nothing about it and so they can not get any in-formation from you. Just trust whoever comes up to you and says 'Churchill's cigar.' I trust him completely and in a little while, I swear, we will all be together again. Take care of the boys." Just a few days later a man in a white suit came up to me, a man I had never seen before, and said something to me that contained the words, 'Churchill's cigar' and asked me to let him transfer Erwin and Jackie to the children's infirmary in the camp in order to see if they had not yet been checked for typhus. Gizzy's kids were also transferred to the infirmary. The man instructed me to come and visit the children at four in the morning and pack a little suitcase or bag for them. So there we were, Gizzy and I, in all our simplicity - which altered its nature all at once into an act that seemed both routine and random - as we all walked out in a sort of procession, walked right out the front gate, and were accompanied by that man to the train station, where we got into one of the noisily crowded cars filled with men and their families headed somewhere else. You were there along the wretched platform. I remember you surrounded there by a mass of the hoi polloi that pushed and pulled to and fro before the train, dressed in a fancy grey suit, sporting a necktie, with a lit cigarette in the corner of your mouth that you tossed away as soon as you spotted us, and you hugged the boys and we all left there together, riding the passenger train that lost no time stopping at any station along the way - your brother, Gizzy, and their children headed for Grenoble, and we on our way to Marseille, where we would live until you disappeared once more, though this time without any plan whatsoever. It was the first time in your life that you were caught without a plan.

But if you had only been there with me now some plan would have formed in your mind and you would have done what I had never quite managed to teach myself to do, or perhaps you would not have been able to rebel after all, and I would have maybe been the one more suited to an uprising this time around. I guess we will never know.

It was only when we began to make our way into the freezing cold outside that I turned my thoughts to the fact that neither I nor the boys had removed our overcoats inside the overheated police station. Even indoors we had been on the outs, I mused to myself, and we remained just the same as when we had arrived. And that was how we headed off once more. I had no idea if prisoners keep their coats on once they are locked behind the bars of their prison cells simply because they have imported a certain chill with them that can find no suitable pores in the skin's surface through which it might escape. Perhaps the prisoners are forced to remove their coats for the simple reason that there is no regime in the world which allows one climate for all its regular citizens and another climate for those it chooses to persecute. But the boys will not remove their overcoats when they get to the convent, I thought. It is cold there, holds an eternal chill.

Today, when I think of it, it seems so foolish to me to admit that these were the completely deluded thoughts that rushed through my mind at the time, as I made my way to wherever it was that I was headed, accompanied by that lady officer and the two male officers, with the boys still by my side, accompanied in turn by those two nuns with their glowing, everlasting smiles, heading off to wherever it was that they were then headed; and I had no idea when, if at all, we would once more be reunited and head off together to some place that belonged to them and belonged to me, if some place still existed in the world where such togetherness might yet be found. I admit that, at that moment, I once more failed to think of you. But they did not tear you away from us in Annemasse. You already belonged to no other place at all.

Erwin suddenly came to a halt and Jackie immediately stopped in his tracks as well, and though I did not even have the ability to think anything one way or the other, I froze too. We were standing next to one another but an invisible wall already separated us from each other - I was surrounded by my police escort and the boys were confined by the convent. There was no way for us to scale our respective walls, the-re was just no way at all.

"That is our mother," Erwin said.

"But of course," replied the officer, who sounded like he was far away even though he stood right nearby, and the two nuns repeated as one, "But of course," and they, too, sounded like they were speaking from behind some barrier, gate, or fence. They demonstrated that they were well aware of the fact that Erwin had not simply told them that I was his mother and Jackie's mother as well, but that he had also indicated that it was just absolutely impossible and even prohibited to separate me from them. And if you separate us from each other, he seemed to have added, when exactly are you going to allow us to reunite once more?

That was what all of us there understood Erwin to have said anyway, but other than that "But of course," neither the officer nor the nuns uttered another word, and as Erwin's voice echoed there, rising into the air from some sort of unseen space in which the phrase "That is our mother" seemed to return in layer after layer, the officers and the nuns pushed us into the street and the former led me off to the right, while the latter led the boys off to the left, and it seemed to me that I could hear the words "That is our mother" bouncing back at me from the deepest recesses of every house in Annemasse,and off every corner of its convoluted streets. Yet even though the whole world seemed to be hearing me, that selfsame world did not raise a finger on our behalf. They heard but held their peace, saw all yet stayed silent, as I continued to make my solitary way just as the boys made theirs, and none of us had any more strength inside us than the visions in a dead man's dreams.

I will never know what the convent looked like where they took the boys that day. Erwin never told me anything. Jackie tried but he was never able to get beyond a sort of superficial description of things, such as one might resort to in trying to describe the mere sides of a box, without delving into any further details, such as the glue that keeps them all together or the screws spun tight to keep them all in place - upright, or at an angle. Erwin, I know well, could certainly have told me these things, he could have described the glue and the screws, as it were, but he never once said a word, not right after we had at last been reunited, and at no point thereafter either. There was just one time that he began, "The nuns and the monks were not allowed to..." and when I asked him just what he was getting at he simply repeated the fragment, saying, "They were not allowed to..., and Jackie would also repeat things of that nature, as a certain sort of pride that was well aware of its own power would begin to spread across his tiny features, and his eyes would fill with a sense of bound-less admiration for his older brother. I know that there is no way that convent could have passed from the stage of the world inhabited by our boys without exacting its price from these little scions of the Jewish people. Our sons refused to speak about the cross but they bore the weight of its burden across their frail backs. That is just how things had to be. The cross wounded their flesh, but since the mark that it left was minor they denied the scar that had formed along their frames.

I suddenly remembered the block of soap. It was still sitting deep inside the bag I held in my hands. I almost lost my mind at the instant that I recalled its presence. My fear mounted with every passing moment. I feared for the past as well. How had they man-aged to overlook checking inside my bag aboard the train? And what would I have said if they had checked there, after all? All the money I had was hidden in there. I had no idea how much. What are diamonds worth? Everything. Nothing. Who knows? It does not matter. It was all I had and it was hidden away and reserved there for a time of emergency. It was impossible to make out the line where you had sliced through the block of soap, you could not see even the faintest outline of an erasure where the string had passed. But all of a sudden I was seized with fear. A block of soap, if it is any sort of hiding place at all, is certainly not a suitable hiding place for journeys such as these.

I felt my blood burning inside me over all the things that had already passed, over what was and what was yet to be, not out of any particular wisdom or foresight but purely by that random chance on which it was impossible and prohibitive for me to rely. I should have removed the diamonds from the block of soap as soon as we had decided definitively to disappear from our apartment and I should have hid them somewhere else. In the hem, perhaps, in the collar of my blouse. I should have swallowed them. But a block of soap? The trains were crawling with Vichy and Gestapo officers whose sole purpose in life was to suspect everyone and everything. How had this fact escaped us to begin with, and why had we not done what was necessary from the outset? I was now headed off to prison. I was carrying a suitcase and I was carrying my handbag, and the block of soap seemed to be burning a hole inside it. In prison the guards toss out everything inside a suitcase out atop some table and count every item, they make a list. That was as far as I knew. That was what I had heard, or maybe that was what I had read in some book somewhere. They would turn out the contents of my handbag onto the table as well. A handbag is an item of greater interest than a suitcase after all. And they check everything, they ask questions, they investigate, they plumb the why and the wherefore of every nook and cranny. Why a block of soap? What is a large, brand-new block of laundry soap doing inside a lady's handbag? Why is it there, of all places? Why is it not in the suitcase? What had you gotten me into when everything you had given me so that I would be able to run for my life had been hidden inside some cursed block of soap whose presence I could not possibly explain to a single soul, and certainly not to so-me suspicious prison guard, be it a man or a woman. And how could I anyway ex-plain anything to anyone at all if I was mute, and now that Erwin was no longer standing beside me, what if my mute play was exposed and was no help whatsoever and the failure of my little pantomime only served as one more strike against me, what then? How was I supposed to explain, using the dozen words of French at my disposal, the presence of this mysterious block of soap, to which it seemed that I was so fearfully attached?

I proceeded to make my way alongside my escort in a state of absolute terror. Just a moment ago they had taken away our children, but that was not my foremost concern. The boys had disappeared in the company of those kindhearted, nauseating nuns and were headed for captivity in a house of borderline blasphemous compassion, so I was not terribly worried on their behalf. It was the block of soap that caused a growing sense of terror to rise inside me into a paralyzing crescendo. It was that soap that would have me sentenced to death. How could you have failed to understand this fact, and where were you now when I needed more than ever your support and that magic touch with which you reached out to fate and seemed to shape it in whatever image you desired? But you were not there, no, you had not shaped fate after all. You never had. That was just an illusion. You had no magic touch. You left me with this traitorous bar of soap and you had disappeared. Those moments there - moments during which I felt that you and I were guilty of the fact that I had tried to run for my life, and save the lives of our children along with mine, along with the life of our unborn child that I was carrying inside my womb; moments in which I felt that this block of soap would not have been with me if we had not committed the unforgivable sin of foolishly trying to repeal the fateful edict that had so clearly been issued against us - those moments are seared in my flesh like the thistles and thorns of some oppressive poison. I think back now to those moments and I am ashamed to recall them.

I felt completely empty inside. I walked on without any strength left whatsoever. I could not see where we were headed. Everything disappeared - the city, the street, the men. No one was accompanying me anymore. It was as if I were being carried along by someone who was not even there to begin with. I kept walking, heading nowhere at all, as my legs led me on of their own accord. Everything everywhere was null and void. I became nothing at all. There was no sense of time anymore. My mind died inside me with a resounding roar, at once an insult and a rebuke. I could hear it exploding between my temples just a moment before I fell. And then there was silence. I sat in the middle of the street with my legs spread out in front of me. With one hand I held on to my handbag and the other hand rested on my belly. I saw the contents of the suitcase where they had spilled at my feet. The woman leaned over and wrapped her arms around my shoulders. She did not try to pick me up. I did not even feel her touch me. She said something. Perhaps she asked me if I was not feeling well, or maybe not. What do you ask a woman who collapses in the middle of the street?

The other officers stood over me and did not move. Not a single one of them bent over to collect my things and put them back inside the suitcase. People heading out to work the morning shift passed us by. They did not stop for a single sliver of a second. And I did not care. I did not belong to any world anywhere, and there was no world that owed me anything at all. My exhausted eyelids came down over my eyes. I did not see a thing. I did not see you. I did not see the children. I did not see my life flash before me nor my death for that matter. All I could see was that idiotic block of soap, not the diamonds inside it, just the primitive mass of soap itself. The woman said something that sounded like, "You can get up now." But I did not respond. She stood up then, straightened her skirt and shouted something to the other officers. One of them bent over and haphazardly returned the spilled contents to the suitcase and closed it. He then placed the suitcase next to me, stood up, and said nothing.

The female officer then added something else and hurried off who knows where. I did not move from where I sat. I began to notice slight pangs arriving in all sorts of spots throughout my body, some lasting but a brief moment, while others appeared to last longer. I did not make a sound, no groans, no sighs, I simply did not move. I remained seated right there where I had fallen, staring out vacantly into the nothing that stood before me, my breast heaving beneath my over-coat, rising and falling, my breath alternating between deep and shallow, drawn as one. The officers did not speak. They stood rooted to the ground like dark, elongated logs. People kept rushing on by wherever it was that they were headed. The sight of a woman sitting in the middle of the street and the sight of these officers standing beside her were like a little clip of some urban landscape that could not possibly interest anyone at all.

A short while later the sound of the approaching, intermingled gait of a man and a woman reached my ears. As I looked out of the corner of my eye I saw the officer in shirtsleeves from the station. He was now wearing a completely unbuttoned cardigan. You could tell that he had rushed out into the cold. The female officer stood beside him breathing hard. He crouched down in front of me, right before my very eyes, and stared into my face as he surveyed my weary gaze. The woman then leaned over me as well. She felt for my pulse beneath the sleeve of my overcoat. I did not move. Do whatever you want with me, I mused, and it was the first thought that went through my head since I had fallen to the ground. The female officer said some-thing. The man in the shirtsleeves shook himself loose into a standing position and said, "Take her to the hospital." I still did not move. The woman leaned over once more and asked me, "Are you not feeling well?" but I did not respond. She was clearly concerned, as was the man in the shirtsleeves. After a few moments of absolute silence, a car arrived on the scene. I suppose they had ordered the vehicle when the news reached the police station that I was not feeling well. The officers helped me get up and the man in shirtsleeves sat down next to the driver. I was seated with the female officer to my right and one of the men to my left.

We rode around for quite a while. Morning broke but the view of the mountains was rather grey - the cypress trees, the stones, the snow, everything, even the farms that passed by in the window; there was every possible shade of grey. It seemed to me as if I were travelling through a picture postcard photographed in black and white. I was surprised to see that Geneva was nearby, a sign by the side of the road said 'six kilometers' - what is six kilometers? Nothing. So that means Geneva is right here, means Geneva and Annemasse are one and the same, side by side along the horizon where God forgot how to set proper borders. But people know how - that is all they know. They also know how to turn nearby Geneva into a city so distant that one will never actually manage to make it there. And never is quite a long way off. Between Annemasse and Geneva the devil stands on the mountainside smiling his wan, wintry smile. I have witnessed it with my own eyes, and that is the truth. That is what happens when a woman like me goes for a ride in a vehicle with three police officers for company to keep an eye on her and make sure she does not, God forbid, go free. At that moment she sees things more clearly than anyone else on earth.

We were still outside the city passing through a sort of suburban village. A loose gravel path led up to a modest sized white house that looked like the servants' quarters on the grounds of some large land-holder. The entrance, which seemed a bit too wide, was crowned with a sign that said clearly, in large, dark letters, 'Clinique.'

The officers helped me out of the vehicle. I was a bit unsteady. A nurse appeared in profile in the window and then immediately disappeared from view. The door opened before me. The man in shirtsleeves hurried on inside as he entered the infirmary. Through the open door I could see him talking to the nurse who listened and cast a glance in my direction, then listened some more as her glance seemed to grow more and more distant. I suppose the story was a rather lengthy one. The female officer supported me as I slowly made my feeble, painful way inside. The two other officers who accompanied me walked right beside her, heel to toe. I suppressed a bitter burst of laughter. This madness, I thought, just will not let you be. This woman here is simultaneously trapped among you and at the same time does not need you whatsoever, yet you play at being police officers whether or not there is any real purpose to the game.

In the waiting room the female officer offered me a seat. I sat down. Through the thin slits of my weary eyelids I saw the two officers rising high above, to either side of me. The man in shirtsleeves who was holding a bundle of papers in his hands was still speaking with the nurse and alternately looking down to examine the documents. I closed my eyes. Nothing mattered to me anymore.

The female officer brought me a cup of water. I took a sip and waited a moment before taking another. I stared at the cup in my hand. I was still a human being - look, they are giving me water, they are taking care of me. They have given me a chair to sit down on and they are taking me in to the infirmary to be examined. They are concerned for my welfare, they are concerned for the welfare of the unborn child that I am carrying inside me. But I am also here because I am suspected of being someone who has no right to actually be a human being. They separated me from my children who were sent into exile beneath the dominion of another god because this very matter - whether I am worthy of being left alive or not - is suddenly in need of tremendous clarification. Absolute clarification. Like in some laboratory somewhere. This war puts millions to death in the blessed name of the Lord, casts down adolescence itself as it spills the young innards across flaming military fronts, lays low those who run for their lives down paths ordinarily trod by horse and carriage, murders mere children trapped inside rubble and ruins, but at the same time this war enlists a host of male and female officers to ride the railroad tracks and patrol the streets of a lost city like Annemasse in order to determine whether one particular woman, among all the other members of her myriad sex, is indeed a mute French woman in accordance with the letter and spirit of the law, and whether her place is among the free men and women who still have the right to live, or if, in fact, she is neither French nor mute and has committed the mortal sin of trying to keep herself and her children alive.

So let them deny me my cup of water. Let them just say no already. Let them stand me up against the wall. Let them leave me here to collapse atop the unborn child in my womb without any compassion whatsoever - that compassion that only ever exists for those who do not really need it - without that pity that has nothing at all to do with the Master of Mercy up in heaven but concerns only the human beings here on earth, all huddled together in one camp, who rise up in order to wipe out all the human beings huddled over there in some other camp. I am writing you now of the anger that I felt as I stared, in between sips, at the cup of water they had served me. But anger is not really a story of any substance. I know that. Better to stay silent on that score. Anger anyway has no words. But I am describing it here as I write you because a mere statement of the facts, any statement of the facts for that matter, is not worth anything at all. Anybody can tell that story. But I am the only one who knows the tale of the anger inside me, the only one who knows if it was me-re vanity or empty passion, and even if you skip these passages or read right through them, the things that I write when I recount the feelings that flooded through me at that moment are all that I can describe when I try to address you here, those feelings are all that I have, all that is left of what I was, in whatever sort of terms I can manage to find to help express what it was like, after all the time that had passed since they first sat me down in that infirmary, where I waited, simultaneously uncertain and yet so sure of what it fate held in store for me.

A little while later they put me on my feet and led me off into a little room with a neatly made bed, a small white dresser, a table with a rather deep, outsized bowl on top that held a white ceramic pitcher, a small dish with a minuscule brick of soap, and a towel hanging from a hook along the wall. A big, brown, homespun closet, that seemed rather out of place in the room, stood right next to the door. As I entered the room a male nurse dressed all in white came in and brought two wooden chairs that he placed on either side of the bed. The female nurse who had handled my admission said to me, "The toilet and the washbasin are outside, right next door. You are the last room down the hall." My face remained blank and attested to the fact that I had no idea what the nurse was saying. She sensed that I seemed not to have understood. Her gaze met that of the man in the shirtsleeves, as though trying to seek his advice with a silent glance as to how to communicate the items of absolute importance to me and then repeated, "The toilet… outside." I nodded my head to show that I now understood. I had no idea if I was still mute, did not know if the moment had finally arrived, that moment when I ought to put an end to the insipid pantomime of my muteness that was anyway just embarrassing and altogether improbable, if not downright impossible. But I did not know how to do that, and what exactly should follow, and what would be better after all, in the long run - exposing myself, or allowing myself to be exposed.

The female nurse asked the men in the room to turn around. The man in shirtsleeves left the room. The nurse and the female officer helped me get undressed, handed me a white, cotton gown, white woollen socks, and then helped me up onto the bed. Today, when I think back to that moment, I realize that it must have been humiliating, but at the time I did not feel anything at all. The man in shirtsleeves came back into the room. The other officers once more turned to face me. The nurse folded my clothes and placed them in the closet, hanging the clothing that needed to be hung and settling the items that were folded into one of the drawers. One of the officers picked up the suitcase, as though in response to some unspoken order, and placed it in the closet as well. "We can check the suitcase later," said the man in shirtsleeves. "You can put your handbag in the little dresser next to your table. We shall have to check that as well. Later." The nurse told me to get some rest and that in a little while the doctor would come around to examine me. She recommended that I try to sleep until that time because it was impossible to foresee what might delay the doctor from getting to see his patients at the appointed time. "You are tired," she said, "but you will get over it."

Everything was said in French, and an effort was made to try to use simple, earthy language, and it was all accompanied by explanatory gestures, a type of mimicry that verged on pantomime, and I nodded repeatedly to indicate that I understood, which seemed to leave the nurse rather pleased. The man in shirtsleeves smiled as well. The male nurse returned and placed a cup of water on the table. One of the officers who had accompanied me checked the window whose thick glass seemed to be glazed with an eternal layer of frost. The window was locked. The officer then took a seat on one of the chairs, moved back a bit from my bed and maintained his silence as still as the plaster coating the walls. Everyone else made their way out of the room and left the door partly open. I could see the second officer who had accompanied me standing stiffly like a sentinel in the doorway, but all the others left. I was all alone now, all alone with the officer sitting next to me and the other officer standing just outside my room. I was a prisoner in an infirmary that was like some white wing of a dark jailhouse.

I believe that I immediately fell asleep. I have no idea if I dreamed at all or if I awoke from time to time from a deep sleep, wavering along the threshold of wakefulness as I shuttled back and forth between thoughts both near and far. I suppose that it just had to be that way. It seems to me that at that time dreams disappeared altogether from the landscape of my sleep.

But we were born to be displaced, uprooted. More than once I had told you stories about my family and my childhood and you would tell me things as well about your own childhood, your own family, and here I am now telling you about me and you, and our children, and the unborn child that I was carrying in my womb, telling all about you, and me, and them - and we were all displaced, uprooted.

You were born into the world in your little village in Romania and I was born into the world in my little village in Hungary. Our sons were born in Belgium and now I am carrying this little child inside me and praying that the child will be born in Switzerland. You are not here now. I am trapped inside the prison clinic and the boys are being held behind the convent walls by the entourage of the cross. If we even survive, where will we all be tomorrow? Where will you be, where will the children be, where will I be? I hope that God possesses sufficient strands of heaven from which to watch over us from above. I am not praying to God asking Him to take care of me and you and the boys. I am simply praying for Him to exist, and if He exists, then let Him take care of us, for if He does not take care of us, then what does it matter to me if he exists or not, after all?

My eyelids came down once more on these bitter thoughts as I plunged the room into darkness, blotting out the weak light of the sun that faintly made its way through the sealed window, and the single lightbulb overhead that had been left on. My father had elevenchildren. He married another woman after my mother, who had given him seven children and then died. I have no idea if she loved me. Some said that I was like a servant around the house while others said that I took all those tasks upon myself because that was just what I had been made for. The fear of the Almighty was ever-present in our village home. Reb Mordechai Zalman, my father, was like some nobleman, always sporting a pair of well-polished boots and flourishing a thin, carved walking stick that never left his hands. His clothes were always immaculate and a thick, gold chain fell in a wide arc from the buttonhole in his lapel to the coat pocket where it rested, attached to a watch like no other in the world and it was a source of pride and a sort of hidden feather. His beard was groomed, his sidelocks always smoothed back behind his ears like after a ritual dip in the *Mikva*. And even though he had fallen on hard times and the properties that once were his, it was said, were now leased to him at quite a high rate, yet he never once seemed to give in - though it is true that he did not quite rebel - and he carried himself like every inch the nobleman, a pillar of the community in our little village synagogue, and that was how he was known throughout the neighboring villages as well.

We attended a school where it seems to me that all the students learned together in a single, large room, but my father did not think that this shabby little Hungarian school was enough and so he hired private tutors for us. One of these tutors, a boring, old pedant of a man, taught me German - reading, writing, and conversational *Hochdeutsch* - with fluent precision. Another tutor, a young man whose eyes forever flashed, as a smile played on his lips when he taught us - though he was rather re-served when he taught our brothers - was in charge of imparting Biblical Hebrew, teaching us the Pentateuch with Rashi, and teaching us the daily prayers from a Siddur with Hebrew letters, along with a High Holiday Prayer Book that contained a German translation as well, in fearful-looking Gothic lettering. My brothers used to put in a day's work in the fields, harvesting, picking, working in the animal pens, but then they studied as well. Some of them were rather diligent while others were a bit lazy, some filled with joy while others were rather introverted, but they all strictly observed the commandment 'to honor thy father and mother,' even that mother that was not really theirs. Our mother had died some time back and the current wife had married my father as soon as the thirty-day mourning period for my mother was over. There was no way of knowing if she had any love for the children of the woman who had preceded her, but the boys still honored and re-spected her quite a bit all the same. There was only one rebel among us children, my sister Monye, or Manya, the one that we had wanted to go visit now in Saint-Claude. She would strike out against what-ever was within striking distance, so long as there were witnesses to testify to the act. If the rest of us said 'yes,' she would say 'no,' and if we all said 'no,' she would immediately respond with a resounding 'yes.' And you could tell that she was always rather happy during those moments when everyone around her was angry with her and the things she did. On the other hand, she was rather bored when nothing of any importance went on around her that could possibly be connected to her. Our lives looked as though autumn had already arrived and the leaves that still clung to the branches were already yellowing and about to fall. All the trees in our sparse forest were already naked, even though they did not quite seem so just yet.

We never read the newspapers, though my oldest brother used to tell me all sorts of things... He was Father's favorite because of the way he constantly applied himself to learning Torah, along with his diligence at work on the farm, and his natural charm and grace, his innate wisdom, and the fact that you could tell just by looking at him that he recalled his mother who had passed away, with a silence that was entirely his own, and it was only my father, I believe, who truly knew how to read him properly. He would tell me about a world that lived in bankruptcy, of people who toiled away, forgotten and abandoned by time, whose groans and sighs went unheard, of the winds of change that blew through Hungary when Béla Kun came to power full of new hope, but disappointed everyone. I loved him like a soulmate, but I was not under the impression that he was telling me things that I truly wanted to know about in all their intimate details. I was afraid of the freedom that he had adopted for himself. He used to tell Monye, his sister from father and mother, things as well, but she would make him tell her more and more until he stopped telling her even the half of it anymore. And everything was a secret. God forbid if our father were to find out about our vain conversations concerning matters of the world. To this day I have no idea if Father actually knew or if he just chose to look the other way and pretend not to know.

One day Monye just got up and left. Quite a while later we received a letter from her that was postmarked Belgium. To this day I have no idea how she got there. She never told us who paid for the train tickets that took her there, and we never knew if she just got up and left on her own or with a group - she left us completely in the dark. Only God knows how she managed to get by in Antwerp, that foreign city, as a young girl who had not yet turned sixteen yet. Father did not say a word. He knew nothing whatsoever about it but guessed the truth of it all. The silence that he maintained when we would bring her up was a sort of gesture of excommunication. A breach had been thrown open in the walls of the family house.

Some time later I too got up and left. The family as a whole, and I in particular, did not have a penny to our names, and Father would never have given me what little there was for the sake of such a trip. I went to visit my uncle Andor, who still lived in our little village of Tiszasalka, although he no longer kept the Sabbath nor observed the commandments, had become a Zionist and was one of the leaders of the Beitar movement in our district. He was one of the members of an association that had purchased land in the city of Haifa in the Carmel region in Palestine, in order to build himself a house there. When he traveled to the country by ship in the company of quite a few other members of his group to visit the Land of Israel he found that the land which he had bought was in fact covered by the sea, though he had no idea if it had always been that way since the world was created or if it had only been washed over once they had put it up for sale. But Andor never confirmed the truth of that story. "I did not buy anything," he would say, "and what I did buy is not covered by the sea but once they build on the property you will be able to see the water from the windows, and when am I going to begin construction? In a little while, before the big storm blows through here."

The rumors swirling around this joker were that he had lovers throughout the neighbouring villages. But he was a wise, comprehending man full of sage advice, and I felt a tremendous love for him and he, too, loved me from the bottom of his heart. "You and your mother," he used to say. He never let an opportunity pass without telling me that she was the most beautiful woman he had ever met. I told him that I wanted to go visit my sister Monye in Belgium.

"Belgium is a long way off," Andor said. "How are you going to get there?"

"By train," I replied. He puffed on the stem of his pipe. A spark of mischievousness lit up in his eyes. Belgium is indeed a long way off," he said, "but Monye is even farther away. How much money do you have for travel expenses?"

"I do not have a thing," I said. "I will get there and go to work and save up and when I return I will pay you back whatever you lend me today."

"Girls like you do not come back," Andor said. "Not to a place like this and not these days anyway. You want me to pay to separate you from your father, and your brothers and sisters, and from me, forever?"

"We will meet again, I swear," I told him.

"Where?" he asked. "Well, if a modest young woman like you swears to it, I suppose she knows what she is getting into. If that is the case, then tell me where we are going to meet again - here? In some big city in Hungary? In Israel? On the way to America, in some place where neither you nor I will even have a home? Where? I know we will meet again and I am going to lend you the money. You will pay me back when we see each other once more but I do not want you to feel like you are in my debt until then. It will happen, of course, because you swore, but you did not tell me when when you took your oath and it may well take quite a long time before it ever comes to pass. That is something that neither you nor I have any way of knowing."

Now, as I am telling you about the things that flashed before my eyes as I kept them closed in the clinic just outside Annemasse I must tell you that I have still not repaid my debt to Andor. The deadline of my oath has still not arrived.

I could not possibly swear to you that all the things which I am telling you occur-red to me in the order that I have here put them down. It seems to me that I had a fever at the time, and the images that passed before my eyes came in scattered fragments, in between the sleep that seized me for a brief instant and some troubled moment of rest that washed over me thereafter, and I am only making the connections here now. But that does not matter at all. Today I believe that sanity wages its own war for survival in rather simple ways. Everything that we went through from the day that they threw you in prison and you disappeared from our lives, to the instant when they arrested me and took our children from me, right down to the moment in which I lay imprisoned in this strange clinic high in the Alps, that I was never ever meant to even visit to begin with - all of it was completely insane.

It would seem that the only way to not lose your mind is to clarify just how you arrived at that fork in the road where it seems that you are, indeed, going to lose it. How did this girl get here, this young girl from some little, nondescript village that has nothing whatsoever to do with Antwerp, or Bondigoux, or Brens, or Annemasse, or the Gestapo, or train rides through the night trying to reach the border, or pretending to be mute, or a convent, or prison, or a pregnancy in which the pregnant woman has no idea if the child she is carrying inside her womb is already an orphan, or if that little boy or girl will one day yet be a source of pride and joy for his or her father? How did this woman get here without a single friend, without a savior? It is life laid out as sheer insanity. What is her story? Who came up with it? How did it begin? The difference between sinking and floating along the surface of the water lies in the ability to ask just how it all began. How it all began is a question rife with life. How it all ends - no, how it all ends is, in the final analysis, a dead question to begin with.

I have no idea how long I lay there like that in my bed without any strength whatsoever, returning to all those sights and sounds that once were. I had a watch with me but they had also taken that and put it in the closet, while the nurse cleaned off my face and body with a damp cloth before helping me lie down. I had long ago taught myself to pay attention to time in whatever I do, marking the minutes and the hours that had already passed as well as those that were still yet to come. Time, for me, was always ordered and arranged in neat parcels, packaged together bit by bit. It seemed to me as though the hands of the clock had been created for the express purpose of making order in life, and without them anybody knowing when to get up and when to go to bed, when to head out and when to head back home, and how would children have been able to learn altogether - I mean, the day is not just some random mess, and what does it want from them altogether?

Before clocks had been created in the world time would come to a stop when the sun went down, and the night was like some dark pit in which everything that bustled and rustled around incessantly hid lying in wait, and we used to close our eyes so as not to have to see a thing, until something somewhere leaped out at us all of a sudden, and if we were able to beat it back and best it, then God bless us. Clocks then doubled our lives. They do not stop when the day ends. At any rate, I had always needed a clock or a watch, but now I had absolutely no need for one whatsoever. Time had left me all alone from the moment when they took away my control over my own life and the lives of my children and seemed to rob me of all my strength, and forced me to accept whatever it was that was going to happen to me, however things would turn out, without my being able to do anything whatsoever, however trivial or monumental, on my own behalf, on your behalf, on behalf of Erwin or Jackie, or any of the people who had rendered the world in which I had lived a place populated by people, men and women, who had been quite dear to me, or who had caused me quite a bit of pain, and from all of whom I had now been abruptly torn away. Who needs a watch in a place where time has ceased to have all meaning? That is how it seems to me as I sit here now and write these things to you. It is not the bars, nor the chains, nor the guard on the inside, nor the officer on the outside that constitute a sense of imprisonment. Prison begins when one no longer has any need for time, when one does not need a watch anymore.

I was suddenly uncomfortable with the fact that I was thinking all these things with a police officer sitting in my room right next to my bed. His presence seemed like some prohibited glimpse of things, like an invasion of the space that life had clearly delineated for me. I looked at him out of the corner of my downcast eye in order to try and discern if he was able to see the things that I saw. This was, of course, patently absurd. He did not see a thing. He was not keeping an eye on me. There was no way I was going to escape, after all. There was another officer just outside the door. He was sitting next to me because the spectacle of a prisoner is simply scripted that way - those are the rules, there is to be an officer in the room with the individual who has been arrested. But he was not a mere chair, after all. He was a human being. His eyes were wide open. They were focused rather firmly on some imaginary interstice inside my room, but they had no lids. He stared at the people and the places that I had just left behind as I wandered weakly through the world of sleep, or maybe fever, and guarded the dream that I had not even dreamt. He was the stranger who somehow joined up with the world of the individual who has nothing left but that personal world. You know well that I was afraid of him. He was not going to do anything to me. He was a being completely void of volition. They had put him in a chair and he sat there. If they were to make him stand up, he would stand. Were they to tell him to let the woman go, he would have opened the gates for me and sent me off to freedom. And if they would have told him to take me to the scaffold, he would have personally prepared the hangman's noose for my neck. I myself am, after all, no more than a mere seat in the theater that his life has somehow led him into. He has no real connection to me. I am a mere tool with no name, in a place with no name, in a city with no name, on a day with no name, in a time that has no name, and perhaps he too is merely a nameless entity himself, nameless even in his own eyes, and if he once had a name, perhaps by now he has already forgotten it.

That is how things go, I thought, people that you do not even know imprison people that they, in turn, do not know, chase down people that have nothing whatsoever to do with them and with whom they have no connection at all, and the torture is not meted out by someone that you love or by someone that you hate, but by some stranger who does not put you through your suffering out of love or hate but simply because that is what the nature of this name-less world has become, in which people refer to God by using some bland moniker with no real significance because they are afraid to call Him by His true name. These police officers who sit upon some sort of ersatz throne in the room do not harbor a single evil thought in their hearts, with no separation, no real distance between them and the bed where this woman lies. They are merely the blind, un-seeing agents of the Angel of Death, with his thousand, all-seeing eyes, who has chosen them to do his foul bidding. They are awful.

You told me all about this particular angel with his thousand eyes. I still recall your words. We were walking side by side in Ki-evit Park in Antwerp on a Saturday in the summer as the evening fell. I was still uncertain as to whether or not I was going to marry you, but I was sure that if I did get married, I would only marry you. I did not know if you, for your part, were as certain. You were so good-looking. Tall. Slender. Light on your feet. You held your only felt hat in your hands and walked with your head bared among all the other people taking a walk in the park, almost all of whom were wearing dark, wide-brimmed hats. Your hair was as dark as coal and shined about as bright, with a single, small curl falling across your forehead like some errant twig that had slipped out of the wavy line. You talked most of the time. You were so knowledgeable. For a few good minutes you told me all about the geniuses in Vienna, where you had studied architecture and philosophy for what was actually little more than a year. As soon as you sensed that I was not capable of being impressed by the things that impressed you you began to wax poetic, and when it seemed to you that I was listening intently, flatteringly, though perhaps with a slight touch of ridicule, then you began to talk about the wonders of nature, and then you switched to music, and then proceeded to talk about all sorts of well-known painters whom I had never heard of in my life. You lorded it over me a bit because you could not believe that this rather beautiful girl , from this little village could not help but be impressed. You were wonderful, a real man and a mere boy at the same time, and I just knew. And you talked about life, talked about poverty and wealth, talked about justice and malice, life and death. And then, I still recall, you told me that the will to live was quite a bit greater than the field of death, and the angel that God had appointed to bring back all souls to Him was not able to find anyone that he might convince to agree to die among all the many millions living in the world. So for that reason God had given the angel a thousand eyes and the angel needs every single one of those thousand eyes in order to be able to manage, to find that one individual who would finally give in and give his soul up to the angel after all.

"I am telling you the story of a real believer," you said to me and you put your arm around my shoulders with a smile, "because you know what, I am going to put out the angel's eyes on the day that he comes to look for me and then we are going to just sit there and look at him and laugh."

"Really?" I asked, with a bit of a challenging tone. "And then what?"

"Then we are going to live forever, Roszyka," you replied. "You and me, forever!"

"You are crazy," I said. "What got into your head to tell a young girl like me such silly things? Why do you spend your time thinking about this angel, and who ever told you how many eyes he has to have in order to be able to carry out his mission?"

"He needs every single last one of his eyes," you replied. "And I gouged out the lot of them the day that I met you..."

I did not notice the nurse who had entered the room. She was suddenly standing right next to me and said, "The doctor is here, Madame." Through the slits of my barely opened eyes that were still hidden behind the hardly lifted haze I could see a tall figure dressed in black standing behind the nurse. I was not sure if what I saw was real or a mere illusion. The nurse said, "Doctor," but what I saw did not seem to me to be a doctor. The officer got up from his chair, executed a slight, polite bow before the man in the black robe, and then left my room. "You know Father, Doctor Sir, that the rules in such an instance require that I be present during the course of the examination. Do you have any objections?"

"By all means," the man in black said to her as he stepped around and approached the bed.

The nurse moved the chair over to the door, sat down and folded her arms in her lap while her eyes stared off into the distance and occasionally came to rest on me, with a presence that was not entirely there but could still be felt all the same, as she demonstrated a certain respect for what was left of the idea of my privacy, though without acknowledging any real privacy whatsoever.

His name was DuPont, or so he told me, "I am Doctor Albert DuPont."

I now saw him clearly. He was a priest. The nurse had said, "Father." Now it was clear to me too. His voice was deep and soft. They have sent me one of their angels, I thought to myself. Their angels wear black even up in heaven. Here on earth they are priests. I did not offer him any greeting, as I waited for him to speak. If he was really a physician he would not have said to me, "I am Doctor Albert DuPont," but he was a priest. Perhaps he was a priest who had become a physician, or a physician who had become a priest, or neither of the two, or both for that matter. He was definitely someone from some far away place.

He did not take any notes. He sat down next to the bed, let his gaze fall on me for a bit and then told me that he had heard that I had come a long way by train and that I had been taken off to be investigated in order to address a number of questions that needed to be clarified. The police captain had told him that they had taken my boys away from me and sent them off to the convent. "It is a good place, you can rest assured," he said. "I am the doctor there, and among my other patients I will take care of your sons as well. They will not be there long. They are your sons, are they not? The police captain is of the opinion that in a short time everything will be clarified and you will be free to once more go on your way and complete your journey, you along with your children. In the meantime, there is no better place for them than the convent." I listened and did not say a word. It was not that I did not want to cooperate, but I just could not bring myself to do so. I was too tired, too worn down, too empty inside. An invasive sense of weakness robbed me of my will altogether. I was not even able to marshal that minimal amount of strength necessary to display a certain politeness. He spoke to me and about me but it seemed to me that he was speaking about someone who had nothing to do with me whatsoever.

He examined me. The nurse turned her face away. There are some manners that manage to survive despite everything, I thought to myself. My doctor was a man of refined sensibilities with a rather delicate nature. A woman senses these things. But I refused to acknowledge this fact. I did not respond, I was completely passive. This was the language I chose to use to express the fact that nothing could overcome my forced status as a foreigner. It was clear to me that he sensed just what I was getting at but he did not alter the course of his silent, restrained, rather personal examination all the same. That was the language that he, in turn, chose to use in order to tell me that he was concerned for my well-being, mine and that of the unborn child inside my womb, not the well-being of a mere nameless prisoner who was pregnant and about to give birth. He seemed to be saying "I am your doctor, I do not belong to the police or the prison either." But I did not want to hear what he was saying. That was my sorry little act of disobedience.

The nurse handed him a pitcher and a bowl of water that had been prepared for the purpose beforehand. She poured the water over his hands. He scrubbed his hands firmly with soap, and as he dried them off he said, without turning his eyes to the nurse, "You will have to leave us alone for a few moments, Madame Nurse. The-re are some things that must remain solely between a doctor and his patient and no one, not even the authorities, have the right to be party to these things. I am sure that you understand. I will handle any problems with your superiors, not to worry." The nurse took the towel from his hands. She placed the pitcher in the bowl and left the room without saying a word. I was now extremely terrified and began to cooperate completely. He had become a physician in every sense of the word and I was completely at attention, all of me was now turned completely towards him. The child. He was going to tell me something about the infant inside me. I had lost my child. The child was dead inside me. I am no more than a corpse inside my own body alongside this child. His face did not reveal anything at all. He wore an easy, pleasant expression. The shadow of a smile played across his lips. But he was a priest. There is always the shadow of a smile hovering across the faces of priests and men of faith. They flit through the very worst news in the world with that selfsame smile. All is right in the leaky world their God has sent them to help, once it seems to them that they have plugged up the holes with the words that they have uttered. I waited for the first word out of his mouth in order to rise up from my bed and strangle him.

"I will speak quickly," he said. "We do not have time. I am going to get you out of here. You and the child you have inside your womb. You are both perfectly healthy. But I am going to tell them that you are in danger. You require a comprehensive examination that can only be conducted at the hospital. I will accompany you. The children will be waiting for you there. Do not ask me how. You are healthy enough to board the train and travel. Here you are finished. Your papers are all in order, but you are not. They know that you are not mute. They will continue investigating until they find what they are looking for. The papers will be with me. Do not ask me how. We know who Moritz Mayer was." "Was?!" I let slip in alarm. "Shh... shh... shh, that is just a figure of speech! Who he is, certainly, who he is, not who he was. I hope that he is still with us somewhere out there among the living. Who he is, yes. Do not whisper one word. You do not know how to speak. You are to conduct yourself without any will of your own whatsoever. I, along with the female officer and the captain, will say whatever it is that we will say and you are to do whatever you are called upon to do, even if you do not understand a word and remain mute like a dumb pumpkin in the field. Do you need anything? Now, quickly, anything at all?" "The block of soap in my handbag, in the closet. Now." He had no time to think about what I was saying. He did not ask what block of soap I was referring to. He threw open the closet and by silently moving my eyes around and nodding my head in all directions I managed to tell him just where he might find this soap of mine. He located it immediately. He slipped it into the medical bag that he had with him. He smiled, the smile of a smuggler, not the smile of a priest, lightly patted the leather exterior of his bag and did not ask me anything at all as I, too, remained silent. He sat down and called out for the nurse to return. This all took place in a matter of three or four minutes, perhaps even less. The nurse approached the bed, and out of habit, straightened the sheets and arranged the blanket on top of me.

"I have explained to the lady what her condition is," said the doctor.

"You are truly a genius, Father, Doctor Sir," the nurse said dryly. "Even deaf-mutes manage to hear every word that comes out of your mouth."

"Bravo! Not even the war can dull our sense of humor. We shall have to transfer her to the hospital for a more comprehensive examination. I shall arrange everything with the captain. In the meantime…" he began to write out a prescription on a piece of paper that he had removed from his bag as he simultaneously finished what he had been saying. "…see that she takes this here in the amount prescribed. She must drink a lot of fluids and remain on absolute bed rest. She is not to get out of bed for any reason whatsoever. You are to call me in the event of any change in her condition. See that the light in the room is not too strong, in compliance with the minimum amount required for security purposes, of course. I trust that the minimum will suffice." He got up, bowed slightly as he stood over me and said, "Madame," caressed my head in the manner of priests and left the room. I turned my head to face the window and after a moment I could sense that I was crying as I had never cried before in my life. They were tears that soundlessly rocked my very soul, tears that tore through me in silence, redemptive tears with no crying, no shouting, no thanksgiving, nothing at all other than the purest tears that had ever been shed, cleansed of all else that was not in itself these purely falling tears.

Suddenly my understanding returned. He had spoken to me in German. I had not been aware of that fact while he talked. Every word that he had uttered now reverberated against my eardrums. It had been German with a heavy French accent. But it had been German. "…We know who Moritz Mayer was…" Who are "we?" And how do they know? Are "We" the Gestapo and the Marshal along with Pierre Laval, they and that worm that had eaten through all that was left of France, and now they knew who Moritz Mayer was, and they are crawling in my direction now and they have spiders at their command weaving their wily webs and all of us, Erwin, Jackie and I, are already trapped inside them? Maybe so, and then again, maybe not. Maybe so, because that is just how the world recreates itself anew each day. And then again, maybe not, since I gave him the block of soap without even asking who he was, because I believed in him, because this physician-priest was someone that you put your faith in without examining anything, without checking anything, without any suspicions whatsoever, in a fraction of an instant. How stupid of me. They are the biggest deceivers. Except you simply can not even imagine that the slightest drop of venom runs through their veins. A priest. A priest and a physician, what is that supposed to mean? I should have been more careful. "…We know who Moritz Mayer was…" They knew who I was too. He spoke German, he knew that I was not mute. "…Even if you remain mute like a dumb pumpkin in the field…" There is no expression like that, no such saying. Maybe he was born someplace else. Not in the Alps. This physician-priest is not from Annemasse. Or maybe he is. Maybe he is some sort of a poet. A pumpkin in his eyes is simply the mutest thing that there is in the world. But when you see a pumpkin you do not think that it is mute, that is not the first thing that goes through your mind. You think to yourself that it is a pumpkin. It was the same with me. They did not see a mute woman when they looked at me, they saw a pumpkin, a

Jewish woman whose sentence and the sentence against her children was issued long ago, and she was now trying to escape as though she were not, in fact, a pumpkin. But I am not a pumpkin. I am just one woman, and I want to live.

The priest had come to me from heaven, had taken his life in his hands when he came down here to earth - to me, my children, and my unborn child. I began to cry once more. The nurse placed the palm of her hand against my skin. She was rather cold. *"Fièvre* (fever)," she said. I had no idea what *"Fièvre"* meant, but when she placed a large thermometer underneath my armpit I understood. She took my wrist in her hands and measured my pulse. Her lips moved, but soundlessly; her voice did not emerge. She then sat there and waited for the thermometer, saying to me in a French that was something between what you would use if you were addressing little children and the broken language you would resort to to address a foreigner, *"Demain bébé bien, madame hopital. Calme Madame, calme!* (Tomorrow baby okay, Madame go hospital. Relax, Madame, relax!)" Had the priest's subterfuge dulled her senses? Did she think that she had been asked to leave the room because the doc-tor was going to communicate a difficult piece of news to me concerning my welfare and the welfare of the unborn child inside me, news that even the men and women of the police force were not permitted, in accordance with their faith as human beings, to be party to and hear pronounced by the Man of God, or the doctor, for that matter? Was she too in league with him? Was I inside some clinic that was entirely a put-on, a front that the Resistance had thrown up inside occupied Annemasse? "We know who Moritz Mayer was." Did they know because Moritz Mayer, because they knew where he came from, and they, with their own origins, were all partners in crime, trusted members of the same secret cabal? Had you worked together with them? Had they collaborated with you? Did you have code names, made-up names like they give themselves in those youth groups, like the boy scouts? Was the game you played one that you were willing to play right down to the scaffold, right up to the wall where they would have you all lined up and shot?

Was this all not just a bit too romantic, when in fact the truth was complex enough that it did not need to be camouflaged by some further fascinating fact or tidbit? Be careful, be careful I said to myself. I was running a fever. The nurse administered some liquid medicine, straightened the covers of my bed, caressed my forehead, then went over to her chair and sat down and told me that I should try to get some rest.

It seems to me that I did not, in fact, fall asleep. I slipped into a sense of confidence that suddenly came over me after all the doubts and the fears. I knew, with more certainty than the circumstances would seem to have warranted, that I would be saved. I did not know how. The tale had unfolded and reached a dead end, but then the light of some alternate form of salvation had suddenly appeared at the end of the tunnel, in the form of this priest. I suddenly had complete and incontrovertible faith in him, and from that point on the story continued to twist and turn, and the priest was no longer on the scene and there were figures that I recognized and others that I did not, in places I had already been and places I had never even imagined before in my life, and they led me right up to the legendary peace and tranquility of Switzerland, but right before I crossed over into that promised land something happened and I did not make it. If I were to tell you that everything seemed to be happening as if I were sitting in some movie theater somewhere, and just when the plot seemed to be on the point of some sort of resolution, the film tore in half and the room went dark and everything started over again from the beginning with a new reel - if I were to put it that way, you would just say that I have a penchant for overly simple metaphors.

In one version of the story I take a path that leads to a big gate, with Switzerland written overhead, and I run in that direction, with Erwin and Jackie running on ahead of me even faster, first Erwin, and then Jackie right behind him. And there I am running along behind them with my pregnancy rendering me somewhat awkward as I go, a little suitcase in my hands, running forward and retreating, forward and then retreating, as they keep running on ahead and off into the distance, and suddenly I can not see them anymore and I do not know if they already went through the gate, and if I head through the gate in their wake, how will I find them, and am I on the verge of losing the children I guarded so carefully throughout our time in captivity now that we are finally free, or did they maybe make a mistake and miss the gate and run right past it straight down into the basement in Marseille, and the train station in Lyon, and all the other places we had already run away from? In the end this reel broke off as well and everything started over again once more from the beginning, with the priest, and the boys, and a plot that unraveled in the direction of our salvation, only to be cut off once more before it got there. That was what the absolute confidence in my approaching salvation looked like, that confidence that filled me with a calm that could not quite find satisfaction nevertheless, but, all the same, there were moments of hope and positive thoughts which it would seem I was terribly in need of, even though every faint ray of hope seemed to be extinguished as soon as it had begun to shine.

I did not sleep at all, though I was not completely awake either. I felt like you had slipped into my room without anyone noticing and that you stood by the side of my bed and watched over me as I slept and you did know that I could see you, even though I did not open my eyes and did not reach out my hand to touch you, nor did I turn my head in your direction, and I did not say a word of all the things that were hidden away in my heart, simply because I loved you so much in that moment as you stood looking down at me. All that there was between us was this extremely loving gaze of yours, along with the fact that I swore that this magical moment would last forever and would not finish in the hurried declaration of a love that was so innocent, complete, and pure. Kievit Park was ours and it filled the white room of the clinic where I lay with the vibrant colors of the falling autumn leaves.

We went walking there often after that summer evening - do you remember? Every Saturday afternoon, each *Shabbos* straight through till Rosh Hashanah. That was when the entire Jewish community in the city came out in order to do *Tashlich*. I know that I was not among the great believers when it came to getting rid of your sins from the past year by tossing them into the wide canal that ran through the Park. "It is a wonderful tradition," you said to me. "A real fairy tale. Sins are never reduced to mere crumbs, they remain large forever, heavy, weighty, you can not toss them into the deep blue sea, they float right up along the surface. But how wonderful it is that they do not believe in this awful truth and do *Tashlich* instead, and then return to their lives like some burden has been lifted, without looking at the scales where we are being judged just before we leave."

"You're arrogant," I said at the time.

"No," you uttered, "not arrogant. Anyone who loves the fairy tale as much as I do can not possibly be arrogant. You know, *Tashlich* is perhaps the most magical moment that there is. Here I am walking along by your side. There are thousands of people all around us, milling around, standing in place. Some have a little prayer book, a little *Siddur* open in front of them and they are praying. Children's baby strollers are parked right beside them. The man and the woman recite lines from the Bible in unison, and here you are, and here I am, the two of us all alone in the midst of the masses, and I am telling you that even though I have said some things to you that were as heavy as cast iron, my entire being is as devoid of sin and light as the wind, and here I am now whispering in your ear, Roszyka, the time has come, today is the day. We will leave here and head straight over to see my brother and your sister and the entire family and we will tell them everything. Yes. We are going to stand under the *Chuppah* after all, we are going to get married." You were not the least bit embarrassed. I sensed that you yourself did not even know that you were going to say all this to me a moment before you actually said it, but all the same I felt like you had prepared your words rather beautifully somehow in advance, right down to the slightest detail, and you had recited them from some invisible text that you had memorized, like someone reading out a proclamation from a scroll that had already, in fact, disappeared.

I was enthralled and yet could not believe my ears at the same time. That was just the way it had to be, given how deeply I was in love with you. You were a sort of bohemian. You sang, you painted, you wrote poetry. There was not a single thing about you that could have convinced me that you were not a vagabond wanderer in every fiber of your being, even though not a day went by that you were not hard at work, trying to make a living and to get by however you could, trying to earn a few cents even when money was harder to come by than some minor miracle. You were responsible, diligent, faithful, but it was impossible for you to hide the wild gipsy that you shoved into a sort of holding cell within your greater personality. That part of you was trapped inside, but it was there. I could see it. I loved you and I was scared and yet still loved you. I knew that you were a sort of adventure that was almost too wonderful for words.

You were so different from your brother Zollie. You both came from the same rundown, godforsaken little village right outside Satu Mare. Your parents were extremely poor. Your uncles and other family members lived in the neighboring villages and you would go visit each other on foot along endlessly winding dirt paths. Zollie became an apprentice at a tannery. In the *Cheder*, the single room where the two of you went to school together, even though you were a bit older than him, you over-shadowed him until he absolutely hated school. You, they said, were a genius. But you ran away. You were just a child and already that world was too small for you. To this day I can not believe the story, but I know from Zollie and your sister Chana that things actually did take place exactly the way that you described them, and that the tale is, in fact, accurate. You just suddenly disappeared, without a warning, with no prior notice, from one day to the next. Little Moritz was swallowed up by the forests bordering the village. For months they had no idea where even to look for you and a heavy sense of mourning slowly descended on your family's home, until someone arrived in the village with you in tow. That person, or someone else, perhaps, had found you in Turkey. A child of only eleven years old. Turkey was very far away. You told me that they never asked you how you got there, and so you never told them. There were no rebukes, you were not beaten, nobody troubled or tortured you at all. Everyone simply thanked God for performing this particular miracle and for the fact that you were, after, all alive. It was as though the whole thing had never taken place and was merely some sort of fairy tale or childhood myth. The only thing that you would say if anyone ever tried to resolve the mystery surrounding the miracle of your disappearance and return was "What else could I do but go to Turkey, after all..." They did get you to calm down. I have no idea how. They sent you off to a Yeshiva in Satu Mare and you quickly developed a name for yourself among the masses as a budding Torah giant and God-fearing Jew, whose future held a rather certain promise of greatness, a promise that had not yet been fulfilled and yet was already being realized at that very moment.

But not you.

The same way that you had suddenly up and disappeared the first time, you once again disappeared, shrouded in a cloud of mystery. You went off to Vienna. At the *Yeshiva*, before you left, you had been secretly studying German and Math and had read all sorts of different books, and I do not know what else you devoured in order to nourish your knowledge-starved mind. They accepted you at the University to pursue studies in Architecture. You were a rather diligent student, and you became a member of a private circle that was devoted to the theories of the philosopher Hegel - about whom, to this day, I know absolutely nothing and have no idea how he managed to earn your admiration - until things got to the point that you were no longer able to stand the awful crisis into which you had been plunged and you left everything behind and took off for Charleroi in Belgium. There were no other countries in the world quite like Belgium. It was an ostensibly properly closed, introverted country, that was in fact rather open, and the stream of Jewish hu-manity that was being torn up from its roots all over the place found its way there, if they were not able to sail across the ocean instead. In Charleroi, or nearby, you found work in a coal mine, and after a little while, given that you were not able to handle this humiliating, backbreaking labor, you made your way to

Antwerp, and that was where you found me, among the other family members who had already been exiled to the city. You immediately wrote your brother Zollie to tell him that he ought to come over there as well, and he lived in our midst right alongside us, and Gizzy Scheck, the daughter of one of my father's nephews - a man with a small operation raising and selling poultry, who was nevertheless a widely reputed student and scholar and the first to leave Hungary for Belgium - became the object of your brother's affection and desire. He admired her in all his innocence for the fact that she was a stately woman, endowed with both beauty and intelligence, and it was clear to him that she would deign to marry him if she would just take a single day off from her rather incredible dealings as a small-time businesswoman and momentarily overlook the discrepancy between what she was and what he, in turn, was.

We were all somewhat homeless. It was not that we were orphans, God forbid. To that day none of us were actually orphans. We had lost neither father nor mother - not you and not me, and not any of the entire group of refugees who left our villages behind, guided by some invisible hand towards Antwerp. They included our real blood relatives, as well as those who felt like relatives, though they were not, in fact, our family and some young men and women with whom we had been friends since childhood. We connected with one another and turned into a large, extended family of foundlings, as it were. Not a single member of our entire group - with the exception of perhaps you and Gizzy - managed to learn the language spoken in Antwerp. We did not read the local papers, we were entirely consumed with the need to earn of our daily bread, to procure proper shoes and clothing to pay the rent on the little rooms and apartments where we lived, and to think all the time about the future that was always so close at hand, no more than a day or two, at most, beyond the horizon. You and I made sure to write home to our parents once a month. I do not recall us ever confessing to one another that we felt like we were committing a sin as each day passed with us in Antwerp while the rest of them had been left behind in the old country. It was just that sort of a moveable world order at the time, which seemed to sift its youth and let them fall where they may, while leaving the elderly behind, caught up in the net from which the latter listlessly refused to disentangle themselves. Today I can recall that neither Erwin nor Jackie ever heard a thing from me about their grandfather and grandmother, other than the occasional pronouncement that I was "sending kisses to Grandma and Grandpa from them," before, or even after having already sealed the envelope in which I had secretly sent off my weekly letter home. They had no concept of the fact that grandparents were something that belonged in any way to their world. And, in fact, they did not. They were no more than the name of a far away town. What a sin, and a rather strange one, at that - our entire group, consisting of our immediate and distant relatives and the childhood friends that were there with us too, were all guilty of this sin, without acknowledging the guilt or the very nature of the sin. We were the first generation of émigrés. What had preceded us could not possibly continue and what would follow was our own children, and our children were just like us, another first generation of émigrés.

In the midst of this mix of people you flowered like a prince crowned with an enchanted aura. If the world that still stood at that time had in fact already been destroyed, you certainly would have found your way to some Paris or London or other city, and there you would have married a member of the royal family, or an actress or a poetess. But here you were instead, in Kievit Park, which the local Jews, who were always fond of a certain sense of self-ridicule, lovingly referred to as 'Cholent Park,' and you were saying to me - this lost little village girl - that you were intent on marrying me. And during *Tashlich*. The fairy tale holiday. I took ahold of the large palm of your hand and held it in my own fragile palm and linked my fingers with yours as I said to you, "Let us go and see your brother and sister."

And now you were here by my side, in my room in the clinic in Annemasse, staring at me through the foliage in the trees in the park all decked out in their autumn hues, and neither one of us was saying a word that might disturb this wonderful sense of togetherness that we shared.

The days passed in a dense blur, or at least that is how it seemed to me. The hours were endless. The female officer in my room was ever-present, as were the two officers standing outside the door. I have no idea if they had replacements or substitutes, and I can not recall if they slept, and when they slept, or where they slept, for that matter. They were part and parcel of the time that stood still, along with the washbasin that they would bring me, and the medicine that they would have me drink at regular intervals, and the bed linen that they would straighten all around me each time, and even changed once, as I recall. But time was not a dimension in which anything at all took place. Nothing, nothing at all took place. Time, and the people that populated it like no more than mere objects, and the objects themselves, along with the walls of the room, were all one and the same - a sense of time that had turned immobile and which I was no longer capable of measuring altogether. Only my thoughts seemed to continue to move. It seemed to me that I was becoming even weaker, wan, waiting for something I was not even waiting on, my entire being a body that was not allowed to rise from its bed because that was the order that had once upon a time been handed down, and no one had ever come by thereafter to check if I was still in need of such watchful care. I was a human being left stranded like a bough that had been cut from the tree. I thought to myself that I must be gathering moss already. Even my thoughts themselves were at times gloomy, as they turned to examine the many faces of fear that look out on what was and what is certainly yet to come; and other times my thoughts were lit with the borrowed light of awe and hope, that what seemed certain might yet not come to pass, as I lost all mental connection with life as it was - all these thoughts that ran around inside my head, round and round, until it seemed that they too were standing still like time itself.

I thought of the children incessantly. I had no idea if they were still in that same convent, and what they were doing there, and what was being done to them, and if they were silent, or crying, or scared, or in a state of catatonic shock, or filled with all sorts of little wild strategies to escape and make their way to me. But if they even knew, would they also know how to find their way to me? Did they know where the officers had taken me? Did they know if I was still alive or already dead, nearby or far away, so far away that it would never again be possible to bridge the distance that the officers in Annemasse had thrown up between my children and me? You know, the worst thing in the world is to knock your head against all the walls of uncertainty within which your children have been imprisoned until your skull bursts, not from the blows that it has received externally but as a result of the desperation that strikes from within. It is something that you just have to go through every single day. For you I am trapped within these walls - me, along with this child of yours that I am carrying around inside me, along with our two sons. You have no idea that I am here in this clinic. You have no idea that they ordered me off the train, just as you have no idea that I ever boarded the train to begin with. You have no idea that the children are no longer with me, just as you are completely unaware of the fact that their convent exists, or Annemasse for that matter, or a priest who intones, "We know who Moritz Mayer was." Your skull must be more damaged and wounded from within than even mine is. Or maybe not. Maybe you are managing to survive some other way. Maybe the pain you are suffering is of a different sort. Maybe you are being held and bound within yourself to the point that you can not even bang your head against the wall. Perhaps you have been stripped of everything, or perhaps not; perhaps you already escaped and are off somewhere out there running down a wide, intricate path, endlessly searching, and not stopping to ask yourself what has happened to me and the boys, but concerned only with where we are, with where we might be. Then again, perhaps all these thoughts are mere empty, worthless vanities, and the reality of the situation is something that I can not even begin to imagine, and the truth is something that will never, ever really be

PART TWO

Then suddenly, without any prior notice or even the slightest hint that something was about to take place that would change everything, the door flew open. "Voila!" The officer in shirtsleeves stood there between the threshold and lintel. The officer stationed outside the door and the one stationed within, along with the female officer, all jumped to attention. The priest was also standing in the doorway. The officer in shirtsleeves addressed me without checking to see if I understood or could even hear him, and informed me that the doctor was going to examine me. If you are healthy enough to get up and walk then he will accompany you to the hospital for a more comprehensive examination. After that we shall see, he said, as he scratched the hair at his temple. "Voila" he then said, once again, and added, "I will leave you now with the doctor. If everything is alright, then you will be able to take all the things that you have in the closet with you. If everything is alright then you will not be coming back here, and if not, then you will remain in the hospital. Voila." And then he walked out as the door closed behind him. The priest waited a moment and then whispered, in German, "I am not going to examine you, not even for the sake of putting on a show. You are going to leave this place behind completely. Do everything that I tell you to do. In French. Whether or not you understand what I say really does not matter to me at all. Just do it, like a good Prussian soldier. I will be waiting for you in the hall." He opened the door and said to the head officer and my faithful female guardian that I was well enough to get up and go to the hospital. No, there is no need to help her get dressed. She has been through a lot. Perhaps too much, for that matter. But now she is strong enough to go. She will manage. Yes, she will pack her things, and you can help her by carrying her little suitcase. She can handle the handbag on her own. I suppose she could handle the suitcase as well but it would be better not to overdo it.

A black vehicle was parked right outside the clinic. It was difficult for me to walk, and not because of my pregnancy or because of any sort of illness or physical pain whatsoever but simply because I had not moved my legs for some time now and the over and entirely superfluous bed-rest - I was certain of this as I thought about it - had weakened my limbs and allowed a certain fatigue to inch its way inside me unobstructed. The suitcase was heavier than I remembered. The strap of the hand-bag at my shoulder dug into my bones. Just a few steps separated the clinic I had just left from the vehicle towards which I was headed. How many steps were there between the hospital and the place to which I was supposed to escape? Who has the strength for all this? I stood still for a moment. I filled my exhausted lungs with air. My entire escort stopped along with me. The priest stared at me and I immediately began walking once more.

I got into the vehicle. The female officer sat down next to me. The priest sat up front next to the driver. The head officer opened the car door that had already been closed and handed me a bundle of papers.

"Voila Madame," he said. "Your documents. You are French, Madame, for the time being that is how you will be examined and that is also how you will be registered and admitted to the hospital, if need be. Afterwards the papers will be returned to me. Then we will see whether the investigation shall begin. The priest will hold on to your documents Madame, that is why there are trustworthy priests in the world, much to our good fortune." He himself placed the documents in the priest's hands. Just before closing the car door he added, "I am certain that we will meet again, Madame - I certainly hope so. As far as I can see, at least, you seem to be in perfect health."

We drove off. No one said a word. The windows were cloudy and I could not see a thing. Through the front windshield I could barely make out the road in front of us, but I did not make all that much of an effort. I did not have the strength to free myself from all the doubts and questions and fearful hopes and concerns, or even the simple element of curiosity that snuck into my mind amidst all the rest. I lacked the strength to overcome it all. It was cold. I was trembling. Just hope we do not have to drive too far to get there, I told myself. I can not take it much longer. I absolutely have to get there. I do not know where that is but I can not hold out much longer until we get to wherever it is that I have to go now.

Suddenly the car slowed down. Through the window I saw a soldier holding up his arm as though someone had told him to get his hands up. The vehicle came to a halt. We were at a checkpoint. The driver rolled down his window. A German soldier looked over the passengers inside the vehicle. The female officer seated next to me said, "French police," and showed him her ID. The soldier examined the card somewhat superficially and then handed it to the soldier standing right next to him and the latter then handed it back to the officer. The driver handed over his papers, as did the priest, who also handed over my documents as well. I was tense. Why would a priest be holding the papers of a Frenchwoman who was traveling with him by car? Why would the woman herself not be in possession of her own papers? They had given my documents to the priest to make sure that I did not try to escape with my papers in my own possession and now here I am, due to all this caution, suddenly exposed to all the questions that I could not possibly answer, not with this female officer seated right beside me and those soldiers standing at the door. I was trapped. But in the end, nothing at all happened. This time I was afraid for nothing. What luck. The soldier once more looked over the documents somewhat distractedly, then handed all the papers back to the priest, including my own documents, and indicated with a wave of his hand that we were free to proceed. The vehicle slowly started once more. I think that I did not even begin to breathe again until we had covered quite a bit of ground beyond the checkpoint. I threw my head back against the headrest atop the back seat in the car and took a long, deep, loud breath. "You were afraid," said the female officer, as she lent her words an explanatory gesture. "It is only natural," said the priest from the front seat. "Women in her condition are always afraid. Pregnancy and fear, they say, go hand in hand." The late winter afternoon began to grow dark. Now I could not even see a thing out of the front windshield, other than an occasional pair of passing headlights. I suddenly heard the vehicle turn off the paved road and start down a loose gravel path. I could make out a large house in the shadows with a few lights on inside. We came to a stop and the driver got out. The priest and the female officer remained seated where they were and neither one said a word. I tried to make out the nature of the large building in front of us but the darkness was too thick and I did not really have a precise idea of where it was that we were parked. A few brief moments later the driver came back and told the priest that everything was ready.

"Please come with me, Madame," the priest said to me. He was already standing outside the car and the female officer was standing right next to him. I got out. I was now able to make out that the building which rose up before me was a convent. There was no mistaking it. It was not the hospital. It lay there like a huge, heavy brick on the ground. There was a tremendous front entrance right in the middle. At one of the edges of the gently sloping roof the profile of a tiny steeple rose into the air. The top of the steeple disappeared into the darkness. There was a cross atop the steeple but I could not make it out. It was too high, always too high - lordly, unseen. But it was there. The crosses do not suddenly come down off the steeples. Not even in the days when the Germans come to power. They remain on high to rule over all in their open mystery, their hidden revelation. Was it the priest's home? My home? My children's home? There was a little door built into the large front entrance. Even before we had a chance to announce our presence against the door with the copper knocker cast in the shape of what seemed like a fist, a slit of light shot open in the middle between lintel and threshold. It was hesitant at first, the opening, but then it grew wider. There was a nun, with one hand inside her habit and the other hand resting on the doorknob, and she bowed her head slightly and indicated to us that we should come in. The door closed behind us. The nun made a sign to us that we should wait and then went off somewhere inside the building. We stood there waiting on a gleaming floor of alternating black and white marble squares. It seemed to me as though there was not a living soul inside the entire building, just that one nun who had disappeared and a host of ghosts. The silence inside a convent is like the stillness of a world without any echoes. How can you possibly pray inside a building like that, where even the very heavens would seem incapable of pronouncing an answer? People fall silent inside a convent. They do not even have to be told to be quiet, they just fall silent of their own accord. It is not because of some vow. There is a sort of soundproof glass screen that seems to descend. The priest stood still just like me, just like the female officer. Was he a regular visitor? It can not be, I said to myself, it just can not be. He is a stranger inside this convent. Or maybe not. Perhaps a priest is not even at home in his own house. Convents scare me.

As though floating along the waves of black and white squares beneath our feet, like a figure altogether without legs, a rather tall nun approached us from afar. She came alone and stopped. "Father, my dear Doctor DuPont," she said. "Welcome one and all," she said, turning to include us as well. She began walking away. The priest drew close to her and walked by her side, talking in low tones about things that I could not quite hear. We walked in their wake, the female officer right by my side, all along the corridor that was lit by a few sparse bulbs high overhead, hanging right beneath the arched ceiling. The sound of my footsteps was all that I could hear. I made an effort to walk on without making a sound. The nun seemed to be hovering. Her footsteps made no sound at all and the priest hovered along right beside her. I was the only one plodding heavily down the hall. Even the female officer did not seem to be walking. She was as agile as a black cat. I had no place down this long, dimly lit corridor. I had never learned how to walk such a hallway properly.

We went up the stairs. Right outside a door along the hall stood the nun whose name was Jolanda, or Marie - it is all the same - one of those two nuns who had been at the police station in Annemasse, both bespectacled, sweet, and forever smiling. She was smiling now too. "Hello Madame," she said. "The children are well."

I did not even have the time to burst out inside me with that powerful sort of explosion that assails an individual in a fraction of an instant when all his or her sup-pressed expectations are sudden-ly, surprisingly, deeply fulfilled. My children!

The door opened. I was taken aback. Erwin and Jackie were standing against the wall facing the door, far away from me. They did not move. They did not run to me. They did not throw them-selves around my neck. They did not cry, they did not scream. They were like two wax sculptures, stock-still and submissive. I could not make out their faces or their eyes. I could only see that they were standing there, together, like two condemned prisoners. They were wearing the same clothes that I had dressed them in when we left. My children. The other nun - whose name was either Ma-rie or Jolanda - was standing right beside them, with her hand ex-tended from the sleeve of her black habit and resting on Jackie's little shoulder. She smiled. Oh, to hell with it all! She was smiling as though that smile had been frozen into her features forever and ever, although it was as though the smile contained nothing more than that frozen gesture, no joy, no good wishes, no hello, nothing, nothing at all other than the mere reflexive gesture of the smile itself. I should have run over to Erwin and Jackie and swept them up in my arms and held them to my heart and said their names incessantly, but I, too, was not able to do any more than simply stand still where

I stood just as they did, as though the hand of the nun - that Jolanda or Marie, or the two of them as one - had forced me to remain in place as though I, too, were just another one of the statues in the convent, those one or two statues that I had seen, I now recalled, as I made my way along the long, dark corridor below. "Come kiss your mother," said the priest. "She loves you both. She has come to visit you." I could have strangled him at that moment.

Erwin and Jackie did not move. I made my way over to where they stood. I got down on my knees. I pulled them close to my humiliated heart, first Jackie's little head and then Erwin's somewhat more grown-up head, and after a moment I sensed that I was kneeling there on the ground and crying soundlessly. The children still did not move. I could feel Jackie's little hands caressing my neck and pressing against my flesh until they were almost causing me pain, pain that I was more than happy to finally feel, whereas Erwin caressed my hair and I could hear him whispering 'Maman' over and over again. My child. He had not forgotten to call me mother in French. They had never called me 'Maman' at home. My eldest child was at war. He did not let down his guard for even the slightest instant. Just for that 'Maman' alone you can be eternally proud of him my love, forever and a day.

The priest gently separated the children from me, slipped his arm around my waist and helped me rise. The children resumed their previous position and stood there facing me, while the nuns, Jolanda and Marie, stood to either side of the boys. How had our boys been trained in such a short amount of time to submit so completely to some unseen command that had not even been voiced? The statuesque nun who still stood by the side of the priest now addressed him without taking her eyes off the boys and without turning to face him, saying, "It is only natural that we would have agreed that the children, under your tutelage, Father, should be allowed to spend a few hours in the company of their mother, a prisoner - may God help her set things right and be set free as quickly as possible. She has every right, it is a most human, humane thing, and the children, who are completely free of wrongdoing, who are not even suspected of any wrongdoing, have the same right all the more so. But the hour is rather late. I was thinking that perhaps we ought to put it all off until tomorrow, and after a good night's rest both the mother and her children will derive greater benefit from the few hours that we are permitted to allot them for their visit."

Oh, such compassion, just dripping with kindness. From what well filled with freezing waters do they draw forth this kindness in order to sprinkle its drops all around, as the very soul of God on high melts from an excess of delight?

"Forgive me, my most merciful Mother Superior. That is just not possible. The mother is to head directly for the hospital when she leaves here. She is expected. She will spend but an hour with the children, no more, under my watch, in my capacity as both a priest and a physician. That is, after all, what we had already discussed."

"Indeed, indeed," said the woman who, on the basis of this brief exchange, was apparently the Mother Superior. "I was only trying to help, in order to afford the mother and her children something more than a mere hour. But let it be as we already discussed. We only speak out of love. You can squeeze quite a bit of love into an hour, sometimes even more than you might manage in quite a few hours, or even en-tire days, months or years, for that matter. So let it be, Father." The children still did not move from where they stood. The Mother Superior now turned to the two nuns, Jolanda and Marie, and addressed them saying, "See to it that the children wear warm coats and cover their heads. It is rather cold outside and there is quite a wind blowing."

"Please, Father, do not tell me," she said, turning once more to address the priest, "where it is that you are taking them. I am certain that you have found a warm, pleasant place for them, but until they get into the vehicle and once they leave the vehicle, it would be better if they were wearing the warmest possible clothing. Follow the good sisters," she now said to the children. "Your mother will wait for you at the front entrance. They will, of course, accompany you on your way."

I took my leave of the Mother Superior with a curtsey and followed the priest, the nun who had initially received us, and the female officer back down the long corridor below. I will never again make my way down this hallway, I said to myself, never again. But where am I headed? As I walked along I asked myself how there would possibly be space for all of us in the car that had brought us here. I could not believe that we would all squeeze in, or that they would put one of the boys on my lap. That is not the way you treat a pregnant woman who is on her way to the hospital to be examined. I was certain that the priest had devised some excellent plan, but I had no idea what it was. I was dying to know, but I had to wait in silence without the slightest idea. But who did know? Only the priest? Was the female officer in on it as well? The driver? The Mother Superior? The senior police officer? Were they all in on it? Or was the priest the only one who knew? And the priest, for that matter, did he know everything, everything from A to Z, or just A and Z, as it were? Like throwing dice. Life was like a throw of the dice, like dice in the hands of the good and dice in the hands of the evil, dice even in the very hands of God, and dice in the devil's hands. At the end of that long hallway in the convent I found myself thinking all these thoughts about man, and God, and the devil.

There were now two cars parked outside. There was the vehicle that had brought me here and another, much smaller vehicle, as well. The driver was standing next to the smaller one. The children came out accompanied by the two nuns. "Here, get in this little car of mine. It is no limousine, but it is rather comfortable all the same," said the priest. "It has only one drawback. I am the driver. You too, Madame, please get into this little car of mine along with the boys. The second vehicle will follow us. I hope that you will all excuse this sweet little carriage of mine. It is small, but still regal." And so saying, he opened the door for the boys and stood there as though he were their footman. The children, who did not have any bags with them, got in and sat down without saying a word. The priest asked his driver to bring over my suitcase, which he took and placed in the trunk. Then he opened the front passenger door, bowed ever so slightly, stretched out his hand in a sort of invitation and said, "Madame…" I was confused. I sat down. My handbag was still in my hands. I put it down in my lap. I looked over my shoulder for a moment at the boys. Erwin smiled at me, put his finger to his lips as though warning me not to speak, or to let me know that he was not going to say a word. Jackie was terrified. He stared hard at me and his eyes were filled with fear. The priest was standing outside the car exchanging a few words with his driver and the female officer. I could not manage to overhear what he was saying. He patted the driver on the back before the latter got in to the other vehicle. Then he exchanged a few words with the female officer, who then got into the other car as well. The priest then got into the car with us. The two nuns stood facing us, already waving their hands in farewell before the cars even got started on their way. I could not see their faces but I was sure that they were smiling. I thought to myself that they were waving for quite some time already and smiling even longer than that. The priest made himself comfortable in his seat and then turned his head towards the back of the car and asked if the boys had enough room for their legs. "It is not so simple," he said. "You are already quite a serious set of young men. It would seem that your legs are already far too long for this little carriage of mine."

He turned the key and started the car. It made an awful sound and began to rattle even while it was still parked. Then there was the sound of an engine bursting some sort of a throttle, as the car suddenly broke free from its standing position with a jolt that was immediately reigned in and relaxed. And we were on our way. Where to? The headlights of the car that had left the lot behind us followed along in the rearview mirror of our car. We were not alone. I did not dare speak. Neither did the children, nor the priest. He simply whistled a tune that was almost unbearably beautiful. I did not recognize it. Perhaps it was taken from some folk song. It was very melodic, somewhat mournful at first, then filled with joy but a moment later. He kept repeating the tune over and over again. After some time all I could see were the beams of light out in front of our vehicle along the narrow road. No light now danced in the rearview mirror and there was no other car following along behind us. We were alone. The night swallowed everything other than us. It was a miracle. When would I be able to speak again?! The priest did not stop whistling but he began to speak as well. To me. In German. He whistled and talked, in short sentences, almost keeping time with the tune, talking along and whistling as though he were merely emphasizing the lyrics of the song.

"We are going to stop at an inn along the highway," he said. Period. A little while later he added, "We will have something warm to drink there. You and the children. The owner of the inn is a friend. He loves soap. You will enter with me but you will leave without me... We are not going to separate. You are to run away. Not on foot. I said on foot. You are not going to escape on foot. A little truck is waiting for you there. I have no idea. I heard nothing. I saw nothing. You and the children. You are not to say a word. The children will not say a word either. I am not aware of anything at all. But I am the only one who will speak. You have no name. You are just 'Madame.' The children are not yours. You collected them from the house of their parents who were handed over to the authorities. They are not to ad-dress you as their mother. They have no idea what is happening to them. They are in shock. You will just have to tolerate this situation. There will be a whole conversation during the course of which you are not to say a word. But you have passed more difficult tests than this."

I was on alert, but the way he spoke in the midst of all that whistling dulled my brain. This priest was a madman. Where did this God of ours manage to find him? Erwin understood a bit of German. I do not know where he picked it up. I sensed that he was following fragments of the words that were spoken. So curious. Filling in the gaps on his own. There was no way that Jackie understood a single word. He was holding my arm tightly. He was by no means relaxed but neither was he afraid. From time to time he squeezed my arm a bit tighter, as though trying to tell me that he was checking if the strange words spoken by this whistling priest were putting my mind at ease, checking to see it they were the words of someone who was with me and not against me. He was so helpless but nevertheless he tried to signal to me that he was there to protect me. From the time that I had first seen the children they had not said another word to me. They were simply unable. Everything went by so quickly. I have no idea how they managed to contain themselves and employ all their faculties in a way that they had by no means been prepared for, in these roles that they were now playing in a show whose text was completely foreign to them and that they had no way of know-ing before they became its lead actors. It was impossible for it all to not be well beyond their innate capacities. And yet they managed. You had to have been there with us to acknowledge this amazing feat, to witness and yet be incapable of believing that what you were seeing was indeed taking place. But believe it. If you are reading these words that I have written you then you simply have to believe.

The car came to a halt. The priest got out first and helped me get out next, then opened the door so that the children could get out. "Leave your things in the car. Trust me. Someone will come to get them immediately. But take your handbag with you. Come with me." It would seem that the hour was rather late. There was a faint light behind the glass door of the inn. There was no one inside. The priest pulled on the string that rang the doorbell. A light went on in one of the windows. A moment later the door opened. A tall man wearing a heavy winter sweater, wide woollen pants, and leather sandals with wooden soles on his feet addressed the priest, saying, "There you are Albert," and led us over to one of the tables, where he took down the overturned chairs and indicated that we should sit down and told us that he was going to prepare something warm for us to drink. We sat down. The priest began to whistle once more. He stared at the ceiling, looked around the inn inquisitively, and kept whistling. It was cold. He tried to warm himself up by energetically rubbing his arms, then stopped whistling for a moment and said, "It is rather cold, is it not, Madame?" And it was indeed cold inside. A woman who was apparently the wife of the owner of the inn came down the stairs wearing a rather large, warm robe. Her hair was a bit unkempt but it was not exactly wild.

"We waited for you, Albert," she said. "Is everything alright? Do they have bags with them? Bring in their bags," she said to her husband, addressing him by name, though I have since forgotten what it was. "I will take care of making them a fine cup of tea." The children and I silently followed the strange midnight spectacle in which we were now playing an active part, shaking from the cold but still certain of the kind turn that destiny was in the process of dealing us. We had no idea where it was taking us. At that moment it could only have been good. The owner of the inn came back with my small suitcase. The lady of the house came over to us with a tray carrying a steaming set of tea cups. "We have hot chocolate with milk for the boys, tea for you, Madame, as well as for you, Albert." The owner of the inn got up from where he was sitting and came back holding a bottle of wine in one hand and four rather ample, round wine glasses upside down in the other, which he placed right-side up on the table, as he set about removing the cork from the wine with a joyful pop and then poured wine into the waiting glasses, wine that must have been rather chilled at that point, even though its color was a flaming red. His wife sat there holding her head in the palms of her hands and watched us as we sipped the hot drinks that had been placed before us. I did not touch the wine, while the priest did not even take a sip of his tea.

"I must leave you for a moment," said the owner's wife. "I will be back soon." The priest removed the block of soap from his bag and handed it to the innkeeper.

"Is she aware of the arrangements?" the owner asked the priest.

"She is aware!" he replied.

"Can I open it?" asked the owner, as his eyes remain fixed on the figure of the priest.

"Go right ahead." I offered no response. The children's eyes rushed back and forth over me and the priest and the owner of the inn and came to rest for a moment on the large block of soap. Erwin's eyes were carefully inspecting everything, while Jackie's eyes were filled with confusion as they settled on my own. The innkeeper suddenly had a long, thin string in his hands that looked like it was an animal's sinew or some such thing. He sliced into the large block of soap with an expert hand and exposed the paper that turned out to be that of an envelope just like those used by the diamond dealers in Antwerp. The children's eyes shone wide as though they had just witnessed a magician's sleight of hand. The owner of the inn opened the envelope. There was a bunch of small diamonds inside along with a few larger ones. The faint light inside the inn glanced off the diamonds. The innkeeper pulled a jeweler's magnifying glass out of his pocket, affixed it to one of his eyes and began to roll a diamond or two between his thumb and forefinger, then a third, and said, "I will need these here, as well as these. The rest can go back in the safe." He smiled. He seemed to like his little joke. He looked up at the priest in order to obtain the latter's okay with a nod of his head. The priest looked at me. I nodded at them both.

The children never had any idea that I had these diamonds inside the block of soap. I could see the amazement in their eyes. They searched my face for an explanation for what they had just seen. They were completely clueless and yet it seemed that they understood everything. They were with me. Did they think that I was rich? That I was some sort of thief who sold illegally on the black market? Did they think that you had prepared everything in advance, and that you were our savior in this hour of our need into which we had fallen without you? Or did they not think anything at all but simply trust me and the priest and the owner of the inn, with some sixth sense, that all the strange goings-on that they could not have possibly foreseen were simply the outer manifestation of a struggle between luck and being, between tragedy and complete cessation. Could it be that all these thoughts were only able to rush wildly around inside my mind, while they were incapable of running around inside our children's heads, where it was impossible for me to have even the fain-test idea just what they were truly thinking?

Life, I know, is not as it seems. Life is the story of what we think as we live it.

The innkeeper brought forth a diamond envelope as though conjured by some magic wand and placed the diamonds that he had chosen in there and then shook the remaining stones into the center of our own envelope. He carefully refolded the paper along the existing creases, closed the envelope and put it back inside the hollow within the block of soap. He looked at the priest and said, "I will give her what she deserves and what she deserves is exactly what she needs right now. Agreed?" He pulled a roll of bills from his pants pocket and began to count them out.

"Agreed!" said the priest, as he looked over at me. I did not say yes or no.

Who dares to quibble over the price when one's own life hangs in the balance and is completely out of one's control? The innkeeper put a pile of bills in the priest's hands and told him to count. The priest shoved the roll of bills into his pocket without counting. I had no idea how much money had just changed hands, and I did not know why or what for, I had no idea why the money had been given to the priest. I knew absolutely nothing whatsoever about the entire proceedings. I did not even know who this priest was, or who the innkeeper and his wife were, or where the female officer in the police car had disappeared to, or what would be given to the people waiting for me in the hospital, and what would be given to those waiting for my children to return to the convent, to those smiling nuns and their statuesque Mother Superior - I knew nothing whatsoever about any of this. I was just a mere backdrop in the play of my own life.

I know that I tend to draw comparisons between real events and the life of the theater a bit too much. I only went to see a play once with you. I was not particularly fond of what I saw. But I knew that it was true, all too true. It was a truth that got up onstage after they had filtered out the fallout from life. It was a truth that was hard to take. The owner of the inn placed the other half of the block of soap on top of the one where he had inserted the envelope with the diamonds inside and, with a practiced hand, as he wet solely the inner surface of the block of soap with a finger that he had dipped into a glass of water, he glued the two halves together as one and erased the line where they had been joined. By the dim light it was impossible to see it. Afterwards I had a rather difficult time making out the line even by the light of day.

The innkeeper got up from where he was sitting and said, "I am going to go get him. My wife will be down any moment now. She is getting a few blankets and covers ready. I am going to put out the light. I will only leave the light on outside the door. You will manage. I will be back in about a half an hour. It is not much." He slipped a large, heavy coat over his shoulders, removed his sandals and put on a pair of boots and walked outside. I could hear him starting a car but I did not see the headlights come on. The children and I remained seated along with the priest in almost complete darkness, and a chill that simply would not let up.

"Let us drop this little farce of ours," said the priest. "You do not speak French but you understand it. Whatever you do not understand, tell me and I will translate for you. I want the young men to understand as well. They are old enough. Destiny might just need them yet. It is important that they know what is going on as well, if necessary." He spoke slowly. He pronounced each word precisely out of concern that I should hear them each separately and understand them. He stared hard at the boys as he spoke while taking small sips of wine from the glass that seemed to refuse to empty itself. "You said Saint-Claude. That is what I read in the protocol of the investigation. I would not go to Saint-Claude if I were you. The city and the surrounding countryside are crawling with Germans. But you have a sister there. Apparently she has managed to get by. That is certainly an advantage. We will take you to Saint-Claude.

Now. Tonight. Here all is lost. They are already out looking for you. It could not have been otherwise. They only trust me up to a certain point, and once that point is surpassed then they begin to suspect me. Yes, even me. But no matter, they have already suspected me for quite some time now. You just have to live with it. They will not do anything to me. They would not dare. At least for the time being. But if they suspect me, then they must be looking for you. What shall I tell them? I know. I will tell them something that does not explain a thing. They will accept it. They will have no choice, at least for now. And by the time they do have a choice - if they ever shall - I myself will already be in Saint-Claude, or some place exactly like Saint-Claude. The Church is a merciful mother. I will pay the innkeeper and his son. I have already paid them. What he gave me was the change, I will give it to you before you run away. The innkeeper's son will take you. He went to get his son from his house just now. It is his son that has the little farm truck. He and his son both know every single little side road, here, along the way, all along the border, everywhere. They live off smuggling, smuggling across the border. They are righteous people, they risk their lives day in and day out, night after night, and what they are paid is little more than charity. Small change. It sounds like a lot but it does not even begin to cover what they invest in time, precise preparations, the truck, risking their lives. You are to wait at your sister's until they call you and tell you that it is okay to proceed into Switzerland. This will perhaps take some time. It is not a simple matter. You can not make it across every night, you understand. The German look-outs are planted where they are. They do not move. But there are armed border patrols moving back and forth between the lookouts. You have to know when and where. But you will make it. You are a brave woman. God is on the side of the brave women. Always. Do not smile. I can not see your face but I know that you are smiling. Abraham's Sarah smiled as well. She was ninety years old. Too old. The angels told her the news and she smiled. However, nine months later, less in your case, Madame, much less, by the grace of God - she was holding a newborn son in her arms. And they called him Isaac, Yitzchak. God gave her her smile and a son. So it is written…"

I smiled to myself. I was carrying a son inside me. What was he talking about?

"My Hebrew name is Yitzchak," Erwin suddenly whispered. There was a moment of silence, the silence of wonderment in the darkness of the most solitary, wintry inn in the world. How had Erwin suddenly managed to recall the name that we had given him when he had been circumcised and entered into the covenant of our forefather Abraham? We had never called him Yitzchak. 'Erwin,' 'Erou,' 'Erouka.' We had told him that he was named Yitzchak after your grandfather Isaac, but we had never cal-led him Yitzchak. Perhaps we had in fact told him about it all sometime I am sure that we must have told him; we must have told him about it, but we had never called him by that name. But it was his, and he knew it. The name, the name, the name - Hashem - the Guardian who never sleeps. It was as though the priest was struck dumb and after a moment he said to Jackie, in a voice that could not hide his expectations of an additional wonderful surprise, "And you, young man, what is your Hebrew name?" Jackie answered without hesitation, immediately, in a voice brimming with confidence, "Yaakov, Jacob." The wonder of Jackie was even greater than that of Erwin.

In the darkness I could yet make out the shadow of the innkeeper's wife coming down the stairs. On a table next to ours she put down a pile of covers and blankets as she said, "He will not be long. He and my son will be here within fifteen minutes, at most. Would you like something else to drink? I prepared a large thermos for you and filled it with hot chocolate. The milk is top quality, fat, nourishing. You will need it." She sat down next to us and continued speaking. "This war is sheer madness. What is it all for? I have no idea. The soldiers have no idea. The generals have no idea. One day rushes headlong into the next, through the winter, the same summer, identical autumns and springs, they are all the same as ever, but the war does not care about anything other than the crosses in the cemeteries, and the deep pits without any crosses at all, and the children in the orphanages, and the widows scattered about who knows where. The snow is the same snow, the rain is the same rain and the sun remains the same, but the men are now soldiers and no longer farmers, the women are now widows and no longer beloveds, and the children are now out on the roads instead of in school, or by the side of the well in the town square. That is all. And when the war is over, what will be then? There is always a before and after. Afterwards, what will be? Just as it once was. The victors will not be any better than they were before, and the losers will not somehow be wiser, and the mountains will be no higher, and the pasture will not be any greener than it was before. Books, yes. More books will be written. Oh, if only they never wrote them. I do what I can. Me, my husband, and my son. That is how it is. That is just the way we are. Whoever needs us, we are here for them. We do not stand on circumstance. The rich, the poor, loners, whole families, ravishing young men and women, the elderly who still want to survive. And why not? There are Jews too, of course. They do not say anything, but we know, we take care of our end as though it were nothing at all. We do not do it for the sake of the afterlife. It would seem that there is no afterlife, after all. Forgive me, Albert, we have known one another for such a long time, you were quite a heretic yourself in the days when our blooming adolescence was driving us both out of our minds, so you must forgive me. That is all, we do not do it for the sake of God. Where is God, after all, that is what I want to know - if there is a God at all. We do what we do because we simply could not possibly do things otherwise. Not when we have an inn in a location like this.

"I hate the Germans. They sit here sometimes and drink. They speak German in loud voices and laugh their irritating, thunderous laughter. The soldiers sit there with their awful helmets covering their ears. And the officers place their elegant hats on the tabletop. They seem perfectly okay. But I hate them when they come in, and I hate them when they leave. I serve them what they want and I do not hate them then. But they are so German, these Germans. And I am a French woman. That is the whole thing in a nutshell. It is in the blood. And not just the blood that gets spilled. It is in the blood that runs in our veins. It is very thick, that blood. And it became thicker one evening, two or three months ago. They arrived, armed to the teeth, stepped out of some armored vehicle. There were two officers, a blond, obedient woman with her hair pulled back, well-dressed in green, two helmeted soldiers, long rifles, pushing an old man along in front of them, and a young woman, just like you, or almost, Madame, and a young girl who was all eyes, big, dark eyes filled with fear. The officers and the woman sat down to have a drink. The regular soldiers in their helmets stood across from them guarding the old man and the woman and the little girl. They placed a generous tip on the table even before I had a chance to bring them their beer and, of course, before they paid. The woman drank beer as well. One of the officers got up after a few moments and asked for the bathroom. I showed him where it was and he went inside. He came back, buttoning up his pants as he went, sat down once more and got lost in the conversation and the beer. All that time the old man, the woman, and the girl stood there between the two helmeted soldiers with their rifles. I could see that the girl was darting her frightened eyes in the direction of the young German woman as though she wanted to ask something but did not dare. I walked up as naturally as I could to one of the soldiers and asked about allowing their charges use the bathroom. It was then as though some hermetically sealed window had been thrown open in the middle of a storm in the night and that same officer leaped at me, the one that I had seen buttoning up his pants as he returned, and in halting French screamed at me that it was no concern of mine.

"He sat back down. The soldiers in their helmets did not move. The other officer, the lower-ranking one, it would seem, and the well-dressed blond woman who was probably I would rather not say what, were sitting there, with their glasses of beer raised to their lips, and drinking in silence. The first officer sat down, slammed the palm of his hand down on the table and said something that I could not understand and then raised his glass as well. The three of them began to laugh. I froze where I stood. I stared at the old man and the woman and the little girl with the big, scared eyes, standing there between the soldiers in their helmets and armed with their long rifles. I noticed that the little girl's knees were dripping. She did not leave her spot, did not move a muscle. She stood there in place, along with the old man and the young woman, and their knees all ran with a liquid that began to pool at their feet and stream in rivulets along the wooden floor. The officer noticed it as well. He stood up and screamed, 'Take them away!,'" put his money on the table, donned his high hat and followed the soldiers out the door as they hurried back to the vehicle with their prisoners, followed by the other officer and the female soldier. I saw all this with my very own eyes. And that was when I swore that what my husband had already been doing for some time now, along with my son who had joined him in his efforts quite a while ago, is precisely what needs to be done. I was always with them, as you well know, Albert, but now I knew that it was also due to the blood that boiled in my very own veins. I am a simple woman. I am a woman straight out of real life. I did not learn a single thing from books because I never read them. And I never learned anything from the newspapers since what are the papers to me, after all? What I learned from the image of that young girl and the terror that seemed to root her to the ground as though she had been nailed to the floor is something that you could never manage to learn from all of your sacred books."

At that very moment there was the sound of a car parking outside, followed immediately by the sound of another vehicle hitting the brakes. The priest, who had not taken his eyes off the innkeeper's wife as she spoke and nodded his head from time to time as though to affirm what she was saying and the thoughts that lay behind her words, now said, "You are a good woman," and rose in order to greet the innkeeper and his young, well-built son who entered alongside the owner and kissed his mother on her forehead.

"Everything is ready,"said the innkeeper. "The road is open now. We are on our way. Come with me, all of you. This is my son, Phillip." Phillip bowed his head slightly in a sort of greeting.

"He knows the job well, isn't that so, Phillip? You are in good hands with Phillip," said the innkeeper's wife. Phillip smiled. The innkeeper rebuked his wife with a kindly look on his face, saying, "Woman, we do not have time for all this talk. Let's go."

The innkeeper's wife went over to the pile of covers and blankets but before she reached them she stood still and said, "Everyone is always rushing, rushing everywhere, but first let them use the bathroom, excuse me, but whether they need to or not, they really ought to, you must excuse me." Jackie grabbed my arm tightly. He was already standing, without moving. Erwin stood up as well.

"It is out in the yard," said the innkeeper. "Let me show you the way, young man. Perhaps you should come along too," he said to Jackie. "You might as well."

Jackie hesitated and then separated himself from me. He went over and stood next to his brother and the innkeeper led them both out into the yard. I waited for them and then I went outside myself. When I got back, the priest was standing with the two boys and talking easily with the innkeeper and his son. The innkeeper's wife was standing right nearby and her arms were full. We all went outside. There was a small truck parked along the gravel path and the cabin was closed. Phillip got into the truck from the back. Using a large flashlight he lit up the open cargo space. There were huge jugs of milk, something that looked like the long handle of a plow, and bales of hay. He moved two of the bales aside to reveal a low door, which he proceeded to open. The innkeeper helped us up into the truck, holding my hand and leading me into the small compartment where there was a narrow bench along the wall. Then the children were lifted into the truck and the innkeeper helped them get inside the compartment as well. They were careful to avoid the various obstacles along the way as they sat down next to me. I could see a black hole in the roof through which the cold air rushed inside in abundance. I saw the innkeeper's wife hand her husband the blankets and covers. He stuck them inside the little compartment and wrapped us up in them. I heard Phillip open the door to the driver's cabin and a moment later the entire truck shook as the engine started up.

The innkeeper stood still. For a moment the priest stood by his side. He bent down, I believe, actually got on his knees in the utter darkness and said, "Good luck, good luck, Madame, good luck Masters Yitzchak and Yaakov." It seemed to me that these were the words to the prayer offered by this wonderful man. The innkeeper could not see in the dark that the priest had handed me the bundle of worn bills and was not able to overhear him whispering to me, "These are yours, Madame."

It was only some time later, Moritz, that I realized that everyone who was in on this deal had to be paid off. Even a priest was suspected of treason if he were willing to risk his life solely on the basis of his fear of God or out of mere compassion. It is an unwritten rule in this world that there is no God during wartime, not for an innkeeper, not for a priest, and if God does exist, then He only exists underground, Moritz, in the shadows, in the darkness, in the frailty of a whisper. And it would seem that He does, after all, exist. I saw Him. I heard Him.

We sat huddled in the dark. The children did not ask where we were headed. They trusted that I knew, but in fact, I had no idea whatsoever. I knew that the train had brought me to Annemasse, but in Annemasse itself I had been led around from place to place as though my eyes had been covered with a black scarf and I had no way of knowing if we were still in Annemasse, or the surrounding countryside, whether the clinic and the convent and the inn were all within the town limits or right nearby, or even far away. I knew where I was headed, to Saint-Claude, but I had no idea where I was coming from and I had no idea where Saint-Claude was, for that matter. Yet the children trusted me.

I had placed my life in the hands of the priest and the innkeeper and his son and I had purchased an escape route that seemed to hang by a string of doubts and helplessness with the money that you had so carefully set aside for that very purpose, in your attempt to control whatever might eventually befall us. Yet who truly rules the matter - does wisdom have the upper hand over chance, or does chance actually run things while wisdom is merely a bystander? Perhaps wisdom is in charge, despite everything, I mused, trying to calm myself. Without wisdom there would not even be any instance of chance altogether. And then again, perhaps there is neither wisdom nor chance but just things that are dictated in the moment as they are occurring, and in this play that we are living out there are no lines that have been prepared in advance whatsoever. This play has no author - it writes itself. Perhaps.

I had no idea how long this forbidden journey was going to take. It was cold. We were dressed in our heavy clothing and sat huddled together in the darkness, breathing the air that rushed inside through the hole overhead that we sensed up there in the night - all of us, me, the boys, and the unborn infant inside my womb. I thought of that little being now, not in the way that I had been aware of my pregnancy in the clinic, or in the priest's car as it hurtled along the road in the night, or at the inn. My pregnancy was by and large something private, something that only concerned me. That was not the way I conceived it, but that is just the way it was. Now, though, I found that I was telling myself, "He is taking four sorry souls on their way to Saint-Claude, and he will not make it if they stop him and search the vehicle and find the four of us, and the four of us will not survive, yet he is riding along as though it were nothing at all, in this frozen chariot of his, through the thick, black night, along these pitch-black mountain paths, and who knows if when he gets where he is going he will get anywhere other than this absolute darkness, while I, the mother, along with my sons and the unborn child that I am carrying inside me will all be lost in that darkness; and you, in your own darkness where you were taken prisoner, will never know what happened to us."

Jackie whispered, as though he were afraid that someone might be able to hear what was said in this little hidden smuggler's compartment as the truck flew through the night, "Are you cold, Mom?"

"Are you?" I whispered back.

"No," he replied. "But you are, I can feel it."

Erwin may or may not have overhead what we had whispered and he himself whispered in turn, "Be quiet. There's no talking in here." And his word was our command. We did not speak or even whisper anymore until the truck screeched to a halt. We did not move. I did not know if we had stopped because we had reached our destination or if we had perhaps stopped just so that the innkeeper's son could get out and stretch his legs. I did not know if we had stopped because police officers or soldiers had ordered us to stop and we would soon hear them tapping the thin walls of the hidden compartment and then see them breaking in and be caught like thieves in the night as the beams of light from those huge military searchlights exploding in our faces. It would seem that similar scenarios were flitting through the children's minds as well. They held me close in the thick darkness as they trembled, both of them, or perhaps only one of them, I could not tell, but the tremors were rather forceful and I began to shake as well. We were all one single, shuddering mass.

I heard the sound of a car door slam. I heard the rear door of the truck hit the ground as it fell. Then there were footsteps and the sounds of metal vessels being dragged back and forth and suddenly the door to our little hidden compartment was torn aside and a dull but determined light burst inside with a certain brilliance. It was day, though dim, and it shone. We sat there huddled together holding on to one another waiting for the innkeeper's son, whose profile we could make out in the frame of the compartment's doorway, to tell us what to do, that we should get up and go, or stay seated where we were and wait.

"This is Saint-Claude. We are right outside your sister's house, Madame Ravel. Her name is not Resnick, as you stated during the interrogation, but Ravel, as you told the priest. Ravel. Quickly now. We do not have a lot of time," he said.

"Does she know?" I asked, as I made an effort to get up and Erwin lent me a hand.

"Does she know what?" asked the innkeeper's son, dryly, as though he were somewhat put out that I should be posing an unnecessary question.

"That we are here… at her place…"

"I have no idea what Madame Ravel-Resnick knows or does not know," the inn-keeper's son said, as he helped me and the boys emerge from the hidden compartment. "All I have is the address, and I have brought you to that address, Madame. What she knows or does not know is none of my business. That is your business, if I may say so, Madame. Quickly now, here, let me help you."

He took me by the hand and led me through the piles of hay and the jugs of milk, jumped down from the truck, placed some carton on the ground and held out his hand to help me get down. The boys did not wait for his help. They had already jumped down and were standing by his side and also stretched out their hands to help me, even though there was no way that they could really be of any help. The innkeeper's son put my little suitcase in the narrow road right next to us without saying a word. He jumped lightly back into the truck and hid the door to the smuggler's compartment once more, dragging hay and jugs across the floor, straightening things out a bit, then jumped back down and put up the rear door of the truck, breathing hard as he stood next to us and said, "Shall I walk you to the door?" He did not wait for a response but picked up the suitcase and walked up to the front door of the house we were standing in front of as the boys and I followed him.

I did not look around, but while the innkeeper's son was otherwise occupied I took a good look at the house to which he had brought us. It stood there, with its snow-covered roof, along a steep path. Similar houses stood next to each other. A thin layer of snow that seemed to have frozen over covered the street. There were heaps of snow that had been piled up on either side of the street and smaller openings in the drifts that led to the front doors of the houses all along the sidewalk. There was not a single living soul to be seen along the street. All the blinds were down in all the windows and not even the slightest hint of light shone behind them. It was as though I were standing there with the children in a town that had been emptied of all its residents and where winter now reigned, solitary and supreme. I looked around for a dog, at least, but there was none, not even a cat, or a lone priest heading out to the house of worship. There was nothing at all. I was completely alone, all alone with Erwin, Jackie, and that unborn infant in my belly. I did not even recall the presence of the innkeeper's son. The little truck was waiting for him to disappear. It was as though he had left already.

In the middle of a wooden plaque affixed to the front door was a single name carved out in ash. The name was not Ravel and certainly not Resnick. The innkeeper's son pushed open the door and to my extreme surprise it was not locked and simply gave way. We entered a silence that seemed to lie in wait like the house of a hunter. There was a door with another sign and another name that was also neither Ravel nor Resnick, and a second door facing the first with yet another name written on it, neither Ravel nor Resnick. There was a set of stairs that we began to ascend and at the top there was another door with yet another sign and another name, though not Resnick. And then there was a door with no name on it. We stood facing this door and knocked. At first there was no response whatsoever. Then we heard some faint noises behind the door and a key turned in the lock with a grating sound. The door, which was firmly locked with a chain opened slightly and I heard a voice say in broken French:

"Who is it?"

"Manya!!" I immediately shouted.

The chain then came off the door. Manya, without her glasses, squinting as only she knew how, stood there as she let a forced glance fall on me and a shout of "Roszy" left her lips as we threw our arms around each other, embracing, bursting out crying as the tears that we could not hold back flowed down our cheeks. For a brief moment we would separate from one another and then embrace each other once more, paying absolutely no attention to the two boys who stood by in shock looking on at this spectacle, until Manya separated herself from me definitively and turned to the boys, saying "Erwin" as she covered him with kisses and tears, and then "Jackie" covering him too with kisses and tears in turn, as the boys wiped their faces with the palms of their hands and the sleeves of the coats that they were wearing, somewhat shamefacedly and embarrassed. We stood there in the doorway until Manya took a small step backwards so that I could see how large her nightgown seemed, with her large belly I blurted out in surprise and amazement - for indeed I had had no idea - "You are pregnant" and she looked at me and uncovered my own stomach beneath my overcoat, saying with her typical sarcasm, "My sweet sister, I have news for you, you are pregnant too," We fell into each other's arms once more, and I could feel our bellies touching each other, pressing up against one another, and I felt, just as I believe she did a brief moment so full of joy such as I had not experienced for a very long time.

The innkeeper's son was no longer with us when we finally entered Manya's room. It was more spacious than the average rooms with which I was familiar. A large wooden bed whose sheets showed that it was still warm took up a considerable portion of the room. But there remained a rather generous amount of space for an imposing closet, a heavy table that could be surrounded by quite a few chairs - although there were only three in the room - along with a stool that stood next to a long, narrow kitchen table, with a washbasin and a pitcher on it. Right next to it was a black iron oven with two round rings in the stovetop where a low flame burned and gave off a pleasant warmth. The room was remarkably clean. There were not many objects lying around, but whatever there was appeared well-ordered and in modest good taste. This room was the entire apartment. We stood there and did not know exactly what to do. We did not know where to put our heavy clothing if we took off our things and so we remained standing there dressed just as we were. Manya was rather emotional and said, "Sit down," as she began straightening the sheets on the bed. Then left off before actually rearranging them and turned to pulling back the woven curtain that cove-red the win-dow to let the light of the new day into the room. However, before completing this operation she was already holding a large iron kettle and said that she wanted to go get water in order to put the kettle on the fire. Just before leaving she turned and recommended that if we needed to use the bathroom we really ought to go with her since the floor that she lived on had a single, communal bathroom. When she noticed that we were not removing our overcoats she ran over to the children and took their coats off, saying that she was going to lay them over one of the chairs where I should put my coat as well,. Then she lifted all the coats off the chair saying that we were the ones who would have to sit down and not the coats. She then hung one of them from a hanger that was attached to the door and placed everything else down on the table. She saw that there was no way she could go outside in that nightgown of hers, and so she quickly picked up a robe and sat down with it in her hands saying, "All at once I just lost all my energy, it is all the emotion, my sister, emo-tions unlike any other. I am expecting a child. Maybe today, maybe tomorrow, perhaps in two days from now, who knows? The baby is here already and will come out when it comes out. The main thing is that you made it here in time with Erwin and Jackie. Where did you come from…" We were still standing there as she burst out cry-ing rather loudly, shaking all over and saying, "And if Moritz is not here now, if you came by yourself, and he is not here, just as Jack is not here, and Zollie is gone too, along with Joss - they have taken away all our men, dammit, one by one, they did not overlook a single one, and they are gone now, and we women are all still here and this damn war could not care less because it is out to eliminate everyone, the ones that it takes away as well as the ones that it leaves behind."

She threw her robe down on the floor rather angrily and then immediately picked it back up and placed it on her knees. She suddenly stopped crying. She sat there with her head hanging down as we remained standing where we were. It was if we were not even present there in the room with her she began to talk to herself. It seemed that she was almost addressing me, saying, "But the war will not get us, sister, even though it has taught us to be stripped completely naked, we will remain and we will never forgive…" She raised her head in my direction and added, "You see, I have calmed down a bit, I am pontificating again…" Then she got up, put on her robe, walked over to the boys and kissed them each gently and pulled them over to have a seat at the table and then she kissed me too and said, "Come, wash your face off, you look like a tombstone." She pulled me over to the pitcher of water, told me to hold out my hands and poured some water over them as I began to wash my face. She then took a towel from the closet and dried me off with a great show of love, as though I were another one of her patients and she were once more a nurse as she had been in Gurs.

Manya, who excelled at a sort of excess laziness throughout her life, was exceptionally diligent when it came to taking practical care of her immediate needs. I still remember her passing many long hours on an almost daily basis in the cafes along the De Keyserlei in Antwerp, as though time had absolutely no relevance to her. At the same time, she could rush around to clean and cook and go shopping and make decisions as though she had no spare time whatsoever to weigh her options. Now too, in than a few brief moments we had all already washed our faces in the tub of water that was somewhat less than lukewarm, and we had each eaten a slice of bread spread with jelly and had had a little something to drink. The boys lay down in Manya's spacious bed, which was covered with a colorful coverlet so that the children should not dirty the actual sheets themselves, still wearing their clothes, though having removed their shoes, of course, there they both fell into a deep sleep, and I despite the fact that Manya urged me to put my head down as well on the bed right beside the boys. I remained seated across from her as we talked.

First she wanted to know what had happened to Moritz. Even

before I had a chance to tell her she was already saying to me that she had no interest in hearing such stories at that moment. "They took him away," she said. "That is the whole story. I could talk for hours about how they came and took away my Jack. Out in the street. Just like that. How he left me with this swollen belly of mine. How I ran away. How I got here. But it does not mean anything at all. The real story is what is going to happen tomorrow. There is one thing that I must say about Moritz. You thought that he was in love with me. Nonsense. He loved me, certainly. But it was no more than that. He was in love with you. I think you were never really sure of that fact. Were you? If you say so then I guess you were, perhaps. There was no way that I could have lived with him even though I was more suited to him than you. The difference is that I have the ability to be with wide variety of men, even someone like Moritz who was a charming, bohemian intellectual, someone for whom being young meant really standing out, being flashy; and I could be with someone like Jack who was faithful in a simple, courageous way to his father and mother, to the point that he pretended for their sake that he still observed the Sabbath and kept kosher. Jack put me on a pedestal like I was some sort of princess and for whom being young meant being athletic. But there was no way that you could have been suitable for anyone other than Moritz because you were in love with him like he was some sort of a demigod. You knew that he was not, but you loved him just as though he were all the same. But that is not what I wanted to say. I wanted to say that he managed to save us all with the French documents that he forged for us, but he did not manage to save himself or a single one of our husbands. And it is not fate. There is no such thing as fate. This wonderful man made a mistake somewhere along the line. He thought that the war was being conducted in accordance with a set of albeit ugly rules, but there were still rules, at least. And he was sure that he had managed to decipher them. But that is not the case. The war does not devour when it is hungry and does not take a break when it is full, it does not kill when it conquers and it does not show pity when it is victorious. It is completely senseless, idiotic. The generals make their plans but the war does what it will because it does not even begin to comprehend the generals and it had no time for Moritz either, although his poor, kind soul failed to grasp that fact.

"Stop me, I am pontificating again. And here we are now, without them. I will tell you what I have been doing and you will tell me what you have been doing and then we will see what we can do together and what we will not be doing together but will each have to handle on our own."

"You have not changed," I said to Manya. What she said to me about you she had already told me more than once in the past. She knew that she was torturing me and she took pleasure in the torture, and not because she did not love me with all her heart but simply because she was born - as you were well aware, even more so than me - to love herself first and foremost, not at the expense of her love for her sister, but in addition to it. Any love that she experienced had to come to terms with the fact that the deep love which she felt for herself always came first. So she may well have tortured me, but I did not really suffer. Perhaps.

"I do not know how to change and I do not think that I have to," she said. "Everything changes anyway. The question of whether I have changed or not has no real value altogether. My plan is to give birth. Here, in Saint-Claude. I am registered. Not as Resnick. Moritz decided that my name would be Mariel Ravel. The mamzer. He was crazy about Ravel's 'Bolero.' The clinic is a good one. I have been there. They examined me. Nuns. I don't care. There were crosses everywhere. I don't care. I'll get out of there after eight days and I am not coming back here. They are going to take me to the border, in an ambulance. I have already paid for everything, in advance. I will head to a village that is half French and half Swiss and that is where I am going to cross the border with the little infant boy or girl, who knows which, though it is all the same to me. Whatever it is, it is, and what it is, is what will be. I do not know what I am carrying. All I know is that we are committing a grave sin, you and me, bringing children into the world in the middle of this war. Who are we relying on? This idiotic war? Are we some sort of heroes? Perhaps you are, since you are already a mother of two, but me? I am just plain stupid. How am I going to make it through the war for myself and a child if I am having the time of my life trying to make it through by myself? Is that normal? But it is spilt milk. The two of us will get by. They will not get me. Forget everything I said. Even if you remember it - forget it. This rented room is paid for up until the middle of March. You will live here until then, with me while I am here, and by yourself once I will have left and until you leave as well, but not a moment after the lease is up. Once the lease is up they will turn you in without batting an eyelash."

She did not hesitate at all as she laid out her plans. Everything was set and the lines were clearly drawn and there was no room for any questions or recommendations. This woman had no problems whatsoever with the future. She was certain that she had it under control and that her control was unique and would tole-rate no objections or naysaying, and that if the future existed altogether it was there only in order to serve her.

Manya got up from her seat. She stood facing the large mirror that was affixed to the closet and looked over her figure as she continued to talk. From time to time she turned away from the mirror and looked at me in order not to lose the connection, then went back to addressing the mirror as though she and the image of her reflection were all alone in the room. She had been like that ever since I had known her. People would rebuke her for this odd habit when she was a child but even then the criticism had had no effect on her whatsoever. "What do you care," she would say. "The main thing is that I am talking to you, the mirror anyway does not hear me. Respect? Manners? Really now, what does it all have to do with respect or manners. Nonsense." And that was the end of that.

"It will be a bit crowded for you during your time here. It will be crowded for me too. But we have no choice. I have no more than a single room and there is no way that you can go and rent anything else without stirring up unnecessary curiosity. The curiosity seekers are the ones who cause all the tragedies in the world. They see something and then they want to see more. They go snooping around. They talk too much. Curiosity is the broom with which they sweep the place clean of foreigners. You are not to enter a single bakery more than once in order to buy bread. The first time you are a guest just passing through. The second time you are already a familiar face that is nevertheless unfamiliar. Such a thing exists. And then the investigation is already underway. That is the way I have done things. I am going to go out in a little bit to buy a few things for the house. I have been here for two months already and I still make an effort to do things this way. Until I give birth you are not to leave the house. The boys must stay inside as well. Once I go to give birth you will have no choice. You will have to take chances, but you will be careful about it."

She took evident pleasure in reciting this laundry list of instructions. I believe that she was searching the mirror for evidence of the authority that she felt ought to be reflected in her face. She was clearly satisfied. I did not object to a single one of the things that she told me. Even if I had wanted to, I could find no grounds for any possible objections. I could not possibly imagine how we were going to survive even a single day, much less two or three, or more, in a single room with a sister like Manya, all of us together. How were we going to sleep, how were we going to bathe ourselves, how would we eat, how would we get through the day without going crazy? But when she told me that she was about to give birth any day now I was terrified of what would become of us when we would be left there all alone, just me and the children. Manya seemed to sense that I had received her instructions rather fearfully and she came over to me, pulled up an empty chair, hugged me close and said, "My sister, we are on the run, you and I, and the only way for us to make it out alive is not to move, you hear me? Not to move. When the time comes, we will run. But if we run now there will be someone behind us who can run much faster than we ever possibly could. So we must just sit and wait. You are here with me and I am here with you. All we have is each other. Later on we will separate. If we make it, we will be separated but we will meet up once again. If you do not make it and I do, or if neither one of us makes it, we will never meet again. Whoever makes it will survive. Whoever does not make it must not kill the survivor with sorrow. There is no such thing. Sorrow does not kill. You live with it the same way you live with a disease that has no cure. For now we are on the run, we are fighting for our lives. Is it a little crowded? The war crowds everything. Does it seem like we will not have the strength to take it? That is how things look when you are fighting for your life. I think we will win. Am I sure of that? Well, yes, my sister, I am sure, I am ready for whatever, even success." She let out a rather loud, rolling burst of laughter and hugged me close, then let me go and said that she had to go out now and would be back a little while later.

I fell asleep in the chair. A short while later I woke up, stumbled in a daze over to the bed where the boys were already lying and lay down in my clothes by their side and fell into a deep sleep myself.

When I woke up the table was set and Manya, Erwin and Jackie were seated around it, talking. I did not move. My eyes were wide open, but the three of them did not sense that I was awake. I listened to the conversation. Manya was only speaking Hungarian and that was the sole language she had used in speaking with me as well. She had spoken fluent, of course, Flemish in Antwerp with her friends in the communist cell in the city and occasional passing acquaintances of hers and Jack's who were not Jewish, and she had read the leftist paper in Flemish, from which she drew all her truths - the news, and, above all, all the opinions that came to form her outlook on the world. She knew a few words in French, but they were phrases one used to shop, or in other basic situations, which would not carry a full conversation with Erwin and Jackie, who had already almost certainly forgotten all the Flemish that they had known up until about three years ago. Erwin understood a little Hungarian, which he had picked up from what he overheard when I spoke with you and the other members of our family, but even that consisted of only the most basic vocabulary. Yet despite all these limitations the three of them were managing to carry on a real conversation. Manya was at ease with the boys, putting on a kind face and overflowing with warmth, love and understanding. The boys were rather unreserved and expressed their thoughts openly, resorting to a rather amusingly lexicon. I listened perhaps a bit too long until Jackie sensed that I was awake, jumped up and came over to embrace me and lay down by my side and curled up with me saying that he was glad I was already awake.

What did they talk about? About you. The first thing that I overheard was what Jackie said. He made use of his hands and fingers and all sorts of odd words in order to say that he had seen you when "the men", as he called them, took you away in the night from the house in Marseille, that you had kissed him and told him and Erwin not to be afraid, since there was no doubt whatsoever that you would be back shortly.

"Daddy true, Daddy no leave," Jackie warned, waving his finger.

"Because he is Daddy,"Manya said in a soft, compassionate tone, as she added, in her confusion of languages that you would join them in Switzerland, because you knew the way, since you had already helped quite a few people out and so you knew how to help yourself, as well.

"True," Jackie said proudly.

Erwin did not reject this but he was doubtful. He said something like,"Daddy disappeared now and then for quite a long time, but he always came back. He will be back this time too. But where will he go? Where do we live now? Nowhere. How could he possibly find us?" Manya caressed his head. He pulled back. She hugged him but he broke free of the embrace.

"Fathers know how to find their sons…" Manya said to him. Jackie agreed, vigorously nodding his head.

"How?" Erwin asked.

Manya said that she did not know how but she knew that this was how things were. Fathers know how to find their sons anywhere in the world. Even Jack, she said, would find her and their child that was soon to be born. She pointed to her belly and said that even le bebe was waiting for his father, and she took Jackie's little hand and placed it on her stomach and said, "Can you feel the bebe? No? He is going to kick any second now. There…" Jackie was taken aback and removed his hand. I had never allowed myself to pull down the barriers that stood between me and the boys the way that Manya did, quite naturally, and, I must admit, rather gracefully. She laughed. Jackie began to laugh too, somewhat hesitatingly and still in shock. Erwin would not let up and said to Manya that he had been to the Gestapo headquarters in Marseille. He had seen the trucks and buses taking people away.

"Where did they take them?" he asked, and immediately replied. "They took them to work for the war. They will not be back before the war is over."

"It will be over soon," Jackie said.

Erwin seemed to rebuke his little brother, who was more naïve than he, and said, "If it is going to end soon, then why did we run away from Marseille, why are we on our way to sneak into Switzerland?"

"Because there the war already ended completely," Jackie immediately replied. "And here it is only going to end in a little while, that is why, smarty-pants. And any-way, we have to escape to Switzerland because that is the only place where Daddy is going to look for us because that is where he sent us."

"That is actually correct," Erwin gave in, having no other choice. "He prepared passports for us to go to Switzerland if need be. That is what he knows from before we ran away, that we would be waiting for him there. That is all that he could possibly know."

"How do you know so much about passports?" asked Manya.

"You know just as much."

"True," Manya admitted with a smile.

"True, I also know quite a bit." Jackie sensed that he had the upper hand now in this conversation and he said once more, "He will come looking for us in Switzerland. That is why we are going to Switzerland."

Erwin's gloomy mood or perhaps his argumentative spirit would not let him be and he uttered, as though to himself, "…if we make it to Switzerland…"

"We will make it," Manya said. "I will make it and you will too. Here in Saint-Claude we are almost in Switzerland."

"Is it far away?" Jackie asked.

"No, everything here is near Switzerland."

"But Switzerland is not near here," said Erwin.

"How could that be," Manya asked, and added, "What is the matter with you? Your father would not believe what he was hearing. He would have looked into your eyes with those two shining green eyes of his and he would have told you that anyone who sets out on their way reaches their destination. And then you would blink and look away. You remember his eyes. What is this 'if we make it', what is that supposed to mean, young man?"

It took her a little while to express these rather involved, convoluted ideas using broken bits of language and an array of gestures, but she stuck with it, with a bit of feigned anger, a little ridicule, and those gestures that added a certain gravity to her rebuke.

"That's how it is," said Erwin. "I know that's how it is. Switzerland is a completely different place in the world. The Germans did not seal it off, it sealed itself off. Daddy told me that. He once told me about Switzerland, that it was sealed off. Who sealed it off, I asked him, and he told me that the Swiss themselves had sealed it off. I asked him why and he told me that Switzerland was only worried about Switzerland, and it had sealed itself off so that the whole world would not descend on them. And the Germans, I asked him, why don't they open the country back up? He listened but did not explain it to me. He talked with me about everything, but he never gave me all the details. Like when he told me about kids."

"What does that mean - 'told you about kids'?" Manya asked, in curious amusement.

"How kids are born," Erwin said, without any embarrassment.

"And he told you?" Manya asked.

"Yes," Erwin responded. "I basically knew already but he explained it to me so-me more, though not the whole story."

"They are born," said Jackie, "and that is the whole story."

"You don't understand a thing," Erwin said, and Jackie replied that he understood everything, certainly more than Erwin did, at any rate, and then he noticed that I was awake and he came over to me.

He needed me. He had not lost you because I was right by his side for him to hug me. I believe that in his heart we were like one single being, you and me. If I was there, then you were there too. A distant father, but a father that existed all the same. A father whose arm may not wrap itself around his shoulder anymore, but a father who loved him every moment of the day all the same and was always present, no matter where he might be in the world. That is my interpretation of what he felt and what he was going through at the time. He was not afraid that we might not make it to Switzerland. He was with me. He would make it there with me. Erwin did not need me. He knew that I needed you. He was there to protect me. He stood by my side because you were far away. If I were to have asked him if he believed that you were going to return, deep down inside, he would have resented the fact that I doubted whether he believed it. But I am telling you that he is not sure if it is at all possible to come back from those trucks that took you away, as he witnessed with his own eyes. He is afraid that we might not make it to Switzerland. He does not know this for a fact but he feels responsible to make sure that I make it, even though he is only a child. He tells himself, even if he is unaware of this fact, that you prepared the way for us, and now you are gone, and so he is the one, the only one - there is no one else. It is insane.

I am constantly taking an inventory of the thoughts of our children, according to the things that they say and according to the silences in between, and the way they move, and the way they hold themselves, and I tell you that I can not even be certain that these thoughts are really what I think they are. I do not know how the children are experiencing the war in their minds and hearts. How can anyone possibly know such a thing? Adults never learned how to go through a war, and there are things that happen during wartime that even they could not have imagined. All the more so in the case of children. Though it may well be that they are more prepared than their parents, because they never had a chance to live any other sort of reality.

For Jackie and Erwin life was essentially a city that you left behind, a train that got bombed, a village that was in reality a holding pen, a camp that was all humiliation, a plague, rife with disease,. Marseille was no more than a deception, a grand illusion, and a father who was taken away in the dead of night, their mother helpless and imprisoned, separation, the convent - what had gone on in the convent? - a crowded, camouflaged compartment in a truck traveling through the night to a godforsaken town, and an aunt who told them that all the women in the world had been left alone and had no husbands anymore. All this while one of them had been but four years old when it all began, and was now seven, whereas his brother had been five and had now turned eight. How can children possibly begin to understand the life that they were now living, having lived like this the majority of their days on earth? And how would they conceive the life that they would yet live, from here on? I still hold out hope, for them, for myself, even for you. Do not make fun of me. I am not holding out hope in vain. It is hope itself that I am holding out. And that is not the same thing. That is allowed. I do not indulge in thoughts that never ever lead you to a good place. And I am constantly thinking about our children, imagining them. They are the riddle of my life.

That same night we all slept rather deeply. I passed a night lost in dreamless sleep atop the blanket that Manya had spread out for me on the wooden floor of her little apartment, along with the boys - Jackie in my arms and Erwin right by my side, though I do not know if they dreamed anything at all. Manya, who I think might just be incapable of dreaming anything altogether during the night, was all alone in her large bed.

I opened my eyes to the sound of utensils knocking around. Manya was standing by the table fully dressed, setting out forks and knives, plates and mugs, with a single hand. After I had a moment to wake up, I rose cautiously from the floor, making sure not to wake the boys, went over to Manya without her noticing my presence and whispered into her ear in Hungarian, "You are insane."

She was surprised but immediately retorted, "I may be crazy, but I am not insane." She stood still for a moment, planted a large, generous kiss on my face and added, "The time has come. I already went to see the neighbor. I had to wake her up. Her husband took his bicycle and went to call a taxi. Why did you have to wake up? I would have gone without saying a word. I was afraid that you would all be left without any breakfast. But you beat me to it. I have everything. I am ready. I am taking nothing but a small suitcase with me. You know that I will not be back. Why would I leave, then, without saying goodbye? Because it is hard to say goodbye when you do not know if you will ever see each other again. You know that I am not at all sentimental. But now you woke up and it is going to be hard for me to say goodbye. Do not wake the children, I would not be able to take it."

I sat down on a chair and said to her, "That is no way to give birth."

"I know just how I am going to give birth," she said, and sat down across from me.

"You never gave birth before. Are you even ready for it?"

"Basically. I am not going to wait here until I am ready. I am going to get myself ready at the hospital. Who is going to help me here? You? The children? The neighbor? The noise out in the street? I am going to scream, Rozhi, I am going to scream until even Jack hears me. Is that going to help me at all? I have been hiding away here to the best of my abilities and a single moment of weakness, just one instant of absent-mindedness and the entire block will be aware that there is an unknown woman in their midst who is giving birth. Does that make any sense? Do you know what that would be like in a little out-of-the-way street in a small town? The time has come, Rozhi, and I am in control. How do I know? I just know. And besides, I am showing signs of a new sort of pain."

"So what are you waiting for?"

"The taxi, there is a taxi service in Saint-Claude. Two or three cars. They confiscated the rest of them. The neighbor does not have a telephone. I paid her off so that her husband would call me a taxi when I would need one. And I need one now."

"Does he know that we are here?"

"He knows. Now he knows. I paid him off for that as well, just this morning. If you have any cash handy then you can pay me back now. If not, then you will pay me back when we see each other again. If we ever do. Do not feel like you owe me one. Without money, nothing is guaranteed. Even with money, things are never certain. You never know who else has been paying someone off. But it makes no difference. Whoever wants to live has to pay. Even if there are two people and only one is going to make it. You can come visit me by taking the same taxi. Call for him in another two or three days, if your contacts have not come to get you already by then."

"You said we may never see each other again."

"That's right. I am going to give birth, Rozhi, I am strong and I am going to get through it just fine, but you never know. I am ready for whatever. They're knocking at the door!"

She went over to open the door. The neighbor's husband was standing in the doorway, a short man, wrapped in a coat that was a few sizes too big on him, fastened with a cloth belt at the hips, with a cap on his head, wearing glasses and sporting a moustache. He did not say a word. He stood there in the doorway and looked at me and the boys who were sleeping on the floor and nodded in a slow, measured fashion, and kept nodding away like that until Manya, who had already managed to slip into a large coat made of rabbit fur, and take up her small suitcase, was there standing by his side and said, "I am on my way." Before I even got a chance to go over to her or say goodbye, or anything else for that matter, the door had closed, and my sister had left, off to bring a child into the world.

I stood there in room and I had no idea what I was going to do when the children woke up. The light of the new day was taking its time coming in through the windows. I was completely cut off from the world, trapped within these four walls, all by myself. The worst part of it all was the terror of having no one to talk to, and that I had these kids with me for whom I was going to have to speak. I suddenly realized that the muteness which I had feigned during the train ride and at the police station and in the clinic had all merely foreshadowed my real muteness. The little play was now done. I was a cripple. A person who has no one to talk to is mute. Even once the children wake up and we begin to talk with each other there will still be no one at all in our world here that I can talk to, until the neighbor's husband will perhaps come over to take me in a taxi to see Manya, though even he will not say a word but will merely nod away endlessly and look me over the way you stare at someone who has no idea that she is already essentially dead. But I was not dead and I had no intention of dying. I could not afford to let myself die.

I remember that I once imagined what it would be like to see the Angel of Death sitting there as though he were trying to hide from view, crouching on his heels, waiting patiently, mockingly, for the moment when he would get up and take me away, that hour that he alone would choose, an hour that might be anticipated somewhat or even postponed a bit, and I told myself that if he was waiting for me, then he was waiting in vain. I will not be there when he gets up. Now it seemed to me that the Angel of Death was the neighbor's husband. He did not deserve this. He had been paid off. When he comes, he will open up the world from which I have been sealed off with a taxi that will take me to see my sister. Perhaps she and

I are still meant to escape together into Switzerland. She had no idea and I, too, have no idea how things will play out, and common sense would seem to dictate that it can not possibly happen that way, but for some reason, in that brief moment when I sat looking at the neighbor's nodding husband, fragments of the strangest tales suddenly came to me. There were these black butterflies, all of whom suddenly became very colourful just before falling to the ground.

I looked over at the table all set for breakfast and smiled. It seemed to me as though it had been set in a rather random, pell-mell fashion. I did not have the strength. I did not want to lie down again on the floor next to the boys because I was afraid to wake them up. Manya's bed was made, with the blankets folded at the foot of the bed. She had managed to put down new sheets. When had she had a chance to rest? And here I had been sure that she was lost in a deep sleep just like me. I threw myself down on the bed and closed my eyes, but I was unable to fall asleep.

You know that it was impossible not to love Manya. It is a mystery and I do not know exactly what it means. Everyone was well aware - which was not all that hard, since Manya never concealed a thing - that she took pleasure in lording it over her loved ones, sometimes even to the point of humiliating them, though they all always forgave her, first and foremost her loved ones. She would always be playing this rather transparent game whose goal was to make a person lose their mind. And when that happened, she would burst out laughing rather loudly and swear that she was surprised that the 'sacrificial lamb' of choice had not managed to figure it out from the outset that the whole thing was no more than a mere amusement for amusement's sake and the 'sacrificial lamb' would end up apologizing every time. She was not a bad woman. On the contrary. She was capable of displaying tremendous love and compassion, to the point of even shedding tears, but when her self-love was awakened - and it stirred rather often - it came before all the other loves in her life. She was convinced that this was in fact the most proper, fitting way of the world. No one was more capable of this stance than her, and even those who liked to gossip about her openly in our circle of relatives and acquaintances secretly envied her and forgave her all these odd thoughts.

Manya went straight from the train that brought her from Hungary to the house of our cousin, Mannes Schick, the *Shochet*, who no longer worked in the slaughterhouse and his rather pious wife, Madame Malvin-Neny ,who was always carefully planning her next step. The couple had already arrived, two or three years before we arrived, with four daughters and a son. They had opened a poultry shop on a street corner in the heart of the neighborhood overflowing with Jews, barely managing to make a living. They lived in a shabby little rental apartment right next to the Hassidic Study Hall, the *Beis Medrash*. Mannes quickly earned the respect due a family man whose fear of God reigned in his cunning and his acumen, and who therefore - though perhaps, as well, because it had been decreed in Heaven - never managed to make more than what was minimally necessary for a man and his family to get by.

Manya, of course, had not notified him or told him that she was coming to live in his house. I have no idea where they put her up, perhaps she slept with Gizzy, or Sarah, or maybe with Tsiku, or even Rozhi. All of the girls, with the exception of the last one, Rozhi, the most beautiful one, who was either just plain lazy or simply lacked practical initiative, were diligent and hard-working, who made a living by accepting all sorts of work, like knitting, or negotiating on behalf of small-time diamond dealers, or as salesgirls in bargain clothing shops.

You and I had met people in Brens who, when they heard that we were from Antwerp, immediately pictured us as certainly having been - and thought that we perhaps still were - diamond dealers and cunning members of the wealthy elite who doubled and tripled their holdings everyday between Amsterdam and the Diamond Exchange, and spent the weekends in Knokke. Who knows better than you that this was not the Antwerp that you and I fell into when we got there. There were millionaires, but I do not know where they were. From time to time someone would go bankrupt and then his name would get out, whether it was the first time he had declared bankruptcy, or the second, or if this had become a sort of incurable ha-bit with him that was not even worth the derision. But we did not know anyone like that. What we knew was a jostling mass of hustle-bustle Jewry, all of whom had come from Hungary, Czechoslovakia, and Poland, people who were dirt-poor and grasped at anything that might enable them to earn francs. There were ragmen, small-time shop-owners, diamond polishers who had learned the basics of the trade for an exorbitant price. The clever ones earned what they could at work and then brought in a little extra in all sorts of minor business dealings, selling whatever they could get their hands on and turning whatever profit they could manage, until they prospered and turned into respected merchants. There were tailors, shoemakers, seamstresses, tutors, synagogue managers, and intellectuals; and there were the idlers and the musicians who played chess in the coffee houses, like you, who would disappear in there for hours at a time, thinking that I had no idea where you were, although, of course, I knew.

I do not know if there were many Belgians among the Jews of Antwerp. There must have been, but who really knew? Everyone was a Belgian. You were a Belgian if you had Belgian citizenship, and you were a Belgian if you had foreign citizenship, you were Belgian if you were 'Statenlos,' had no citizenship whatsoever. I have no idea how it all worked out. The Jews looked like Jews, they dressed like Jews, they stuck together like Jews, they struck deals on street corners outside the Diamond Exchange like Jews, they talked like Jews, and they went to the synagogues on *Shabbos* and holidays just like Jews. The schools were full , whether the *Cheders*, filled with boys sporting their beautiful *Payos*, their side locks, and wearing high black satin hats or the girls' schools, filled with young girls in their long, beautiful dresses. There was *Tachkemoni* and *Yesoday* Torah where the students spoke in Hebrew, and there was *Mesivta* where the boys learned Yiddish and *Loshen Koydesh*. The city was full of Hassidim and ultra-orthodox Jews, the learned and the lazy among them, along with Jews who did not believe in anything anymore, and the idealists, the Zionists, and the revisionists, and of course, the Reds, the Communists.

There was a theater where the biggest names in the Yiddish acting world would perform, and there were choirs - you were even the director of one of these - where the members would sing folk songs from the land of Israel in Hebrew. None of this came from the millionaires that we never got to know. It emerged from the ranks of the common Jews, the ones who got by, the creative ones, the refugees who had arrived just a short while ago, and those who had been there since forever, all of whom were Jews in transition, in various stages of getting settled. Who would ever have thought of leaving Belgium if the World War had not come along scattering us all in every direction. We, thank God, or thanks to you - I have no idea how, but thanks to you, even if I, too, put in my time - as we managed in the few years that passed between the time we had arrived and the day we ran away, to rise from that awful poverty to a certain level of material comfort. We were not rich, far from it, but we had more than a mere crust of bread.

Manya was completely in her element in that world. She managed to do things that magnified the extent to which this was *not* her world. It was so comfortable for her to ridicule everything with her actions and set herself apart from it all with the things she said. She went to work as a dishwasher at a rundown Kosher *Limehadrin* restaurant, but she would not hesitate to sit around after her shift was over along the boulevard in a fancy cafe no Jew had ever set foot in and order a portion of Belgian waffles laden with whipped cream, or a crêpe made with Grand Marnier, or chocolate, and a steaming cup of hot coffee. She would sit there offering her greetings to any Jew who happened to pass by and look at her, not as though she were issuing a sort of challenge, but as if to demonstrate her absolute freedom. People forgave her. Gizzy once told me that at home she was careful not to turn on the lights on *Shabbos* in front of Mannes and Malvin-Neny, but when it was just the girls, who had been brought up to steer clear of everything tainted, she did not hesitate to do whatever she felt like. While the rest of them were *Bentsching*, saying the Grace After Meals, she would lower her head and wait for them to finish mumbling, and from time to time she would raise a single eyelid and try to steal a glance from one of the girls with a wink that was clever but never conniving, as a vague smile passed over her.

One day, not in some private tete-a-tete but when the entire family had sat down for a meal, or had perhaps been called together for that express purpose, Malvin-Neny demanded that Manya find another place to live. Mannes was sitting in the room at the time but he did not get involved in the conversation and could not look anyone in the eye. The four girls sat around the table in silence with their heads down while Malvin-Neny did all the talking. She did not rant or rave, she was not angry, she was not trying to cause any undue suffering and she did not resort to preaching, but her mind was clearly made up.

"This is not the way you used to behave in your father's house," she said to Manya. "We love you, but you are bound to become a bad influence on our girls and cause them to go astray."

"I left my father's house," Manya replied. "I have been respectful towards you. In your house I have respected the fact that it is your house. I am eighteen years old. There is no way that I could influence a single one of your daughters to go astray if they did not want that for themselves. And they do not. They are not built for it."

"You say that you respect us, but you do not," Malvin-Neny answered her, and then immediately added, somewhat dryly, "You smoked a cigarette in our house on *Shabbos.*"

"In my room."

"This is not a hotel. You do not have a room here!"

"When I am alone in the room, I do," Manya responded, and then added, as she shrugged her shoulders, not as though she were trying to protect herself, but like a person telling herself that everything was all so terribly silly, "I hate smoking. I have never smoked in my life and I am never going to smoke. It looks good. And it would really suit a young woman like me. I suppose that it would actually fit me, my personality, but it just disgusts me."

"That is rather strange. It disgusts you but you smoked to your heart's content in your room - that is, if you even have a room."

"I had to try it."

"But why on *Shabbos*?"

"That was the test."

"But why in my house?"

"That was also part of the test. It will not happen again. There is no reason that it should. Now I know what it is all about."

"You are to leave here tomorrow. I found a room for you."

"I can find one on my own," Manya replied, though she immediately followed that up by asking, "A room where?"

"With some fine Jews. The Resnicks. They're Czech. She buys her chickens from me. I am not sure that they actually keep *Shabbos*. When I say them, I mean her and her son. She keeps *Shabbos*. But as for her son, I am not so sure. The husband was a fine Jew with his *Hadras Panim*, his beard, but he did not have *Payo*s and he wore a common cap. He was not the most industrious sort but he was an honest man. He died just a few months ago and now she could really use the money. You will eat with us on *Shabbos*."

"I knew this was going to happen," said Manya. "I wanted it to happen. It was time already. I am a free person, Malvin-Neny, but in order to truly be free you have to have a place to live. That was what I had and I was free. You gave me that, you are family and I accepted it with gratitude because I too am family. That's all. It is done now. I will come back for *Shabbosim*. When I can. Take me to the Resnicks. Not tomorrow, now. I have to work tomorrow." Manya kissed each one of the daughters goodbye, went into the room where she slept and within a few moments she was ready for the Resnicks, with her little suitcase in her hands.

It was at the Resnicks that her romance with Jack began. He

had a childhood flame, one of the most beautiful girls in all of Antwerp, or so they said. Whether it was just a mere legend or the actual truth, people also said of that she was the daughter of a wealthy family who had become a communist. When Manya arrived - Manya, whom you could not exactly call one of the most beautiful girls in the city - when she came to live in that room at his mother's house, Jack was swept away by her charms and his relationship with that childhood flame quickly cooled off until it was completely doused and destroyed. He used to wait for Manya right outside the restaurant where she worked, but often she refused to go anywhere with him because she claimed to have made a date with someone else. Most of the time this was not even true. She loved Jack. She even adored his exemplary devotion to the ageing Madame Resnick, which was why she never bothered him with even the vaguest reference to the fact that she, Manya, was second in his eyes to his own mother. All the same, she could not resist taking a certain continuous pleasure in creating tension and expectations and uncertainty in his soul as far as the future of their relationship was concerned, a relationship that both of them desired with every ounce of their being. In this way, abusing Jack's kindness to no end, Manya, in her typical fashion, managed to express her complete fidelity to this wonderful young man, who, in time, also became your close friend, despite the fact that, in actuality, there was nothing that might sensibly explain this great bond of friendship that formed between the two of you.

Jack was an innocent communist. He was not looking to fix the world. He would consider the fate of his family, uprooted from Czechoslovakia only to fight through tremendous hardship trying to put down roots in Belgium; his own daily routine in a life that offered little promise of improvement; and the Jews of Antwerp who, in his eyes, were a group that tried to deny the unavoidable conclusion that sticking to a dying religion or the rebirth of Zionism were equally devoid of hope. He was not angry. He was a young man with a positive disposition and his brand of communism was a local, familial, personal sort of hope. Nothing more.

Manya may well never have become a communist herself if she had not met Jack, but she looked down on his narrow outlook. Manya actually used to speak of fixing the world. She would read the headlines in one of the leftist newspapers and then repeat them as though she had written them herself. One day, I still recall, things almost got to the point of actual physical violence. Jack and Manya, as well as your brother Zollie, were all sitting around at our place, and you were late coming home. I got angry. I was certain that you had once again stayed too long at the chessboard in one of your coffee houses. You wrapped your arm around my shoulders in an attempt to appease me and said that this time you had a different excuse, as it turned out you had gotten a chance to learn some Torah with Rav Amiel. I do not think that I looked all that appeased.

I knew of your great affection for Rav Amiel. You once told me that he was the most knowledgable Rabbi you had ever known, and that in between the bits of Torah that the two of you exchanged you also spoke at great length about the philosopher Hegel. I assumed that you spent more time discussing Hegel than Torah, but, truth be told, I had no real knowledge of these matters whatsoever and the fact is that they did not interest me at all at the time. Zollie, who in his entire life had never studied any more than what he had managed to learn in the *Cheder* in that godforsaken little village of yours in Transylvania, heard the name Amiel and immediately clapped you on the shoulder and told everyone how proud he was to have a brother that was a real *Talmid Chacham*, a real Torah scholar. And he then turned to me and told me not to get angry but, on the contrary, I ought to thank God for the fact that it was my lot to live with an *Iluy*, a genius such as you.

Jack was already standing at the door ready to leave when he said, "Moritz, you're a good-for-nothing genius. They say Amiel is also a genius. But he is a Rabbi, and you are a worker in the diamond industry. Amiel makes a living off the rabbinate, but Amiel is not going to provide a living for you or Roszy with all his learning."

Manya jumped in at this point and added, in a loud voice, "Amiel is the opium of the masses."

You looked at her with an amused air and said, "And how would you know? Where did you read that one?"

"It was in the paper today," Jack said, in complete innocence, without a trace of sarcasm.

Manya turned to him as though she had been bitten by a snake and said, "You, you're crazy!"And then she immediately turned back to you and said, "What papers? My newspaper has more in it than all those books that you spend your time reading. Your wife does not even read the papers, and here you are talking to me about books? You neglect her and go off to sit with your Rabbi and study all sorts of silliness with him, things that neither edify nor stultify, and you do not care about the fact that you have guests at home who came expressly to see you, all you care about is spending time with the Rabbis and with the chess players when it is about chess. And anyway, you are a heretic. I know all about you. I know you inside out." I do not know to what extent she was truly possessed by any real anger, but I do know that she certainly appeared angry about it as though it were real. She was enraged. There was no better way for her to react to the insult that she felt she had suffered. She was breathing fire.

Jack tried to calm her down but he did not stand a chance.

Zollie, who, by his nature, was a man of peace and inclined to just let things be, said to her, "Go home, Manya, I know you didn't have a drink, but you're drunk."

I remained silent.

You showed no pity. You laughed and said to Manya, who was ready to scratch your eyes out with every one of her painted finger-nails, "You have no idea what a wonderfully charming little girl you are when you lose your mind. It is all so much more entertaining than Karl Marx' *Das Kapital.*"

Manya stood there facing you and said, "Shut your mouth!"

You stared at her and smiled. With her mere glance she tore out your laughing eyes and feeling insulted to her very core she pulled

Jack after her and left, slamming the door behind her. It was awful, but just a few days later it was as though nothing had ever happened.

I opened my eyes when I sensed that Jackie was lying next to me and hugging me with his little hands and pressing his head against my neck. Erwin had already washed up and was ready, standing at the window and looking outside. I kissed Jackie on the head.

He looked up at me and asked, "Where is Aunt Manya?"

I told him that she had gone to the maternity ward in order to give birth.

"I am afraid," said Jackie.

"Why?" I asked.

"Because she is not here anymore."

Erwin dragged a chair over from the table and sat down next to the bed. "I told him, but he does not believe me. I told him that she had to rush to the hospital and did not want to wake us up, though I am sure that she woke you up, but he refuses to believe me."

"I believe you," said Jackie, and suddenly pulled away from me and jumped down off the bed, stamped his feet on the floor, and screamed, "I believe you, I believe you, but why did she have to go?" Erwin did not move from where he sat still. It seemed to me that he was looking at his brother with the mocking gaze of an adult as he said in a measured tone, "She left because a pregnant woman eventually has to go. Women give birth at the hospital, Jackie, not at home. The time has come for you to understand such things." But Jackie would not calm down. He began to cry, and as he cried and really wailed away, broken fragments poured from his mouth that I did not understand. I could not possibly repeat what he said. He was afraid. He was convinced that Manya had been taken away. He had already been told that his father would return, but his father had never come back. Now they were telling him that Aunt Manya had disappeared in the middle of the night because she had to go. The evening before there had been no such need yet the next morning she was gone because she suddenly had to go. There is nothing that you just suddenly have to do.

"If they took her away, maybe they are going to take you away too. And even if they do not take you away but you just leave all of a sudden in the middle of the night because you are expecting a baby and you do not tell us anything at all, and just leave us all alone, what will happen with me and Erwin, all alone in a place like this? Where will we go?" There was no way to quiet him. He only stopped when he ran out of words. He came back over to me and hugged me tightly. Erwin got up from his chair and said, "It's impossible. I can't take it anymore."

I got off the bed, went over to him, pulled him close with both my hands so that he was standing right in front of me and said to him, "I can take it, and you can too. You are his big brother." The child stared at me for what felt like an eternity. It seemed as though he was waiting all too long to respond to what I had said, as though he was weighing up whether or not to say something that might cause me a certain amount of pain.

In the end, all he said was, "That's right," although he kept staring into my eyes as though he was checking to see if I had understood the difference between what he said and what he had left unsaid. We sat down to the breakfast that Manya had prepared for us before she left. We had plenty of time. We all knew, the children as well as I, that it was imperative that we not leave our little room the entire day. At first we exchanged little commonplaces while we ate, but I could sense that these exchanges did not hold any interest for Erwin, and when it came to Jackie I could tell that the conversation was not going to pull him out of his depression or take away his fears.

Erwin pushed his plate aside and, without any connection to the things that were being said, blurted, "This isn't something new now, it was like this in the convent too." Jackie stared at him for quite a while and waited for him to say something else.

I had never asked them what had happened immediately after the nuns took them away, or what went on in the convent itself, never asked how they had felt, or who had looked after them.

I never asked and they never told. At every instant we were merely concerned with what would come next. We were on the run. This stripped us of everything that was not connected to the escape itself. At this point I felt that I had sinned when I had failed to find out what had happened to my children while they were in the convent, and I felt that my fault was even greater for the fact that they did not even know how to ask, or were simply incapable of asking me, anything about all that I had been through while I was being held in the prison or at the clinic. I never gave them a chance to ask. We had been bound together from the moment that they had taken you away from us so it was simply impossible for us to absorb the fact that we had been separated from each other in Annemasse, and we had no idea what the other had been through that period. This stirred our fears that we could well be separated from each other again and again, over and over, and that the next time there would not be anyone to bring us back together.

Jackie was afraid that they had taken Manya away and could well take me away too. This fear was his sole concern at this point. But Erwin's fear was of a different sort. Perhaps he himself was not really aware of his fears. He now wanted to talk about their time at the convent. Perhaps Jackie was afraid of what would still be. But Erwin was afraid of what had already been. Just like me. I could handle whatever would come next. But how could I deal with what had already happened? Erwin spoke at length about their time in the convent. He was not telling a story. I am certain that he did not feel that there was a story there. He felt like something had happened to him there. I listened attentively until I understood that that was the entire story. Jackie lay his head n in my lap and did not say a word even when Erwin began to talk about him. From time to time I checked to see if he was sleeping. But his eyes were wide open. He was completely alert, and listening.

"The nuns were completely unbearable," Erwin said. "Jackie was afraid of them." Erwin was disgusted by them. He told me of how kind they were. All the time. Constantly. They spoke so sweetly, never raised their voices. They never got angry, never rebuked the children, never pressed them. They gave orders, albeit pleasantly, but orders all the same, when it came to everything. And with a smile. "I hated that smile of theirs." There were also other nuns, nuns who never smiled. Their faces were always rather severe. "They were old," Erwin said. "But there were no wrinkles in their faces, just these eyes that saw everything without ever moving in those little holes of theirs, and these thin lips that barely seemed to move when they spoke, just this skin stretched taut across their thin faces, such pale skin, extremely white, and smooth, and cold."

You know how much Erwin loved chess. You believed, you were even convinced of the fact that he would one day become a prodigy. But it never happened. There are no prodigies in wartime. I was not surprised when he told me that the nuns were like those black pieces on the chessboard. The floor was entirely covered everywhere with those squares, marble slabs that had been polished until they shined, alternating in black and white. That was the only association he could have possibly had.

"Were there white pieces on the board as well?" I asked, with a smile.

"No," he responded, with almost exaggerated severity. "There are no white pieces in a convent."

"But I was told that there are certain nuns who wear white," I tried.

"Not at my convent. In my convent there were only black pieces."

The nuns who never smiled were the ones who tended to everyone. They ruled over the children with a nod of the head, or the flutter of an eyelid, with sentences that were no more than a single word. The children were not afraid. They obeyed without feeling a thing, not even fear. At night, in their rooms, they would break the code of discipline somewhat, until the nun on duty was forced to silence them by getting up out of her chair, which was placed at the front of the room where she sat and watched over the entire space, over all the beds that stood right next to each other in two long rows along the walls. The nuns who tended to Erwin and Jackie were rather loving. They would talk with them at great length, explaining things. It was impossible not to do what they asked. The explanations, in actuality, were of no real use. But the nuns continued to explain things all the same. They did not explain what the cross was for. There was no need to explain that. And they did not explain who Jesus was either, since that, too, did not require any explanation. He was everywhere, both with his cross and without it.

Erwin had no idea, or at least could not understand why Jackie was afraid of the nuns. And it was not the stern-looking nuns that he feared, either. He paid no attention to those nuns. "It was our nuns, the ones who took us with them when we left the police station. It was the same fear that he feels now when he says they took Aunt Manya away. The same way he is afraid that they might take you away too. Maybe it was just because of the fact that our nuns were the ones who took him away from the police station. Is that it, Jackie?" Jackie did not stir in my lap. He heard every word but he did not move. I sensed his gaze fixed on my eyes. I looked at him. He did not look away.

"Are you not afraid that they might take me away?" I asked Erwin.

"They are not going to take you away," he said.

"You won't let them?" I asked, cautiously. Erwin did not respond.

"They already took me away once," I continued.

"They did not take you away. You're here."

"They took your father away." "They will not get you," he said tersely, with a ring of confidence that was completely unassailable.

After a moment of silence he took up the subject of the convent once again. "Jackie never wanted to get undressed," he said. "Why? Why, Jackie"

I turned to Jackie himself. "You did not want to get undressed, when you went to sleep you did not want to get undressed? Why, sweetheart, why?" Jackie did not move in my lap. Erwin said that he refused to get undressed when they took the boys to wash up. "Perhaps he was embarrassed in front of the nuns," I said.

"There were no nuns there then. Just monks. All of them, all the children got undressed. But Jackie refused. Even I got undressed."

Erwin told me how he stood naked next to his brother, trembling from the cold and asking his brother to get undressed as well. "Just like everyone else. But he refused. A monk came over," Erwin continued, "and told Jackie, gently, without the slightest trace of anger, that there was no way to wash up in your clothes. Jackie sat down on the long bench and sort of folded up into himself. The monks let him be. Everyone washed up, got dressed and began to file out in the direction of our bedrooms. The nuns were all waiting in the hallway for everyone, and our nuns were waiting there for us too. That monk came over and spoke with them in a whisper. They raised their eyes as he spoke and looked over at Jackie. Jackie, for his part, looked them right in the eye. It seemed to me that at that moment he was not afraid of them. One of our nuns came over to Jackie and caressed his head. At that point he was afraid again. I could tell that he was terrified." Jackie refused to get undressed once back in the dormitory as well. The nuns let him be. All they asked was that he take off his shoes. Erwin said that he refused, since he himself had to put his brother in bed by force, almost throwing him down on the bed as he struggled to remove his shoes. Jackie put up a fight. He kicked. He gnashed his teeth, but he did not make a sound.

"But I could hear him," Erwin said. "He was screaming, shouting, but not a single sound came out of his mouth. It was terrible."

The other children looked on from their beds at the two new boys, brothers, fighting, the older one attacking in an almost violent fashion, as the younger one tried to defend himself desperately until he almost gave in.

"The nun on duty did not separate you?" I asked.

"No," Erwin responded. "Did she not see what was happening?"

"I think she saw it all. Everyone saw it. She must have seen it too. But she did not separate us. I had to do it. When it was all over she told all the boys to put their heads down on the sheets and close their eyes and go to sleep. That's all she did. Nothing more."

As he continued to tell the story, Erwin said that that night the brothers began whispering to each other.

"I told him that there were rules. Particularly in a convent there are rules. In a convent they did not forgive someone who did not pay attention to the rules. Jackie said that they had not done anything to him, but I told him that they were going to. I told him that we had no idea what they were going to do. If he continued to refuse to get undressed they would throw him in a cell and he would never see you again, and he might never see me again either. He whispered back that he did not care if they forgave him or not because he in-tended to run away before they had a chance to throw him in their cell and he would see us again, nobody would get in his way, not even you and me - even if we could not see him, he would see us all. That's just Jackie. I asked him how that was possible and he told me that he figured it would be impossible to run away if he were to get undressed. You cannot run away without your clothes on. I did not believe him. There was no way he could run away. Nobody could run away, I told him. The convent, for us, was like a jailhouse. Only the nuns know where the front entrance is, they are the only ones who hold the large key that opens the iron lock. Anything that en-ters that door will never leave if the nuns themselves do not agree to open it. If you re-fuse to get undressed like everyone else and at the same time as everyone else, then one day they are going to open that door up for everyone else, but not for you, and not for me, either.

He said to me, "Let me go to sleep," and lay there the entire night in his bed, fully clothed.

I fell asleep. I do not think that he fell asleep. Perhaps he spent the entire night thinking about how he was going to escape. But the morning came and he was still there.

I listened to Erwin's story and when he had finished I remained

silent for quite some time until I finally said to him, "You know, Erwin, we are Jews. Jackie knows this too. Isn't it hard to be a Jewish
child in a convent?" I sensed that Jackie was stirring uncomfortably
in my lap. Perhaps it was something more than mere discomfort. He
did not say a word. It was Erwin who spoke.

"We are very well aware of the fact that we are Jews, Mom. It
was not at all difficult for me to be a Jewish child in a convent. I
did not go there in order to become a Catholic. It is difficult to be a
Jew when you go there in order to become a Catholic. But we did
not even go there altogether. We were taken there. I felt like someone who was visiting strangers in a place where he does not belong.
They offered us a very warm reception, they were very accepting.
But I never accepted them. They were oblivious to this fact. There
was no way they could tell. But I knew that I would never belong
to them. It was just impossible. Jackie also refused to accept them.
But he let them see his refusal. I was afraid for him. He was so
obstinate that I was sure in the end they were going to have their
way with him. They did not suspect me at all. Even if you had never
come to take us away and I had to stay there, they never would have
done anything to me. That was just the way I behaved, and that was
how I would have continued to behave. Even if you would have
waited another year to show up, I would still have been the same as
I am today."

"Are you sure?" I asked.

"Yes," Erwin responded, after a brief silence. "Except for one
thing. The prayers. Ma, their prayers are so beautiful. The sisters
sing so beautifully. The little chapel is an awful thing. With everyone
sitting around in silence along the benches. Nobody moves. Everyone's eyes are riveted on the priest up in the pulpit. And the huge
copper candlesticks. The dais. The cross. All the nuns stand the entire time. It's terrible. You're nothing at all. It's as though you too
are built right into the chapel. And then suddenly they start singing.
And it's like the whole chapel is one big organ. I tried to locate the
instrument, but I couldn't find it. Suddenly I could not even see the

nuns anymore. There was just this melody. And it was so beautiful, it was just heavenly. I felt like crying. And suddenly I moved in my seat along the bench. Perhaps I even tapped my feet on the ground, or dragged them a bit. Everyone heard it. They all looked at me. The melody suddenly stopped. The nuns were still singing and the organ was still playing, but the melody was gone. I never should have moved. Nobody should ever have known that the melody had ended. If I had not moved I don't think they would ever have known. Jackie had an easier time of it. I could see him. Out of the corner of my eye, which I was careful not to move, I could see him. He was sitting right next to me. His arms were hanging down along his legs, completely slack, like there were no bones inside them whatsoever. He was not listening. The nuns were singing, but he did not hear them. He was afraid to close his eyes. But I think he was actually fast asleep."

I must stop myself and reread what I have already written. I can not believe that Erwin spoke like this. I want to erase something, but I will not. That was the way he spoke. And it was so painful for me.

There was a long silence. Jackie was still resting in my lap. Erwin put his head on my shoulder. With one arm I hugged Erwin and with the other hand I caressed Jackie's head. I never should have said anything to Erwin about being a Jewish child. I think that we, in fact, had never spoken about it. It is the same way that one never addresses the idea of the oxygen that one breathes. Or maybe not exactly. Oxygen is a thing that is never in doubt. But what is a Jew? What did it mean to be a Jew inside one's father's house; what did it mean in those days to be a Jew outside one's father's house, what did it mean to be a Jew in the *Cheder*, or the Yeshiva, and what did it mean to be a Jew in Vilna which had so altered the course of your life? What did it mean to be a Jew in the streets of Antwerp, along the alleyways around the Diamond Exchange, in the Study Halls of Antwerp, in Manya's club, in Mannes' chicken shop? Is it all one and the same? What does it mean to be a Jew during a war, what does it mean to be a Jew when being a Jew means you are going to die, and what does it mean to be a Jew when being a Jew is one the thing that you live off? What is it like to be a Jewish child who knows that his father and mother are running for their lives with him because of the very fact that they are Jews and he basically has no idea why? And what does it mean to be a Jewish child who is not allowed to say that he is Jewish? Why did I have to go and say to Erwin that he must be aware of the fact that he is a Jewish child? He was well aware. He had said so himself. But what did he know? Jackie too was well aware of the fact that he was a Jew. But even Jackie, what did he really know?

From the time that we boarded the train in Antwerp we had not had a *Shabbos* that was really a *Shabbos*, or a Passover that was really a Passover, or a Yom Kippur that was really Yom Kippur. The children had not once seen us opening up a *Siddur*, a prayer book, to pray. Being Jewish did not depend on any actual Jewish thing other than the mere fact of being Jewish. That was the most Jewish thing that there could possibly be and that is precisely what they were.

One day Jackie came across your *Tefillin*, your phylacteries. You never put them on. Not once. They were in your little *Tefillin* bag that was always right by your side throughout our endless journey, even when you left the house to travel down streets that I had never seen. I once asked you whether you might not want to put them on. You said to me, "I put them on every day. Not in the sense that I actually put them on my head, or my arm, but in the sense that I never let them out of my sight. Just having the *Tefillin* with me is my way of putting them on. It's like the penitential prayer before Yom Kippur, whirling the sacrificial chicken overhead." I admit that I did not initially understand what you were getting at. Jackie looked at the *Tefillin* bag once and at the *Tefillin* themselves, and asked me what they were. I explained it all to him. I told him that a Jewish man adorns his head with the *Tefillin* and wraps them around his arm, and he asked me why his Daddy did not do that. I told him that his Daddy did, in fact, do it. But secretly, in private, when no one could see. I could not tell him what you told me. Or maybe I did, in fact. At any rate, Jackie was very proud of you. The father who was always shrouded in mystery putting on his *Tefillin* in secret. I do not know if he ever talked about it with Erwin.

But were our children really all that Jewish?

Do you know, Moritz, what comes to mind as I am writing to you of all these things?

I once saw you in Antwerp on *Shabbos*, when you thought that you were all alone and that I was still sleeping, trying to forge something in the gas flame of the stove-top. You were at work on some sort of invention. I never told you that I had seen you do it, I did not want you to lie to me when you would try to explain it, and I did not want you to know that I, who was ostensibly so careful about observing all the laws, whether minor or major, was already well aware of the fact that when it came to such things you were quite prone to lying. You were not one of the most righteous men around. I had already told you that people were in the habit of going on about the fact that you were even something of a heretic. During the war you did not observe anything at all, none one of us did, but you were not a heretic, Mortiz, by any stretch, I swear you were actually quite a big believer. If your eldest son could say that, "We are very well aware of the fact that we are Jews, Ma," and your younger son could be so proud of the fact that you secretly put on your *Tefillin*, then I suppose that you must have projected quite a good deal of faith. They did not get it from me. I was completely incapable of being a parent steeped in faith. But it would seem that you in fact were. But how? That remains a mystery. A mystery that we continue to live. It is a mystery that we are running away with in order to save ourselves from all that it might do to us. Until I find you Moritz we will continue to run with it. We will never run away from it.

The entire day we remained hidden away in that little room. Jackie went over to the window from time to time, pulled back the fabric of the curtain and looked outside, though Erwin would tell him to stop. After this happened two or three times, Jackie came over to me and stood facing me all tense and said, "What Erwin said about the convent is not true. That's not the way things went. I would have run away, but you came. He was not going to let me but I was going to run away even without him, even all by myself if he was not willing to come with me. He would have stayed in the convent if you hadn't come. But not me. He told me that he hated them but that he thought we had to be careful. We would beat them slowly, he told me. I told him that if things went slowly then they would win. He's lying. He told you that he was wise. But that's not true. He would sit there adding things up, in silence. And then he would whisper his conclusions to me. There was always some new result, because he was afraid. He was more afraid of me than the nuns. But I was not afraid of him or them. I could not stand anything there - not the nuns, not the whole thing, and I just had to get away. I knew that if I did not run away I would never see you again, ever. I didn't know where you were but I knew that I would find you. I didn't care if they caught me. I just had to run away. That was all that mattered, just that, to run away."

I looked him over. He was waiting there, a trembling bundle of nerves, waiting for me to say something to him.

"But you did not run away," I said to him. He refused to accept that.

"Because you came. If you had not come, I would have run away. That's the way things went."

I wrapped mys arm around his shoulders and pressed his little body to my breast and said to him, "That's true, Jackie, that's the way things went, and you would have run away, but then I came and we ran away together." I could feel his limbs sort of thawing and softening and his hands squeezing me somewhat hesitantly at first and then firmly, decisively. He pulled away after a moment and went and sat down, eyeing Erwin from afar, and said, "That's the way things went, Erwin, and it's good that Mom knows." Erwin did not respond. He looked up at the ceiling and nodded his head in agreement. Then he went over to Jackie, patted him on the shoulder and went off into a corner of the room dragging one of the chairs and sat down.

We were certainly hungry when we went to sleep. There were

a few things in the kitchen and the pantry, we had tasted a bit here and there, but we had barely really eaten anything, neither the children nor I. I did not tell them that we would be hidden away in the room once more the next day and be unable to go out and buy anything, and that we therefore had to be careful about how much we consumed. I was afraid that if I told them they would ask me what would happen when the next day came, and what we would eat if we remained there beyond that next day for another day or two, or more, for that matter. We ate a bit and did not want to eat any more than that. Eating became a sort of burden for us and the things we chewed seemed altogether tasteless. The long hours spent sitting in a locked room and the knowledge that everything which lay beyond that room was closed to us robbed us of the joy of eating and did away with its necessity. Erwin ate and told me that he was not hungry while Jackie barely tasted any-thing and said that he too was not hungry. I then said that I was not hungry either, and the children did not ask any questions. They were hungry, though. It was impossible for them not to be.

Afterwards, when I thought about why I did not speak with them about the next day and the day after that I came to understand that the children did not say anything for fear of appearing as no more than children who were incapable of understanding the fact that it was impossible to provide them with food as it was impossible for us to take the chance of going outside. It was important for them that I treat them like adults. This was not easy. They were not adults, after all, they were in fact children. Even their need to calm me down by demonstrating that they were mature was no more than the common need of children to be considered adults. It was important that I keep this in mind, though I often found myself wondering silently if they had not matured more than they or I were even aware or than what was good for them. But I would immediately tell myself that they were still just children, and the same way that it was important in their eyes that I consider them as adults there was also a great need that they remain children for me. This is not an easy thing, Moritz, not for the children, I am sure, and not for their mother either, as I well know.

As morning approached Jackie woke up. I could hear him crying. I stared at him. He was sitting at the table and looking over in my direction, as though checking to see if his tears had caused my eyes to open or not. I got up at once. I hugged him and asked, "Jackie, Jackie, what's wrong?" He said a few words interspersed with bits of tears, telling me that he was afraid, that Manya had not returned because they had captured her and if they had been able to take her then they would get me too, because they were intent on capturing all the fathers and mothers, one after the other, all the time, while the children, whom they have no need for and therefore do not bother to capture, are left behind all alone, and how could he possibly survive alone, just Erwin and him, in this room that they were not allowed to leave, if I was to be taken away. I told him that no one had captured Manya, that she had gone off to the hospital to give birth to a baby and that she would come back after the delivery. He could not calm down. If she went off to give birth to a baby, then let her come back with the baby already.

"Until she comes back, I know you're lying. I want to see her already." Jackie had never called me a liar or even accused me of ever lying. I was frightened by the pain that he seemed to be suffering. To call me a liar was like refusing to get undressed at the convent, I thought to myself. It was a way of striking a blow, to demand that I never ever abandon him, by threatening to abandon me himself. It was his way of warning me that he was aware of the war, that it would not stop until he had been left completely alone in the world, or and if I were to be captured and taken away then it would be like I too had turned into an enemy, a sort of partner in crime with the war itself, and any woman, any mother who threatens to become an enemy herself can be called names that you would never ordinarily allow yourself to use when addressing your own mother - liar.

If you are reading these things, at this point you would surely be dismissing them as incomprehensible, feeling they lack any substance as mere words without any truth. Try not to think that, if that is indeed what you are thinking. I have seen it all up close, my terrified eyes facing that desperate child's eyes, as the war brought fear to the hearts of children whose father and almost every other adult male that they knew had all been taken away. Now Manya too had gone away, and I had already been taken away in Annemasse, and though I had been saved, my sentence had been to be captured and so it followed that they would take me away once again, since once they were done with the men it was the women's turn, according to some obscure order of things, some sense of justice, some absurd logic - those women who had shielded their children with their very own bodies, protecting them from being left all alone in the world. And now these women, too, were being taken away. If he could have possibly understood what was happening inside him, little Jackie would have said the same thing that I am telling you. But he could not. Perhaps he never will. Is a tree aware that it is losing its leaves in the fall? I am waxing poetic once more. But I had to do something.

Although only a few hours had passed since Manya left to give birth my sense of time had become rather blurred and dull. I had no idea if she had left us the day before or even two days ago, and if she may well have already given birth or if it was more appropriate to assume that her child had not yet been born But I had to see her. Or not me, really, but Jackie. She had not planned on returning to this apartment and we had to wait until they would come, as arranged, to take us across the border. There was no doubt that she knew with absolute certainty that she would make her escape with her infant directly from the hospital, as she had said, and that every last detail had been carefully planned out. After she would make it across the border, or, God forbid, after she should fail to make it across, where would I ever see her again, and till when would Jackie have to tolerate her disappearance? The terror that was eating away at Jackie concerning the fact that if he would not see Manya immediately then he might never see me again in the future as well was a fear much deeper than that of our getting caught ourselves. I knew that I was not properly evaluating the relative risks involved, but please do believe me that my fear was correct. I could not possibly make Jackie understand. It was clear to me that he was wasting away right before my very eyes. I decided to head out with the children, armed with my papers, and make our way over to the hospital, in order to see Manya, not for my sake, as I have already told you, but for Jackie's sake, just for Jackie, or primarily for Jackie, while the two of us, Erwin and I, accompanied him on the trip and would then return to the apartment where we were hiding in order to wait there - if we ever managed to make our way back - for the day when they would come and take us across the border into Switzerland.

All the same, I was sorely in need of some advice. Not that it would have made any difference. Many times a person seems to be in need of advice even when such advice could not possibly add or detract anything at all whatsoever. It is a deepseated need that does not have a logical source. It rises from the hope that what will be with absolute certainty should be for the best, or from the fear surrounding the fate that has already been determined and which, one hopes, is leaning towards life, though it might, God forbid, be leaning in the opposite direction. I therefore could not possibly proceed without first getting some advice. But I had no one to consult other than Erwin. I was, of course, not about to ask him what he thought of what absolutely had to do. I figured that I would tell him what I had already decided to do, like a fait accompli that I had already consciously chosen to enact, and then try to figure out what he thought of it from his ensuing reaction. I would have to evaluate whatever he might say, or assess the way he held himself, or his facial expressions, or the glint in his eyes, to try and tell if he agreed with me, if his fear was greater than anything he could possibly contain, or if he was really afraid, but nevertheless prepared to overcome all sorts of evils that we might confront along the way. It is crazy to try and seek advice in this manner, and it is even crazier to be doing it with your own child, or with any child, for that matter or with a small boy, to be precise. What I would have given to anyone, in order to be able to get your advice in this situation! But I could not. All the same, I admit and readily confess that I was prepared to rely, whether consciously or subconsciously, on the advice that my son would give me. I was aware of a sense of embarrassment at realizing that I had become dependent on Erwin's outlook on things. It was as though I was an authority figure that had to look elsewhere for my own authority. But I immediately shook off this embarrassment. It was only right that I should seek Erwin's advice. He had grown into the role of the worldly wise advisor, perhaps somewhat against his will and not under the best of circumstances, but God bless him that only I knew this and God bless him that he was not aware of this fact and would never have even imagined that this was what I was up to.

I woke up Erwin. After he had washed up and as he, Jackie, and I sat there drinking something hot, I told him that I thought we would have to head out into town.

He stared at me for a moment before he said, "When are they coming to take us across?"

I told him that I did not know. We would have to wait. Perhaps it would be a day or two, perhaps more.

"Then we have no choice. There is nothing to eat here. But you are not going anywhere. Nobody is going to stop me. I am a child. I speak French. You are still mute, Ma. You can't go out and you don't need to go out, but I can."

"I'm also a child," Jackie added immediately. "Nobody would stop me either. I am coming with you Erwin."

"And what about Mom?" Erwin asked. "Is she supposed to stay here all alone?"

Jackie did not respond immediately. After thinking things over a moment he said, "Nothing will happen to Mommy either if we are there together with her. We rode together on the train. We can head out to the bakery together too."

"You are going to drive me crazy, Jackie," Erwin said. "Taking the train was the same thing as heading out to the bakery? Leaving her all alone in Marseille is the same thing as leaving her with you in this room here for a half an hour? You refuse to go anywhere without her but if she comes along it can only lead to trouble Jackie, for her, for you, and for me, for all of us. You're staying right here." Jackie remained silent.

"They could catch you too," he said, after a few moments. "Then Mommy and I will have to go out looking for you. It's the same thing. I just want us to stay together. We have to do everything together. You are not going anywhere by yourself and I am not going to stay behind without you and Mommy is not going to stay behind without the two of us. We are not going to go outside without her. If they catch us then they are going to catch all of us, together. If they don't catch us all together then they won't catch anyone and no one will get caught. We are not some random collection of individuals, this one, that one, the other one. I've had it with you anyway. I don't have to eat Erwin. But you do. You just have to go to the bakery. You have to eat."

"Mommy has to eat," Erwin replied. "She has what to eat here, if you didn't have to eat then she has what to eat already."

Jackie did not wait for a response. He went over to the window, pushed aside the heavy curtain and looked outside, or at least made believe that he was looking outside. He did whatever was necessary to make it clear that we should not expect him to continue the conversation with his brother or even with me.

I am telling you all this in great detail in order to let you know that these two boys, these brothers who once loved and continued to love one another deeply, who even if they occasionally fought the way that brothers naturally tend to fight with one another, never lost their strong bonds to one another, but these boys had now had begun to scar one another deeply. This huge, awful war that people refer to in terms of conquered lands and continents, wide seas and oceans, kings, presidents, government leaders and generals, attacks first and foremost the men, women, and children whose names do not mean anything at all to anyone in the world. It oppresses them as though all of its pent-up oppression is to be unloaded on a single nameless child, it displays an enmity towards them that is so murderous that it threatens to put this single, nameless child to death, like a lone, fragile tree branch in the midst of the limitless forest of humanity, with no end in sight. It is a war so mighty that it seems a thousand volcanoes all spat their lava out in unison onto the heads of our two little boys.

That is how this war feels.

It is a tempest of fire and fear that shakes and scorches the entire world and all its inhabitants, and it is so very personal. It is like a deluge that God has brought down to drown the entire earth though its sole purpose is to actually cover a single individual, whether a man or woman, little boy or girl, whether my little Erwin, or little Jackie - these two children that you and I had brought into this world which had completely lost its mind. Each of them waged their battles in accordance with their nature and the individual makeup of their souls, waging two different wars against that single, oppressive, threatening enemy, though they, of course, could not vanquish him. That enemy is so immeasurably more powerful than them. But there is no way out, and they began warring with one another in order to prevent the war itself from choosing the winning threat. This may seem somewhat complicated, unwarranted, and beyond the comprehension of children or even beyond my own comprehensive abilities, but how would you explain the injurious tension that arose between our two boys, a tension that stemmed entirely from the terror that what seemed to be the true threat in one's eyes was merely an imaginary threat in the eyes of the other. It is a terror that concerns life itself, Moritz, a terror children feel deeply though they are as yet unable to put it into words - its force, all the same, shakes their very foundations.

It is a fear of death that precedes even the knowledge of what the very word 'death' itself means and what is truly hidden beneath its ominous letters.

If you could only write to me you would likely also be telling me what you were going through, and, in addition, you would not just limit yourself to telling me that but you would relate what was going on inside you as well. What a fascinating story I am missing out on. For the time being. Perhaps this is just for the time being. Though perhaps what I am missing now is something that I will end up missing for all eternity. Perhaps when you finally arrive you will be unable to tell your story. Maybe if you do not write me right away, the same way that I am writing you, then you will never know how to find the words. Or maybe you are unable to write because you already belong to a nucleus of humanity cast together like iron that is entirely made of truth, such that writing of the things that we are going through - you wherever you are and me here with the boys, and for anyone else wherever they might be, or perhaps are no longer, within the confusion of this awful war - would only seem like a mere fiction in the eyes of anyone who would begin to read even the first line of truth that the author might put down, and so the author stops, breaks off, and refuses to write because a truth that will not be believed is a rather fearful thing, since it sounds like an act of deceit, or what is worse, has indeed already become a lie itself. Yes, Moritz, I am afraid that when you finally do show up you will remain silent because you will be afraid that perhaps telling your story would be a sort of sin, and even if someone would come along and tell you that remaining silent is an even graver sin than the telling, you would not heed them. You will not be able to. You will fall silent, become mute. You, more than anyone else that I know, will remain silent, precisely because you, more than anyone else I know, are capable of telling the story in a way no one else could possibly manage.

"Let's also go pay a visit to Aunt Manya," I said, almost hesitantly. Jackie heard me and was clearly listening, but he did not move from where he stood next to the window.

"What do you mean, 'let's go,'" Erwin said. "Why should we? We are not allowed to leave this room, Ma. For bread, that's one thing, it's a necessity. But there is no need to go visit Aunt Manya."

"We have to, Erwin, believe me, we do have to."

"I believe you, but why do we have to? Where is she anyway? Are we supposed to go walking around the street asking where the hospital is? And if it is far away from here are we going to go walking there for an hour or two?" Jackie still remained standing by the window. What Erwin had said was of course rather straightforward and self-evident, to the point that I could not believe I had been so rash to such an unbelievable extent. Indeed, where was she? What was even the name of the hospital? Was there only one hospital, or two? Was it in town, or nearby, was it a municipal hospital or a regional hospital, a maternity clinic or a larger, more comprehensive facility? "The neighbor took her to the hospital," Erwin said, after a period of silence that seemed to me to be interminable. The neighbor is right here, isn't he?" I gave him a look of gratitude. He seemed in fact to be agreeing with me that we really did have to leave the room and take our chances and go and visit Manya. I assume that he actually understood just what made this dangerous visit a necessity, in my eyes, or that he at least understood that it was impossible to prevent me from making this visit for reasons that he perhaps did not understand but which he accepted, all the same. He agreed. I felt that this was important, even more important than the advice to seek help from the neighbor.

Manya had told the neighbor that he should take me to the hospital in the same taxi that he had taken with her, and she had even paid for the trip in advance. I had no real love for the neighbor. There was no real reason for these feelings, as far as I was aware. But I was afraid of him. At the moment that I had seen him looking in to our room I had told myself that I was not going to go anywhere in his company. I was suspicious of him without actually having any grounds to justify my suspicions. That is the most intense form of suspicion there is. For no real reason at all I told myself that when the time would come for me to ask him to call a taxi for me he would demand that I pay him again, in addition to what Manya had already paid. But I did not have any more money than the exact sum that I needed to pay the smugglers to take us across the border. If I would have to incur additional expenses I could not meet them and here I was acting like someone had already demanded additional payment, and so the thought to go and see the neighbor had not crossed my mind. When Erwin now recommended that we in fact turn to the neighbor for help there was no way that I could possibly explain this entire convoluted matter to him. There was no way that he could have possibly understood me, and all that I would have accomplished would have been to arouse real fears of a threat that was perhaps no more than the product of my overheated imagination. So I chose not to say a word instead.

"That's some good advice, Erwin," I said.

"I'll go see the neighbor," he said.

"I'm coming with you," said Jackie, without leaving his spot next to the curtain.

"You do not have to go with him Jackie. When it comes to this particular situation it would be better if just one person did the talking rather than two," I said.

"I am going with him!" Jackie suddenly screamed as he angrily pulled on the heavy curtain that covered the window until it came loose at one of its edges and hung there rather low across the entire length of the window, which was now partially revealed. I rather taken aback to see his anger and I told myself that I had no idea how high the fears and frustrations had risen within him, to the point that a drop which seemed little more than a mere trifle had caused the entire thing to overflow and the dam had burst. Why, Moritz, was Jackie capable of harboring such anger? Had this scream liberated him, or was it perhaps, God forbid, just one of the many outbursts that our child was on the verge of releasing, day after day after day? Had we waited too long to help free him from all that was inside him? Dear God - I sang in my heart, thinking of the old Yiddish song - please take care and watch over this child of mine.

After a little while the two boys came back from their visit to the neighbor's. There was a sense of shame written all across Erwin's features. Jackie was once again looking at him with the admiration of someone who knows his place and has no right, or no ability to alter or assist in any way when it came to what Erwin had to handle himself.

"There is a problem," Erwin said.

"There's no taxi?" I asked fearfully.

"No," Erwin replied.

"He can't help us," Jackie added. "He said something was wrong."

"What happened?"

Erwin told me how he had gone to see the neighbor, and before he had a chance to open his mouth the neighbor had asked him, "Taxi?"

"No taxi," I told him. "I do not know anything about any taxi." I told him that we wanted the address of the hospital where our Aunt had gone to give birth.

"What is your aunt's name?" the man asked me.

I told him that her name was Resnick.

He looked into my eyes as though he were digging holes in them and said to me, "Who is Resnick? I do not know anyone by the name of Resnick. What do you want, children, what do you really want?"

"And then," Jackie said, "he slammed the door in our faces and we were left standing there and we had no idea what we had done or what had happened. The neighbor is a bad man, Ma, a very bad man."

I put my face in my hand and shook it desperation, angry at myself.

"Good God," I said. "Her name is not Resnick, it's not Resnick."

"What do you mean her name is not Resnick?" Erwin asked. "Manya's name is not Resnick? What is her name if it's not Resnick?" Something far away, almost too far off to discern, seemed to suddenly burrow underneath his skin and begin to torture him, provoking a minor sense of guilt of which he was not aware or could not quite make out, but no more than that. He was more than just surprised. The reality of the situation seemed to have slipped through his fingers.

Aboard the train we had recalled her name because we had prepared ourselves before set-ting out. But that was such a long time ago. The priest and the innkeeper and his son all knew the name and had pronounced it out loud and used it to seek out her address in Saint-Claude. But now that name had escaped all of our memories and the children had even forgotten that there had ever been another name to begin with. Wonder of wonders. I was well aware of the fact that either I was not real or Manya was not real, or nothing whatsoever was actually real anymore, and Erwin, for his part, was no longer capable of making out where one was headed when reality could no longer be mapped out properly. And it was impossible for me to be of any help. I had forgotten, completely forgotten the cover name that Manya had chosen to use for herself. She had told me the name, it's true. I recalled that you had given her the name and that she had even joked about it a bit. But I could not recall even the first letter of the borrowed name and could find no handle whatsoever with which to call it up from the great beyond. There was nothing, nothing whatsoever. There are things that an individual tends to forget, things that never really leave any trace in the individual's mind. They had been there once, had been pronounced quickly, and then they were gone, carried off on the wind. The situation was serious. The neighbor knew Manya by her adopted name, knew that name as though it were her proper, lawful name, but we were unable to remember it. Who were we, as far as he was concerned? Had he run a certain risk himself when he took Manya to the hospital in a taxi, because he knew - of course he knew - that she was not really a Frenchwoman nor truly a resident of Saint-Claude, and anyone who was caught aiding and abetting those who sought to deceive the authorities here and now had only himself to blame for whatever trouble he got into? He must have been aware. But not to the point that even the name itself was fake.

What was he now telling himself concerning our relationship with Manya, we who did not even know her name but claimed that she was our Aunt whom we had come to visit because she was about to give birth? What had Manya told him? Had she not let him know that we were her relatives? What had the children called her, they who always speak so innocently, without any forethought - 'Resnick?' All these thoughts ran rather quickly through my head and left me for a moment - though no more than a moment - feeling completely helpless in the face of the new reality we suddenly found ourselves in. And the children? I had to explain things to them. And once again, I needed their advice, Erwin's advice.

I told them everything that had happened and explained it all in a somewhat summary though precise fashion, and I admitted that I could not recall their Aunt's new name and I had no idea how I could possibly help my memory.

Jackie immediately said, "He is going to tell on us. We have to leave this place."

Erwin denied this possibility delicately yet decisively. "We don't have anywhere else to go from here. We do not actually live here but we have no other address that we can use. Where will the people who are supposed to take us across the border go to get us if all they know is that we are here and nowhere else but here? He is not going to tell on us, Ma. If he does, then he would essentially be giving himself up too. He is afraid of us, Ma. He does not know who we are, and now, given the fact that we do not know our own Aunt's name, he is not even sure who she really is anymore."

Jackie heard what Erwin said and after a few moments said, "If you had seen the way that he shut the door in our face then you too would say that we better leave this place."

"He is afraid," said Erwin, and added, as though speaking to himself alone, "How could I have forgotten her name, how could I, how could I…?"

Jackie was once again unable to contain himself in the position of the subservient younger brother and ignored his older brother's little confession as he said, rather forcefully, though without even a hint of anger, "He's afraid? - You're afraid. And as usual, whenever you're afraid your advice is to simply not do anything. Mommy, we absolutely can not stay here. We can take the train, go somewhere. We'll find our own way across the border. Here we'll never make it. They'll come find us and take us away, Ma."

"So what are we going to do, Erwin," I asked. "Listen to what Jackie is saying. What he says makes sense. It makes sense, but although we can not just get up and leave this place, there is also no way that we can stay here. At first we were merely discussing going outside in order to buy a few things to eat. We were afraid, but we managed to come to a certain arrangement. Then we talked about going to visit Aunt Manya. We were afraid then too but still managed to figure out a suitable arrangement for that as well. Then we were confused about where to go, but hit on the idea of going over to see the neighbor. But now all of the arrangements that we had made are completely out of joint and do not work anymore. There is no way that we can leave, but there is also no way that we can stay here. The neighbor is no solution, but at the same time we really have not managed to come up with any suitable alternative."

"There is no such thing, Ma," said Erwin. "Nothing was all worked out for us but we managed to work out what we had to do all the same, and we did it. What arrangements are you talking about anyway? What we're supposed to do? We're supposed to talk it over. Let's talk it over, Ma."

"The neighbor won't even talk to you, Erwin. He slammed the door in your face. With whom are you going to talk things over?"

"With his wife," said Erwin. "She did not slam the door shut. Perhaps she would be willing to listen. Perhaps she'll help us. There really is no one else." The child was certainly courageous. I, for my part, truly had no really good advice of my own to offer, and I was careful not to agree with every idea he came up with, but for a moment I let my guard down just enough and failed to hold myself back from expressing the slightest trace of disappointment in my eldest son Erwin's performance.

"You remember everything Erwin, we all knew Aunt Manya's new name, we said it out loud when we were on the train, we said it afterwards too. You spoke up, you were the one who said it. What, you forgot?"

Erwin gave me a stern look and replied, "I forgot, yes, I'm sorry, I forgot her name. I have no idea what it is. You forgot it too. Jackie also did. It was a name, no more than that, just a name. It was even an important bit of information. There's no way to explain why it happened, but the fact is we've forgotten it, all of us, and if we go looking for it we'll only end up forget-ting more things and we'll never even find the name, none of us, not you, not Jackie, not me. I'm going to see the neighbor. It's the only way."

I was afraid and said, "Erwin, you're going to knock on the door, he'll see you and slam it in your face all over again. You said that he was afraid. He is going to be afraid when you come back a second time as well. You will not even get to see his wife. You won't get that far."

"I'll wait until he leaves the house, Ma. He has a bicycle. He'll have to go somewhere sooner or later."

He turned to his brother and said authoritatively, "You stand by the window, Jackie, don't move from your spot until you see him leaving the house. If you get tired I will take your place. We'll wait. Patiently. He has to leave sooner or later and as soon as he does, I will go and see his wife. At least I'll try." Jackie gave in. He went over and stood next to the window, behind the curtain that was partially torn away, and Erwin and I sat down and we all began to wait.

Just a short while later Jackie called out, "There he goes. He has the bicycle with him but he is walking on foot for now. The snow. It's because of the snow." I was surprised.

"Already?" I asked. "He's already headed out? That was quick."

Jackie immediately detected my surprise and exclaimed, "He is going to tell on us. We were just over to see him and now he is already headed out."

"Not true. He was already wearing his overcoat when he opened the door for us. He was on his way out one way or the other," said Erwin.

Jackie calmed down, but I was not quite as convinced. I was not so sure about the whole story of the overcoat. After we had waited a little while longer in order to give the man a chance to distance himself from the building, Erwin got up to go over to the neighbor's place. Jackie did not join him this time. He remained standing on his watch by the window. Just a few moments later, to my complete surprise, Erwin came back with the neighbor's wife alongside him.

The riddle was immediately resolved. The neighbor's wife, grey-haired, tall, dressed likewise in grey, wearing a knee-length skirt that revealed thin legs wrapped in black socks that rather suited her figure, upon entering our room immediately spoke, "You are the sister, or the relative, that's what Madame Marion Ravel told me, isn't that it?"

"This is my mother," Erwin said.

Marion Ravel! How could I have forgotten. The children's faces - Erwin's more so than Jackie's - revealed a slight trace of surprise and the neighbor's wife, with her sharp eyes, sensed their reaction but had no idea why they would be surprised to hear the name that they now clearly recalled. She suddenly said, "I believe that Madame Ravel said you were her sister, so you must forgive me, but that's why I said 'sister,' as well. These days one is not always all that exact. This sweet boy, your son, asked me to come over for a moment because he said you needed a little help from me. Well, here I am." Even her face was grey. Slight wrinkles went down in a line until they met her upper lip and extended from the corners of her alert, green eyes in the direction of her temples. She seemed like a wise woman who had come to terms with wisdom after her instincts had abandoned her. She was still attractive and had certainly been extremely attractive in her younger days.

I was not sure that she was in fact the neighbor's wife. Although I did not really know either one of them, they did not seem to be a real match, as far as I could tell. I sensed that I was prepared to trust her, not merely because I once again had no real alternative at the time, but because my instincts told me, forced as I was to base my decision on them in the blink of an eye. "Erwin, tell her that I do not speak French all that well. I will tell her what I need and you translate for me."

She stared at me while I spoke a language that she did not understand, as though trying to guess what it was that I was saying.

I offered her a chair. She said it was better if she remained standing. So we stood there - Erwin, the neighbor's wife, and I, all right next to the door, while Jackie sat politely at the table and listened to the conversation as Erwin translated, until we all found ourselves seated around the table as well.

At first I apologized on behalf of the children. I had sent them out, I told her, in order to ask your husband to call us a taxi, Madame Marion Ravel had already made the arrangements and paid in advance, in order to ensure that we would be able to go and visit her, as per her request. "I do not know why," I continued with my apology, "but I assume that since the children had not seen their Aunt for quite some time now, they were overcome by embarrassment for a moment and forgot her name. We always referred to her merely as our Aunt, not as a lady with a last name. She is my sister, Ma'am, and who refers to their own sister by their surname, their family name? They knew it, of course, they're smart kids, but kids, as you know, tend to forget the simplest things sometimes." Erwin translated everything I said, but left out the word 'smart.'

She listened and said, "I understand," and looked over the children's faces intently.

I told her that we had come simply to visit Madame Ravel in anticipation of her pending delivery, but here it was just a short while after our arrival and she had already gone off to give birth and we were left all alone without any prior notice in a town that was completely unfamiliar to us. Thank God my sister had had the forethought - perhaps even at the very moment that her labor pains had already begun - to arrange for someone to call us a taxi and take us over to see her.

Erwin continued translating, but before he got to the end the neighbor's wife stopped him, looked into my eyes, put her chin in the palm of her right hand, leaned her elbow on the table and said, "Madame Ravel had no idea that you were going to come for a visit. She was not expecting you. She was glad to see you, but she was not expecting you. I don't need to know who you are. Do not tell me. It would do no good for me to know. Don't tell me where you come from and don't tell me where you are headed. No good could possibly come of my knowing all that either."

She fell silent without taking her eyes off me, except when she cast pointed glances in the direction of Erwin and Jackie, seated together with us at the table. She did not wait for me to answer and continued speaking, as though saying her piece, not as someone really having a proper conversation. "You have to trust me, Madame, you must trust my husband as well. You have no choice. It's not that we are good people, Madame. We make our living off this filthy war. This little apartment where Madame Ravel was living for a few weeks already, or maybe a bit longer than that, and where you are now living with your children, belongs to the mayor of the city. Our apartment does too. We are not your neighbors. We are here to keep an eye on this building. We rent out the rooms and collect the rent on behalf of the landlord. We collect whatever we can for ourselves in the process. There is no more secure building in all of Saint-Claude for people like you and Madame Ravel, Ma'am. They're looking everywhere in town for people like you and everyone is always ratting on everyone else out. When I say 'everyone' I mean the refugees, people trying to steal across the border. Foreigners, Jews. Search parties are never sent here. This building belongs to the mayor. When the war is over we will know if he was a collaborator or a real hero. It depends who will be left to tell their tale. He chose us to help him. I was the librarian here in Saint-Claude, Madame. My husband - though you may have a hard time believing it - was the most prominent pediatrician in the entire town. These days he does not look all that much like a doctor, with his bicycle. The war has that effect on people, Madame, it changes them. No one is immune. I ought to know.

"We had a son, an only son. We buried him just a few days after this foul war broke out. They brought him back in his uniform from some place right near Ligne Maginot. There was a neat hole in his skull. There was not even any blood around the point where the bullet that had shut off his brain had entered his head. My husband was no longer able to work. He was not able to mourn, he simply said good-bye to all the people around him, everyone. He was envious of those who were still alive. He hated everyone still moving. He would just sit around the house in silence. I think that he was hoping that after his son had died everyone else who had not yet died would perish as well. I took care of him. I left my job. We were left penniless. I sold our house. The mayor offered us this job. My husband refused but I agreed to take it. I am the one who gets paid. We offer a sorry range of albeit vital services and collect whatever people are prepared to pay. There is no set price. There are amounts that get the job done and others that don't. It is not a pleasant business. Is it a sin? If surviving is a sin then our job is a sinful one. If there is a God up in heaven then perhaps He will pardon us, though then again, maybe He won't. Nobody really knows what He is truly like anymore. He will have to pardon us, Madame, because for every single one of the people who rented an apartment in this building we could have easily collected seven times the amount of the rent they paid and the money they gave us to help them if we had just turned them in. But we don't do it out of love - God forbid, no, we are forced to, we have no choice. Life forces things on you, Madame. But it is a risky business. Everything depends on what might happen and must not be allowed to come to pass. We can not afford to arouse any serious suspicions. We can not afford to have people who can't remember their sister's name. Even the mayor himself could fall as a result. He might be felled by a French bullet or a German bullet, a traitor's bullet or the bullet from a patriot's gun. I too could fall. So could my husband. So could anyone else who lives here or might yet come to live here, until this filthy war is over, one way or the other. Therefore, Madame, when this young man and his even younger companion stood together in our doorway and could not remember their Aunt's name, my husband had to slam the door shut in their face. What else could he do? I told him that he was afraid over nothing. He told me that there is no such thing, all fears are valid. And then he left. You know where he went? He went to the hospital. He did not know that this young man would come back and knock on our door and ask to speak with us. He went to the hospital to check if Madame Marion Ravel already gave birth. Only afterwards would he be capable of starting to think about what he would do with you. Could he possibly put people like you in a taxi and send you off to the hospital where a woman is lying in bed whose name you do not even remember? He thought that such a move would be tantamount to bringing all the demons that we have spent years keeping at bay down on all of our heads."

I understood every word. I did not wait for Erwin to translate. I could not speak but I knew how to make sense of what I heard beyond the few words that I did not understand. I wanted to say something but she seemed to stop me with the palm of her hand before the words had even had a chance to leave my mouth.

"Let me finish. I am not done yet, Madame. You are not acting wisely by staying locked up in the apartment. You are afraid that they might stop you, might investigate, imprison, and ship you off to we all know where. Things like that have certainly already happened. Everyone knows where they take the people that get caught here. Nobody talks about it. It is as though no one is sure of things, but everybody knows. Anyone who goes outside is running the risk of getting caught. And anyone who stays locked inside runs the risk of having people say that there are people hiding out in there. That is even more dangerous, both for you and for me. I have to look out for myself. One more day and they will come ask me who these people are that are living in the building where I am in charge of the apartments. Such a question could very well bury me. Let me tell you what we are going to do. You have papers, Madame, do you not? Madame Ravel told me that you are perfectly French as far as the authorities are concerned. And the children too. I assume that you could not possibly have told me otherwise, and if you can't say otherwise then that means it is all true. You have your documents. If they stop you, at least you have papers. If you don't go outside then it is like you don't even have any documents to begin with. I will go first. I will walk around town. I want to go and buy bread for the boys. Of course, you do not know where the bakery is and you are not about to stop someone and ask them what everyone else already knows all too well. It could just cost you your life. I will walk by a bakery. I will go inside and come back out immediately and then your son can go inside and buy bread. Do you want some meat? I will stop at a butcher shop. You are to follow me. You are not to indicate that you know me no matter how close we get. Don't look at me like I am anything more than another part of the scenery. If I disappear don't go looking for me. I will find you. It will all go very quickly. But people will see you. Somebody will see that you left this building and someone else will see that you returned to it, that you are alive, that you went out shopping, that you have to eat. You will remain a foreigner. It is impossible to take that aspect away from your appearance. If you remain a foreigner for a bit too long, then they will gradually go after you. But if you do not show yourself at all, as I have already mentioned, then they will go after you right away. It is a damned thing being a foreigner. When my husband gets back and tells us that Madame Ravel has given birth then you can go and visit her. It is not far. I will walk on ahead. He will wait for me with his bicycle at the entrance to the hospital. As though by chance. That is the only way. The entire thing will not cost you all that much, Madame. Whatever you can manage. Not a penny more than what you can manage. Now don't say another word. I am going to go back to my apartment. Wait for someone to knock at your door." She got up, straightened her skirt, stood by the door a moment before leaving, and it seemed to me that she was the proudest woman I had ever met. Deceit always shows its hand. Always. I believe that I even admired her. But proud? Her? This woman, who was so broken, was also proud?

We sat down at the table and stared at the door for some reason, all of us together like that, Erwin, Jackie, and me.

"Do you believe her, Ma?" Erwin asked me.

"I have no choice," I said. "But even if I did not, I believe her."

"Me too," said Erwin. "Do you have enough money?" He added, "She said whatever you could manage. That's a lot."

"I always have enough for whatever I can manage," I said with a smile, and I got up to tend to this minor matter.

"And if we lose sight of her?" Jackie suddenly asked. "What if we are following her and suddenly lose sight of her?"

I went over to Jackie, put my arm around his shoulders and said to him, "We will not lost sight of her."

"But we might," Jackie said, as he slipped from my embrace. "Then we will not know where to go. We will not know how to get back. That might happen."

Erwin, in his heart, either dismissed the concern that his brother had expressed or did not believe that Jackie really felt that way after all, and said, "There are three of us, Jackie, three people do not lose sight of one person. Three people see everything."

"We are three people all together," Jackie said. "She is one person all by herself. The three of us do not know the way. She is just one person, but she knows the way. There are three of us but not a single one of us knows anything about her. She could leave us in the dust for all we know. She is just one person but she knows everything about us. She has no reason to fear us. We are not going to run away from her."

"You do not believe her," Erwin said decisively, refusing to be dragged into a fight.

"I don't know. You don't either."

"I told you that I believe her. Ma," Erwin turned to me, "Did I say that or didn't I?"

Jackie, who also refused for his part to be dragged into a fight did not wait for my answer and said, "So you said so. So what? Swear that we will not lose sight of her. Can you do that? No, you can't. Swear that she will not suddenly disappear on us. Can you do that? You can't do that either. But you believe her. Why? I did not say that she was going to disappear or run away. All I said was that she might. Admit she might, that's all." Jackie was not speaking like someone who was arguing his point of view but as though, for a change, he had managed to prove that his reasoning was sounder than that of his older brother. But his older brother would not admit it.

"Why should she run away from us?" Erwin insisted. "She did not have to offer to help us. She could have refused to come over and see us altogether. You want to stay here? You want to go tell her, excuse me, Ma'am, don't go walking in front of us because you might disappear on us?"

"I have nothing to say to you," said Jackie, giving his brother a demonstrative glance and then getting up, going over to the window, and looking outside, when he cried out suddenly, "The bicycle! He's here. I can see him. We have to get dressed!"

Now that Jackie was ready without any reservations for our strange little trip I suddenly found myself thinking that the doubts he had expressed were in fact rather valid. I laid out the overcoats and footwear for us all but, at the same time, I told myself that the child essentially was right in what he had said. Erwin believed the neighbor's wife and I trusted her just as he did because we had no choice but to believe her and put our trust in her. But the more it becomes apparent that the lack of options is the only possible option that remains, the more that very option becomes all the more unconvincing.

The little trip that we were ready to head out on was altogether unclear and rather problematic. There were all sorts of threats, both apparent and hidden, threats that we had considered beforehand and which we knew might well catch us completely by surprise all the same, all tied to the decision to leave our secret little sanctuary in this foreign town. And why? To go see Manya? That was pure insanity. Just to cater to Jackie and alleviate his fears? This was a rather unreasonable concession. To get food? We could get by with less and less, perhaps even starve ourselves if necessary. There were a tremendous number of risks hanging in the balance, and each and every one of them shone like the sharp blade of an unsheathed dagger, while the other side of the scale was weighed down with our hearts' desires and a series of obligations, all of which suddenly seemed rather trivial and banal.

The risks involved were not the deciding factor, but all the same, as you well know, when a person lives with these threats on a daily, even hourly basis, and is fighting for their life so as not to slip or stumble and fall prey to the Angel of Death - lurking there in ambush for anyone who might succumb to a moment of weakness - such a person may wish to maintain their sanity. But it is impossible to do so, Moritz, unless that person is willing to take a fateful decision in favor of those heartfelt desires which always pose something of a risky gamble. And after countless decisions in favor of a sense of caution, suddenly there comes a moment in which a conscious decision is made in favor of life, like some grand masquerade of obligations and necessities covering a series of rather simple, commonplace needs. It is like inhaling a little oxygen without permission in a world that requires you to choke just in order to exist. It is an admission that, after all, every roof that you try to seal up against the coming storm will nevertheless contain some slight crack through which the rain will manage to penetrate and pelt your head - and just because it can, it will. It is a gesture that involves being captivated, even if only for a moment, by what you had taken such great care to prevent, even though you knew that it had to happen no matter what. It was what Jackie meant when he said, "I did not say that she was going to disappear or run away on us. I just said that she could. Admit the fact that she could!"

PART THREE

That is what our life looked like on the run up to this point, Moritz. I did more than I ever thought I would be capable of in order to lead our two boys and the third child that I was carrying in my womb to the only land of salvation that seemed to exist. I am just one single woman heading down all those paths that lead to the locked gate which takes you across the border, sworn to burst on through, because there is nothing other than that sealed border between me and the death to which I absolutely refuse to succumb. At every moment along the way I am well aware that success, by any normal calculations, and in accordance with the ordinary nature of things, is in fact impossible, but precisely because it is impossible I refuse to give up until I manage to accomplish this impossible feat.

Erwin was not built for this. He believed the neighbor's wife because he believed in himself. He trusted her because he had decided to trust her. Erwin was sure that we would make it to Switzerland because he was with me. Now and then he was afraid, and the fears rattled him. When he was uncertain if he had the strength necessary to face a particular situation he would grow afraid. Not like Jackie. When Jackie was afraid he was absolutely terrified. As for me, I was afraid and terrified at the same time. They were just children. What was fear for the one and absolute terror for the other were things they were conscious of differently than I, and the emotions that gathered inside them were what I referred to as the fear and terror that accumulated inside me. And yet, perhaps, they were aware of a lot more than I thought they were capable of at their age. Who knows how many years will first have to pass before I will manage to learn to discern exactly what went on in our little boys' hearts? Even though I was with them every waking moment of the day I am still unsure that I really know what went on inside them. And you, who are not here with us right now, will you, when you show up eventually - and I just know that you will - will you manage to recognize your sons whose lives were turned upside down when you left us and went off wherever it is that you went? My heart, my heart goes out to you. It is so hard to bear this pain.

There was a knock at the door. Jackie ran to open it. The neighbor's wife was standing in the doorway, wearing a rough pair of winter boots, holding a heavy over-coat and a thick knitted cap. "I have to speak with you," she said, and without waiting for a response she made her way over to the table, sat down, waited for the three of us to sit down with her and then said, "Madame Ravel has given birth. I do not know if she gave birth to a boy or a girl. A secretary told my husband that the mother and the infant are in good health. He asked for permission to briefly visit with the mother. The secretary told him that Madame Ravel had left instructions that only Madame Mayer - I suppose you are Madame Mayer - and a gentleman whose name I can not remember were allowed to visit her. That's all. So it seems that Madame Ravel is expecting you." She did not wait and continued, "This makes a lot of things much easier. It makes things easier for my husband. He was not sure about you, but now he is. You can go there by taxi. You will manage to get by in the hospital, you will know to use the name Ravel without making any mi-stakes or getting confused at all, and you will know that your name there is Mayer. The trip is already paid for, my husband has no further reasons to suspect you at all. But you can not take a taxi there, there is no driver right now. Up until a day or two ago there was still a driver, but now there isn't one anymore. The kid disappeared. The driver was just a boy, a young farmer, the son of a prominent, well-to-do family here in Saint-Claude who left for a villa in Como, in Italy, and never came back. This diligent young man was a rather successful individual, both because of the taxi that he had and also the facility with which he expressed himself. He knew enough to say that he admired 'Il Duce' and was following in the footsteps of his father and mother who both admired him and had therefore joined his empire.

"These days, here in Saint-Claude, and in France, and perhaps in the entire world, are not simple. I must be careful. I will walk on ahead of you rather cautiously, by which I mean that I will proceed as though no one is following along behind me. I will stop along the way and exchange a few words with anyone who still bothers to converse like that in the street. I will take my time looking in a display window, if the-re is still anything to be seen anywhere in town, and then I will be on my way once more. I will go as far as the hospital, and the children will follow me. I will not lose sight of you and you are not to lose sight of me. You will look straight ahead and I will remain within your field of vision the entire time. I will rely on the eyes in the back of my head to tell me if you get lost or are delayed along the way and I will not lose sight of you. In this way you will stay in contact with me and I will stay in contact with you and we will make it there. But do not keep your eyes peeled to my back. Do not let anyone see that you are following me. You, Madame Mayer, must walk along the streets of Saint-Claude like a woman who takes pleasure in her pregnancy, affectionately holding the hands of her two little boys who are so proud of her that she is get-ting ready to give them a new baby brother or sister. I say brother, but who knows. Your pregnancy, Madame, your pregnancy is what is important. You must let them see your belly. Let it show in all its glory. These rotten Frenchmen are still rather respectful of pregnant women.

"On the way back we will go shopping. I will stand outside a bakery, and a little grocery store, and a fruit and vegetable stand. I know where we can find milk and where they might sell this young man a few eggs without asking any unnecessary questions. He will make the purchases and you will go for a little walk. That's all. Ah yes, my husband. He will not come with us. He will not be out and about while I am. It is better that way. He will wait for me to get back. It is hard for him. The poor man gets no respite is always riding around on his bicycle in order not to stay at ho-me. I tell you all this just so that you will not have to ask. He can seem to be a strange man in the eyes of anyone who does not already know him. But I know him. And I understand. I have told you everything now. Get dressed. It is cold outside."

It was wonderful walking around the streets of Saint-Claude. It was a clear day. The sky was frozen and polished like some azure steel. The cold stole through the little holes that the extended stay in the closed apartment had formed in our skin and worked its way inside our blood as we stirred back to life. The warm clothing protected our bodies and the chill that hit our foreheads, cheeks, and lips was pleasurable, refreshing, and liberating. We strolled around like free people. The town looked like a theatrical backdrop. Its houses were all rather modest stone structures with grey roofs, somewhat mournful. There was no way of knowing who lied inside them. Then there were larger houses, perhaps the homes of the wealthy, of community leaders who had disappeared, or maybe even aristocrats, or the knights of old. It seemed impossible that anyone still lived in these homes. The stores and shops all along the way were rather small, the average collection of signs announcing 'Bread' and 'Patisserie,' 'Wine and Other Beverages,' 'Fruits and Vegetables,' 'Clothing for Men, Women, and Children,' 'Shoemaker,' 'Pharmacy,' and then the sad-looking cafes in which a few sorry lights still shone, though there were those that were without a single light on inside, and the doors all seemed to be locked, despondent and abandoned. We walked around this sad town in a rather joyful mood, though there were virtually no other people out in the streets but us, and anyone we did come across walked by without looking right or left, mostly staring straight down the entire time at the frozen, grey sidewalk underneath their feet.

We walked by a little cemetery that surrounded a church with a towering steeple built from stones that had clearly been quarried locally. There were trees with their naked branches and knotty trunks twisting into the air among the gravestones. White snow was piled high beside each tree trunk and stood out against the grey piles of slush that were heaped on either side of the footpaths. There were human footprints in the snow among the gravestones. Two old people wrapped in black overcoats were sitting there on a bench. Their faces, beneath their dark hats, looked like the very face of winter itself. They were silent. It seemed as though they had come the-re together in order to sit and proclaim that their union of many years was a rather private affair within the margins of time inside this town, and they were there to allow their personal memories to do the talking while they themselves did not get involved, they just sat on the side and listened.

In Saint-Claude death was like a member of the community among the living. I knew that during the summer young women went walking among the tombstones keeping an eye on little children who played in what was for them a mere garden. And in the spring, as the evening fell, some young man walked along with some young woman, holding hands and proudly displaying the pregnancy that graced his youthful partner's figure, responding with a grateful nod of the head to the well-wishers who eyed them as they went. The souls who lay beneath the tombstones were not the dead, reminding everyone that life is gone in the blink of an eye, and that man has barely arrived on this earth when he is already turned into ashes and dust. No, the dead who lay there threw themselves on their memories of lives filled with desire just as they had been while they were still living, and from their vantage points in death they attested to the fact that they had absolutely no reason up in heaven to look askance at the simple joy that was busy celebrating its modest little holiday down below. They envied the living. But now that joy, too, had passed away. All that was left were these two old folks seated there side by side in silence, alongside the mute tombstones, now envying the dead. And there was but a single, solitary woman walking along the footpath, and there was no one else out and about who might take note of her pregnant belly and grace her with even so much as a glance of blessing and goodwill.

The neighbor's wife, whom we were following, passed like a ghost or mere gust of wind before the little cemetery by the side of the church. Neither the living nor the dead said a word to her. I was convinced that she was thinking solely of the task that she had set for herself, she did not think of me as a woman, or of my sons as clinging to me, nor where I had come from or where I might be headed in the future. The only secure space in her life were these tasks, not wondering about what had already been or what might be, not asking why or wherefore but just how, that immediate how that does not get one all caught up in thoughts and considerations that completely rob one of any sense of calm, just tasks that only have value if they succeed and do not demand too high a price should they happen to fail. The three of us - Erwin, Jackie, and I, with my pregnant belly - were her current task. And she went about it as well as could possibly be expected. She hurried along at times, then slowed down, would stop for a moment and look in at a display window, as though she were interested in the few things they had out on display, in order to give us a chance to catch up with her and make sure we had not fallen too far behind. She did not talk to anyone along the way, though you could tell from the way she walked, or slightly nodded her head, or occasionally swung the sleeves of her coat when she came across someone that she did indeed know. The task that she stuck to wholeheartedly was to lead us to the hospital.

Her entire life at that moment was consumed with getting us to our destination. I was filled with a sense of gratitude. I knew that if she failed she would simply disappear and no one would ever connect her to us, and she herself would no longer see any connection between us whatsoever, and she would simply head back home like someone returning after an accident that simply could not have been avoided. This did not bother me one bit. I did not think of her in terms of being a good person nor did I think of her as someone who might turn out to be a bad person, for that matter. I simply thought of her as a sort of road map. You just thank God and follow the signs. You put your faith in the map because you do not have anything else to go by.

I did not exchange a single word with the boys as we walked along, and they, for their part, did not say anything to one another either. It is not that we were concerned that someone might overhear us and recognize that we were foreigners on the basis of our accents or the language that we spoke. There were very few people out in the street and none of them showed any particular interest in us. If there had been any real need, we could have whispered to one another, but even this simple consideration did not cross our minds. Without having discussed anything at all, we simply adopted various preemptive measures as though we were already old hands and experts in the rules that governed this war of ours. These preemptive measures were no longer accompanied by any real fear. We were not afraid. The refreshing cold air, the sky-blue winter heavens overhead, the brisk, self-assured walk through the streets of the town, all filled us with a sense of confidence, as though for a moment we had become like birds flying freely through the air who, for that brief moment, were not threatened by any nets that might ensnare them or any predator that might yet hunt them down. If anyone had asked me why I was remaining silent, I would not have had any idea what to reply and I very likely would have simply broken out in song. Brief moments of freedom in between the long days of being on the run like slaves - even if these moments were mostly imaginary in nature - had a way of doing the heart more good than the mind could ever logically comprehend. We were thrilled.

And suddenly it all came to an end.

The neighbor's wife came to a halt. We saw her standing at an intersection as though she were rooted to the ground. She stared straight ahead, then turned and gazed in our direction for what seemed like an eternity, then turned back and looked once more at what only she could yet see. We came to a standstill as well. It was clear to us that something had happened, that the neighbor's wife had run up against some sort of a threat and was trying to warn us of it from afar. We had no way of guessing what the threat consisted of. We were paralyzed, and though we did not want to just stand there, we had no idea where else to go. It was imperative that we not hesitate more than a brief moment but it was also impossible to decide what to do in that instant.

Jackie looked up at me as though I knew where our next step might take us. Erwin stared straight ahead at the distant figure of the neighbor's wife who turned once more to face us from afar as she remained standing still. Though she was far away she did not retrace her steps nor did she continue on in the direction that she had been headed.

The entire town suddenly seemed to us like one big trap. And then, as though he had swooped down from the very heavens without anyone noticing his arrival, a man walking a bicycle passed by us without looking in our direction, just kept on walking along at a leisurely pace down the street where we stood, turned at the corner into a narrow alleyway, where he stood still for a moment, then turned back in our direction and with a wave of his hand, indicated that we should follow him, and then walked on once more.

"The neighbor," Erwin said in an undertone.

I mumbled something from distant memory, "Elijah the Prophet," and we followed that man down the narrow alleyway, as the neighbor's wife off in the distance disappeared from view as though she had never even existed to begin with. All of Jackie's prophecies had now come to pass. But he had not foreseen the arrival of the neighbor.

As we walked along in his wake I told myself that he had tailed us in complete incognito from the moment that we had left the house behind his wife and that she, in turn, had told us he would be waiting for her at home even though she had lied and knew full well that he was secretly heading out after us to keep an eye on her from afar. Or, perhaps, she had not known and he simply had not had the strength to wait at home and had headed out to follow us at a safe distance, or, yet again, perhaps I really do have my own personal Elijah the Prophet in this world who shows up from time to time who knows, from where, in order to watch over me and my children. Either way, I followed him. He did not look back even for a second. He headed up the little street, then crossed into another narrow alleyway and turned to take a foot-path that led through a field where a few houses stood rather far apart from one another. It is not just that we were completely unfamiliar with the town itself, but this particular footpath was one that we very likely would not have been aware of even if we were regular residents of Saint-Claude. I was afraid, but I walked along as though I knew full well where we were headed. I could sense that the children were afraid as well but were walking with me simply because that is what I was doing. There was not a living soul along the path, just the figure of the neighbor bent over his bicycle, turning black against the backdrop of white snow that covered the field and the roofs of the big homes and few barns that were scattered about the wintry hills. We walked along like this for quite a while. We had no idea if we were simply walking in circles, or if we had covered quite a considerable distance. The path led us back to an alleyway, and the alleyway led us to a street, which, in turn, opened onto a boulevard, at the end of which stood a massive building that there was no mistaking - the hospital.

The neighbor stepped off the boulevard with his bicycle and took the path that led up to the wide entrance to the building, but he did not stop. He kept walking along the path, completely ignoring the trio of police officers and four soldiers in French uniforms who stood next to a police car, then stepped back into the boulevard and headed back the very way that he had come. The three of us, the children and I, looked out of the corners of our eyes at the officers and the soldiers, who did not seem to be on the lookout for anything or anyone in particular, talking easily with one another as the greyish cigarette smoke that was clearly visible in the cool, blue air rose in their midst. We took a deep, collective breath and entered the hospital. At that moment I did not concern myself with thinking about where we would go after we were done with our little visit in the hospital, who would direct us, whose lead we might follow back to the house. From this point on, Jackie and I were in Erwin's hands. There was no need for us to say a word to him. He knew how to play his role as though he had trained for it in lengthy rehearsals on the stage, and it seemed that he trusted us to have learned our own roles by heart as well, in this new play that was unveiled at that very moment.

Erwin went up to a man who seemed to be a sort of security guard, or information clerk, sitting just inside the entrance wearing a uniform that clearly was not a military outfit, and told the man that he had come to visit Madame Ravel, and asked where he might find her.

The man pointed him in the direction of a large hall. Two women dressed in nurses' outfits stood behind a long counter. When Erwin said that he had come to visit Madame Ravel, the nurse who was busy jotting something down looked up at him, examined his face for a moment and said, "It is clear that you are either the son or a close relative of Madame Mayer. Where is Madame Mayer?"

I was standing right nearby and I could clearly overhear the nurse as she spoke. I walked over and stood right in front of her, nodding my head slightly in order to indicate that I was, indeed, Madame Mayer.

"Are you Madame Mayer?" asked the nurse, and then added curtly, as though it went without saying, "Your papers, some ID."

I dug around inside my handbag, pulled out the documents for me and the boys and held mine up for her to look at.

She gave the document a brief, perfunctory once-over, no more than that, seemed satisfied and then handed it back to me, saying, "You came specially from Marseille. How touching. Are these your children? Wonderful. Madame Ravel left instructions that only you were to be allowed to visit her, or rather, she also indicated that another man, whose name I, of course, can not disclose to you, might also visit her. I assume that it will be alright if the children accompany you, seeing as they are here as well. I am sure that if she had been aware you were bringing them with you she would have authorized their vi-sit in any case."

I said, "*Merci*," in the hope that I would not have to pronounce another word in French and could wrap up the entrance procedure without saying anything more or arousing any undue suspicions. There are very often conversations in which only one person does the talking and does not really have any need for the other to respond in any way. This first person makes do with the things that he or she says and is even left with the impression that it was a rather interesting give-and-take. This lightweight thought flitted through my mind like a brief ray of hope.

"Go up to the second floor. They might not let you in. Visiting hours are officially over for now, but perhaps Madame Ravel will step out for a moment to see you. There is no way of knowing, it depends on who is on duty up there. Tell them that you came all the way from Marseille. They will understand. I am sure of it. Be well, Madame."

I said, *"Merci,"* once more, and added, *"Au revoir Madame,"* like a born and bred Frenchwoman, then headed over to the wide set of stairs that led up to the second floor, accompanied by the boys. Were they as proud as I was that I had managed to carry on an entire conversation in French using just two words?

A somewhat elderly man who seemed clearly amused sat in the entrance to a wide hallway. The belt from which his rather large gun hung was connected to another wide, diagonal belt that swept down from his shoulder to the nether regions of his rather narrow figure. He wore a round cap on his head as though someone had stuck it there as a sort of prank. A wayward strand of his greying hair fell across his forehead. His cheeks were pink and the tip of his nose was rather reddish. His uniform seemed quite worn, but his boots were highly polished and shone as though the entire uniform was there but to set off those clearly painstakingly polished boots.

"Here we are, Madame," he said with a smile. "Good day, pretty lady. A good day for the glorious future of France. What good news have you brought with you to our little house of joy?"

"Our aunt, Madame Marion Ravel, recently gave birth," Erwin quickly replied. "We were given permission to visit her."

"Of course you have permission," said the ageing police-officer-cum-security-guard. "If you did not have permission you wouldn't be here. Marion Ravel, you say? Well, you see, I have no idea who the authorized mother is. I do not know her name and I do not know any other name for that matter. This is not the information desk here. And even if it was, there's no way I could possibly know who gave birth yesterday and who gave birth the day before and who is going to give birth today and who will be giving birth tomorrow. Anyone who would ask such a thing would be demanding more than any soldier, even a veteran like myself, could possibly manage. I am a soldier, you see. I was with the Marechal at Verdun. That was back in 1916. He was a real hero and we were all heroes right alongside him. So you see, I know a little something about the army, and what it means to be a military man. Marion Ravel, is that what you said, young man? She must be a woman from out of town. I know all the new mothers of Saint-Claude by name. There's no Ravel in Saint-Claude." You could tell that he was a natural-born talker, just looking for the chance to revel in a little meaningless chitchat.

"Madame Ravel," Erwin dryly cut in on the meandering discourse of the rather loquacious police-officer-cum-security-guard, as though demanding a succinct response to a single question - 'where is Madame Ravel?'

For a moment a look of dismay stole over the officer's features in the face of these three uncultured visitors, who preferred straightforward, simple facts over the fine art of smiling, convoluted conversation and said curtly, "There is a nurse to your right in the large hall. She is always busy. Tell her the name. If she has no time, repeat the name. She never responds the first time. That's the rule."

Erwin and Jackie had already turned to go and had perhaps not even heard the final words that left the mouth of this veteran soldier who had been relegated to the life of a security guard.

I uttered my standard, "*Merci,*" which I already considered a sort of skeleton key, and rushed into the hall ahead of the children.

The double doors were open wide. Down a long hall almost twenty different women lay in beds that fairly touched one another. The nurse, who was otherwise occupied at the bedside of one of the new mothers said, without raising her head, "No one is allowed in here," and without waiting for any sort of a response she repeated once more without raising her head, "You are not allowed in here. Visiting hours ended quite some time ago." She now raised her head and gave us the rather lengthy, meaningful stare of some self-important matron as though waiting for us to simply disappear from the doorway.

The three of us, Erwin, Jackie, and I, all managed to quickly scan the faces of the women lying throughout the hall. Manya was not among them. Jackie was rather clearly troubled and in an instant he had turned into a somewhat restless child. Erwin's features, on the other hand, betrayed no more than mere alertness. What did the children see in my face when we looked at each other? I have no idea.

Manya was certainly somewhere in the hospital. The woman at the reception desk downstairs had known that she was here. But she was clearly not in this wing of the maternity ward. Where was she then? There was no way that I could ask the nurse who was already bending over the bed of yet another new mother. It was not simply that I had no idea how to relate to a woman like that, but I was afraid of getting entangled in some new complicated situation. I could not remain mute and yet, at the same time, I could not speak.

Erwin, of course, understood my helplessness and therefore said from the doorway, "We have come to visit Madame Marion Ravel. Where can we find Madame Ravel?"

The nurse raised her head and spoke from where she stood, saying, "Madame Ravel is not here," waited a moment for her words to sink into our consciousness, then repeated once more, as though demanding that we remove ourselves from the doorway, "I have already told you that there is no Madame Ravel here."

Suddenly an almost hesitant voice rose from the distant recesses of the hall, saying, "She was here. She was not feeling well so they came to take her away," was what one of the women offered.

"Nobody asked you," the nurse chastised the woman, who was, of course, not the only one in possession of the information that she had provided, but all the other new mothers had remained silent whereas she had clearly not known that she too ought to remain silent, not because anyone was expecting her to keep a secret, but simply because in this ward, it would appear, the nurse was the only one who spoke, whereas others might raise their voices only randomly and then only on condition that they had been granted express permission to do so. Of course, no one had actually made these rules explicitly clear. People these days simply no longer trust that they are truly free when a single woman or man adopt for themselves any sort of an air of authority - whether great or small - simply because they can.

We absolutely had to see Manya. What had happened to her? What did that woman mean when she said that they had "taken her away?" Where had they taken her? Why had they taken her away? Who gets taken away altogether? Had some-thing terrible happened to her? Was that something terrible the secret they were supposed to keep? Was the lady at the reception desk downstairs unaware that something terrible had happened? She certainly had not addressed us like someone who knew that something terrible had happened. It would seem that Manya was still right nearby, right there next to us, so close by, really, but there was this single nurse standing between us and separating us from each other, this woman who clearly could not get enough of the power that her position of authority afforded her in her minor little kingdom. Just like that, in a matter of seconds, you feel like you are losing your mind. We slowly made our way over to the staircase at the start of the hallway, as I tried to think of what I might do without running any unnecessary risks.

I was simply unable to accept that trivial roadblock that the nurse had thrown up in our path and head off wherever it was that I was headed without ever knowing, perhaps for all eternity, what had happened to Manya, and just turn to leave sadly without even seeing her. But I was likewise incapable of bursting on through this foul roadblock, and afraid of making a mistake in a time and place when any misstep might turn out to be my last. I was afraid of that nurse. Erwin picked up the pace, went on ahead and stood next to the soldier-cum-security-guard sitting in the entrance. We came up behind him in turn. Erwin and the soldier were already talking with one another. "What do you want from me, young man? I told you that I do not know anything at all about Madame Ravel or any of the other ladies. My entire responsibility is simply to be a soldier. I already explained this to you. Now let's see if I can be of any assistance. Who are you, Madame?" he said, turning to me, and without waiting for a response he continued, "a cousin or an acquaintance, it does not really matter one way or the other." He did not say 'sister.' Why not? I will never know. I said, "Yes," and nodded my head significantly, although the man was not actually awaiting my response. It had no importance whatsoever in his eyes. "Now then, Madame, let me tell you directly what I have been trying unsuccessfully to explain to this young man here. I am but a humble soldier. We are not at the front here. That is true. This is a hospital. But my responsibilities are clear. You might well ask what am I doing here, and it is good that you asked. I am here to maintain order. I am here in the event that they bring in the wounded. There is the war on, and where there's war, there's the army. I am here to make sure people know. Right now, of course, it just so happens that all we have here are new mothers, and new mothers are not exactly the wounded or the war, for that matter. So you see, I can't rightly say. But you are a fine-looking woman and you have a wonderful family, so if I can possibly be of any assistance I would be glad to help. If Madame Ravel is not in this hall here, then she must be in another room in the hospital. If the nurse did not tell you why she is in another room, or where this other room might be, that is simply because this nurse here never tells you anything at all. All that matters is that she knows. And once she knows whatever she knows, there is no need for anyone else know it. That would not be of any additional benefit to her. So you see, you have no way of finding out where Madame Ravel is."

I lost my patience, said thank you once more and was about to go, when the man stopped me. "Look one of the younger doctors is coming down the hall heading in our direction." Before I had had the chance to respond, the ageing soldier was already up on his feet, clicking his heels together and waving his arms with a formal flourish to welcome the arrival of the doctor. "This honorable lady here is the cousin of Madame Ravel who recently gave birth but is not here in our wing of the hospital. The nurse, as you well know, has no time to speak with anyone at all. I am a simple soldier. You have known me well for some time now, and I, for my part, have known you, Monsieur le Docteur, for some time as well. I have always shown you the utmost respect. I already told the lady that I would try to assist her in any way possible. No sooner had the words left my mouth than you come along as though you fell from the very heavens on an express mission from God Himself." The young doctor smiled. He looked at me and said, "Everything is fine, Madame. Your cousin suddenly found that she was not feeling very well. We moved her for observation into a smaller room for four patients, though at the moment hers is the only occupied bed in the room. There are three empty beds. That is something of a rarity. She is lucky. There ought to be a nurse sitting with her but we are unfortunately a little low on human resources at the moment. You may well find her all by herself just now. You can go in, if she is alone. I have already examined her. She is in good health, but just to be on the safe side, you understand, we chose to provide her with the chance to get some extra rest under our supervision. By the way, I should mention that the birth itself was relatively easy compared to what she seems to have thought of it herself at the time she was giving birth. By tomorrow she should be well enough to return to the regular maternity ward here, and within two or three days she should be able to go home again. I am glad that I was able to be of assistance." He bowed his head in a show of deference and turned to head off once again.

The security guard, who had remained standing throughout this brief conversation with the doctor, now differed to him by removing his cap as he left and said to me, "These young doctors are still doing their residencies, Madame. They have already been to the front. They come back here for short stays at a time, then they head back once more to the trenches. The entire hospital depends on them, while they are here, and on the older members of the staff who no longer go off anywhere at all. They tell me everything openly. I am like an older brother to them, perhaps even a sort of father figure. I do not ask questions. That is not my role here. I am a soldier, as I have already told you. But they respect me. After all, they are soldiers too. Yes, in fact, I would say they are soldiers. But they are still young, so they still tend to talk to you when they see you. Now you are no doubt asking yourself where this cousin of yours can be found. Well then, let me tell you. If I could, I would accompany you there myself. But, you understand, that simply is not possible, as a man like me never leaves his post for anything in the world."

We were shown down the dimly lit hallway on the first floor. The door was closed. In the square of light at the other end of the corridor figures could be seen walking back and forth. There was a distant, dying din that seemed to be coming from a neighboring building. Where we stood, outside this room, it was dark. The silence felt hollow as there was not a soul in sight anywhere in the vicinity. It was as though we had entered another building altogether. We stood there for a moment, wondering whether we had indeed come to the right place, or if there was someone waiting in ambush on the other side of the door for anyone who dared enter. After another moment's hesitation, I knocked lightly at the door, just loudly enough that anyone inside might hear. There was no response. The children and I looked at each other, as though waiting for some prearranged response to my knock at the door, but all that I heard was my own heart beating hard in my breast. I knocked once more, a little bit louder this time. The sound echoed a bit. There was still no response. Suddenly the door swung open and an old woman, wearing a white robe that was a few sizes too large for her, stood there in the doorway. With one hand on the doorjamb and the other resting on her hip she said loudly, in a hoarsely strident voice, "You are off-limits here and are about to wake up my patient. You must leave at once." But her words came too late. Behind her we could make out a big white bed, where Manya lay in all her glory in the midst of a large, puffy quilt. I had the chance to notice that her face was made up, her hair was combed. Her delicate eyeglasses were perched on her nose and that well-known squint of hers, which she had never taken the trouble to correct, was ca-sting about joyfully in all directions. She waved her hand and cried out in Hungarian, "A boy, I gave birth to a boy!" Then she immediately added, once more in Hungarian, "I will be leaving this evening," and she blew us a big kiss filled with warmth and heartfelt desire. The old woman slammed the door somewhat loudly in our faces. The silence immediately returned. The children and I stood there in amazement before the door, and then, without saying a word, we slowly turned around and began heading towards that square of light at the other end of the hallway in order to leave the building. We stepped back out into the street we headed back to the place we had left behind.

I was thrilled. I had managed to see Manya, even if only for a moment. But I had seen her and the children had seen her. Jackie had seen her, that was the main thing. It was the reason I had come. She was the proud mother of poor old Jack's baby boy. In the brief instant in which we had seen her, her face was glowing with that unique beauty of hers. She seemed to be strong and in good health. Her voice was clear, steady and joyous. I had no way of knowing how, but it was clear that she had overcome everything that might have hampered , delayed, or cancelled her plans and that she was prepared to make the big trip to the Swiss border together with her newborn baby.

How long I had taken to prepare myself and my children for this visit. How I had looked forward to it. How far we had come just in order to make it here. All the strategy employed by the neighbor and his wife to lead us safely through the town that was so littered with traps everywhere. In the end, all it amounted to was a visit that went by in the blink of an eye. It consisted of the exchange of no more than a few words, and yet it had fulfilled all our expectations. It was perfect and complete in every sense of the word. The children walked by my side. I could sense that they were at ease and that they understood - albeit not necessarily in the same way that I did - that they had had a glimpse of their aunt in a brief moment of hope and promise. It was a sort of omen. The few steps they took to reach the front entrance of the hospital were light and filled with joy. I could sense it. We had only seen Manya for the briefest of instants. Even if I wanted to, I could not possibly tell if we had seen her for a mere second or two, or ten, or twenty for that matter. One brief moment, yet so full, we had seen her and heard her and all four of us - Manya, as well as the boys and I - were beside ourselves with happiness as a result. Anyone who saw us, if they bothered looking at us at all, would merely have seen us walking along, but I knew that we were in fact dancing.

In my mind those rapid-fire thoughts flew by, thoughts that fathom all the eye has seen and all the ear has heard with a certainty that re-quires no extra time to mature. I was sure that Manya was the leading lady in a play that had taken place backstage, behind the curtains of its own performance. The entire hospital had turned into her own private theater. Everyone there was playing the role that she had assigned to them. She had written the script. She had set up the smugglers that she had told me about, had them at the ready, had arranged everything with them, all in accordance with that very script that she had created, telling them she would wait for them in an isolated room. Only one of them - that man who was the only other individual besides me that was authorized to visit her, he alone could come. It would be virtually impossible for anyone to be cunning and shrewd enough to get her out of that large hall in the maternity ward without arousing unnecessary suspicions. She had taken sick for this express purpose and pulled the wool over the eyes of her doctors. The staff had all fallen in line and were now all filled with genuine concern for her well-being. She would get out. I did not know how, but I was sure of this with a certainty that would tolerate absolutely no objections. I was sure that she would hold her newborn son close and overcome all the supervisors and security guards throughout the hospital as she made her way with her infant child to the freedom that so surely awaited her. She would see to it that the baby was wrapped in the warmest possible clothing she could find I had no idea how but she would have brought them to the hospital for that express purpose. She would tramp through the snows of salvation. She would make it; she would be victorious; this time. This woman would be victorious; this time. There was no other woman who could compare. For a moment I asked myself: our old soldier in the hall-way, the young doctor, even the ill-willed nurse and the old woman in her oversized robe standing there in the doorway of that isolated room - who were they? All these figures themselves - who were they? Were they mere characters in that same backstage play behind the curtains whose true role was only known to Manya and to them. Perhaps only Manya herself knew? Then again, perhaps even she did not know their true role. Even if she was ignorant on that score then who did know? Dear God, who truly did? I had no idea then and to this very day I still do not know the answer.

But now, where were we headed? The neighbor's wife had disappeared. The neighbor himself had shown up with his bicycle but now he too had disappeared. We stood there in the entrance to the hospital. Alongside the joy we all felt at having seen Manya, the terror rose inside me as I realized our complete and utter dependency on the couple next door, our neighbours - or at least one of them. In reality I did not know anything at all about him or her, or the two of them together, for that matter. Once again we were damned if we waited around and damned if we left. Jackie looked up at me. Erwin stepped outside to look around for a moment to see if he could spot anyone that might lead the way, but just like me he did not see a soul. We were completely on our own. The trio of police officers and four soldiers were still standing around, just as they had been standing around when we had arrived, talking amongst themselves and smoking their cigarettes. They were not examining the few passersby who came and went passed them. We also could have walked right by and they would have paid any particular attention to a pregnant woman leaving the hospital accompanied by her two sons. But dissemblers are constantly exposed. They know the truth and so they are convinced that the people pursuing them - even if those giving chase are literally blind - are fully aware of this truth as well. Reason refuses to acknowledge this rule, but reason is the philosophical luxury of the professional. For an average woman like me, fear is more reliable than reason; and I was afraid, I was terribly afraid.

We had only been in the hospital for a few moments, but the weather had quickly changed. A chill wind was now blowing, as the approach of a gloomy mass of clouds stole the light from the cold, retreating azure of the sky. The sky turned grey, even those patches that were not yet covered with clouds. The sun is a wonderful thing in these wintry mountaintop towns, but it is always on the run. Even if we had known the way back to our hiding place, the storm was going to catch us, and we would be left to wander through the wind and snow along the streets and alleyways of the city. But we did not even know the way. A cold chill slithered down my back like the narrow coil of a snake. A single, tremendous tremor went through me and shook me to my very core. Erwin sensed it and caressed my shoulders. Jackie sensed it too and a corresponding tremor went through him as well. I turned back, reentered the hospital and went up to the stairs as though I were just beginning my visit. I needed this little window of time to work out the next steps I was going to take. I did not intend to go upstairs to the large hall or down the first floor back to Manya's room. Nor did I intend to remain there inside the hospital walls more than a mere minute or two - the time it would take for my thoughts to coalesce and allow me to decide just what to do. Before I had a chance to lift my foot on to the first step I heard a voice that I immediately recognized as that of the nurse who had greeted us at the reception desk when we had first arrived at the hospital. "You did not manage to find the place, Madame. Here I was thinking rather foolishly that I had actually explained it all quite well. It would seem that I did not explain it all that well after all. I will be right back and take you to the room myself. Wait for me here." I said, "*Merci*," as a matter of course, but she did not hear me as she was already rushing off to wherever it was that she was headed.

Now here I was doubly trapped. At this point I could not leave the hospital, and yet I could not stay either. I could not wait there for that kindly-looking nurse to return, though I could not run away either, I could not even think of my next step, nor could I ask the children for their advice. My entire being became this utter inability to do anything at all. I froze on the spot. I saw the nurse coming back in my direction, moving rather quickly. It is a terrible thing when an act, or mere display of kindness or innocent assistance suddenly constitutes such a petrifying threat. Nowhere in the world is the 'a' truly an 'a', the 'b' a 'b', or the 'z' a 'z'. The bigger picture has a way of altering the fine print. I was sorely in need of some miracle to save me from the sentence of this nurse's good intentions. She began heading up the stairs in front of me, stepping lightly and quickly along the stairs, and here I was heading upstairs behind her, as though my hand had been forced by the very kindness that she was showing me. In just another moment the old soldier was going to begin wondering whether or not he was dreaming - having just seen me there mere moments before. The nurse will send me on my way with daggers in her eyes, as she begins to suspect that I am some sort of a scoundrel and not a mere idiot. The young doctor will walk by telling himself that something is not quite right, seeing me return to this floor once more even though there is nothing for me there. I will be at a loss for words and be unable to explain myself. But the spider web that ensnares the helpless was already wrapped tightly around me, as I headed up the stairs behind that kind-hearted nurse, towards the certain disaster that awaited me at the top.

Just then I heard a strong, sharp voice call out, "Madame Mayer!"

The nurse went up another step or two but the children and I stopped at once and all looked back over our shoulders. The neighbor's wife was standing at the foot of the stairs and spoke once more in a voice that seemed to me to echo off the walls of the hospital in the forceful tones of a command that absolutely must be obeyed, saying, "We are waiting for you!" We paid no attention to the nurse, who had certainly heard what was said but assumed that the words were not directed at us. The children and I hurried back down the stairs in the direction of the neighbor's wife, who had already walked out the front door of the hospital. We headed quickly for the open door of a waiting pickup truck parked in the entrance, the sound of whose running motor seemed to fill the whole world from end to end. We got in - I got in first, as the neighbor's wife pushed me from behind - then the children, though they did not want any help from her. She herself then sat down on the narrow seat where only the driver seemed to have ample room. He was an older man with a spent pipe stuck in his mouth. We left the hospital and rode down the boulevard into town, where it seemed winter had returned in full force.

No one said a word. We did not ask any questions. The driver took the pipe out of his mouth, knocking the remains of burnt tobacco from the bowl out the window, which he had opened for a moment despite the cold wind that flew in through the opening, all the while holding the rattling steering wheel with his other hand. He then picked up a pack of cigarettes, took one out, stuck it in the corner of his mouth, lit a match with which he in turn lit the cigarette. With a single puff the entire cabin of the car was filled with a thick veil of smoke that gave off a nauseating smell. Jackie began to cough but immediately controlled himself. I had no idea if he had coughed because he was choking or simply in a show of protest. I, for my part - even if I had known where the handle was located that might have opened the window, even if I could have reached it - I would never have dared to do such a thing. I was completely unable to move my limbs, and my hands even less so - neither the hand that was pressed firmly against Erwin's own hand and back, nor the other hand that was fixed sternly against my own ribs, to prevent them from brushing up against the driver. In this smoke-filled bubble with its thick, heavy smell, where we had been crammed in together right next to one another, there was no room to move, no room to even say a single word, to the point that it appeared as if anyone who might move or make the slightest sound would actually be risking their very life. I could not see a thing out any of the windows. The steam of the breath leaving our mouths and the smoke from the lit cigarette completely obscured our vision. Even the front windshield was covered with the steam rising from our mouths. The driver was constantly wiping it off with a red cloth. The town, or what little we could make out through the wiped down pockets of the windshield grew dark and overcast. All that I could see was the bluish light from the truck's headlights along the road we took between rows of houses that bordered the street like no more than thick clumps of shadow. Lightweight snowflakes fell diagonally through the foreshortened sheaves of light. The long black arm of a windshield wiper whisked the snow from the glass. I told myself that the trip could not take too long. Even though the walk on the way there had taken quite a while, the trip by car could not possibly last too long. But I was suddenly not at all certain that I even knew where we were headed, whether our destination was in fact near or far. When a person has no idea who is even serving as their guide, then they also have no idea where it is that they are headed. The neighbor's wife knew. She knew everything. What bothered me was not so much the question of where it was that we were headed, but whether any of us would manage to hold out until we got there - the three of us, the children and I. These little boys remained so much more silent than one could properly expect children to be. They even refused to allow themselves to cough.

The truck then came to a halt. The neighbor's wife opened the door on her side and nimbly stepped onto the sidewalk. Through the open door that she had not managed to close I could see her quickly run in to some store, keeping her head down in the face of the falling snow. The driver leaned his body out across the boys and me in order to slam the door shut. At the same time he threw his cigarette out of the cabin, sat back up in his seat and immediately lit another cigarette. He inhaled the smoke deeply into his lungs, clearly taking pleasure in the smoke that he then exhaled rather loudly, almost impertinently. He did not say a word. He did not apologize for leaning across us like that. It was as if we did not even exist in his eyes. Jackie pulled his arm free and began waving his hand in the air to get the smoke out of his eyes. Erwin grabbed his brother's palm and placed his hand once more between his knees. The engine was still running and rattling the cabin where we all sat perfectly still. The three of us were shaking in a single, solid mass to the rhythm of the rumbling engine. The driver leaned across us once more, feeling around for the handle of the window, in order to throw it open. The smoke was on the verge of overwhelming him as well. A chill gust of wind whistled through the cabin.

After a little while, out the open window, we saw a man in a white apron emerge from the store with a wooden crate on his shoulder. The neighbour's wife, who rushed out behind him, overtook him at a run and then stood in the street facing the truck's cabin as she indicated to the driver that he should get out. At first he seemed to have some difficulty understanding what she wanted from him but then he immediately did indeed get out of the truck and disappeared. The man in the apron also went around to the back of the truck, with the neighbor's wife following him. A brief moment later the driver threw open the door of the truck and we saw the man in the apron hurrying back inside his shop. The wooden crate had disappeared from his shoulders. The driver helped the neighbor's wife get up in-to the truck. She sat down in the narrow space left for her, as we crowded together even more tightly than before. She shook her back as though trying to get rid of the chill in her bones. She did not say a word. The driver, who came back around and got in behind the wheel did not say a word either. I was silent, and the children remained silent as well. It was as though the whole world were muzzled as we drove away.

Just a few moments later the neighbour's wife called out, "Stop. We're here. This is it." The driver pressed down on the brakes and the truck came to a halt all at once. The neighbor's wife got out first, followed in turn by the children and then me. We stood on the sidewalk facing our building. It seemed to me at that moment that we had been living there for years. It was as though the house had been waiting for me, expecting me, it seemed somehow compassionate. Ridiculous. No house like that, in a town like Saint-Claude, could possibly be compassionate. At that moment, like some sort of otherworldly wonder, the neighbor materialized out of the darkness. He was walking with his bicycle by his side, bent over the handlebars, wearing a sort of over-sized cape that even covered his head. The falling snowflakes clung to the fabric. He did not look up in our direction, as though there was no one in the world but him. He just leaned the bicycle against the wall of the house and stepped slowly around the back of the parked vehicle, whose engine was still running. The driver got down from the truck. At this point I noticed that the back of the truck was covered with a dark sheet that hung down over the low wooden rear door of the truck. The driver re-leased the catch and let the door fall on its hinges. The sound of the smack of the wood echoed down the empty street. The crate from the store was inside. The neighbor lifted it onto his shoulder and, without saying a word to the driver, he walked up to the entrance to the building, passed right by us, and disappeared into the stair-well. We stood there waiting for the neighbor's wife. We saw the driver lift the rear door of the truck and fasten it once more in place. He then hurried off to return to the front cabin. The neighbor's wife stood by the door waiting for him. She pressed a wad of bills into his hand. He counted the bills, then put his finger to his temple in a sort of salute, stuck the wad of bills in his pocket, got back in the truck and drove off. The neighbor's wife waited until the truck was out of sight and then entered the house. When she saw us she said, "What are you all doing standing here in the doorway? Are you waiting for the gendarmes?" She did not wait for a response but went upstairs ahead of us to her apartment.

The wooden box was sitting right up against the bottom of the front door of our apartment. There was no way you could miss it. I opened the door and we went in-side, stepping over the crate. It was meant for us. That was clear. But no one had told us that explicitly. We did not want to bring the crate into the apartment with us as though it went without saying that it had been prepared expressly for us. We could see that there were two large loaves of black bread inside the crate, partly wrapped in wrapping paper, resting clearly in view atop of other essential items. There was the white neck of a bottle of milk peeking out from the crate as well. We had not ordered a thing. We had not asked for any of it. We had not paid for a single item. There was however also no way that we could leave the crate out there on the landing. That might be interpreted as some sort of a sin, an in-sult, or a simple show of self-righteousness. Before locking the door from inside Erwin said that he would step out for a moment to see the neighbor's wife and ask her about the crate. He realized that this was the only possible solution. He came back a moment later, barely managing under the weight of the crate, and lifted it with a rather extraordinary effort onto one of the chairs in the apartment. We took off our heavy clothes and the three of us sat down with our legs spread wide. We were extremely exhausted from the long day that we had just put behind us. It had been more eventful than we could really take, so demanding in its reality that it was almost beyond our ability to bear. Although we had not buckled under the burden and had bravely born the yoke - yet now it was as if we simply could not take it any longer. We did not even look inside to inspect the contents of the crate. It sat there on one of the chairs, while I sat on another, Erwin sat on a third chair and Jackie on a fourth. The coats that we had thrown off rested on yet another set of chairs, with our winter shoes beneath them. The single light bulb that we had turned on when we entered the apartment lit up that little room as it closed in on us with a muffled silence that seemed almost merciful.

After a little while had passed, during which none of us spoke, Erwin said, as though speaking to himself, "She said that she would stop by in about an hour." I did not respond, nor did Jackie. I got up from my chair. I went over to the crate and began to empty it out. There was bread inside. There were two large bottles of milk. There was a pile of loose, rather dark potatoes. There was a paper bag filled with brown sugar, a bottle of oil, salt. There were also a few large apples that looked like they were a little rusty. There was a big jar of marmalade and three or four cans of sardines. The basket gave off a scent a little like coffee. Perhaps it was chicory. There were no eggs. There was a sheet of paper torn from a notebook, with big block letters that read "Receipt" with every item on the list, including coffee, with the price right next to it. At the bottom of the entire list, once again in block letters that were underlined twice for emphasis, there was the word, "Paid". I put all the items in their place and left the empty crate next to the front door. I took the receipt and sat down in the same chair I had previously occupied. I looked over at the boys who had fallen asleep in their chairs, in postures that looked completely spent and exhausted. A huge wave of sorrow washed over me. It completely overwhelmed me. Tonight Manya would be setting out, along with her little newborn baby - I did not even know if she had already given him a name. And the baby, Jack's one and only son, his firstborn - I had not gotten a chance to see him. And what of my sister herself - would I ever see her again? I was soon fast asleep myself.

As though in a dream, I heard a knock at the door. At that moment the sound was still so far off that it did not at all concern me. My eyes were open but I was still in the throes of sleep. I did not even have the strength to rouse myself. I submitted to the need to keep sleeping, but then came a second knock at the door, somewhat more forceful than the first. I immediately got hold of myself and leaped up from my seat. The children were still sleeping in the very same positions that I had seen them in before I had fallen asleep myself. I must have only slept for a few brief moments. Erwin had said that the neighbor's wife would be by in about an hour. It could only be her knocking at the door. But I had not been asleep for an hour. All was silent. There were no more knocks at the door. I opened it halfway but there was no one there in the doorway. I went back inside and woke up the children. Erwin was immediately awake, stood up and asked, "Did she come?" But Jackie refused to wake up. He curled up, grumbled, twisted up his face and pressed his eyelids firmly shut. Then he got up and walked like some little drunkard over to the bed, threw himself down on it, curled up once more and fell asleep.

"Forget about him," Erwin said. "He is a very heavy sleeper. How do you know that she came?"

"There was a knock at the door, Erwin. I opened the door but there was no one there. But they knocked. You said it would be her."

"She told me that she was going to come over, in an hour, that's what she said. Has it been an hour already?"

"Wash your face," I said. "Cover your brother with a blanket. Let him sleep. Actually, wait for me to wash my face too. In the meantime, take the coats and put them away. The shoes too. If it was her - and I suppose it was - then we have to get the place ready for a visitor. Even if she is just stopping by to collect her money."

"Does she deserve it?" Erwin asked, as he went about making some order in the apartment.

"If she says she does then she does. How much? Whatever she says. And then there's the receipt. In the basket - the crate, that is

- why did I call it a basket? The receipt is in the crate. There was a bunch of food in the box, Erwin. I put it all away already. There was bread, and milk. Everything. And the receipt." I went over to wash my face and brush my hair.

"Do you have it?" asked Erwin, as he stopped me in my tracks.

"Do I have what?" I played dumb.

"Money, do you have as much money as she wants? How much does she want? Do you have it?"

"I have it all, Erwin, I always have it all, whatever is necessary." I stood still for a moment, caressing Erwin's head, and I added, "Are you hungry?"

"Maybe. But not now, Ma. Now we have a visitor."

"I'll put up a kettle of water. First let me wash up."

I stood in front of the mirror. Moritz, you would not have recognized me. It's not that I had suddenly aged. The time that had passed, washing over me in wave after wave, with a force and a regularity that I did not know time was even capable of, had not ploughed any new furrows in the field of my face. My eyes had not lost their luster. I was still me, still a young woman, perhaps a little bit thinner than before, perhaps a bit paler now. But you would never have recognized me. I was a completely different woman, a woman you had never known. I slowly brushed my hair, gathering it in a bun over and over again, taking my time staring at myself in the mirror, trying to make out what it is that you would have seen if you had come to me then. I was asking my reflection if you would love me now the way that you had loved me before I had turned into this other version of myself. I was not all that sure. Moritz, I know that this moment standing there before the mirror, this moment that I am describing for you now in print, was a painful moment. If I had not written about it I would have been simply deceiving you. But now that I wrote it down, I know that it was not the truth. I would never be anyone else for you, you would never be able to see me that way, ever. Oh, how I longed for you, with every ounce of strength that I had left. Forgive me.

I went back over to my chair and sat down, and waited. I got up to put the kettle on the fire. I would never have bought myself such a kettle. It was heavy, iron, painted in flaming red. It was good that things were that way, it reminded me that I was not in my own home.

I sat down once more. Erwin came over and sat down next to me. "You know," he said, "I have no idea just what happened today. What are we going to do when Manya gets back? You don't even know when she will be back. You didn't say a word to her. What is going to happen tomorrow? We have no idea when we are going to be leaving this place. But we also have no idea what to do while we are here. She has a new baby. Can the baby grow up in this place? Everything is all too confusing, Ma. And what about the neighbor's wife? And the neighbor? And the pickup truck with that scary driver? And all that smoke. You know what? That smoke was awful. It didn't even seem like smoke to me." "What did you think it was?" I asked in a tone that held a little bit of levity. "I don't know," Erwin said. "I thought I was going to die..." At that moment there was another knock at the door. Erwin rushed over to answer. The neighbor and his wife were standing there in the doorway, one right next to the other, without moving. Their heads hung loosely and they looked at us as though staring up out of some unknown depths. The wife asked, "May we come in?" And I got up to welcome her and her husband, saying, "Please do. We've been expecting you." She stepped inside with a firm gait. Her husband slowly made his way over to one of the chairs, sat down as though completely separated from Erwin, and me, and his wife, stared over at Jackie sleeping, and then let his chin slip onto his chest like an old man who had fallen asleep.

"I am glad that you had a chance to see your sister Madame Ravel. You said that that was the reason you came here from Marseille. I thought to myself that even in a world where it seems anything is possible it would be impossible for you to come such a long way, you and your children, for nothing, and then go back where you came from without even getting a chance to embrace your sister and her new baby boy. It was a boy, I believe, was it not? That just now came into the world, whether he wanted to or not. Now you can go back to Marseille. The weather is a bit more comfortable there, is it not? Here it gets very cold, Madame Mayer. You know that I know your name is Mayer. I called your name out loud in the hospital. Who told me that your name was Mayer? Madame Ravel? Perhaps you yourself told me? I can't quite recall. At any rate, the weather is pleasant and much warmer along the coast of the Mediterranean. I don't know if the city of Marseille ever even saw snow throughout its entire existence. Here, as you can clearly see for yourself, we are in the land of snow. Here it truly gets cold."

I had no idea if she was mocking me, or if she was preparing herself to tell me certain things that required a sort of introduction. I had no doubt that she did not for a second believe what she herself was saying. I had nothing to go on in order to try and decipher her true intentions. For all these reasons I did not say a word. I was cautious and waited for her to come to the real purpose of her little speech. But she never got there. Instead she just seemed to prattle on aimlessly. "I have no idea," she continued, "if you have already made arrangements to leave at once or if you will be departing in another day or two, or even three, for that matter. You are free to go. The same way you knew how to make your way here - though it remains a mystery to everyone else - I am sure that you will know how to make your way back now, without anyone else having to be in on the mystery of your travels at this point either. Do not respond to that. I am sure that you have understood by now that I am not all that innocent myself. It is not as though I truly believe that all the things that I witness here in Saint-Claude - and I have witnessed quite a bit - are indeed exactly as they seem or precisely what they pretend to be. What once was is now set in the past. What happened once is now over and done with. Things are not like that anymore. This cursed war is like some front where deceit fights lie, and the lies subjugate deceit. We had better watch out for the loser in that battle, just the same as we ought to steer clear of whoever proves to be the victor in this war of subterfuge. You're better off being well aware of the fact that if something suddenly seems to be the very spitting image of the truth itself, then it ought to be absolutely clear, beyond the shadow of a doubt, that it is an out-and-out lie. Show me a loyal citizen and I'll tell you he's a traitor; show me a traitor and I'll suspect that he is in fact one of the loyal few. I have to steer clear of them both with equal caution. Show me a lover and I'll be sure that he's just another trap I better not fall into. Show me a trap and I'll leap into its arms like the very arms of a lover all the same. What am I, Madame Mayer, an enemy or a felon, a patriot or a traitor, a well-behaved woman, or just some common scoundrel? What am I, who am I altogether? You have no idea. And what is my husband - is he the victim of aggression or just another aggressor, the oppressed or the oppressor, another human sacrifice or a violent avenger? What he once was he is no longer. I too, I am no longer what I once was. And so I sit here and you have no idea why I was willing to play the tour guide for that risky little trip you took today to the hospital. You have no idea if I did it for my sake or yours, on your behalf or mine. As for my husband, what is he altogether? Is he a living human being or no more than a mere ghost, a phantasm, a product of your own imagination? You do not know the answer to any of these questions and there is no way that you possibly could. It all sounds like some sort of odd monologue in a play written by a rather inexperienced amateur. But that is precisely the point, Madame Mayer. This whole cursed war - who wrote the script if not a bunch of inexperienced amateurs, hmm? Even once they are all grown up - as I hope they will have the chance to do, this war will be no more than a distant memory because there will have been others in the interim that will surely take its place. Your children will remain incapable of explaining - either to themselves or their own children - how it could have possibly been that the act in the play in which they themselves were assigned their roles was written by such imbeciles, just a bunch of rank-and-file people who took over the world simply because they themselves had gone insane."

Erwin stared at her in amazement with his mouth open wide. From time to time he would translate something if he thought I might not have understood, but he himself - at least so it seemed to me - could not believe all the things that he was hearing. At the same time I was certain that he would never forget all those very things that he may not have understood. She was a nimble woman. We had seen evidence of that in the way that she had walked through town. But when she spoke she was very measured in her cadence, carefully enunciating and choosing her words. She placed the emphasis on certain items where the emphasis alone might alter their meaning. At times her voice fell to a whisper in order to focus the attention of her listeners. She spoke as though she had learned her speech by heart. It was not one penned by some anonymous other, but a text she carried around in her own breast. She was an actress playing the role of her very self. And it was no stage act, for that matter. She could be trusted. A woman whose heart has been broken is someone you can trust. Her husband, for his part, did not move a muscle. I could see him out of the corner of my eyes, constantly. He was a living statue, a statue still breathing. It was disconcerting. He was present but silent, and his silence was saturated with a meaning I could not quite make out. It seemed to me that she had ordered him to come along with her when she came over to see us, in order to listen to what it was that she had to say, but I knew that things could not possibly have gone quite like that. Yet the truth of it all was something I could not quite comprehend.

"I boiled up some water, can I offer you both a cup of coffee?" I asked. Erwin translated for me. She laughed.

"You have coffee? Where did you get coffee?"

"You bought it for us. There was also some coffee in the crate."

"Coffee? That coffee is called coffee precisely because it's not coffee. If it was coffee they would call it by any other name in the world than 'coffee.' Who wants to get called in to be investigated and do time for doing business on the black market? You can pour me a cup, in a little bit, afterwards, I'll gladly have a cup. I'm used to it. First let us wrap up the few things we have to take care of."

Jackie stirred. He rose slowly from the bed, came over next to me, wrapped his arms around my hips and put his head down in my lap. I turned his face up in my direction and told him to go wash up. He refused. Erwin gave him a stern look. But Jackie would not pay him any mind. "He wants to rest a little longer in your lap, Madame. He had to walk quite a long way throughout a rather long day. He is exhausted, much more tired than his brother, that goes without saying. At an age like that a difference of a year or two between brothers is quite a significant gap. But you know all this, I'm sure you do, in every way." I asked myself if this sudden display of humanity was merely a put-on, or if it was something that this cursed war had not managed to eradicate along with all the rest of the innocence it was out to destroy. I believe that I actually felt love for this woman. I was careful with her, though perhaps it was not her that I was trying to be cautious of but the very confidence that I felt I had in her. I did not have the slightest impression that I was making a mistake. She could have very well become my friend, and I would not have asked her a single question, and I would not have judged her in any way whatsoever, and I would have simply accepted her the way she was. But I was no longer the sort of woman who could make friends;f any kind of friend. And it was not because I was suspicious. It was not that I was overly cautious. It was simply due to the fact that I had become the sort of woman who has no choice but to steer clear of any sort of closeness or human connection. I had apparently lost whatever ability it is that enables one to make friends. I was rather troubled by this explanation of things as it expanded inside me. But I could not refute it. Different, so different - I had become a completely different woman.

"First let me tell you what happened along the way, Madame Mayer. You still have no idea. Everything went exactly as I told you it would. I walked along precisely as I had planned and I did not falter, and the three of you followed along behind me and you did not falter either. Perfect. We were like some team of secret agents. You were all able to see me and I was able to see you, but I could also see what the three of you were not able to see. I was like an additional set of eyes inside the sockets of your own that went walking some 200-300 yards ahead of you. Perfect. And then, right around the bend in the road, I suddenly saw a checkpoint. There were soldiers. French as well as German. There were military vehicles, those motorcycles with the sidecars, and a line of people, about twenty or thirty men and women, who were clearly not standing there because they were waiting to buy some Italian salami. The soldiers were checking the people one by one. Slowly. Rigorously. A man who was walking a little bit ahead of me and had gone just around the bend was stopped. The soldiers made him get in line under the guards' supervision. If I had taken one more step around the bend myself and the three of you had followed along behind me, you would have been stopped too and ordered to get in line. They had put up wooden barbed wire barriers at either end and sealed off the entrance and exit from the street. Anyone who came around the bend from the street we were on was trapped. There was a truck there with armed guards standing next to it. There were people in the truck who had been on line just a moment before. I saw all this and I immediately understood what was going on. They had already seen me but they had not seen you. I had to get you to stop in your tracks. I myself had essentially already fallen into the trap. If

I had stopped walking along and had turned around the way that I had come, they would have stopped me and subjected me to an inquiry - not in that line there, but in a place no one ever comes back from unless one is willing to admit to things that never even happened. I was not afraid of that line of theirs. Here in Saint-Claude I have nothing to be afraid of for the time being. Not their lines nor their checkpoints, not the German soldiers nor the French soldiers, not some police officer, whether plainclothes or in uniform. But an inquiry, in some place I had never even seen before, that was enough to make me afraid. So I walked along naturally, freely, through the street. I was terrified for you. Anyway you look at it, all by yourself, in a town where you do not belong, with two little boys - you're a suspect, Madame Mayer. No matter what you might say, you are a suspect. Not even your pregnant belly would have saved you. Not from a group of soldiers who were sent here for the express purpose of conducting their inquiries and taking their prisoners. Not when it is a group of French and German soldiers together who take it upon themselves to try and demonstrate which of them is more effective in carrying out the atrocities that they have been assigned. Yes, the atrocities, Madame Mayer. Basically, this whole foul business that I have learned to live with simply because I decided that I had no better choice than staying alive, is one big atrocity. I stopped for your sake. When I saw that you had understood and stopped as well, I walked on.

"This man sitting here with us, this man that I told you would be waiting for us at home, was not, of course, waiting at home. He was with us the entire way, seeing all and himself unseen. I would not have led you through the streets if he was not leading me. He thinks fast, Madame Mayer, he does not stand around wondering what to do, he just does it. He does not stand there asking himself how to get out of a situation that had not been planned for in advance. Anything that seems as though it was not foreseen he has actually already planned for. For all the questions that no one had even bothered to ask, he already has an answer. All of life is either one way or the other, it is either filled with the expected or the unexpected. Like a throw of the dice, Madame Mayer, like a throw of the dice. He already knows every number that the dice can turn up. He does not try to predict the future or what fate has in store. To hell with fate. No one among the living has any control over it. But this man here has managed to work out in advance what fate seems to have decided just a moment before the dice are cast and the sentence is issued. That's how it is. This man here can not change a thing. Not even when fate strikes him person-ally, or la-shes out at me, for that matter. He knows the villain always gets to where he's going once he heads out on his way. It all happens a lot faster than you could ever imagine. He went on ahead of you through the streets, out in the open yet hidden from view at the same time, even before I led the three of you on your way. He was with us the entire time. You all followed me while he followed our entire group, the three of you and me. It all sounds rather complicated, but it isn't really. Is it a bit miraculous? Perhaps. Yes, you could maybe call it miraculous. He saw what I saw and intuited the same thing that I had understood, and could tell that you had understood enough to stop in your tracks but did not know if you should stay put or turn around the way that you had come, when he suddenly appeared and made it clear that you should all follow him. We did not exchange a single word, as you well know. He and I did not say a word to each other, and he did not say a word to the three of you. Nor did you three say a word to him or to me, and yet we all understood one another with absolute certainty, without any prior preparation, without any instruction, without any training. It was perfect.

"You were not left there to fail. And not out of compassion, or pity, or a sense of justice - all these things, if they have not died al-ready, are certainly dying as we speak. Why were you not left there to fail? Because we did not leave you there - not me, and not him - certainly not him. It is his way, at this point, of showing his hatred for a world that has murdered compassion and pity and justice, and lacks any clear conscience that might torment it any more. You probably think that the things I am saying are rather baseless. You're right. What real basis is there for anything anymore in this world?

"I did not encounter any difficulties when I went to stand in line," she went on, continuing this chilling monologue of hers. "The inspec-tor who was not familiar with me brought over one who was, and this latter individual displayed a rather showy, vocal respect in my regard. Someone in line hissed between clenched teeth 'Whore', loud enough that I might hear, and spat. I did not care. He was right. But it was not right to spit. If it were right to spit then he would have to stand in the town square and spit incessantly at almost everyone walking around this city. Who is not a whore here? To spit in my direction alone is to demonstrate that one has not grasped what this cursed war has done to everyone involved. No, I see you do not agree. You are telling yourself that this woman before you has no idea what she is saying. A war produces heroes as well. True. So what? What difference does that make? Those heroes - if there even are any - isn't it the war that makes them what they are? Isn't it the war that brings them glory? And do the poets not sing precisely because life has turned to garbage? And he has the nerve to spit? I spit on him." I sensed that Jackie shook when she used the word, 'whore.' I could see the horror in Erwin's face. Where had they managed to learn that a word like that existed at all? There was no way that they could have understood what she was saying, but who knows. Who knows what the children know once the garbage - as the neighbor's wife called it - is piled up everywhere, out in the open in secret, it really does not matter anymore, there is no place that is not filled with it. I did not care much for these thoughts I was having. The neighbor's wife had forced me into a language that I did not care to employ.

"When I arrived at the hospital I did not see you. The soldiers who were standing there saw me and asked me, 'Where are you headed? Is someone close to you laid up in the hospital? That can't be. You're taken care of. The mayor would not let a single one of your loved ones fall sick. Perhaps someone gave birth? Even the mayor can't put a stop to that.' And they laughed." She pointed to her husband and said, "He was in the vicinity, outside the hospital. He was waiting for the three of you to come back out. There was no one helping you out inside, and the fact is you could have failed in there even worse than out in the street. I thought you probably needed me. I went inside and caught sight of you. You looked lost. I called out 'Mayer' in a loud voice. The rest of the story you are already familiar with."

This was perhaps the moment to tell her why we had looked lost like that inside the hospital, and to thank her. But she was not finished yet. She had come to our apartment to tell me something that she had not told me yet, and I waited for her, my nerves all taut, waited for her to speak. I remained silent.

"Yes," she said. "I have not yet told you everything. This man," and she pointed at her husband again, who now seemed to me to have turned into a sort of pillar of salt, "this man understood that you would not be able to return on foot. He knows this old smuggler who rides around from town to town in his rusty old pickup truck. By chance he ran into him this morning and had arranged with him to come if he got word that he was needed and take you all back home in the afternoon. Aside from the price, the driver did not ask a thing. In his line of work, whatever does not constitute absolutely essential knowledge is essentially forbidden knowledge. He got the word and came straightaway. He is around in order to try and get by and he lives off the ones sacrificed to their sentences as much as he lives off those issuing the sentences from on high. If there is a hell for the sinners of the black market, then the police are roasting in the fires down there right alongside the thieves. That is who drove you back. I do not even know his name. He once told me that his name is Guy. Then he slipped once and told me his name was Louis." At this point Jackie suddenly piped up in my lap and said, "He is a bad man. He smokes like a fiend." The neighbour's wife nodded her head and said, "Indeed, like a fiend, my little one, I am well aware. I almost choked to death myself." "He didn't care. Everybody almost choked to death. It was so awful that he didn't care." Jackie hid his head in my lap once more. The neighbor's wife gave Jackie a look in which I found an expression of compassion, as she paused a moment and then immediately returned to what she had been saying. "In short, here we are. I bought the groceries, the few things that were available. I did not ask what you wanted. I knew you would want whatever you needed, no more than that, at any rate. The main thing is that you have something to get by on. They won't exactly be royal repasts, but even kings no longer feast as they once did. Now then, Madame Mayer, let us address a few things that we absolutely must discuss between us."

She fell silent for a moment. Out of politeness, before she had a chance to address those few things that we absolutely had to discuss, I would have offered a few words of thanks for what she and her husband had done for us. Simply out of politeness I really ought to have said thanks. In the end, what was self-evident and went without saying, at a time when nothing was all that self-evident or went without saying anymore, was that the two of them had done us an immeasurably good turn. It was not my place to examine why they had done it, nor to try and understand how they had managed to pull all those tangled, interconnected, frayed strings that com-posed the story of what they, my children, and I had all been through that day. It was amazing. How could I possibly remain silent in the face of such a story? But I did not say a word. I wanted her to first tell me whatever it was that this talkative woman and her silent husband had arranged to tell me. And then she said it. Her voice was straight and smooth like a new sheet of ice on the sidewalk at midnight.

"This apartment is paid for up until the middle of March. Madame Ravel paid the rent. Madame Ravel knew that she would no longer be here after the middle of March. There are two weeks left. Madame Ravel will not be coming back here. If you are not aware of that fact, I am, and if you are aware of that fact, then I am not. Together the two of us are both ignorant and in the know at the same time. But she will not be back. Where will you go in two weeks? In mid-March, not a day more than that, a new tenant is going to come to live in this apartment. He has the money to pay. You do not. He will pay, but you have not paid and are not going to pay. That's life. Our lives, Madame Mayer, consist of collecting what is owed to the land-lord. That is our religion, as it were, and we are rather devout about it. The master that we serve will not stand for anything less. So tell me now, Madame Mayer - not a penny is left of the money that Madame Ravel paid for the taxi. I gave Guy - or Louis, whatever his name is - I gave Louis everything and then some. The price is always whatever people like that say it is. I left the receipt for the box from the grocery store inside for you to see. You will settle the bill with me. I already paid the owner. The day that you have been through, as I already told you, comes at a price - a lower price than what one might or ought to expect, but it has its price, Madame Mayer. And it must be paid. There is no other way.

"I assume that you have the money that you owe. I assume you also have the money to buy tickets for wherever it is that you are headed from here, whether back to Marseille or not, the money is there. I am sure of it. I hope that you have more than that because you will certainly need more, a whole lot more. You did not come here in order to stay here. You will not have to pay a penny for your stay here. But once you have settled the whole bill, Madame Mayer, when will you be leaving us? You do not have to tell me right here and now. I have given you fair warning. Consider what I have told you to be a warning. Even if you can only get back to me tomorrow or the next day, we will wait. But you must understand that we absolutely have to know. If you do not tell us in advance and simply get up all of a sudden in the middle of the night, or something like that, and simply disappear along with your children, before the middle of March, and after having settled your bill, that is just fine. If you should need anything between now and then, anything of the utmost importance, that is, as important as life itself - just tell us. We are here to help. That, too, is fine. But it would be better if you didn't. It would be better if you did not stay here until you need something as important as life itself, because by then it might just be too late, Madame Mayer. Can you tell me now just when you plan on leaving us, Madame Mayer?"

She spoke straight, like she was reading from a book, and looked right into my eyes, as I looked right back into hers. Her eyelids did not flutter closed a single time as she spoke, nor did mine. There was no ill-will in her words, and there was no pity either. There was no insult in my silence, and neither was there any sense of supplication. We sat there facing each other and it was as though I was the wax and she were the seal. She spoke like someone who does not have the power to change a thing. I sat there in silence like someone who had been born but to accept it all just as it was. The same woman who had done us such an immeasurably kind turn now quoted us a price that was little more than an itemized bill. It was the same woman, the same couple, but it was not the same voice. At least her voice, at any rate, was not the same. I had not yet heard his voice. He had remained silent the entire time and now, too, he did not say a word.

"Are you throwing us out?" I heard myself say, and as soon as the words left my mouth I knew that I should not have pronounced those few syllables. She was not throwing us out. She did not owe us a thing and I owed her a tremendous amount. We had not come to stay with her. It was Manya who had come, and Manya had signed the contract. It was that contract which we had to uphold to the letter, and not merely because of the fact that this woman's very existence obliged us to fulfil our obligations. So why had I said what I had said - I, who knew full well that my words were rather out of place? Because even if she was not throwing us out, the fact is that I was being thrown out. She had told me how things stood, but the way things stood was that I was being thrown out.

Somebody had to be responsible for the fact that I was being thrown out. I could not very well blame the great, all-merciful God who had uprooted me and sent me on my way to try and save my life and the lives of my children. The Lord was too far away. I needed someone more close at hand, someone I could charge with the insult of my being thrown off the very earth itself. And there she was, even more so than the Germans, more so than the traitorous French who had become the Germans' dedicated agents - either out of weakness or cowardice. She was right there in front of me. She was no less of a casualty than I was, but she was a different sort of casualty. She was on one side of the barricade that separated us from one another, and I was right across from her, over on the other side. I unjustifiably put the blame on her for the anger that a woman feels when she and her children are left with nothing more than the iron rails, the getaway cars, and the backroads running between the frying pan and the fire through strange, alien towns - the anger of a woman with nothing more than the hope that is virtually sure to fail her but which she continues to harbor all the same, despite that fact. A woman like that is like a sailor who refuses to cast his anchor overboard into the stormy sea once the rope has torn. Ropes like that, tropes like that - like the trope of the Messiah - even if they are suddenly found, suddenly show up, suddenly arrive at last - can not possibly help a person who failed to hold on to their anchor, even once the rope broke free.

I felt bad for what I had said. She must have felt insulted. I waited there, admitting the rashness with which I had spoken, waiting for her to let me have it with her response. But this is what she said, "I understand how you feel, Madame Mayer. You do not have to forgive me for the fact that I have to throw you out. I would not expect you to. How could I? After all, the truth is that you are being thrown out. But I am too. Not from Saint-Claude. Maybe you have no place to go, but there you go heading off all the same. Me, I don't have a place to stay, and yet I stay here all the same. You do whatever you can.

Me too, I do whatever I can. Let's not cry over spilt milk, Madame Mayer. The lives we have been left with don't allow for the pleasure of a good cry. We must live our lives in accordance with the rules that the authorities have laid down until they are more covered in shame than they ever would have been if we had cursed them to the high heavens. That's the life we lead. I am hanging by my neck and now I am forcing you to dangle your-self over the abyss. Dear God, how I wish the person that hung me up like that would be forced to give a reckoning for the rope that he tied around my neck. Just like the one he tied around yours. It is the selfsame rope. But that man will never be brought to justice. There is no justice, no reckoning. There is nothing to reckon up. What would you have me do? Would you prefer that I lie to you? At least grant me that. Grant me a certain coarse sense of the truth. At least let me tell it as it is. Don't force me to live in fear of how ugly it all is. At the end of the day, when you tell me 'You're throwing me out', you are blaming me for a rather aesthetic transgression. You must forgive my use of such a rarefied word in a rather inappropriate time and place, my dear Madame Mayer. You must forgive me. This cursed war tore all aesthetics to shreds quite a long time ago.

"I am not throwing you out. But you have to go all the same. You are aware of this fact. There is no reason that you should feel insulted by it. The two of us are standing side by side on some stone. It is the only rock left to take refuge on in the midst of the sewer that has overflowed all around us. The stench is unbearable, but the two of us simply refuse to drown. You stand strong, I stand strong, but we will both drown if we fail to recall the fact that each one of us must tend separately to her own priorities. This is not a pleasant reality. But if we are not cautious on this score we will stumble and fall, and at that point it will not matter if we fall together or if just one of us falls, because the one to fall, as far as I am concerned, will always be me, and from your vantage point, it will always be you. I feel love for you, Madame Mayer, for your children as well, even for the one that is on its way, in just a little while. Stay strong. One day, when this cursed war will have ended - if it even remembers any-more how to end - perhaps we will meet again and ask ourselves if it was really you who sat and listened to me, or if it was really me who did the talking. Believe me, even if we know the answers, we will have difficulty believing them.

"Now let's see here, you owe me..." and at this point she named a sum which I have since forgot, and which there is no reason that I should remember altogether. I had it. It was almost everything I had left in cash.

Jackie had already lifted his head from my lap a little while earlier, he was listening, along with his brother Erwin who was translating what the neighbor's wife was saying in accordance with whatever he assumed I had perhaps not properly understood. All things that would ordinarily never have been said in the presence of children. I got up and went over to the spot in the apartment where I had hidden my money. I counted out what the neighbor's wife thought she had coming to her in front of her. She followed my count. I put the money in her hands. She slipped it just as it was into one of the pockets of her long skirt and said, "You do not have much left of this currency. If you need a moneychanger, just tell me. When you get back to me about what you have not yet told me, advise me on this matter as well." She got up from where she was sitting. Her husband rose as well. He went over to the door first and left without saying a word. Why had he come? Why had he sat there the entire time in silence? Why had he risen to go back the way he had come, like a dead man silenced inside his tomb? I was afraid. I could see in the children's eyes as they followed his measured steps to the door that they were afraid just like me. The neighbor's wife was still standing there, and before heading over to the front door herself, she said, "We did not yet have our coffee. We will have the opportunity yet to close that debt with each other in the near future, Madame Mayer, in the very near future." And then she left. The door shut behind her. I suddenly noted that we were all standing there, Erwin, Jackie, and I, the three of us all studying the door as though that door itself were a living thing.

And this was how the month of February gradually came to a close. We did not leave the apartment. About two or three days later another crate of basic supplies was placed right outside the door with the receipt inside just as before. I sent Erwin over to settle the bill immediately. The cash I had was dwindling but I was hoping to hear some news at any moment from the figure of the priest, Father DuPont, or from the innkeeper, or his son Phillip. I did not stop thinking of them for an instant. Even though they seemed to be taking their time I awaited their arrival constantly with all my heart. They had promised me. I was dependent on them. And so I trusted them. What else could I do? Even though the neighbor's wife had informed me that if I needed a moneychanger I should let her know and she would help me out, I kept postponing the moment. I had to first find out how much I would have to pay the smugglers who would get us out. I preferred being left without a penny while I was in Saint-Claude, rather than ending up short even a single cent of the amount that I would need to get us out of Saint-Claude.

Every day that we spent locked in that apartment seemed to me to be rather end-less. It was perhaps even more difficult for the children than it was for me, but they never spoke about that fact. In the second box of supplies that was left outside our door, there was a chess board and a box of playing pieces. You could tell from the board and the little box with the playing pieces and the pieces themselves, that they had already been put to pretty good use in the past. On the attached piece of paper there was a note explaining that the game was a loan for the children to use. No need to pay anything in that regard. The game would be returned when the time came - the note said - because it was a rather old item and the neighbor had a rather intimate attachment to the board and the playing pieces. The things that I failed to even think of, my neighbors had managed to look after. You, Moritz, if you had been trapped in a little room as I was together with the children, what would you have done? You would have played chess with them. Certainly with Erwin, at any rate. You had taught him to play during the few days that you had spent with us in Marseille. You felt that this was much more important than all the other things that were there waiting for you when you arrived. You dedicated much more time to it than seemed appropriate, though that left me somewhat bitter. But chess was more than just a game to you. Chess was, as you had once told me, the game that God Himself played. "He sits up there in the heavens and plays against Himself in order to take the full measure of His wisdom. Down here on earth, we imitate Him. You think that I play against my opponents? Nonsense. I am always playing against myself, and the man sitting across from me is little more than a living hanger hung with clothes. I sit with his clothes on my back as well. My son shall play chess, Rozhi," you said. "I am taking the time to pass on to him all that I know. That is the sum of my worldly possessions, and it is all for him."

I did not understand the strange things that you said about God, nor the whole matter of worldly possessions that seemed to fall from your tongue almost by chance. I did not even try. It was already quite some time since I had completely given up trying to deal with anything concerning you and chess. But I had a difficult time co-ming to terms with your preference at that juncture for Erwin. Jackie would sit there looking on but you would not say a word to him and did not even grace him with the slightest display of attention. He would just sit there and stare. You allowed him to do that, but no more. "My son is going to play chess, Roszy,", by which you meant Erwin, right? "And Jackie?" I had asked, with pointed resentment. "Jackie too," you replied, without looking up from the board. "When he matures. He is my son. He will play too. When the time is right." I never forgave you for this. Now the two of them sat there and played for hours, using the game that the neighbor had suddenly been so kind as to lend them. Erwin would patiently teach his brother everything that he knew. Jackie would play, and his older brother would kindly show him how he might improve his game, or make a better move. I could hear in his voice the same tones that you would adopt when you spoke. Sometimes Jackie would accept Erwin's advice, but other times he would stand by his own approach. There were times when the two of them would address each other like friends having a conversation. Other times their tones would sharpen like antagonists in a fight. At times they would sit there laughing together. Other times only one of them would laugh while the other would get up and walk away, only to return immediately. This was how they passed quite a few hours in that room, and God bless the neighbor or his wife for not even asking permission to lend us the game that your boys played, as it saved them from the stifling pull of all that time locked in a narrow cell where both child and adult could barely catch their breath. I tell myself that if the two of them will get the chance to grow up, then the chess that they will play will never be the same as the game other little boys will play when they grow up. And you, when you come and join us, and play with them once more, you will no longer be merely playing against yourself. You will have something to learn from them. Even God will have something to learn. That God for whom you said chess is His own game of choice.

The children played for hours, but there was also quite a bit of time when they did not play. Jackie would spend a lot of time next to the window and would report back from time to time on the things that he saw, as though there was something new in these reports. At first we took a certain interest in the things that he saw, but after a little while we did not even hear what he said to us. Just let him go on talking like someone sitting there talking to himself. Erwin would often strike up a conversation with me about all sorts of little things that did not really matter one way or the other to either one of us. At first the conversation would ramble on with a certain interest, but after a little while he would sit there talking. I barely heard a word he was saying and would simply limit myself to offering up all sorts of minor expressions of yes and no that were completely unrelated to anything he was actually saying. He, for his part, would sit there prattling on about nothing whatsoever. The two of us would just sit there facing each other for the sake of appearances and nothing more, when, in fact, each of us was actually sitting across from the other as if on either side of a big glass wall. There were three of us, just the three of us, so attached to one another by spirit and blood, connected through every yesterday and every tomorrow, bound by every single rope and strand, both visible and invisible. Yet here we were, all of a sudden cast our separate ways, each sitting there entirely alone for hours on end within the four walls of that apartment that had become our prison cell.

I tell you, Moritz, a person in prison, even right alongside the people who love them and that they love, is always in prison all alone. There in their cells, the prisoners turn inward between the walls that rise up inside themselves. Free people have no idea that such walls even exist. As far as they know the story of stolen liberty is a tale of two people. The one who was formerly free and the one who took away the latter's freedom. But now I know that it is in fact a tale of three people, including the one who was formerly free. The one who took away the latter's freedom. The prisoner who actually imprisons himself more and more with each passing day. As far as you are from me today as I sit here, my dear Moritz, you know this fact just as well as I do. And that is why I am afraid. You are trapped somewhere out there and I am trapped in here. Have you in fact imprisoned your own self to such an extent that I will not be able to locate you even once you return? And will you ever manage to find me? These walls, though they've been built, shall tumble on the day that I finally embrace you and you hold me close. I must admit to you that when I pray the concentrated sum of all my hopes and desires for that longed-for moment, I raise my voice in terror, Moritz, a terror that, even more than fear, instills a sense of pain inside me that no balm can soothe. Is it the same for you? My dear, distant Moritz, is it the same for you?

If I could manage to actually hear your response I would stop my ears.

During these long, endless days I would spend a lot of time wandering down the alleyways where our memories have made homes for themselves. I did not visit these byways often, and not because I did not sorely miss those homes. I missed them, even though the many joys they held were no longer ours, but I had no time for what had already passed. The present moment that I was living had detached itself from my past. I had to provide that present with a future, a future that I would not find down those alleyways. It was not some grand future, just a future filled with a house that stood firm. A future with a fixed shore, not filled with far-flung voyages at sea. The calm of a couple at rest, not the fascinating storms of one in flux. I was on guard. Constantly. You were certainly a part of this future of mine, but the future I was working towards for the two of us failed to catch your fancy. The big waves were what grabbed your attention. I was like your anchor. Perhaps you thanked your lucky stars when you failed to tear loose the rope that bound you firmly to the ground I had laid out for us, but you could not help trying to break free over and over all the same. I dare to think that I may well have been stronger than you. Whenever the wind lifted your sails and you began to distance yourself from me, you suddenly discovered that you loved me with both of your souls. That wanderer's soul that was ever stirring in your blood, and the corresponding soul of the man at rest at last, which gradually gained ground in the hallowed sanctuary of your heart, as you would return to me once more before you had wandered off too far to find your way back home again.

When you would again set off wandering because you were afraid that you might become too tightly bound, you could find no respite from the corresponding fear that you might just sail too far from shore. I was already waiting for your return even as you set out. I knew when you got back that you would head out once more. Anyone who saw me in my dance, would tell me I was weak. That I gave in too easily. That I allowed the gypsy in you to ill-treat me unjustifiably. You certainly had more than a little gypsy in you. And in loving that part of you, it was I who forced it to succumb to me, and you knew it. Now that our destiny has torn us apart and separated us from one another, and I find myself bound to you unconditionally, while you, I swear, are bound to me as well, unconditionally. All that we can ask for in our prayers is that tomorrow restore us to what was the day before. And so I wander through those alleyways. I walk along, remember, stop, let go, move from place to place as I remember. One day overtakes the other and then gets stuck somewhere in time, until there is no real temporal order anymore to all these memories.

The children sit and play. I do not remember ever playing myself. Maybe when I was three or four, or five for that matter. I guess so. It is not possible that I was all that different from other children. But as soon as I was minimally of age, my father and stepmother had dropped a yoke of domestic concern around my neck, for the care of the house and my younger brothers and sisters. I was required to be intelligent when it came to my studies and wise in my ways, ever-obedient on the one hand, yet independent on the other. Forever joyful from the time I rose until the moment I went to bed. A home that houses 11 children is a home run riot and there is no escaping the confusion. I was the one peacemaker. Everything was out in the open. The full range of sins, from the minor to those that were, God forbid, considered rather major would be attributed from time to time to one brother or the other. Sometimes word would get out about things concerning the boys. Other times it was about things concerning the girls. Even those things that my parents thought they had managed to successfully hide from view often managed to find their way into the whispered exchanges of the gossipmongers. All of my brothers and sisters, even Manya, were devoutly respectful of our parents, but everyone let me in on their secrets. They would tell me all about the whys and wherefores of their differences with our father and stepmother - who was a mother to all of us in our hearts. They would tell me if they had restrained themselves from openly defying our rather forceful parents. They would admit however that a little while longer and they would not have been able to hold back anymore and would indeed openly defy them. If they had secretly had it with the observance of the religious commandments, they all ostensibly seemed to keep them without the slightest objection or afterthought of rejection. They told me all about their hidden dreams and desires. I would keep everyone's secrets and so I was a prime suspect, but our parents respected me and they never told me openly what they secretly expected of me in their hearts. I never talked. I kept everything in. The commandments of my brothers and sisters were stronger than those of our parents. It was my brothers and sisters who were my true home.

In Belgium we had managed to reconstruct something of this home that we had left behind. There was me, and Manya, and Olga, my baby sister - all in Antwerp - and my older brother Yoszy, in Brussels. Seven of my brothers and sisters had stayed behind in Hungary as it slowly sank. I would send letters to my oldest brother from my father and mother, may she rest in peace, in the name of all the Winklers who had been uprooted and exiled. He would write back in the name of all the Winklers who had stayed. That was how things went while I was still single and that was how things went even after we got married. Things continued this way after Erwin was born and once Jackie was born later on too. One day, though, after I had sent off my usual letter, my big brother suddenly stopped writing back. A month or two later I wrote to Yoni, my youngest brother from my father, may he live long, and my mother, who had already passed into eternal peace. He wrote back, quite some time later. In a brief letter on a piece of paper torn from an old notebook, he said that everyone was well, including our eldest brother, who had not received my letter because he was in Budapest where he had joined a Yeshiva and was lost in learning the Talmud and Poskim, the rabbinical arbiters. "Our father," he wrote, "wanted at least one of his sons to become a *Talmid Chacham*, a learned Torah scholar, and our eldest brother, who has always been the most God-fearing of all our siblings, as you well know, was exiled, at his behest, to a Torah hub." I did not believe him. If he had not written the word 'God-fearing,' I might well have had my doubts, but I would have accepted it as true, the way that someone is inclined to accept the unexpected simply because one encounters it in print. And indeed, our eldest brother was strict in his observance of every commandment, both great and small. I had never seen him even drink a glass of water without first saying the *Beracha,* the blessing. He took upon himself and adopted many *Chumres,* strict practices that he did not demand the rest of us to observe. But 'God-fearing'? After all, with me he used to secretly discuss new tenets of his faith. He admitted to me that he had a number of books that revealed a truth that was absolutely incontrovertible. He would only discuss the simplest level of things with me because he was convinced that I would be incapable of fully comprehending the thought processes of his spiritual heroes. "If I had the guts," he told me, "I would tear the cobwebs off the *Aron Kodesh,* the holy ark, right before our father's very eyes. I would show everyone near and far just how dated it has all become, and how the world can not be fixed by simply throwing ourselves on the mercy of a God who gave us all those worn scrolls that serve to ensure nothing more than the rule of the high priests of religion over the ignorant masses." I could not believe my ears. But even more than my surprise at the fact that he had confided in me, I was afraid that perhaps the abyss that yawned between the lies he subscribed to in public and the truth that secretly burned inside him was literally tearing him to pieces. "Ah, but my little Rozhi," he said to me, completely oblivious of the extent to which I was terrified for him, "it is imperative that I not be so gutsy. If I were, I'd probably end up accused of parricide. I admit it. I am willing to sacrifice the entire world for the sake of my father. Not because I feel such a deep love for him, but simply because he is so very deeply my father. Perhaps, if there really is a God, then He will forgive me." He flattered me when he talked to me like that. Here I was worthy in his eyes to hear his confessions. I did not reveal his secret to a living soul. I did not even tell you about it. And here he is all of a sudden being described as 'God-fearing'? Did Yoni also know that it was absolutely imperative that he in fact not know? He could not possibly have written what he had written in complete and utter innocence. He had written, 'God-fearing… as you well know' - did this mean that he also knew precisely what I knew?

After a little while I wrote back to him asking him to kindly send me our brother's address at the Yeshiva. He did not respond immediately, but about a half a year later he sent me a letter saying that he was writing quickly to tell me that the day before there had been a knock at the door at our house in the village. There were two men and a woman. They said that they had come to give us a message from our eldest brother. Our father turned pale. They did not seem like emissaries who had come from the big Yeshiva in Budapest. He offered the visitors a seat, ordered all the children to gather around and then waited for us to enter in an oppressive silence. Once we were all seated he allowed the three of them to proceed with their message. "Our eldest brother," Yoni wrote me, "was in the habit of sending a letter home from the Yeshiva once a month, in which he told us what he was learning, and how he was getting by, how he was progressing up the rungs of faith and Torah knowledge, and all the things that his Rabbis had said in his praise. Our father was always happy to get these letters. He would read them aloud to us and keep each one of them in a special drawer in the bookcase along with the *Siddurim, Machzorim,* and *Chumashim,* the daily and High Holiday prayer books and copies of the Pentateuch. Now listen to this and try not to fall off your chair in shock, because what I am about to tell you is the God's honest truth. Our eldest brother, my dear Rozhi, never spent a single day in that Yeshiva. Not a single day. Everything he had written was entirely made up. He had joined up with a group of young men and women who were out to save the world. He had lied to our father out of a sense of respect. His group had joined the Brigades in Spain. These three otherworldly emissaries had come to tell us that he had fallen in battle over there. They told our father: God bless you, your son is a hero! Our father did not utter a single word, my dear Rozhi. The rest of us all remained silent as well. We were stunned and terrified. Now there is nothing left for you to do but fall silent as well. Do not write our father. He said that if you were to find out your heart might, God forbid, break and stop beating altogether. But our father's heart, though broken, continues beating. And your broken heart shall keep beating too, God willing. Your loving brother, Yoni." I kept this letter, which was written out on fine writing paper, after having read it over several times by myself. I read it aloud to you as well. The letter was left behind in Antwerp. So many things got left behind there.

I could not forgive my brother for having gone and died. You said to me, "You are right. If the dead only knew how much pain and suffering they inflict upon their loved ones left behind among the living they would refrain from dying. But they are ignorant of this fact. The noble ideals, Rozhi, which cause them to raise their eyes and discern things so far off in the distance, blinds them at the same time to what is right before their eyes. Noble ideals are a curse, but the world would be lost without them. I love your dead brother. Try to love him too. You don't have to forgive him in order to love him."

The children sit and play. Where is Manya? If they already took her to the border she probably made it there in an hour. If they did not take her there, how did she manage to make it just a few days after giving birth, and what about the newborn baby? She would not have set out if she was not already certain that she would make it with the baby in one piece and safely get over to the other side. Whom had she bribed? And how much had it cost her? How had she managed to collect the money that she needed for it? And if she had not collected it, who had given her the money? Jack? Did Jack have money? Where had he gotten it? All the women in our family are headed to Switzerland. Manya. Gizzy. Me. Manya is headed there without Jack. Gizzy is headed there without Zollie. And here I am headed there without you. And there is more. I have that block of soap with me. What does Manya have? And Gizzy? What do all these women have - these women whose husbands were taken away from them - as they head down their various paths trying to save their lives by paying sums that seem to have no limit, their children tagging along behind them as they all head to the one and only Switzerland. That is all that is left, now that Spain has closed its doors. Portugal has been sealed off for some time now, and America is too far away. Switzerland, the one and only possibility. But the road to Switzerland is expensive, and if you do not have the money - you are dead. All those husbands who have been taken prisoner, who did not manage to earn even a hundredth of what the road to Switzerland costs while they were still free, how did they manage to provide Manya and Gizzy and me with the exorbitant sums that they all could not possibly have had, but which, when the time came, they managed to come up with all the same? It is not like all of you robbed trains filled with gold in occupied France, or broke into bank vaults before fleeing Belgium. A woman does not know everything, after all, but I know that you were all straight shooters. So how did you manage to come up with these tremendous sums of money? It is not as though we were complete paupers. We each had a little something, you and I had a little between the two of us. Zollie had what he had mostly thanks to Gizzy, Manya had what she had thanks to Jack's mother. But all these little somethings taken together do not even begin to explain how we managed to survive through the war, have food to eat and a roof over our heads. Now that you are all gone, how is it that we are each trying purchase survival, me with my diamonds. Gizzy with her gold - is it gold? - And Manya, what did she have? If you were only here now perhaps I would ask you to tell me. Perhaps you would give me a truthful response. Perhaps you would try to avoid having to give me a direct answer, though I would not care about that, since who really cares where the air comes from when one is dying just to breathe? But you are not here now. I have only myself to ask, since I am certainly still breathing at the moment. Somehow I am still breathing. I have the air to ask my questions, but there is no air that might offer me a suitable response. But that is just another effect of all these cursed wars.

If Manya were here now and I were to tell her the thoughts that are running through my head, she would probably just say something like, "You're losing your mind." She would sit there and stare at me and just shrug her shoulders and stay silent, as though it was not even worth the trouble to talk to somebody like me. But she too was not here now. Had she made it to her destination? They had not caught her. There was no way. That would be simply unnatural. A woman like her always gets to where she is headed, whether she knows where it is or not. But at this point she knew.

The children sit there playing together; two brothers; they will never be separated. Yet my entire world is frayed. My distant father and my siblings, will I ever see them again? Manya, who was nearby, is gone. Will I see her again? Olga, my baby sister, is off in Palestine. Perhaps she is in Palestine - Who is ever going to see her in Palestine? Our eldest brother is dead. I will never even see his tombstone; if he even has one. And you, my dear, where art thou? And where is Jack, if he is even still alive? And Gizzy. And your brother Zollie - I never knew what was up with him. And Joss, and Fannie, and Arzhi, and your big sister Chana, who landed with her husband Mendel in Algeria, of all places. All of them torn apart and sent to the four corners of the earth. And me, me too, here I am torn asunder, just a single woman, all torn to pieces. And the children sit there playing. The two of them, too, are one single torn shred. Or perhaps they too are no more than separate shreds, each torn off on its own. There is no way that they know the answer, any more than I dare to find it out. Who truly dares to know anything at all in a world that is completely frayed, in tatters...

My sister Olga had been like a daughter to me. I was only four years older than her, but we were always more than mere sisters. She had forever been like my shadow, ever since she was a little child. Her mother, who was not my mother, loved her, but our father - at least this is the way I see things to this day - never forgave her for the fact that she was the first child born to his second wife. Her mother was aware of this fact and never forgave our father for it. Olga ran for her life from this mortal coil. When I headed to Belgium, it was not long before she left and came to see me. She was still just a child then. After staying at my place for just a day she said that she would sleep in the street if I did not find work for her so that she could get by on whatever pittance she might earn. That was the truth. That was her, through and through. Steadfast, innocent. The way she looked was exactly the way she was, with her black hair shining in a deep, hidden blue, like the hue of that bird of summer whose name I have forgotten. Her face was shapely and pale, as though some artist had carved her features out of fragile, white porcelain; and she was not all that tall but she seemed a statuesque girl nonetheless. She was beautiful and hungry. Not simply because she had not had much to eat along the way that took her from our little village in Hungary to those rented rooms in Antwerp. That was simply the nature of her beauty. I was a seamstress, but she did not know how to sew. I spoke German, and anyone who spoke nothing more than Yiddish could manage to understand bits and pieces of what I said, and somehow managed to fill in the missing spaces through guesswork. I, myself only understood a little Yiddish and had to fill in the blanks however I could. I quickly managed to get by with anyone I had to speak with, as though I were a locally born Jewish girl. Olga, however, only spoke Hungarian and was completely dependent on me. I am speaking of her, but she was not the only one. The whole lot of us were like so many leaves that had fallen from the tree and been gathered together in a heap by a stiff wind. We were now trying to connect with one another as though we might be able to thus turn ourselves into the foliage of a single tree once more. But the tree itself had been uprooted, and the leaves had all been torn away. Still we tried. Olga, me, you, all of us. It was a miracle, Moritz. We succeeded, somewhat, we were certainly more successful than anyone could have possibly, sensibly expected. We crowded together and connected with one another in order to survive, to live. We began to put down roots. But God clearly did not notice the miracle that we had worked with our own hands. An even greater wind came along and once again uprooted everything. Here we are now, no longer a heap of leaves which had been brought back to life and connected once more at the base to the branches of the tree that we created for ourselves. Once more the blown foliage has been torn away in the storm and scattered in every direction, to the point that none of us are capable anymore of even seeing the falling autumnal leaves of our lives, as it were. Is it possible that there will again be such a miracle? These leaves that had once been brought back to life, and then condemned to fall once more, could yet again be resuscitated, before they dry up completely beyond all hope?

I offered Olga to work side by side with me. She learned quickly, even though that there were two of us, it is not as though we began earning double. Olga was not at all embarrassed to ask around among all the members of our little group to see if any of them had any idea where she might find some more work. But she did not find a thing. I myself did not even bother asking because I knew that nothing at all would come of such inquiries. One day the three of us, Olga, you, and I, went to visit our distant cousins, the Baums. The son, Shlomo, or Shloimy, as we all called him, was there. He was immediately struck by a thunderbolt the moment he laid eyes on Olga. He was a rather handsome young man. His well-meaning, slightly shy smile had a way of winning over the heart of all who saw him. It was almost as though he were ashamed of his own beauty.

His mother Hensche, an ultra-orthodox woman who wore a wig - a wise, rather educated woman. It was even said that she had attended the university in Prague. She sat forever in her chair and ruled over the entire roost from that perch. She loved Shloimy more than any of her other sons and daughters. Not a single one of them spoke German, certainly not the flawless German, that their mother spoke. Nor even some broken version of the Hungarian language that she had taught herself in order to communicate with all the other members of her household.

Shloimy sat down next to Olga. His mother kept her eye on him constantly and her gaze tortured him. It was impossible for this fact to go unobserved, but he did not switch seats. I stared at the two of them. They were incredibly beautiful together. They spoke with one another in between long pauses filled with shy stretches of silence. I could not overhear what they were saying, but afterwards you told me that Shloimy had guessed at the fact, or rather seemed to know definitively, that Olga did not have a suitable job at which she might make a living. He himself was a salaried gem polisher and from time to time he would be asked to convey some of his employers' merchandise to the office of some well-known diamond dealers. You told me that he had informed you that they were, in fact, looking for a young female assistant. You went to see them with Olga. They said that they had never put out the word that they were looking for a female assistant, but if they even were in the market, they would have rejected her because she did not speak any useful language, neither Flemish, Yiddish, German, nor French. The Hungarian that she did speak did not count for anything in their eyes. It was only good for dealing with Hungarians. You told them that if she would be employed as a cleaning lady, there would be no need for her to talk. They relented. Shloimy had no idea how to thank you.

He was the first young man that Olga had met in Antwerp. Throughout all the time that the two of them spent in that city he remained the only young man in her eyes, and, I swear, that is how he will forever remain. They afforded one another a spring-like refuge in the very heart of autumn, and the freezing cold of those winter nights. In poverty, uprooted from the little village where her entire immediate and extended family lived, Olga seemed to blossom. If

I had not had you, I might have en-vied her. But as things stood, I was not jealous, rather I thanked the very heavens for having shone on Olga and covered her and Shloimy with that wonderful sort of love that makes a better person out of anyone who simply lays eyes on such a couple, in all their earthy simplicity. I remember that I said something like that to you once as we were walking arm in arm along the De Keyserlei. We were in love and so we spoke of lovers. You stopped for a moment, looked into my eyes and said to me, "Roszyka, the love story between Olga and Shloimy is in search of a playwright interested in penning a tragedy." I was terrified. I stopped in my tracks and gave you a questioning look, a look filled with rebuke, with amazement, a look that inflicted pain, , a look filled with fear, like someone who can not believe what she is hear-ing but is in shock all the same, and I said, "Moritz, are you playing the prophet with me, or is the-re something you know that I don't?" You told me that it was not at all a prophecy, nor were you trying to tell me that you knew something I did not. "All that I said," as you put it, "was that it is big love, and now just forget everything I said." We walked on a little further until stopping to have a sip of something at a cafe, and we seemed for all the world like any of the other unconcerned patrons sitting around sipping and smoking and chatting away, but the two of us, as I recall, were silent. Big love. That was all you said. But big love between whom?

Olga and I worked together into the afternoon, and then she would leave me alone to work as the cleaning lady at the office of the diamond dealers until late in the evening. Afterwards, she and Shloimy would meet up and while away the hours until midnight in the midst of a group of revisionists, or at their club. Of the girls from back home who were in Antwerp, one became a communist, the second became a revisionist, and the third, being myself, was not looking for anything more than peace and quiet, without all the ups and downs of the road, and so I found myself Moritz Mayer, who looked down, in his heart, on all those folks smitten with their various -isms - as you referred to them - although you yourself were addicted to Hegel, along with the Hebrew choir that you conducted, and sitting and learning with the big *Talmidei Chachamim*, the Torah scholars, and chess; and when you were not already occupied trying to come up with some new insight on behalf of the gem polishers and the diamond cutters, your whole being was consumed with trying to make a living. At night you would spread out a big roll of white paper and sketch the most wonderful charcoal portraits of all the people that you had come across during the day. You would immediately tear up these same drawings, saying that you did not want anyone to possibly glimpse in those portraits any of the dreams, both large and small, that found refuge behind the false front of these acquaintances' features. All of this was more than enough for me. It was almost beyond what I could even handle. Quite often everyone would be invited over to our tiny apartment for a Friday night meal, or for *Kiddush Shabbos* morning. It would get crowded. My sisters and their boyfriends would show up, along with your brother and his wife Gizzy; Josh and Fanny; one or two, or even more, of the Schick siblings; my beautiful girlfriend Erszy, who would show up accompanied by one man one week, and by another man the next week. She had no idea why she had even showed up with the first one, nor why she had broken up with him in favor of the second. Then there was little Edelstein, all ragged and thin, as though he were constantly sick. He was a violinist, a genius, both in his own eyes and yours, who, if he was not invited to play at some paupers' wedding from time to time, was left without even that sorry small change that somehow miraculously found its way into his pockets. He usually brought along with his wife, my cousin Helen, a large, fleshy woman who lorded it over him shamelessly to no end. She was constantly gossiping away in a loud voice, and complaining incessantly at the same time of how bitter her life was. And there were others. We were a lively group that had come to form a sort of little island of our own in Antwerp, as we tried to find our own little patch of heaven for the bit of ground we had managed to occupy. This illustrative metaphor of a little patch of heaven over a bit of ground is not my own, of course. It came out of your own mouth one afternoon after the whole lot of them had left and gone home.

Where are they all now?

In the midst of the continuous confusion of things of everyone busy speaking to each other without even stopping a moment to listen, not taking the time so that they might respond, everyone still knew everything that was said and heard it all. They knew what was and they knew what the prophets said was going to be. They knew all about the street and the city, the country and the entire world, even the goings on up in heaven. The whole lot of us, through all the time spent toiling away worriedly, day after day each day of the week, we bonded as a group into a rising hustle and bustle of joy, and comfort, and yes, even hope. Manya, who was a full, active, energetic partner in this wonderful riot of humanity, would constantly find herself reaching some sudden impasse from which she would emerge almost unexpectedly to launch a hardheaded attack on Olga. She would suddenly come out with some statement against Olga and Shloimy in which the word 'fascist' seemed to find its way, as though it had suddenly fallen into the midst of her discourse out of the clear blue sky. When neither Olga nor Shloimy deigned to offer a response, Manya would stand there staring at the people present all around her as though she were of-fended to the very core of her soul. She would then raise her voice and pronounce rather loudly something like, "Look at these two little fascist lovebirds, heading off to their little clubs at night in their uniforms, and singing their little songs of hellfire, blood, and brimstone, issuing threats in the name of some scurrilous patriotism against their very people, and everyone everywhere throughout the entire universe. I am ashamed to say that I am her sister." She would go absolutely insane when you would hug her, Moritz. You murmured all sorts of affectionate things in order to try to get her to calm down in front of all assembled, trying not to get dragged into the polemic that she was always attempting to bring down on all of us. Her mind would come completely unhinged when Shloimy would look at her and smile his soft, shy smile and hold his tongue without making a sound. She would scream, "What are you smiling at me like that for, like some imbecile? Look at him sitting there laughing at me right in my face. Look at how my sister sits there holding his horny jeweler's hand in her soft, delicate palm, smiling right alongside him and mocking me and the rest of you outright. But you, all of you, what do you do? You see it all just like me but you say nothing, you just sit there and stare and cloak yourselves in your cowardly righteousness. I've had it with the whole lot of you. Jack, you better get out of here. Right away, you better leave. And you're taking me with you. Don't leave me here another second. Rozhi, you're ridiculous the way you invite this absurd little band in-to your home and refuse to toss them all straight down the stairs. But me, me you're basically telling to get lost. Let's go Jack. We don't belong here." She would walk out and slam the door behind her, not with Jack, but making a show of heading out even before he could leave. Everyone would start to smile as soon as the door closed, knowing full well that just a few days later they would all be back crowding into my little apartment, and dear Manya would be right there with them. Her heart would go out to all of them until the tempest would take over once more and waken the demons that were ever lurking inside her, just waiting for the opportunity to run wild for a moment and wreak havoc in the face of all. Ah, my dear sisters.

The days stretched on by. Madame Baum, regal matron that she was, refused to give her son Shloimy her blessing. The word was that she had neither forbidden the relationship outright, but she had also refused to condone it, as though she were hoping that their love would eventually die down like a flame on its own anyway. When it was done, it would have completely consumed the wick as well. But it did not die down. It was never said openly in the mother's name that she had in mind a more fruitful *Shidduch*, a better match for her beloved son than a completely uneducated village girl, a two-bit seamstress who spent time washing the floors and dusting the furniture and display cases at a diamond dealer's office. She was too intelligent to allow herself to talk about the faults, of which even her own children had their fair share. They seemed more the product of Kosice than Prague. Shloimy, of course, could not openly defy his mother's word, but at the same time he refused to give in either to her or to his brothers, who pushed him to accept the reality of the situation, telling him that their mother was like some sort of law of nature itself. For Olga's sake he fought the one battle that he could possibly win - Palestine.

One could easily interpret the choice of Palestine as an innocent one, a sort of passing blemish that would fade with time. A dream that any normal person would have woken from eventually. But it was not possible to ban Palestine the same way that one could ban a certain *Shidduch*. The rules implied by the commandment to honor one's father and mother did not apply to Palestine the same way that they did when it came to weddings and marriages.

Shloimy showed up at our place one day by himself. Olga had told us that he was on his way. When he showed up she said that she had to take care of Erwin. The boy followed her everywhere and she loved him like a mother. Here he was crying, so please, she said, sit down and talk to Shloimy. Everything that he says, know that I am in full agreement with it. Shloimy said that he did not hear Erwin crying and before the boy began to cry it was better if he and Olga said what they had to say to us together. So Olga sat down. I was sure that Shloimy would talk the same way that he smiled, but Shloimy did not smile at all, he just spoke in a low, determined voice. The things he said seemed set in a stone the purpose for which he had quarried quite some time ago. "I have come to ask for Olga's hand in marriage. Here in Belgium the two of you are like the father and mother that she left behind in Hungary. I am not going to marry her tomorrow, but I have come to ask you today that you give her away to me in the future. So why have I come to you now? I have come, as it were, to deposit my solemn word with you that I intend to take her for my wife even if there are delays. Neither my mother nor my siblings know about this oath of mine which I am offering you. But Olga is not theirs. You are the ones who need to know. She belongs to you." I was exceptionally embarrassed. You were silent for a moment and then you broke out laughing and shattered the rather serious moment to pieces. I felt like you were acting like a wild man, like someone completely devoid of all sensitivity.

You clapped Shloimy on the shoulder and said to him, "Now that you've said the piece that I suppose you spent quite a long time working up and learning by heart, we can have ourselves a real talk."

"That's why I'm here," Shloimy said. He was easy, balanced, confident. He said things that seemed to me to be completely absurd.

I knew that he was a revisionist. He referred to himself as Beitar member who had taken a strict vow to make Aliyah and head to Zion. I had never heard the words 'to Zion' before. He said it in Hebrew, as though it were a written part of the sacred Torah. You understood. You were an ex-pert in these matters. But not me. He explained that he was talking about what I referred to as 'Palestine', but that 'Palestine' and 'Zion' were not the same thing. I failed to grasp what he was getting at. But you, it would seem, caught his intention right away. He spoke about a vow to take back our homeland, to conquer it by force, with weapons. I stared at him, this charming young man, the pampered son of an ultra-orthodox family who in their wildest dreams never dared to go beyond the little alley-ways where the deals went down and the haberdashery stood, there where the paradise of maximum economic well-being hid; I stared at him and tried to find the traces of that man heading off to Zion to conquer the homeland and I could not find him anywhere. Olga, whom I could not have possibly imagined being familiar with the jargon that Shloimy was employing so naturally that it absolutely stunned me, Olga sat there listening like she knew full well just what he was talking about. She was nodding away like a complete, sworn partner-in-crime, ready to head off with this kid to Zion to conquer the homeland with cold steel arms in those fragile porcelain hands of hers. You asked him if he and Olga had a certificate and he said that they did not. Despite that fact, however he was intent on heading off to Palestine without the authorization of the ruling powers, and Olga would go with him. They would be married the night before they headed off, and no one in the world was going to stop them.

"And when will that be," I asked in amazement. "How long are the two of you going to go around like this?"

"Until we make *Aliyah* to Zion. That's the date!" Shloimy said.

"And what date is that exactly?" I persisted, while you, Moritz, answered on his behalf, "Any day now, like the Messiah," and you smiled a wan smile, like someone who was in on some secret. I was shocked. But not you. You got up, walked over to Olga, pulled her up out of her chair and made her stand next to you. You asked Shloimy to get up too, wrapped your arms around their shoulders and said, in a tone that, it seemed to me, was a little bit too playful, "*Mazal Tov* to both of you," and you immediately turned to me and added, "Rozhika, he has taken a vow, and you and I are now a party to that vow as well. We are going to make the wedding for you." Olga spoke up for the first time and said that all they wanted was a Rabbi and a *Chuppah*, an official wedding ceremony, nobody needed to be invited or be in on it. "We don't need R.S.V.P.'s, we don't need a party. All we need is the two of you and a *Minyan*, a quorum of men - or even just the two of you, without the *Minyan*." I got up as well, threw my arms around my little sister and covered her with kisses. I felt her skin moisten with my tears. In my heart I could not decide if I was simply standing by while my baby sister was subjected to a tremendous tragedy, or if rather you and I, Moritz, had become accomplices, in that very moment, in affording her something like the secret of boundless happiness.

We did not discuss this situation with a single soul. Quite a bit of time had passed when one day Olga came home and told us that Shloimy was going to be boarding a ship in Italy, where he was headed by train. She would be boarding a ship a few days afterwards that would be travelling from Antwerp to Portugal, from Portugal to Tangier, and then from Tangier on to Palestine, where he would be waiting for her.

The evening that Shloimy was to board the train we prepared a modest wedding ceremony. You brought all of his brothers and sisters to the party, along with my brother and your brother, every man with his wife, each wife with her spouse. And you even got Shloimy's mother, old Madame Baum, to come. Before the actual *Chuppah*, she asked to be brought over to where Olga was standing. She stretched out her hand that was somewhat limp from a partial paralysis she had suffered, and said in a voice almost as limp as her hand, before everyone assembled there, "Kiss me, my daughter." Olga curtsied as though in the presence of the Queen. She took her future mother-in-law's hand and kissed it and then bent down and kissed her on her forehead, stood up tall and said, "I am glad that you are here with us, Mother." She then immediately averted her gaze, looking out over the old woman's head and smiled to the right in my direction, and to the left at Manya where she stood, and then looked out at all the women standing there facing her, more beautiful than any other bride in the world.

After the *Chuppah* and the full wedding ceremony in accordance with every letter of the law, with quite a bit more than the required quorum. Of course, there was a light meal, and then we all quickly got up and accompanied Shloimy down to the train station. There was a group of boys and girls there who were all members of Beitar, waiting on the platform to say goodbye to their childhood friend. They all began dancing the Hora. You joined in. Not me. The steam from the locomotive that shot out from the low belly of the train seemed to slither along the platform and curl around the legs of the dancers. I looked on at the scene and it seemed like you were all dancing in a cloud. Shloimy hugged his wife with whom he had not had even a moment alone since the *Chuppah*, and boarded the train. He stood there in the doorway and joined in singing a song with his friends. That seemed to me like it was the sign for the train to start heading out. He stood there in that open doorway while Olga stood before him on the platform singing with the group of his friends who had come down to see him off. She was the only one I saw. She was the only one that I heard, as Shloimy disappeared in a cloud.

About ten days later just the two of us went down with Olga to the port to see her off. It was towards the end of August. On the first of September she arrived in Portugal and that very day the news went out that no more ships would be setting out from the country in any direction whatsoever. The Germans had invaded Poland, and two days later England declared war and closed off the Strait of Gibraltar. Olga was stranded in Portugal. We received a single postcard from her in Antwerp, in which she wrote, "Don't ask me how I managed to survive in Portugal. The months were interminably long. But it does not matter anymore. Tomorrow I will be heading out to Palestine. I have had no contact with Shloimy, I do not even have an address for him, but I know that he will be waiting for me. All else will be forgotten." When she arrived, Shloimy was not there. He had volunteered for the British army and gone off to war. We only heard about all this two years later, in Marseille. Olga wrote to Belgium and made anyone she had written to swear that they would not tell old Madame Baum that Shloimy had been taken prisoner. She included a letter that was intended to seem as though it had been written by Shloimy himself to his mother. "She does not see all that well," she wrote, "so you will have to read the letter to her. In it, Shloimy tells all about his life in Palestine, about working the land, paving the roads. Includes a few words about the fact that Shloimy, the light of his loving wife's life, is doing well, thank God. It was painful for me to write this letter. I had to overcome a sort of inner revolt at each word that I penned. I tried to guess at what Shloimy would have written, if he had penned the letter himself, what a son who is completely consumed by trying to make it in the Land of Israel would have written to his distant mother across the sea. It was not easy, but until he returns, I will write more from ti-me to time in his name. His elderly mother would simply die if she knew that he has been taken prisoner. She would never forgive me. If he had not fallen in love with some barefoot girl from out of town, he would have eventually found himself a proper girl from Antwerp and given up, in the end, on the idea of going off to Palestine. But I know my Shloimy. That never would have happened. And even if he had not been taken prisoner, she would never forgive me for the fact that that alternate reality did not come to pass. Remember, you are sworn to secrecy about all of this." In that same letter she told me that she was working as a nanny, taking care of the children in the Kaiser family, along with serving as the cook and cleaning lady in their home. I knew Kaiser. He was a fervent Beitar man and had taken Shloimy under his wing. He had headed off to Palestine as a sort of advance scout on behalf of the rest of the group all too many years ago, only to find himself the daughter of some wealthy landowner, whom he married and then promptly cut himself off from all the other Beitar members back in Antwerp as he turned into some big businessman. As a result of his tremendous fondness for Shloimy he had offered Olga a place to live and a sort of allowance in exchange for her services. But she was planning on leaving herself, she wrote, and enlisting with the British army as well. She owed that much to Shloimy.

Jackie suddenly called out to me and cut off my reverie. He had gotten into some sort of minor argument with Erwin over their game of chess. I told him that I did not understand the game one bit, but he said that it was not about chess, but something else.

"Erwin says that if you touch the piece, then you have to make a move with it, but I say that this rule is wrong because everyone is entitled to make a mistake. Part of the game is learning to forgive the other person when they make a mistake. Erwin says that part of the game is learning that when you make a mistake you have to pay the price. What do you say, Ma?"

"I say you are both right. I have seen things happen both ways in my life. I certainly love it when someone is forgiving, but I myself am willing to forgive someone who says that there is nothing you can do about the rules."

"Not me," said Jackie, and he went over to the board, picked up all the pieces rather demonstrably right before Erwin's astounded eyes, and said, "This way you can not play at all. I'm going to sleep." Erwin did not respond. I stared at him and saw the exhaustion in his face. He came over to me, sat down next to me, rested his head on my shoulder and immediately fell asleep. I got up cautiously and picked him up. I put him down on the bed next to his brother and went back to my seat. I said to myself, here I am, thinking about everything I knew to have been under the sun and about things I believed will be and turned out not to happen at all, and things which I had no idea that they could be, nor will yet be, even though I already knew exactly how things went in the past. And then it seemed to me that I could see you so clearly once more, dancing in a cloud on that train platform in Antwerp.

I have no idea if I fell asleep as well. I heard a rustling just outside the door and I was immediately on alert, like someone who has woken

up all of a sudden, or been cast to the ground after hovering somewhere in between waking and sleeping. I fixed my gaze on the door
without moving from where I sat. I saw a white piece of folded paper
slip into the room through the narrow slit between the bottom of the
door and the floor. I waited there, frozen still in my seat. Only after
waiting there a little while did I get up and walk over on tiptoe to the
door, as though it were imperative that no one hear that my children
and I were in the apartment. I picked up the note, went back over to
my seat on tiptoe, and stared at the piece of paper still folded in my
hands. I did not dare open it. The time had come. I had been waiting
for some news. Like all news, it posed a certain threat. I opened the
note. In big block letters written in black ink, in French, it said, "St.
Pierre's Cathedral, Sunday, the 7th of the month, at 11:00, by yourself, inside the church, right inside the front door." It was the doctor,
the priest. The man I had said goodbye to as though I would see him
again ever. I read the sentence over two, three, maybe four times,
or more. The children slept. I understood every word, but I thought
all the same that Erwin might read it and understand the things that
I had read and perhaps failed to understand. I did not wake him. I
understood the meaning of the words. There was no real difficulty in
that - but the real story, what was the real story here? I wanted to sit
with someone and try to decipher every last hidden meaning in that
message, but with whom could I share such a moment - with Erwin,
with Jackie? There was no way that they could possibly have known
any more than I did. I did not wake them. St. Pierre's Cathedral?
What is this cathedral that is apparently so very well known by name
throughout all of Saint-Claude? Its spires can be seen from everywhere, and yet I do not have the faintest idea where it is even located.

Sunday. I was suddenly aware of the fact that I had absolutely no
idea if today was Monday, or Tuesday, or Friday, or even Saturday,
so how would I know when it was Sunday? I had apparently already
lost track of the days while I was at the clinic in Annemasse. Since
that moment it seems I had lived like an animal in the wild who is
completely unaware of the fact that the concept of time exists altogether in the world. It knows only the light of day and the dark of

night, following each other in turn, but nothing of minutes and hours, or days, weeks and months, life and death - nothing at all. When would it be Sunday, the seventh day of the month, at 11:00 - was that tomorrow? The next day? How could I possibly know when it was if I had no idea what day of the month it was today, having lost all sense of time altogether? Whom could I ask? It was clear to me that I would have to ask, but how would I phrase the question without stirring the other's pity, and whom could I ask without arousing their suspicions? By myself. Why by myself? And where was I supposed to leave the children while I would be in that place, on that day, at that time? How long would I have to be there? And the children - I was going to have to leave them somewhere by themselves. How long would it be before they became terrified? Doctor DuPont. Why was he called a doctor and not a priest? Why should he be called a doctor in the cathedral, and not a priest in the cathedral. Where had he suddenly come from once more? When I was sure that they had already tortured him long ago over his betrayal of the homeland. When I had already suffered terribly over the fact that because of me and my children, they had long since wiped him off the face of the earth? What did he want? What was he, in fact? Some doctor-priest for the sake of heaven, a man of God prior to the war and throughout the war as well, who risking his life on a daily basis? Or was he perhaps just some impostor in priestly raiment, a smuggler for the money. Was he forced to be a traitor or had he chosen the role of his own free will? I was secretly ashamed of the fact that I was allowing myself to indulge in such suspicions over the most righteous one of them all. I immediately told myself that I deserved to be pardoned because I was not really being suspicious but was simply posing the questions that anyone who wants to stay alive absolutely has to ask themselves. It is not that I was being overly cautious but I was simply fulfilling my obligation to question everything that was, simply because somebody else had put their faith in it. Either way, I had no choice but to show up at that meeting. I was convinced that my life depended on it, but my life was at that selfsame moment hanging in the balance in any case since how, dear God, how was I going to do what the note, which had been slipped under my door asked me to do?

In the window night had already fallen. The children were still sleeping, but as quite a bit of time had passed since their last meal, I expected them to wake up at any moment out of hunger. I had not yet come to an internal decision as to whether it would be a good idea to ask their advice about the note and what was written there. Would do better to wait a little while longer and prepare myself for the meeting before letting them in on any of it, or before asking them? For a moment I thought of going to see the neighbor's wife and telling her that I needed to exchange some money and asking her to help me as she had said she would. During the course of that brief ex-change I could try to find out from her what day it was, where the cathedral was located and how to get there. Perhaps she could walk on ahead of me the way that she had done that day we had gone to the hospital. But I immediately discarded such thoughts because I had no idea how I would possibly discuss so many complicated things with her without my trusty translator Erwin. He did not yet even know a thing about the existence of this note, and as I was still unsure whether I would tell him anything about it at all I looked once more at the writing. The few words looked more and more hostile to me. That is how things go when a woman is left to weigh up her options all by herself, options that she can not possibly properly weigh up alone. Solitude, Moritz, is part of the torture. But being all alone is much worse. It is a curse. You had not disappeared from my solitude. You were too far to touch, too far to see, too far to hear, but you were there. Perhaps you were no more than a prayer; but you were there. In the face of my being all alone, however, you had completely disappeared. You were gone completely. Not even that prayer was left.

My helplessness paralyzed me. I felt it crawling through me and crushing my heart and my spirit and my mind, until suddenly, a mere moment before it completely subdued me, I rose from my seat. I stood there for a second, filled my lungs with air as though steeling myself to immediately do what I was suddenly certain that I absolutely had to do. I woke the children. Erwin woke up immediately as usual and leaped to his feet, while Jackie, as usual, curled up once more, twisted up his face in protest over the fact that someone had disturbed his sleep, and made little plaintive noises. In the end, he too got up, however unwillingly. He stared out the darkened window. "Are we heading out," he said, "in the middle of the night?"

"Not yet," I replied. "First we are going to wash up, have a bite to eat, and talk."

Jackie grumbled some more. "I am not hungry. I don't like the food here. Let me sleep. Talk to Erwin. Let me sleep."

Erwin had already walked over to wash up. I hugged Jackie's slack shoulders and said to him, "I want to ask your advice, my dear Jackie, I need you now." He hung both his arms around my neck and after a few moments he slipped from my embrace and went over to wash up as well. Erwin was already sitting there ready to hear whatever new events had taken place while he was sleeping, but I told him that I would first prepare a little something light to eat and then we would all talk at the table, the three of us, Erwin, Jackie and I, just as a family ought to do.

Erwin barely touched the food. Jackie chewed his food quickly and asked for more. I slowly drank my tea until it was completely gone cold. I looked at the children and told myself that from the outset I ought to have known that they were the only people I could turn to for advice, and not because I had no one else with me but them, and not because they had the right to have their say when it came to things that concerned their own lives, but simply because I could not have asked for any better, more trustworthy advisors than them, even if I had had someone else to turn to, even if all that was required of me was to look out for them with all my heart like any mother would with her little children. I was proud of myself for being so proud of them.

I spread the note open before them. Erwin got lost reading that single sentence as though it were an entire chapter in a book.

Jackie said impatiently, "Read it out loud," and Erwin read it out loud.

"So what, basically," Jackie wondered, "What, huh? But you're not going to go by yourself. I won't let you. Even if you have to go by yourself, I'm going with you. When is Sunday?"

"I have no idea, Jackie," I answered. "The days have gotten all confused."

"Maybe it was today and we already missed it," Jackie said.

"How could it be today?" Erwin objected. "They only brought the note today, after the 11:00 listed in the note. Could it have been today? It could not have been today. Good thing you understand. I think it must be tomorrow. Today, I think, is Saturday. Sunday is tomorrow. That's what I think."

I looked at Erwin in tremendous amazement. "Saturday? How do you know that today is Saturday?"

"I don't know how. Every day I just know what day it is. That's how it is. You don't have to be all that clever. It's a simply thing, really." Jackie gave me a look of complicity and said, without taking his eyes off me, "If it is such a simple thing and you don't have to be all that clever and you really know what day it is, then why did you say that you think today is Saturday? If somebody knows something they don't just think it. If somebody thinks something then they don't really know it. I do not know if tomorrow is Sunday. Mom does not know either. And neither do you. You just think you do. Mom can't go to the cathedral tomorrow just because you think it is Sunday. And what if it isn't Sunday?"

I smiled, amused for a mere second. My compulsive tendency to turn specifics into general rules remained unremitted. I immediately became serious and told myself that there is never a Sunday anywhere in the world that is not commonly agreed to be Sunday, there is no Sunday and no day altogether for anyone who mistakes it, or for anyone for that matter who is right about it either. The time that Erwin had been keeping track of disappeared with the time that the rest of us had lost. The question of when it would be Sunday became a strange sort of problem for which the three of us were unable to come up with a suitable solution. Erwin let it go.

"Tomorrow or the next day, it does not matter, you are not going to go to the meeting by yourself. I trust the priest. He knows full well that you can not walk through Saint-Claude all by yourself. Why does he ask you anyway to do such a thing? There must be some explanation that we are not aware of, Ma. But you are not going to go by yourself. If you do go, it will only seem like you are alone. We will be there with you every step of the way. As far as the actual cathedral goes, you will enter by yourself, if need be. But that's it." Jackie listened. A moment later he said, "Even when it comes to the cathedral, it will only seem like you went in by yourself. We will sneak inside. Are there guards? Doesn't matter. We're not going to wait for you outside. What if you don't come back? How long are we supposed to wait? Where will we go if we wait and you never show up? Are we supposed to go looking for you in the cathedral? You'll never find anyone who gets lost in one of those places. It's dark. There are columns, crosses. Everywhere. It's terrifying. I saw it once. You're not going anywhere, Ma. I don't trust this priest."

I had no response for the unsettling uncertainties that were constantly assailing me, but it was clear to me that I had to take it upon myself to get Jackie to relax, because there was no way that we could not obey the order we had received in the note. But Erwin, who I was afraid would lose his patience, did not give me a chance and took it upon himself to do the work of getting his brother to calm down with a show of patience that once more left me amazed. "You're right," he said to his brother. "You're right about it all, but how are we going to get out of here, Jackie, if we don't get out of here? How will we make it to Switzerland if we don't go to Switzerland? How would we have made it this far if we had not left Marseille to begin with? We were afraid. The whole way we were afraid. We were afraid everywhere we went. But we went. We had to go. We were afraid to be left alone but we were never really alone. We'll never be alone. Mom is with the two of us, I'm with you, you're with both of us. You're here with me. Nobody is all alone, Jackie."

Jackie listened. I could tell from the look on his face that as much as what his brother said seemed right in his eyes, it was not enough to allay his fears.

"Going to the cathedral is not the same thing as going to Switzerland. Nobody is going to be all alone as long as we all stay together here until we all head off together for Switzerland." As he said these things he turned to me and gave me a look like he was asking for my support, but Erwin turned to me himself and said, "We'll take you to the cathedral, Ma. I think that I spotted it when we went to the hospital. I remember the way. You too," Erwin turned to Jackie, "you also remember it. I'm sure of it. You remember it perfectly." "When are we going to go?" asked Jackie.

"Sunday," Erwin replied.

"What day is Sunday?"

"Tomorrow is Sunday."

"You just think it's tomorrow. Maybe it's not tomorrow. How are going to know if it's tomorrow? I'm not going to go ask the neighbor's wife."

"Me neither. We'll get a newspaper."

"Where are you going to get a newspaper from? What's in the newspaper?" There was no way for Jackie to have known that they wrote the date in the newspapers. I think that up until that day all that he knew of the papers was that they contained news about the war, things that we said we had read in the papers when we talked about them.

"The newspapers tell you what day it is."

"What are you talking about? Just because we don't know? Everyone else knows."

"It seems not everybody does, but either way, that's how it is, Jackie. Every day the papers tell you what day it is. I'm going to go get us a newspaper."

"By yourself?"

"You want to come with me?"

"And Mom is going to stay here by herself?" He looked at me and checked my face, and without taking his eyes off me he said to Erwin, "How do you know where to find a newspaper around here?"

"I saw one not far from here, in a pipe shop, Jackie."

Jackie turned away from me and gave Erwin a mocking look as he said, "A pipe shop? This whole town is full of pipes. Pipes. Pipes are not the same thing as newspapers. You're going to go into a pipe shop and they're going to ask you what a kid is doing in a pipe shop, and you're going to tell them that you've come to buy a newspaper? And you want me to come with you and leave Mom behind here until they're done figuring out just what we're doing in a pipe shop? What are you crazy?"

I could not keep myself from laughing. Jackie was offended. I hugged him, pulled him close to my breast and said to him, "You're wonderful, Jackie, everything is just so very funny."

Jackie pulled away from me and cried out, "What's so funny? You don't have to laugh at me."

"God forbid, God forbid, sweetheart," I said to him, and pulled him close once more. "I wasn't laughing at you, not at all, I was laugh-

ing with you. What's so funny? The fact that we have to go looking
for a newspaper just to find out what day it is today. That's funny. It's
funny that we have to go looking for it in a pipe shop, that somebody
slips a simple note under the door and it completely upends our lives
to the point that we have no idea when we are going to go, or how
to go, or if we should even go at all. It's just a note, after all, Jackie.
That's funny."

"I don't find it funny at all," Jackie said.

"You're right," I said to him. "It's so not funny that I just had to
laugh, Jackie, because it's so very serious. What pipes, Erwin, what's
with the pipes?"

"At the bottom of the street," said Erwin, who was standing there
waiting for us to calm down, "there's a pipe shop where I saw they
also have souvenirs, and postcards, and newspapers. It's just a five
minute walk. I'm going to go there now, buy a newspaper and come
back, and that's it. As far as I'm concerned I don't even have to go
because today is Saturday and tomorrow is Sunday, and I know that,
but you don't and neither does Jackie."

"And you're not even sure!" Jackie immediately added.

"That may be," Erwin said. "That's why I'm going."

The children looked at me. They were waiting for me to decide.
"It's dark, kids. I think the shops are probably closed by now."

"So what are we going to do?" Jackie asked, as it seemed he had
already come to terms with the idea that he was going to head out
with his brother, and now, after that whole struggle, here I was dashing all their plans. There was a hint of severe disappointment in his
voice. I understood him perfectly well. What I had said when I pronounced the words, "It's dark, kids," was a sort of announcement that
there had never really been anything to begin with to our little battle
over whether or not we were going to make the first move in taking
our fate into our own hands, because it was not at all in our hands,
whether by the light of day because it was light outside, or in the
dark because it was dark, or at any time whatsoever, simply because
that was the wrong time, whatever time it might be, since time was
in charge of us and we were no longer in charge of time. But then -
perhaps because I apparently did not put all that much faith in this
last thought that flitted through my mind, which seemed to contain

too much desperation for a woman like me who, along with her children, had made it from Marseille all the way up to this point precisely
because we had not allowed time to rule us any more than we ruled
it - I said to Erwin and Jackie, "Perhaps the darkness outside is just
due to the early nightfall in winter and not because it is really all that
late already. Get your coats. The three of us are going to go buy ourselves a pipe. We'll give it to the priest when we see him tomorrow. A
woman in a pipe shop is a bit strange, but it's no worse than a few kids
in a pipe shop." In a matter of seconds the children had their heavy
overcoats on, and I put on my shoes and wrapped myself in my own
coat and put a warm scarf over my head, tying the ends around my
neck, and the three of us left to go buy a newspaper at the pipe shop
as though we were not completely filled with fear and utter terror.

There was absolutely no one in the street and it was completely
dark. A few lights glinted from afar on high, some red, some green,
and a very few were plain white. The snow swallowed the sound of
our footsteps. The heavens overhead were like some chilly, purplish
sheet of steel, and the white scythe of the moon was planted there like
some artist's signature in its shiny, metallic sheen. We did not hold
hands. We were like three murky shadows moving through the chan-
nels of the freezing night heading nowhere for no reason whatsoever.
We had only reached this path to begin with because we had decided
to act like free people for a moment and stand up to our fears. I knew
well, as I am pretty sure the children knew too, that it was completely impossible that there was any open shop on that particular night,
down that particular street, in that particular town.

Suddenly, through the darkness, we saw the figure of a familiar
shadow pass us by like the wind, and we noticed that it came to rest
as though it had flown down from the very heavens and landed a
little way off in the street and was now walking along hunched over
ahead of us. We stopped in our tracks, scared at first. Then we took a
few more steps, and without exchanging or saying a word, we turned
around and went back the way that we had come in the direction of
the house, and we did not look over our shoulders until we had gone
up to our little room and closed the door behind us. We took off our
coats and put them away, sat down at the table and did not say a single
word to one another. It was not clear to any of us - at least it was not

clear to me, and I suppose it was no clearer to Erwin or Jackie for that matter - why we had stopped walking like that and turned back the way that we had come. The children did not ask any questions and did not demand an explanation, and I, for my part, did not ask them anything and did not offer any explanation. I had turned around because I had panicked. Not because of the shadow. I had panicked because I realized that I was not free after all, that there was someone watching my every move, that before I even knew I was headed out in the night, that someone was already out there walking on ahead of me, and whether that shadow was actually a person or simply some sort of a ghost or a mere gust of wind, I felt threatened by the very fact of being exposed, and it would be better if I ran for it, even if just to return to a place where I could once more nourish the illusion that my privacy had not been completely violated. The children had panicked as well. But they had certainly not panicked for the same reasons that I had. One of them had perhaps panicked because of the shadow, while the other had perhaps panicked because of the wind, or ghost, or whatever it was. Both of them had perhaps panicked as one simply because of the murky mysteries through which they suddenly found themselves shuffling along.

A moment later there was a knock at the door. When I heard it, it seemed to me like I had actually been expecting it. Of course, the neighbor's wife was there in the doorway. She did not come inside. Erwin, who had opened the door, stood there next to her. From where she stood she surveyed the room. I got up to greet her and offered her a seat. She did not answer me but simply said, "You did not have to run away from us like thieves in the night. My husband and I deserved better than that. We have been looking out for you like our very own flesh and blood. I offered you more assistance than you could ever have expected. My husband did not even close his eyes at night for fear of not being on the lookout for any saboteur who might be lurking and come looking for you. It's not about the bill. You paid everything that we were owed. But to run off like that as though you suspected that we might turn you in if you left - that, we did not deserve." She spoke softly. She hissed each sentence between clenched teeth as though she were afraid that her anger might throw her jaws so wide open that she would no longer be able to contain it altogether.

I was taken aback. I remembered that she had said to me, during the course of her previous visit, "You people are free to do as you please. The same way you knew how to make your way here, though no one knows how you did, so you will know how to leave without anyone else knowing how either." I remembered it word for word. I remembered the tone she had used when she said it, and yet here she was, like some wounded wild animal simply because we had done, as it were, precisely what she had said that we were completely free to do. I did not know whether to tell her that we had not been in the process of leaving but were simply headed out to buy a newspaper and then come back, and not simply because it seemed that she would not even believe me, but also - and perhaps primarily - because I refused to pawn my freedom simply in order to appease her anger, and also because I did not know if it was proper to remind her of what she had said previously, since that probably would not have helped at all, one way or the other. She felt herself betrayed to the point that I was sure she would fervently deny what she had said anyway. So I remained silent and waited for her to continue her attack against our apparent ingratitude.

"You are a strange woman, Madame Mayer. You did not set foot anywhere in Saint-Claude without me. And your fear was not for nothing. By right you should have been even more afraid than you actually were. You were not and are still not aware of how many snakes there are lying around beneath every single stone, all kinds of snakes, and they are all poisonous, and they all bite. I am well aware of this fact. My husband is well aware of it. We did not owe you a thing. We felt love for Madame Ravel just as we felt love for you and your children, and even though we did not believe you nor Madame Ravel, we said that we would help you out because the day will come - in heaven or even here on earth - when it will be good that they know up there, or down here, that we did something on behalf of someone who could not actually do it for themselves. That's all. If you really want to know, that's all there is to it. And all of a sudden none of that matters. All of a sudden somebody comes along and sticks a note underneath your door. He came along in secret but he had no way knowing that in this house nothing done in secret actually remains a secret. Who is he? What does he want? What is he planning? Why does he come and go like that, like a thief? My husband sees everything. He has eyes everywhere throughout all the rooms in this house, in the entrance, on the stairs, along the hallways, from the front door up to the rooftop, from the sidewalk right up to the top of the chimney. He put me on alert and there I was, sure that you would come to me with the note. But you never came. Instead you suddenly got up, in secret - and I have already told you that there are no secrets in this house - and you head out with the children in tow. Where to? To some meeting? And then when somehow - I don't know precisely how - you make out my husband's shadow in the darkness, that husband of mine who has risked his health and his very soul in order to protect you, you panic because if he God forbid sees you at your meeting he might turn you in - I don't know to whom - and you all immediately turn around and cancel your meeting. Is there some other explanation for all of this, Madame Mayer? You have nothing to say. There can be no other explanation. Who was waiting for you, and where? And now you haven't even told that someone that you are not coming after all. Perhaps they are still waiting for you in some darkened ruin and have no idea that you are not going to make it, simply because my husband saw you heading there and you were afraid that he might turn you in. But he could have turned you in already any day he wanted, at any moment. Would he do that? You are a scoundrel, Madame Mayer. Only a scoundrel would think a thing like that. To think a thing like that does not demonstrate a proper Christian ethic - I don't even want to say just what sort of ethic it does demonstrate. I don't pretend to be some sort of a saint, Madame Mayer, but out of self-respect I refuse to mention just what sort of ethic this demonstrates, and I am willing to swallow my words and stay silent on that score.

"But you are out of here, Madame Mayer, the very day that Madame Ravel's contract is up - Madame Ravel, who also did not tell me that she would not be coming back, since now I see that she is just like you, two sisters like two peas in a pod. Not a minute more, Madame Mayer. And by yourself. You will leave all by yourself. The same way you were able to go out by yourself in the street tonight, you will be able to head out in the street by yourself in just a matter of days. Today is Saturday, Madame Mayer, March 6, 1943. On Sunday, March 14, at midnight, you're out of here, Madame Mayer, you and, I'm sorry to say, your kids too. Have I made myself sufficiently clear?"

What I was most sorry about was that Erwin had to translate all these foul things. I understood what he had not translated as well, I did not need the words themselves in order to clarify what this lady next door was saying and what she meant to convey. Her voice, her tone, this speech of hers standing there in the doorway, the monotonous, demanding stream of a sort of lecture, the projection of the figure of someone who is insulted, who feels insulted by my very presence, the complete confidence in facts that had no basis anywhere but in her mind and which had been entirely fabricated therein, who could no longer stand the pressure of the awful contradictions her life presented, all these things did not need words, which could anyway only have served to unduly soften their reality. But Erwin was forced to translate. He had to stand there and hear the things that she accused us of both explicitly and implicitly, and he had to cloak the things she said with words that did not rely on impressions or sensations and which were driven like tacks into one of those cork boards filled with slanderous character assassinations. Erwin, who had certainly understood everything, stood there and translated like an automaton completely devoid of emotion that was not built to understand the things it said, and it was only when the neighbor's wife seemed to say by chance, "Today is Saturday, Madame Mayer" that his eyes lit up and he looked over at me and Jackie like a victor mocking those he had defeated.

But Erwin was not some mere automaton devoid of emotion. The soft wax slate where life left its imprint was now filled with words that were sprayed into the air with a hatred that was completely baseless, but which nevertheless based itself on a wealth of imaginary evidence. When he would grow up and the slate would have hardened like marble, these traces would have become set in stone, and these words would stand like pillars planted firmly in the hard mountainous ground, and no amount of time would cause them to fade. My son was condemned to remember it all. Jackie too, who was silent and, it seemed, could not possibly have completely understood the full extent of everything that he heard, could not possibly empty his heart one day of the refuse that this situation had filled it with. This, for me, was an even greater source of pain than what we actually went through.

But I had no time to feel the pain or wonder about what had come first - the lash or the loss of order - whether this woman was angry at the fact that we had challenged her absolute rule in her little minor realm and were no longer her obedient subjects, or whether we had completely negated the last bit of love she had left in her life, and she was unable to forgive us for that. Right now I had to protect myself from this anger, whatever its primal cause might be. I believed her when she said that her husband, our neighbor, would not have turned us in. That had never even entered my mind, not out in the street that night, and not now, though now that I believed this fact it had, indeed, come to mind. To believe something is to admit the possible doubts related to it and then lay them to rest. That was what you once told me, and who knew better than you when it came to such things.

I wanted to act proud. I wanted to slam the door in her face, wanted to respond. I wanted to contradict all the facts that she had invented in order to justify her animosity that she had apparently been repressing and carrying around inside her and which had never actually needed any real facts in order to exist. I wanted to express my superiority in the face of her aggressive weakness. But I decided that the moment was not right for all this. There is never a right moment when it comes to helplessness. Her weakness was more powerful than my superiority. My superiority was a much more sorry thing than her weakness. I went over to her, took her hand and pulled her gently to me and said to her in her language, "Sit down." She freed her hand from my grasp and turned around in order to return to her room. I leaped like a young girl, although I was roundly pregnant. My life depended on it. I stood before her and blocked her path and said in a pleading voice, "Please, Ma'am," and I almost pushed her backwards until she had reached one of the chairs at the table and sat down. I had to tell her everything, I had no means of escape, no way of hiding beneath any cover. It was not that I could not come up with any better option than confiding in her everything about the note - what was written, who had written it - and the disorienting loss of a sense of time as the days no longer corresponded to the usual signposts along the way, and our heading out to try and reclaim that sense of time in the pipe shop - but I also thought that I had no other choice. I spoke quickly. I did not give her the chance to ask a single question, or to clarify anything that she might not have understood right away. And Erwin, as well, without our having arranged anything in advance, translated the entire stream of sentences that I pronounced before I even had a chance to complete them, and he did not leave even the slightest pause in between the sentences where she might insert herself whatsoever. My voice was like a rushing stream of water that did not stop and did not change, while Erwin's voice was dry and monotonous, like gravel.

She listened alertly but somewhat reservedly. Then after a while she was simply alert, and in the end, she dropped her forehead into the palms of her hands and said, "Enough, enough," straightened up and then asked, "And now what? Now you know that tomorrow is Sunday. Now you are going to go there tomorrow. How are you going to go? You have to go alone, even though I do not know why you must go alone. And the children? I will take care of them. Perhaps they won't want me to, or they simply won't be able to tolerate that. What was this priestly doctor of yours thinking, what did he think you were going to do with the children when he asked you to come all by yourself? The fact that you are going to Switzerland - that's what I thought the moment I laid eyes on you, but the children, where are they headed?" Jackie was suddenly on alert, like a jack-in-the-box, and said, "Mom's not going anywhere!" Erwin put an arm around his brother's shoulders and said, "Mom is not going to go to the cathedral by herself. We are going to go with her." The neighbor's wife gave the children a look that seemed to contain a bit of admiration, or at least so it seemed to me. "Of course," she said, "she will go, and you will both go with her, and I will go too, and that way there will be someone there to keep an eye on your mother while she is all alone inside the cathedral. Allow me to tell you, Madame Mayer," she added, turning to me, "that it is dangerous to head out from here for Switzerland. Many people have tried but only a few have made it. And even fewer managed to actually make it across the border. There were those who came back after making it to the border and were not allowed to cross. There were those who never even made it to the border and never came back. Saint-Claude is no more than a stone's throw away from Switzerland, but you have no idea how far away it actually is. It is just one side of the bridge if you do make it across, but it is the very gateway to the cemetery itself if you don't. No one else is going to tell you how things truly stand the way that I have, Madame Mayer." She fixed her eyes on me and waited as though either checking to see if I looked like someone who had properly understood what she had just been told, or perhaps simply waiting for me to speak up and say something. I remained silent.

"I can see the cold chill running down the length of your spine, Madame Mayer. And the children? We ought to spare them such things as what I have described, they must be protected, we ought to take pity on their gentle souls, right? I was also once a bourgeois mother just like that. I too thought that I was the one who was in charge of drafting the life stories on behalf of my son, in accordance with my own choosing, at the appropriate time, using just the right words, all of it. Nonsense. We are not in control of anything, Madame Mayer. These days children are aware at a rather young age of things that we were not even aware of when we were already much older than they are. This cursed war, Madame Mayer, has drafted them all into its army of men and women walking about among the ruins and the graves and the lies, without any illusions and without any false hopes. There are no children left who are still mere children, Madame Mayer, and if there are then they demand that we let them in on everything - above all, the truth - that we trust them to be no more fragile than we are. So yes, between Saint-Claude and Switzerland death itself lies in wait, Madame Mayer. It is as cold as the snow that covers up to its eyes roaming among the trees in the forest, right up to the barrel of its rifles that shoot you like rabbits if you have not already been captured and sent to die some time later on down the road. That's how things stand, if you care to know. And the children ought to know it too. They are just like us, Madame Mayer. I do not know this priest of yours, Madame Mayer. There are priests and then there are priests. God only knows if what they have beneath their habit is a bottomless pocket or a beating heart, or both, Madame Mayer - yes, sometimes, rather often, in fact, it is both. When it comes to this priest of yours I must say that I have my suspicions, since as far as I know from what you've told me he is a proper doctor and a proper priest, and there is no conceivable explanation for such a phenomenon these days as far as I can tell. But I understand that you have every reason to trust him, since he brought you here from Annemasse, and that indeed went off without a hitch, and he told you that he was preparing the way for you from here to Switzerland, although that has not yet happened. You do not know anyone else in whom you might alternatively place your trust. So you are going to go to the cathedral, Madame Mayer. You can't trust me. You can't trust my husband either. We're just Saint-Claude moles. We are familiar with every burrow in the area, and we know how to get by on what's left in the barns and the vineyards, and the stables and the pens, the mud and the filth, Madame Mayer, but as soon as we set foot outside Saint-Claude we are as blind as a pair of bats and are likely to fall prey to the rats and vermin that are not above preying on their own kind. As far as the priest and the cathedral, you've got me, but once you leave the cathedral - and I don't know why it has to be the cathedral, of all places - you have only him, him and that God of his, Madame Mayer, since you don't really have anything better to fall back on."

Even as these words were leaving her lips - those lips that seemed to me like they would never stop moving - I saw out of the corner of my eye that another note slipped in under the door. Jackie saw it first. Following his eyes, which were fixed on the threshold underneath the door, I looked that way as well. Erwin immediately caught me looking that way and then the neighbor's wife in turn and noted the white slip of paper waiting there on the floor for someone to pick it up. We all stared at the note where it lay. Not a single one of us stirred. The neighbor's wife said to Erwin, "Do you have trouble bending down? You think it's any easier for your mother? Bring her the note." Jackie caught my attention. I looked at him. He was ready to drive a spit straight through this woman simply with his eyes. Erwin hesitated for a moment. Jackie moved first. He brought the note over to me, opened it up and placed it in my hands, and then drove the daggers of his eyes into the neighbor's wife once more. "The truck, Phillip, 10:45, in front of the church house door. By yourself. DuPont." I recognized the French letters. I read it all in an instant and then handed the note to Erwin who read it himself just as quickly and then showed the note to Jackie, and whispered its contents in his ear. The neighbor's wife gave us all an inquisitive look, and you could tell by the way she was looking at us that she was checking to see if we were going to let her in on what was written in the note or not. Erwin handed it back to me and, without re-reading it, I handed it over to the neighbor's wife. She read it rather slowly, at length.

"They are coming to get you. Who is Phillip? 'By yourself'. Again, by yourself. What does he want with this always asking you to come 'by yourself'? Amateurs. With your luggage? Without it? And then what? What's next after the cathedral?"

"I don't know," I said. "They're the ones who know. I trust them. I have no choice, as you yourself said. I'm tired. As far as the priest and the cathedral you have me, as you said, that is, I have you, at least that's what I understood from what you said, and then after the cathedral, you said it was just him and his God, since I don't really have anything better to fall back on. Let's leave it at that for now. Let's all get some rest and later on we can talk some more. Tomorrow, early in the morning. I'm just so tired right now." Jackie came over to me, hugged me, and placed his head on one of my shoulders. Erwin did not move as he monitored every muscle in the lady's face. She got up and said, "I understand you, Madame Mayer. Rest now. I'll come back in a little while. Send the boy to come get me. I'll come over whenever. It has to be today, Madame Mayer. Though things could well go differently. There are people who come to get you, who give you things, who bring you places, help you hide, are there to redeem you, who look after you, save you, guide you; and the ones who are good are good because you were born into this world simply in order to give them the opportunity to do something that passes for good in their lives as well; and the evil ones are evil because they could not squeeze any further benefit from you; and you are on your own, completely on your own, all alone. Because there is no good and there is no evil that really needs you when they come to call. I don't want that to happen to you. Not here, not as long as I - who suffered the same fate - am still around in Saint-Claude. Send the boy to come get me when you are ready." And she left.

It was hard. I was alone, all alone with the children. My plans were all in disarray. I could not make order out of them all by myself but I did not have any strength left after this woman's long speech: yet she addressed me as if I was just a single woman, by myself, small and weak. I was, some sort of crowd gathered in the town square, or a witness that would one day be called to the stand in some heavenly court, where anyone who ever walked the earth stands in need of someone who will testify on their behalf, attest to their good name - and all the more so in the case of those who walked the earth in wartime. She could well be of assistance to me. Perhaps, she was the only one who could help me, but I needed a few moments of silence in order that all the springs that had sprung inside me would have a chance to recoil and relax, and let my soul come to rest once more, for whatever peace of mind I had left could return. I knew that the boys also wanted to talk with me without any further delay. But I could not handle it just then. I was terribly in need of that absolute silence that I had experienced from time to time, when, after a long, hard day I would sink my body into the warm bathwater at our home, and let the water rise until it reached my lips, enveloping and making off with my body, hiding me away from my very self, as though my entire mind and body were no more than so much water themselves. I sank down into the chair and began to immerse myself within my own being. The children stared at me and remained silent as they waited respectfully.

I remembered that you had once told me that, as far as you were concerned, the *Ninth of Av* was more important than Yom Kippur, the Day of Atonement. You had said things that, at the time, had not seemed all that important to me, something about the fact that on Yom Kippur the individual prays for his own soul and asks forgiveness for what he, with his own hands, brought upon himself, and for which he certainly bears the blame. On the *Ninth of Av*, however, the individual cries over what God did to him, to him and to the entire Jewish people, and basically demands that God - who apparently bears no small amount of blame Himself - asks us to forgive Him and pardon His sins, as it were. This conversation, which had descended into utter oblivion, suddenly rose in my mind, as I thought to myself that I needed a fast day that was neither a plea of atonement nor the remembrance of some iniquity but a sort of process of purification that might ensure that I would in no way be tainted by anything that might justify my death, if I were to die, whether my children would be there with me or would survive me - it was one and the same at that point - and so that I might be pure, not before God, or before man, or even before my own self, but that I might be cleansed of any blame anywhere, ever. They have not yet instituted such a fast day for us. They have not yet written the liturgy for such a day, there is no *Kol Nidrei* like that, no such Book of Lamentations. Perhaps these prayers will never be written. Who would write them, after all? The dead can not exactly write, and what would the living write - and the survivors, why would they even read it? And those who did not manage to make it, in vain do we hope that they might rise from the dead one day simply because some scroll remains somewhere in the world, in some tunnel, in some cave, inside some bombed-out ruin, where it might read itself. What would happen Sunday, that Sunday that had already come to greet me in the night and gone to wait for me in the cathedral? By myself? As of today there are still people who know that I exist. The priest knows. Here, look, Phillip knows. The neighbor's wife knows. And her husband too. I am still here. But tomorrow? Perhaps by tomorrow there will not be a single soul left who remembers that I was ever here. If you eventually read what I have written here then you will one day know, but if not, if God forbid you never do, then even you will not know of my existence, and those fingernails of mine that I dug into the cracks between the bricks in the walls of my life as they closed in on me, trying to dig out an escape hatch for me and my children, those fingernails will simply turn blue, and there will be no one anywhere in the world at that point who will know that the blood has left every last one of my fingers and that I am no more.

I fell into bed as though I were on the verge of a collapse. I fell into the sort of sleep that would seem almost humanly impossible and I was terrified constantly, as though I were swept away on a river of fear. There was a waterfall. I found myself dragged in that direction. I was standing up on the very walls of the abyss. I knew that the children were staring at me. I knew that they were being assailed by terrible fears of separation, seized by some sort of panic beyond all the other kinds that they had already known. And for a moment I imagined that I too was bidding farewell, that it was done.

And then everything changed. Suddenly, I knew that all of the questions I was asking were in vain, and that all of the fears that I felt were for nought, and the whole thing could not possibly be so intricate and complicated, it was simply that I was unwilling to dare to believe that it was all so clear, and simple, and straightforward. Were there snakes underneath every stone in Saint-Claude? Phillip would take us straight through those stony fields. Was the priest too holy, and for that reason was it impossible to completely cleanse him of any and all suspicions? From Annemasse up to this point he had certainly been a saint, why should he now turn into the devil? And the children? This crazy lady next door was going to protect the children with her very life. And her husband? Nobody has any control over the wind, no one knows what secrets it holds. And that death which lies in wait along the way from he-re to Switzerland? It is out there waiting for anyone who dares to just pronounce its very name. I am going to live. I am not going to pronounce its name or even the mere hint of its name. I was determined to such an extent that it ought to have been a source of concern for any normal thinking creature. How wonderful those moments are, even if you can not be certain that the next day there will be any memory of them, and all that will be left will be the refutations, contradictions, and illusions.

I do not know how much time passed from the moment I succumbed to my exhaustion and the moment when I awoke. I opened my eyes where I lay. The children were still sitting in the same spot where they had been when the neighbor's wife had left us. They were staring at me, as it would seem they had been doing from the moment she had walked out. The skin of their little faces was stretched taut and seemed almost transparent, and I could clearly make out the concern, or perhaps the fear, that was frozen there from their foreheads down to their thin lips and on down to their necks. They noticed that I seemed to have woken up and waited rather expectantly to find out from the first words I would utter what our fate was going to be. I looked at them for a long moment and then I smiled. I sat there smiling silently. Jackie ran over to me and kissed my face over and over again. Erwin got up, stood next to me, caressed my shoulder and said, "I knew that every-thing would be okay, Ma." I stretched my hand out, pulled him close to me and hugged him, and as we sat there with Jackie holding me and me holding Erwin, I said to them, "Let's eat something first, we are going to need a lot of strength for tomorrow, and then we'll call the neighbor's wife to come over after we've eaten. But first we are going to eat like kings." Erwin laughed. Jackie looked at him and hesitated at first, not knowing whether he ought to laugh as well, and then he just burst out into an almost uncontrollable fit of laughter and began dancing a little close-legged dance on the floor, as he said, "Gonna eat like kings, gonna eat like kings, a little appetizer, then a first course, second course, third course, and then we're gonna explode from all those little nothings and just die laughing." Then Erwin took his brother's hand and mine and the three of us began dancing in a circle, pawing the floor with our feet and singing, "Gonna eat like kings, gonna eat like kings," until we all fell onto the bed, breathless, out of our minds, and happy beyond belief.

In the end, though, we did not eat like kings. We did not even eat at all. We did not feel like we needed to before having wrapped up everything we had to take care of. I sent the boys over to get the neighbor's wife. She came over at once, accompanied by her husband. As soon as the door opened, he went over to the chair where he had sat throughout his first visit and sat down, as though he were returning to his regular place, put his hands together in his lap, let his head fall onto his chest, and just sat there in silence. His wife carefully surveyed the room, and her eyes came to rest for a moment on the bed from which we had just risen, and I could see her sort of making out a certain frivolity that seemed to hang in the air of the apartment, as she said, "I see that for some reason there was a little celebration here. I don't exactly know why, but that doesn't matter. What matters is that we don't have much time now. Why are we standing in the doorway like this? We already know each other, don't we? We can all sit down, right?" And we all sat down at the table. She spoke and the rest of us listened.

"Sunday is on its way, though we have no idea how it is going to end. Perhaps God knows how, but He never lets us in on what He knows in advance. But we have some idea what is going to happen up until a quarter to eleven this morning. That much we know. This

Phillip mentioned in that note of yours is going to be waiting in his vehicle, and you are going to go with him to our little Saint-Pierre's Cathedral, and enter the building at 11:00 sharp, but from that point on neither you nor I have any real idea what will be. I am not in the habit of making plans for things that I do not know. But I can handle what we do know. So listen to me. You will pack your things tonight, though if you're too tired you can pack early in the morning before the sun comes up. Pack everything you own and don't leave anything behind here in the apartment that might reveal the fact that you were here. If you come back, you can unpack, and if not, then there won't be anything left to give away the fact that you, the children, and Madame Ravel all stayed here." She looked over at her husband who was sitting there like some statue in a garden without hearing a word, although, to my surprise, he suddenly nodded his head ever so slightly. She continued. "At a quarter to nine, the boys, dressed in the warmest coats that they have, will kiss you goodbye and leave the apartment. They will see me standing two houses away, wearing my black hat and my Sunday winter clothing. They will see me, just as I will see them, and then we will proceed the same way that we walked over to the hospital, with me out front and them following along behind, and I will lead the boys to Saint-Pierre. I will stop right near the cathedral. They will approach me as though they were simply walking along casually and then we will all enter the building together, as though they came along with their devout, God-fearing aunt in order to attend mass. We will sit in the middle of the church. I will sit along the aisle and they will sit right next to me. By barely even turning my head - a gesture that not a single soul will notice, other than the gossipmongers who anyway see everything, even those things that have not actually taken place - I will have a clear view of who enters the church through the only door left open for the faithful these days.

"The children will not say a word to me. They are not to look in the direction of the door. They will not pray. They don't know how to pray. All they know how to do is come along with their aunt. That's what their parents told them to do, insofar as these parents exist... as it were. If I get down on my knees, then they will get down on their knees too. Out of politeness. When I stand up, they will stand up too - once more, out of mere politeness. Anyone who sees them will note that this war has not yet vanquished a good, old fashioned upbringing. Is that clear, boys? Of course it is. Next. All of your luggage - though I see that you don't have all that much - along with the boys' luggage - though they don't really have too much either - is to be left at the door. It will all find its way to you, if necessary, whether you come back here or not. Don't worry. Now we're talking about 10:40. You will leave the apartment and take everything you need with you in your handbag, as though you were never going to be setting foot in this apartment again. Everything. Your papers, your money, every-thing you have with you that only you know about. You will lock the door. My husband will catch up with you on the stairs." She looked over at him. He nodded his head ever so slightly once again, barely raised one hand, and then let it fall once more into his lap as he sat there, perfectly still, not moving a muscle, like a completely lifeless mummy. "He will come down the stairs as though by chance, but you will know that he is coming. You will give him the key while you are both still inside the building. You will meet this Phillip of yours and then head - I hope, no, I know - over to the cathedral. You will not see him," she said, as she waved a thumb in the direction of her husband, "but he will be there on his bicycle, and he will see everything, and keep an eye on everything, and, if necessary, he will let you know whatever you need to know. He is the patron saint of Saint-Claude, Madame Mayer. Whatever happens afterwards is out of his hands. But I am hoping for the best.

"I do not know why this priest of yours wants you to show up alone, as he has asked you to do. When the time is right - and only you can tell when that moment will have come - you will tell him that you are not alone."

"He already knows," I immediately responded. "He knows the children. He loves them. I don't know why he wants me to come by myself. But he certainly knows that the boys are with me and that they are just as dependent on him as I am."

"Don't get offended on his behalf," she quickly said. "You say he knows every-thing, but so do you. So do I. But nothing is certain, nothing is ever certain, Madame Mayer, you can never be sure that three people who all know everything actually know the same thing.

Let's not complicate matters any more than necessary. Things are rather simple, as they stand. There may be a moment when common sense will dictate that you ought to tell him that you did not do as he asked and that the children are there with you in the cathedral. Then again, that moment may not come. You, and only you, will have to be the judge. I'm sure that you would have addressed this issue even if I had not brought it up. Now, if you end up having to do it, you will be doing it because I told you too as well. That's all." Her husband moved his head slightly where he sat. He nodded, and then froze up once more. Jackie squeezed my arm tightly without letting anyone see. He was either afraid himself and trying to draw strength from me, or sensed that I was afraid and was trying to buck up my spirits. Throughout this entire conversation, filled with such detailed instructions, Erwin did not bat an eyelash. His eyes were carefully inspecting every little shadow that passed across the neighbor's wife's features. He was on alert. My little patron saint of Saint-Claude. Jackie, my angel.

The neighbors got up and left. Jackie waited until the door closed behind them and said, "I hate them. And now I'm hungry."

"Why should you hate them?" I asked. "The day will come when you will never forget that they helped us, helped us quite a bit, more than we ever expected. But I'm hungry too - so are you, Erwin, aren't you?"

"They hate us," Jackie said. "I don't need their help. But let's eat. Something. I have to eat something." I went over to prepare a little something to eat and heard Erwin say to his brother, "We are going to do exactly what she told us to do, Jackie, exactly, you hear me? Eat, relax, and forget about whether you hate them or not. We don't have time for that. You heard her. A quarter to nine, and a quarter to eleven. It's all very precise. And you need their help, and so do I, and so does Mom."

"I don't need their help," Jackie said, stamping his feet. "I don't need it, and I don't want it! I hate her for the way she talks and I hate him for the way that he just sits there saying nothing. Didn't we go all by ourselves to the pipe shop just in order to find out when Sunday is? Nobody caught us, but we came back. Why did we come back? Because we were afraid. And why were we afraid? Because we're cowards. Now we know that tomorrow is Sunday. Can't we go to the cathedral all by ourselves? You don't know how to get there? So go with me. I know the way. But... but... but... Enough already! Let's eat and then pack and then get some sleep and enough already!" Erwin did not respond. He helped me set out the sparse offerings on the table. After we had eaten Jackie said, "I don't have anything to pack, so I'm going straight to sleep." He lay down on the bed, with his eyes wide open, and stared at us while we packed up our luggage. From time to time he would remind us that we had forgotten something and we simply acted like we were obeying him and did not say a word to him until it was all taken care of and settled and ready to go, and the entire apartment had been cleaned of even the very dust that a person leaves behind when they simply breathe, and then Erwin and I also got in bed to try and catch a few stolen moments of rest before the sun came up in the morning.

The children were already fully dressed about a half hour early. Erwin just sat there, while Jackie stood next to the window, with the curtain drawn back a bit between his fingers as he stared outside. "There she goes," he suddenly said, and immediately went over in the direction of the front door. Erwin gave me a little kiss, looked up at me and said, "See you in a little bit, Ma," and then joined Jackie and opened the door to go out. Jackie took a small step out the door, then immediately turned around, ran over to me, gave me a big, forced, trembling hug, as he pulled my face down to his, gave me a kiss, and then ran back over to join his brother and left. After the door had closed behind them I found myself standing there mumbling things to myself that could not have been anything other than a prayer, although until this very day I am not entirely sure that I was not actually swearing wildly. I went over to the window and pulled the curtain aside. The two of them were walking along hand in hand. I could no longer see the neighbor's wife. I stood there until the two boys also disappeared from view.

At the appointed hour, I too left the room. As though the neighbor's wife had scripted my part for me in some play, her husband passed me on the stairs, took the key from my hand like he was some sort of thief trying to hide his haul from any prying eyes, even though there was only the two of us in the stairwell, and then he disappeared. When I left the building he was nowhere in sight. The priest's car, the one he had used to convey us from Annemasse, was parked outside the house, with the engine running. Phillip opened the door for me, without leaving his seat, and before I had a chance to say a word we were already on our way, with the wheels screeching beneath us as he released the brakes. He may well have offered me some brief greeting, and I may well have responded in kind with some few words, but the fact is I do not think we actually exchanged a single word. I stared out the window, and even though I had already spent quite a bit of time in Saint-Claude, and had already walked around quite a bit of the town, it seemed to me as though I were seeing it out of the window of the little car for the first time and felt like I had fallen in love with the place. From time to time I caught sight of snow-covered mountains with wide swaths of darker terrain that must have been forests. We drove a bit of the way alongside a river where the wintry waters flowed among large boulders that caused the water to foam, and the flow seemed fairly frozen as it sent a chill down your spine just looking at it. We passed by a stone bridge and then the car began to climb as Phillip said, "Do you see the clock in the missing steeple?" I did not know just how one was supposed to see a missing steeple, but I noticed the clock, which was not all that large or particularly impressive, and which clearly did not sport any bells. "I am going to stop the car, then you are going to get out and wait beneath the clock. I am going to park the car nearby and be back in a second. We will enter the cathedral together." That is what he said, and that is exactly how things went.

At first I had difficulty making out anything in the dark inside the church. My eyes roamed around, trying to discern my children among the few members of the faithful, but I did not see them anywhere. Phillip stood by my side. He held my arm and whispered in my ear, "He is waiting for you in the confessional." He walked me over to the end of the large nave, where two or three pairs of confessionals stood, and left me standing before the wooden latticework covered with a curtain inside one of them. A hand reached out and lightly pushed the red curtain aside, from inside the confessional, and I heard the familiar voice of the priest say, "Kneel." I was terrified. I lifted my head. In the darkness inside the high-ceilinged cathedral sheaves of dimly colorful light intersected overhead, as the sun shone through the elongated windows, and the roses along the walls on either side, and in the facade up front. An infinite number of dust particles swirled in the haze of faded light, and seemed to me like a cloud of stars on the run. Where the pillars and arches seemed to swell high overhead, the darkness seemed to lift and the mystery seemed almost vibrant, but the lower they fell, closer to where I was, the deeper the dark seemed to fall, until it seemed as though it reached the very depths of an abyss whose bottom could not even be discerned. I got down on my knees on a plank of wood covered in felt whose color was that of a dim rose, facing the confessional window that separated nothing more than the very heavens from the earth.

The priest spoke in a whisper. From time to time I lifted my head in the direction of the latticework and could see his face in profile. He addressed me while speaking straight ahead into the space of his little cubicle within. He spoke quickly, but he was no longer whispering. He spoke softly, but clearly, though not a soul other than me could hear a word that he was saying. His sentences were precisely measured and he did not wait for any response from me. He told me that he was the one confessing, not me. But what? The fact that he had let so many days pass since we had arrived in Saint-Claude. "We had no choice. The checkpoints along the border have been increased. They caught a woman recently." He spoke in German but said in French, "It is a rather big deal for all the smugglers. She had come from Saint-Claude. They had stopped her along the fence at a barbed-wire gate - the woman and her baby. "There was a whole squadron of Germans. They tried to drag her back to occupied Jura. She screamed like a woman in labor being taken to the slaughter. But they would not let up. Another squadron of soldiers that had been alerted by her screams stood on the other side of the fence and watched the awful spectacle without lifting a finger. She freed herself for a moment from the clutches of the Germans and threw her baby over the gate. A Swiss soldier caught the baby in midair. It basically fell into his arms like a ball of some sort. The Germans were shocked. They opened the gate for her and disappeared. We know all this from the Swiss. They see everything, but they do not always step in and do anything. It is not everyday that a miracle like that happens, and it is well known that such a miracle comes at a rather steep price. A smuggler who was caught that same day has not been seen since, which means that he has already been taken out and shot, or is going to be taken out and shot. So we waited. We had to.

"But the road is clear now. Not that one, a different one. It's all the same, or not - whatever. You will head out tonight. We will discuss the details later. I called you because you are going to be traveling quite a long distance on foot, in the snow, and you are not alone, that is, other than your two boys, Yitzchak and Yaakov." That was exactly how he referred to them, 'Yitzchak and Yaakov', "And you are carrying another little boy inside your womb. The ones already outside have learned to fight. They have more strength than God ordinarily gives to boys their age. And the one who has not yet emerged is going to have to learn. Will he manage? Will you manage? Just days before the little child first emerges into the light of day? I told you to come alone because I am going to take you for an examination now. We can't go there with the children. That's just how it is. We must be sure that you, you and your unborn child, that is, will be able to withstand the journey that is to begin tonight. That is the end of my confession, Madame Mayer. You will rise in a moment. There is another person already standing in line to confess. Cross yourself. It looks good. It won't hurt you this one time. Get up and go over to the front door. The same Phillip that brought you here is the one who will take you now. Where are the boys? Don't tell me. I am sure you must have made arrangements for them before coming here today. I trust you."

The curtain fell back in place. The confessional was shut, sealed. I rose slowly and stood up. I stared at the latticework. I wondered if the person hiding behind it was checking to see if I was making the sign of the cross. I was sure that he could not care less. I turned to go. The man waiting in line came over to take my place. He knelt down. I stared at him a moment and thought to myself - a sinner from Saint-Claude, confessing to a priest from Annemasse? Perhaps. They confess before their God via any priest they come across. Perhaps this is the smuggler who will be taking me across the border? Perhaps he is another fellow traveler? Perhaps he is another member of the tangled nighttime world of dawn and mid-

night martyrs hearing the confessions of Jewish women in their ca-
thedrals, in order to lead them to that land that has been set aside in
paradise for wartime refugees? And then again - how had the priest
put it? - cross yourself, it looks good. Perhaps. All of paradise is
surrounded by the fires of hell, and it seems that one has a better
view of things on the outside from inside the confessional, than the
other way around. Who really knows.

I looked around for the children once more. I was certain that
they could see me, but I did not spot them anywhere. Phillip stepped
from the shadows, and I found him walking along by my side, guid-
ing me quickly to the front entrance. I gently gave in. We headed
over to the missing steeple and I stood there once more beneath
the clock. "Wait here a moment, don't make a single move. I will
be back in a second." I seemed to hear what he said from a great
distance. He hurried off at a slight run. The hands of the clock had
barely moved since I had stood in this same spot just a few moments
earlier. But my entire world had changed. Time itself had shifted.
That woman who had thrown her infant over the barbed wire fence.
That woman. God, dear God, where was that woman now? And her
baby, where was her baby, was he alive or dead, was he, God forbid,
a living corpse, or a lucky, healthy little child - where was that baby
now?

Phillip came back breathing hard, grabbed my arm and said,
"Come, quickly." I walked along, or was rather led, wrapped up in
that thought of that woman and her baby, but when Phillip opened
the car door for me it was as though my own children had burst
through and had come to stand before my eyes, staring straight at
me and demanding that their insult be avenged - and I grew frightened as I stood still and would not enter the car as I said to him,
"Phillip, I am not going anywhere. I am heading back to the missing
steeple. I am going to wait out there in the cold. Do not ask me
why." He looked at me as though he were looking at a woman who
had lost her mind and said, "But you can't." I began to walk in that
direction. The sound of the rattling engine of the car seemed to roar
from one end of the city to the other. Phillip did not pay it any attention and hurried after me to try and stop me in my tracks. I knew
that he would not dare do anything to me that might draw the at-

tention of the people who always seem to appear suddenly from nowhere, even in a town that seems absolutely empty, and I continued
walking ahead. He overtook me with catlike agility, placed himself
before me, blocking my path, and said, "Tell me what happened,
I can help you. I have to help you. You can not stay here another
second." I stood facing him. I stared into his eyes. I gathered all my
strength and I said to him, "The children. I am not alone, Phillip.
The children. They are inside the cathedral." "I don't believe it,"
Phillip hissed between his pursed lips as he froze where he stood before me. "You are not alone? Who is with them in there? God, what
have you done - you're going to get the whole lot of us burned at
the stake. Where are they? You were told to come alone. In our line
of work, my dear lady, you must obey. 'Come alone' always means
'come alone.' Whether or not there are children, you must obey, it's
life or death, you've got to obey!" We fixed our eyes on one another
like the flash of polished steel.

The engine echoed in the empty square in front of the cathedral.
The car door was wide open. I had no idea what I was going to do
in another second, and Phillip, too, had no idea what it was that he
was about to do. "I swear to you," he said in a whisper, "that you
are not going to leave here without the children. I will bring them
to you. You are not going to stand around here and you are not to
take even one more step in the direction of the cathedral. Get in the
car. I will take you a hundred paces from here and you will wait
for me. The chances are not that good, but it's the best we've got.
Here you don't even stand a chance." I took a few steps backwards
and said, "I believe you. You swore." I turned around and walked
quickly over to the car. He went ahead of me and was already at the
wheel when I sat down. He pulled the open door shut from where
he sat, slamming it closed, and in the same instant drove away for a
brief moment, and then stopped the car. We were now behind the
cathedral. He turned off the engine and said to me once more, "Sit
here and try to make sure that no one manages to notice that you are
in the car." He got out and started running in the direction of a little
semi-hidden door along the side wall of the church and disappeared
inside. I stared after him and told myself that someone really ought
to explain to me just once what God was thinking when He created

these people who always complicate everything in His world of simple, foreseeable things, people who were able to take a mere yard of rope and tie over a thousand knots and still leave over just enough to hang themselves with. I was furious with myself, furious with the priest, with the neighbor's wife, with her husband, with Phillip. I was furious with every single person that I knew by name and everyone else in the world as well, for that matter. The children were the only ones who were spared my anger. They were the ones that I asked in turn to pardon me, to forgive me.

Suddenly there was a knock at the window of the car door. It was the neighbor. My eternal guardian angel. He was gripping the handlebars of his bicycle in one hand and motioning for me to roll down the window of the car door by making a circular movement with his other hand. I was frightened. I could not find the handle. I looked at him in desperation. His face was, as ever, blank, expressionless. He gestured to me as though to say that I ought to follow him, but, not knowing whether he wanted me to get out and walk after him or just sit there waiting and drive away, I began to scream inside the car - whose window I had failed to open, to my infinite shame and embarrassment - screaming, "Where?! Where?! Where?!" He placed his mouth against the glass of the windowpane, and in a voice that was barely audible but which I was nevertheless able to make out between the crush of his tongue and lips against the glass, the syllables, "Children home" came through. At that same instant Phillip burst in at a run. The man got on his bicycle with bewildering dexterity and disappeared like a ghost into thin air. The priest, with his coat and hat still in his hands, half running, half hurriedly walking over in our direction from the church, came next, but Phillip got there first, opened the door, sat down in the car and, breathing hard once more, immediately asked me, "Who was that? The children are not in the church!"

"You swore," I said.

"What can I do?" he replied. "Who was that strange man - what did he want, what did he say?"

I did not get a chance to make even the slightest reply as the priest had already gotten into the car and was sitting in the back seat. His deep breaths seemed to fill the entire small space inside the vehicle.

"You've caused quite a number of complications," he said. "Drive," he commanded Phillip. The latter turned the key in the ignition but the car did not move.

"Where to?" asked Phillip.

"As planned. For now." The priest shifted his body in the back seat in the direction of my spot up front, leaning with both hands against my seat as he said, "You've caused quite a number of complications, my dear Madame Mayer. The children. All alone in the cathedral? Perhaps you were not all alone? It would seem, in fact, that you were not. With whom, then, Madame Mayer? And where are they now? That man. Who is he? Where did he disappear to? Where did he go? Who has he gone to see? You have no idea. But I do. People get turned in and die around here for a lot less than that. Make a u-turn, turn around, until I tell you otherwise. You, Mada-me Mayer, you have some explaining to do before we continue, *if* we continue, for that matter."

"Take me to my apartment, Doctor, Father, sir," I replied in controlled near-silence.

"Have you gone mad?" he replied. "Why?"

"The children are there," I said.

"Not in the cathedral? Phillip, didn't you say they were in the cathedral?"

"She told me that they were in the cathedral, Father, sir."

"Did you say they were in the cathedral?" he interrogated me, hurtfully, impatiently.

I tried to keep my cool. "They are back home. You told me to come alone. If I am alone, then where else would they be?"

The priest held his tongue for a moment, leaned back against his own seat once more and then said, in a voice that at least seemed to be calm, "If that is the case, then there is no change in the plans, Phillip. Make another u-turn."

"No!" I screamed.

Phillip stepped on the accelerator and the little car shot like an arrow down the steep street.

"Stop the car or I'm going to scream," I shouted. "And the whole city will come down on us. Stop the car! Stop or I'm going to jump out of this car. Stop," I said. "I'm not going anywhere. No plan is going to make me go anywhere. Let me out here. They won't turn you in for that, and they won't kill you for it either. Stop the car!" Phillip did not slow down. I began to kick against the floor of the car and pound my fists into the dashboard and against the windshield.

The priest was not moved but said in a soft voice, "Make another u-turn, Phillip, make a u-turn. Do you know the way, Phillip?"

"Yes. I've already been there. Twice." Phillip stopped the car, took a deep breath with which to completely fill his lungs, as though he were exhausted from all that had passed in those few brief moments inside the car, turned the car around and began driving normally, though it seemed to me that he was actually driving exceptionally slowly. The priest did not say a word. Phillip too remained silent, until he suddenly said, "Look, father, that strange man is riding along in front of us the entire time. The city is completely empty except for him."

"I suppose he is just some sort of ghost or demon on a bike," said the priest, and then fell silent once more.

Suddenly I saw them. They were walking hand in hand along the sidewalk. The words, "There are the children, stop!" slipped from my mouth, but we had already passed them by. We passed the neighbor's wife too, as she walked on ahead of them, in the street. I looked back and pleaded with them once more, "Stop the car."

"Stop the car in another hundred meters, Phillip," said the priest. "They are at home, you said. If they are out in the street then they are not at home. It would be better if we knew where we were headed, Madame Mayer." Phillip turned sharply in-to a convenient little alleyway and stopped the car.

"Talk quickly, Madame Mayer," said the priest, clearly restraining himself, speaking softly, in a tone that was at once controlled and threatening. "You have two minutes to help me understand. And it would be best if I understood. If I don't, then you'll be getting out here and you'll never see me again ever, Madame Mayer, and I am afraid that that forever - given the current circumstances, and the circumstances that have only recently been created - is not actually going to last all that long. Now talk!" I talked. I don't know if I talked for two minutes, or more, or perhaps even less, for that matter. I do not recall precisely just what I said, but I said everything. I told him the whole truth in little fragments, one after the other, every last one of them, and in each and every fragment there was some little piece of fiery truth. He believed me. Phillip, on the other hand, did not seem to believe me. But he did - the man of God. "And the phantom?" he said, half serious, half amused. He saw him, and I saw him too, standing there leaning over his bicycle at the spot where the alleyway branched off from the street where the children were walking along. "It's a mystery, what do I know. You'll explain it to me afterwards," I said. He laughed lightly and said, as though talking to himself, "It's a good thing that there are still a few riddles left in the world. Drive to her house, Phillip. Is it still a long way?" "No," Phillip said. "We're almost there already."

I could see out the window that we were nearing the apartment and I was already holding the handle of the car door impatiently as I said, "Stop the car," but the priest said, "Drive on a little bit further," and then immediately said to me, "Don't get upset, Madame Mayer. We are going to stop right away at a spot from which we will be able to see the children when they arrive, although they will not be able to see us. We will wait until they have gone inside. Then we will take you home right away. We will stop the car for a moment and you will get out and go upstairs. There you will have a chance to embrace your children and then in about another half an hour either Phillip or I will knock at your door. At any rate, God willing, you and the children had better be ready to head out as soon as it gets dark. Are you relaxed now?" I said, "No," and did as I was told.

The apartment door was wide open. I burst inside. The children stood there rooted to the ground, staring in the direction of the door. I embraced them both. I did not pay any attention to the neighbor's wife who was standing there next to them. They did not respond to my embrace with one of their own and when I kissed them both neither one of them kissed me back. They hung their heads. Both of them were wearing expressions filled uniformly with indifferent blame. At that very instant I suddenly sensed that the three of us constituted a shabby little group of helpless creatures being moved about like playing pieces on a board of black and white squares re-presenting life and death, as though our hearts were made of wood, and we were being tossed back and forth, taken to the cathedral for no purpose whatsoever, and then herded back into the apartment for nothing at all, separated from one another and hopelessly lost, and then together again without it actually doing us any good - all of it in accordance with a series of rules that we ourselves were not responsible for and which, in fact, seemed completely mad. It was insulting, above all else. The neighbor's wife stood there among us in silence.

"I must thank you," I said to her. "I know that you saved our skin. They flew the coop. I admire the fact that you managed to keep your cool like that."

She caressed Jackie's head, as I noticed he let her do so, and she said, "Don't talk about keeping one's cool. I was as scared as a nurse in the operating room would be if they suddenly kidnapped the doctors and left her all alone facing a bleeding patient on the gurney. A nurse like that is seized just as I was with a sort of terror at what she absolutely has to do - and immediately, at that. This priest of yours is insane, and we did not manage to think of everything in advance, Madame Mayer. But here we are. I am going to leave you now. Do you know why I will never ever forget you and these boys of yours? Because, I swear, there isn't anyone left in the world anymore for whom I would be ready to go to the cathedral like that. We re-member all the things that could not possibly have happened but which came to pass all the same, we remember the things that will never ever come back again. I will always remember the three of you, but you, if you manage to survive, you must forget me." She left. She stood in the doorway a moment, on the threshold, and without turning around to face us she said, "Go in peace, Madame Mayer. My husband and I would like to let you know that you do not owe us anything for the trip to the cathedral. It's on us. Take good care of yourselves along the way, Madame Mayer. You are going to find yourselves so very alone now." And Erwin translated for me.

And then she shut the door and left.

The next person to come to the door and knock was the priest. He came in as though he was familiar with the apartment since forever, sat down immediately at the table and said, "The cathedral was a fiasco. But you know exactly what I am refer-ring to. I can not let you head out like this before checking your health and the health of the baby you are carrying inside you. A man should not be sent off to die along the very road that he is taking in order to live. I look after the souls we have down here with us because I am a doctor, I am not merely the priest that looks after the souls we take with us up to heaven. But what are we going to do now?"

"We go, that's all," I said.

"I certainly hope so. But you have no idea what you are talking about. Do you know what it means to go in this context? Do you know where you are headed? Do you know if you are heading out to walk a mile, ten miles, twenty, or fifty for that matter? Did you ever even walk a mile in the snow where your legs sink up to the knees, just one single mile, light as a doe, in the snow, have you? And if it's more than a mile, in the Jura snows of early March, and if you are no longer light as a doe, and can't keep up with the children walking along beside you, or the unborn child you are carrying around inside you, can you possibly imagine the amount of strength that you are going to need to make that trip and reach your destination - shouldn't we really check first to see if you altogether have some hidden reserve of strength for such a trip somewhere inside you?" He did not look at me as he said these things. It was as though he were talking to himself within earshot. "Do I have a choice?" I said to him.

He leaped to his feet and said to me in the voice of a rather angry man, "No, you don't. But I do. I am a doctor, not just some sort of a pimp for a band of smugglers. I am not going to take or pass on a single cent if I am not already certain that your health stands a decent chance of making it, even if you don't have a choice. A good friend who knows how to keep a secret and has helped us before was waiting for you and me, at the appointed hour, at his clinic in the hospital. He was willing to risk his life for me. He was going to examine you as well as anyone possibly could. You could well go into labor along the way, Madame Mayer. All alone, in the mountains. What are you going to do if that happens? Who will take care of you? You can not stay here another day, because every day brings you closer to the moment in which they are going to swoop in and capture you and your children, and God have mercy on your souls if that happens. You must leave this place. Can you make it? If need be, do you have any medication among your things? You see, this medical friend of ours is gone at this point, Madame Mayer. He left. You did not show up and so he left. That's all. He told me a time, a precise time at which I was to show up, neither before nor after, since he was running quite a risk, as he too wants to live through these awful days and manage to survive."

The children moved off a bit as though they wanted to step out of earshot of the things that the priest was saying. They stood by the window, pulled aside the curtain and stared off into the night that had already settled in the streets of Saint-Claude.

"I do not quite understand what you are actually telling me," I said. "Are we not leaving? You are a doctor, Father, sir. If your conscience will not permit you to send me off on my way without first conducting a medical examination, then why don't you examine me yourself. I trust you. You were good enough to examine me when I was a prisoner, so I trust you to be good enough to examine me now that I am on the run. The doctor who was willing to risk his life in order to afford me topflight treatment at the hospital - and to whom I am grateful beyond anything that you could possibly imagine - that doctor will forgive me. In your case, God will be the one to forgive. Examine me now, Father, the children are hidden behind the curtain. They have even turned their backs to us. They anyway already know much more than children their age know, or could, or even should know, for that matter. They have already forgiven me and you, and even God Himself. I think."

He stared into my eyes and a smile rose across his rather severe features. "You think," he said, and then he repeated it, "You think. I am not going to examine you here, Madame Mayer. Let us rather try to make do with a quiet conversation between a woman and her doctor. Are you ready? It will be the best possible examination, since at this point it is not possible to do any better." He asked his questions in a whisper, and I gave my responses, likewise in a whisper. He checked to see if the boys were still hidden behind the curtain and listened to the sound of my baby's pulse, with his naked ear. He had no stethoscope. He had not even brought his medical bag with him.

He got up from his seat and went over to the window. He stood behind the curtain with the boys, and with his hands around their shoulders he walked them over to where I sat and said to them, "I am not going to examine the two of you. You are both in good health. You must be in good health. Your mother is also in good health, as is the baby that she is carrying inside her. You are both well aware that this child is on the verge of emerging into the world. He has almost completed all the necessary preparations, this little boy, or girl, for that matter. Now, the three of you are to put on the warmest shoes that you have and get dressed in the heaviest coats that you have brought with you to Saint-Claude, for you are about to set out on a long and difficult journey. You two are rather brave boys. You must take care of your mother along the way. One day, when there will no longer be police officers aboard the trains and no soldiers on the platforms and no guard dogs to sniff out escapees at the borders, you will come back to visit me and you will tell me how the journey went. It may well be that as you tell me your tale you will suddenly realize that you were both in fact heroes and were never aware of this fact before."

"We'll never find you," Jackie said. "You never stay in the same place. How will we ever find you?"

The priest patted Jackie's little shoulders - lovingly, or so it seemed to me, at least - and said, "When the time comes, that won't be a problem anymore. At that point I will have stopped running around and you'll know where to find me."

Jackie lifted his eyes and looked at the priest and then, to my extreme surprise, I saw him embrace the priest around the waist and press his head against him for a moment. Erwin was embarrassed. He stood there next to the priest and his brother and looked at them, and then came over to me, wrapped his little arms around me, and placed his head in my lap. We were ready. The priest stepped over to the door and said, "Phillip will be here any second now," and he left.

Phillip did, indeed, show up almost immediately. He gathered up all our luggage and quickly made his way downstairs. We quickly followed him, wearing everything that we could possibly wear, me with my handbag in my hands, and the children with little knapsacks on their shoulders. I did not look back to see if the neighbor or his wife had stepped out of their room in order to say goodbye to us, but I could sense their gaze on our backs as we left. In an instant we were in the car, the three of us crammed into the narrow back seat, and the priest and Phillip, who was driving, sat up front. Saint-Claude was completely dark, but I recognized every bend in the road, every house, every tree, every little patch of grass. We did not say a word. At the checkpoint on the way out of town the guards stopped the car. The priest stuck his head out the window, waved a greeting to the soldier who had requested his papers, at which sign the latter immediately allowed us to pass, saying, "Safe travels, Father, sir." The vehicle drove straight into the thick of the night.

"That was one of ours," said the priest. "There are no more the rest of the way. I will leave you at Lamoura. You will spend the night there in a granary by the lake. It is frozen. That is where you will also meet up with the smuggler who will take you across. He is a good man and you can trust him. I trust him, at least - don't you, Phillip?"

"He is one of a kind," Phillip said, without taking his eyes off the road as it wound its way through the forests filled with pine trees laden with snow.

Erwin asked, "Is Lamoura far?"

"Nothing is all that far, child, but here, these days, every-thing is much further away than it was before. We no longer live in a world of meters and minutes. These days everything is measured in patience. Do you have it? Then we'll be there in a little bit, be patient, as you said, we'll get to the intersection and turn off the main road onto a dirt path. Then we'll take that path all the way to the lake, although the car might fall to pieces, but it will make it, nonetheless. There we'll find our way to an isolated farm and from the farm we'll find our way to the granary. At the granary we'll find our way to a warm bed. You never had such a warm bed in all your lives." I listened without saying a word. I told myself that the priest was being a bit too playful. Why? Just a moment ago he had said "There are no more the rest of the way." So we were all alone in the forest then, the three of us and him, right alongside us - why did he feel the need to talk so much? Perhaps it was fear. Perhaps he was afraid that we ourselves were fearful. Perhaps he had played too many different roles in his life and simply could not keep track of them all anymore and so he just kept playing and playing. He was a priest, a doctor, a member of the resistance, a smuggler. Was he a saint for the sake of heaven or was he a man of means for money? Perhaps he was both. He was a single man with many disguises. I was evaluating him unfairly and I knew it. I did not want to think about it all anymore. I did not have the right. This man had been a truly righteous figure. That is what he was then, that is what he had always been, and that is what he would always be.

In the darkness the structures of the farm were totally black. The vehicle came to a stop in a murky yard. The sky overhead was full of stars that looked like snowflakes that had been scattered in a storm and frozen in place. Phillip got out first. The priest whispered that we would wait for him to return to the car and he slammed the door shut. The windows were all closed. There was not a soul in sight, but the priest whispered the entire time as though the very wind itself were listening. Empty nights like that are always full of lurking demons. We remained silent. If we could have, we would've even stopped breathing. The sound of our breath in that bubble of silence was loud and threatening and I could even make out the sound of my beating heart. Phillip came back. He opened the door. The priest got out and we got out after him. From somewhere in the dark a man emerged with a pale lantern in his hands. We followed him. He came to a standstill and illuminated the bolt of a huge wooden door. Phillip opened it and a warmth hit us in the face as a sour scent rose to our nostrils. We could not see a thing. The children held my hands and I have no idea if I was the one trembling or was it them. The man entered, put the lantern down on the ground and stood between the light and the entrance, waiting for us all to enter and for Phillip to pull the door shut. I looked into the faces that were barely lit by the wick burning at our feet. They all looked to me like masks without any bodies attached, dangling over an abyss in absolute silence. The man picked up the lantern. To either side we were struck by the shadows of cows all around, some lying down, some standing, some still chewing away, all of them seemed relaxed as their breath rose like some sort of otherworldly vapor of peace and quiet.

The man walked on ahead of us. He went up a wooden ladder,

and we followed him. He pushed at a door that opened onto what seemed like a small space but very dark. He put the lantern down on a cabinet. Phillip closed the door. It turned out we were now inside a rather large room and we could make out another door that opened onto another narrow dark space that looked like some sort of corridor. A large wooden table stood in the middle of the room. The man motioned for us to have a seat. "You can remove your coats now. The cows downstairs warm the place up. You will spend the night here." We did as we were told and we sat obediently together on one side of the table. The man uncorked a bottle of wine, set out glasses, poured one for the priest and another for Phillip, and when I refused the glass he offered me, he added another few drops and then clinked his glass with those of his two friends, mumbled some blessing or other, and then after all three had taken a sip, he said, "You were late. We were expecting you at nightfall. Fine, the-re's always something. Don't even tell me. It's too late now. The guy was here but he left. He'll be back in the afternoon. You will be here then. We have to settle everything."

The priest looked at Phillip and said, "I think that if you can provide us with a little corner ourselves, we too will spend the night here. Less time spent on the roads is more time spent still living. What do you say, Phillip?"

"If you're spending the night here, I'm spending the night here. I already know the guy. We better stay. If he said that he would be here in the afternoon he may well show up immediately, or in the evening, or whenever works for him. Might be a minute from now, might be the next day."

"You're giving him a bad name, Phillip," the priest said, in a tone that had a slight rebuke in it. "He's a professional, Phillip. I know him too. He's a bit of an intellectual, a bit of a bohemian, but he's a professional. He'll be here in the afternoon in order to set out tomorrow night when there's no moon. We waited specifically for a night like this. You can't play games with the moonlight. A day, or two, for that matter, but that's it, after that you've got the world's biggest lamp hung right up there in the night sky and even a fox wouldn't manage to steal across the border into Switzerland. We'll spend the night here."

"That's no problem," said the man, who was no doubt the owner of the farm. He turned to me and said, "Two or three good pieces of advice, Madame. One: you are not to leave this room. That means the children are not to leave the room either, is that understood?" Erwin immediately responded that this was indeed understood.

"A young man after my own heart," said the owner. "Two: Madeleine, my daughter, will be here in the morning and she will prepare something for you to eat and drink. Until that time, I am sorry to say, Madame, but I don't have anything to of-fer you. That means the children will have to go to bed on an empty stomach. They may as well be aware of that fact at once."

Erwin translated and said, "That's fine. We're used to it."

The man laughed softly and said, "That's actually something you ought not to get used to. Three: there is no bathroom here and there is no running water, Madame. That means that I am going to take you to go to the bathroom in a place where there is a bathroom now, and afterwards you will have to wait until Madeleine shows up in the morning. That means the children had better understand what I am getting at, you follow?"

Erwin translated and said, "That's no problem. We understand."

The priest patted Erwin affectionately on the shoulder and said to the owner of the farm, "That's a bit cruel, my friend. I, for my own part, can't give you my word."

"With all due respect," said the man, "there are demands one makes on the ave-rage man but which one does not make on a man of God. But all kidding aside. We must discuss everything. The Germans are constantly roaming the area. There is no reason for you to be afraid, but you ought to at least be aware of this fact. They co-me here to buy milk, cheese, eggs, chickens. I gladly sell to them. I pray of course that they choke on what they eat or drink but I am glad that they are at least parting with their money at my place. A few days ago they were preparing for a coming storm and they came here to ask if they could spend the night in the barn. I told them - why not? What else could I tell them? Somehow it didn't work out. I received the two officers who seemed especially friendly. They did not insult my wine. They stumbled drunkenly along the short path to the vehicle that stood there waiting for them quite some time, and for some reason they never came back - neither the officers, nor the soldiers under their command. I had to weather the storm all by myself. Do you pity me, father?"

He did not wait for a response but turned to me and said, "Come, Madame. I will show you where you are going to sleep. I will leave one lantern there in a secure spot - the little one. You will quickly get used to it. Then we will make our little trip to the bathroom. You, Father, and Phillip, will wait here for me until I get back."

In the room there were two beds without frames or linen, although there were quite a few blankets on top of each bed. Erwin felt the mattress and said that it felt like his was made of straw. I told him that I had felt mine and that it was in fact made of silk thread.

"Let's switch," Jackie offered playfully, and Erwin immediately responded, "That won't help you. Mom's silk will turn into straw if you lie down on it and our straw will turn into silk if Mom lies down on it."

"That's true," said Jackie. "Mommy is a magician," and he lay down on his mat-tress fully clothed and I had to pick him up and spread the blankets underneath him and Erwin had to give me a hand, because the boy had already drifted off into a deep sleep.

As I lay down fully clothed I thought to myself that I was turning the page on a Sunday that had been fuller than a single day could ever possibly be. I told my-self that if I were a queen I would have created a land in which they did not count the days in order, but in accordance with all the things that you managed to cram into them. I would have a plain old day, and a light day, and a regular day, and a full day, and another day that would change all the others - both the days that had already been and those that were still yet to come - whether they would pass in play or tears, in sound and fury or absolute silence. But in such a land, I thought, I could not possibly be a queen other than for myself alone. If such a kingdom actually existed where every individual was blessed with his or her own individual days, and these days were measured and named and set in accordance with whatever they held for each and every individual, then even the trains would not be able to run in such a place, even if the entire kingdom was covered in tracks, because in order for the trains to run you have to have a country where all the people keep the same time, measured in the seconds and minutes, hours and days. And when my idiotic thoughts brought me to a consideration of the fact that there is no individual whose world is actually the same as that of his neighbor, although time in all these worlds is nevertheless one and the same for each and every one of these individuals, the salvation of sleep came along to resolve all my tangled, unripe problems, and I drifted off into a land where I did not even dream a single dream.

We all woke up as one to the youthful, ringing sound of a voice calling out, "Good morning." Madeleine was a rather round girl, though an amazingly agile, and her laugh was clear clean and full of the sort of joy that needed neither rhyme, nor reason. She spoke of nothing other than the very thing that she was busy with at that particular moment. She showed us the way to the bathroom, which she called the 'toilette', and when it came time to wash up, she pronounced the word, 'soap', then she made us coffee, telling us that she was making real coffee and not chicory, then sliced some thick black farmer's bread, placing a firm slab of fresh, white butter alongside it, saying 'bread', and 'enjoy', and a few other things of that sort. Her eyes flashed with a simple intelligence, and I had no doubt in my mind that she used so few words although she was actually a rather talkative girl by nature, but they had taught her that the most effective way of exercising caution is to avoid saying the wrong thing and to simply refrain from speaking altogether. She had, no doubt, and limited her words to describing precisely what was already clearly visible to all concerned. In this way she managed to avoid getting drawn into a conversation, or being asked uncomfortable questions, or being tricked into revealing secrets or giving away any difficult riddles. She was an important part of the secret network that thrived at the crossroads between the world where those who wished to live were willing to sacrifice everything in order to escape, and that world which you could not put too high a price tag on and which all those lost souls wished to enter. I had not yet been asked to pay up. But I knew that between the priest, and Phillip, and the farm owner, and the man that they referred to as 'the guy', who was going to show up in the afternoon, and this Madeleine here who took such wonderful care of us in the morning, and who knows who else, I would be asked to pay in the form of those diamonds inside my block of soap.

The man showed up precisely at noon. Nobody noticed when he actually arrived since the three of us - the children and I - were all hidden away in our little room, and neither the priest nor Phillip nor the owner of the farm were waiting there with us at that moment. He did not knock at any of the doors. He was suddenly in our midst, with a leather jacket under his arm, a fur hat in one hand, a rather tall man, with silvery shoots of grey in his smooth, black, well-combed hair. His starched collar was adorned with a flowery bowtie that fluttered above a woven vest of Scotch plaid, fastened firmly to his waist with little ivory buttons. He was wearing a brown unbuttoned mohair sportsjacket that hung down past his narrow waist. His brown slacks had been sewn up to suit his heavy winter boots, which were polished till they shone as though they were not intended for a stroll down the street but were meant to go on display in the window of the fanciest haberdashery around. He said, "Madame, call me Fernand." I was completely surprised. I had not expected our smuggler to sport such a name, or cut the figure that he did. I was on the verge of placing my life in his hands, mine and the lives of my children as well. In my mind I had imagined a sort of shadowy figure, a man who blended into the background as he moved about, a man who did not catch the eye of the casual passerby, a man no one paid any attention to, and here I was face to face with a dashing dandy, a showoff who was clearly no more than a boastful impostor, not the seeming intellectual that the priest had described, nor some bohemian - and so I wondered if he were truly a professional after all. And what profession would that be anyway? He looked like the dashing seducer in some romantic movie, in which I could not be anything other than the tragically deceived leading lady. All these thoughts flashed quickly through my mind as soon as I saw him and heard his silky voice. I felt trapped, felt like some sort of prey that had no choice but to ensnare itself. The children looked up at me. They did not know if they ought to be struck dumb by the spectacle that they had before them, or if they ought to let the situation unfold, and so they seemed to be waiting for me to pass judgment on their behalf. I was paralyzed and all I managed to say was, "Bonjour

Fernand."

At that very moment Madeleine entered and gave expression to her surprise by leaping into Fernand's arms and planting a series of kisses on his forehead and cheeks as she giggled things like, "Fernand, you're here! Fernand, there you are! Fernand, how did you manage to slip inside? Fernand, you cat, you!" Fernand absorbed all this affection without moving from where he stood and without moving his hands, in which he held his coat and hat, as he said, "You are as wonderful as ever, my beautiful Madeleine. Where are the good gentlemen? After all, I told them I would be here at noon. I keep a strict schedule, as you well know, Madeleine. Precision, my girl, is the foundation of all the secrets of our noble trade. Would it be too much trouble, or asking a tad too much for that matter, if I were to request that you kindly call the good gentlemen to come here?"

Before the good gentlemen showed up, Fernand put his leather jacket down on a chair, But first he cleaned off the chair with a large checkered handkerchief that he pulled from his pocket then carefully folded the coat and placed the fur hat on top of it Then he sat down, crossing one leg over the other and beginning to drum with his long fingers on the tabletop to the rhythm of a rather patient tango, in silence. He pulled a flat, fancy silver box from the breast pocket of his sportscoat, took out a cigarette and, after lighting it with a rather delicate silver lighter, as he followed the perfect bluish smoke rings that rose before him towards the ceiling of our little room, he said, "You will allow me to have a smoke, of course, Madame. I never smoke once we are on our way. That is why I always smoke once I have reached my destination, or before setting out, for that matter. I thank you. Dear God, they are running rather late." His free hand went back to drumming on the tabletop and I almost lost my mind, while he hardly acknowledged the children and me with so much as a glance.

As soon as the priest and Phillip finally arrived, the three of them began talking amongst themselves as though I were not even present. They spoke in tones that were barely above a whisper. I could hardly make out a word of what they were saying and I only understood a small part of the little bit that I heard. The farm owner joined us after a little while, but he did no more than lean in to the circle of his friends and listen, as he rose from time to time in order to offer his guests some food or drink. A little while later, Madeleine came and set the table as she hummed some joyful folk tune. The owner pushed aside a few of the plates that Madeleine had already set out and spread a tablecloth across the table. Then we all leaned in and listened to the brief speech that Fernand gave, accompanying his words with a closed black fountain pen that he moved over the top of the tablecloth. There were questions, but no arguments, and there were answers, but no objections. Fernand knew what he wanted. He was quiet, serious, calm, and confident. I no longer noticed the way he was dressed or heard the thrum of his fingertips on the tabletop. I stared at him for quite a while and said to myself that the priest knew what he was saying when he had rebuked Phillip by referring to him as "a professional".

Fernand got up and said, "But we are committing a rather grave offense against Madeleine's wonderful cuisine. The scent has risen into my nostrils and it is fairly driving me mad. Let us eat, and at the same time we can tell this good lady what she must be dying to know. We have been acting rather barbarously, gentlemen. We have been ignoring her. We have been discussing things as though she were not the very subject of our discussion. There can be no pardon for such an offense, isn't that so, father? Let us eat, then, and so cleanse our conscience." He pulled up a chair, offered me his hand, and said, "Madame", and when I was about to sit down he pushed the chair beneath me towards the table and then did the same for the boys, as he said, "My young men." This charming bluffer was so transparent that even a woman of rather refined tastes like myself ought to have been put off by him, but I was not.

The meal was filled with delicacies. I am not sure if even in the very best restaurants in Paris - where I have never, in fact, dined - do they serve such excellent food. I did not have an exact idea what I was eating, but when 'the guy' gently wiped his mouth clean with a napkin that had been inserted into his starched collar and said, "The rabbit is wonderful. God bless the rabbit," I knew that I was eating something that I had never before thought I would ever eat. And not because it was not kosher. We had long since let go of those dietary restrictions, as you well know Moritz, almost from the very day that we had run from Antwerp. But it was the rabbit itself. It was because of the fact that there are certain things that the stomach of a woman like me simply can not bear, and that is just the way things always were, ever since I was born. But here this too had now come to pass. And I ate. The children stopped chewing for a moment and looked at me, and when they saw me eating away, they too began chewing their food once more. It had been months since we had eaten such an abundant, full, tasty meal like that, and, when I think of it, perhaps we never had. A last supper, I thought to myself, a last supper - and the priest, who had perhaps read my mind, said, "Eat as much as you want, Madame Mayer. This is, of course, not a last supper, but until you reach your destination who knows what there will be to eat, if anything at all - who knows? Ask for seconds, boys," he said to the children. "Today it is certainly allowed, even according to the strictest etiquette there is." And so the boys asked for seconds.

Madeleine cleared the table and then served a large cake with a crumb top-ping that gave off a rather sweet scent, as she set out a series of plates decorated with pictures of wild forest herbs alongside pretty little utensils, and teacups into which she poured hot tea, at which point Fernand said, "And now, Madame, a few very important things." The priest pushed aside his teacup as the steam rose into his face, cut off Fernand as he spoke and said, "First let me tell you, Madame Mayer, just who this Fernand is. It is critical that you know. He knows everything that we know about you, so forgive me if I do not mention anything that has already been said. It is not for a lack of manners, God forbid, that I do so. Fernand has not once failed to convey his charges across the border, and there have been quite a number of them. You are one of ours now, Madame Mayer, and your children are right there along with you. It may well be that it was a miracle which brought us together, though it may well also be that if more miracles existed in this world we would never have even met, but all that does not matter now. You are one of us. We have entrusted you to his care. He will not fail this time either. It would not be a good thing if you knew too much about this Fernand of ours. If, God forbid, anything should go wrong, your ignorance would be a blessing - for you, for us, and for Fernand as well. One thing I can tell you - if you only knew his name you would no doubt ask yourself how such a well-known individual managed to become a smuggler. I will not mention just what he was so well-known for, but you yourself can well imagine. He has not stopped being what he once was, but he will also never again be that same man, since as far as the Book of Jura Chronicles is concerned, in these mountain forests, as you well know, he will be remembered as a mere legend. Put your trust in him just as you put your trust in me. You will be with him through nights in which you will not be able to tell the difference between the silent snows, fairly fainting from the cold, and packs of wolves roaming the forest in search of easy prey. But he knows. Like a man of God - as you have heard people refer to me - I tell you now that Fernand, from this moment on, is to be your God and the God of your children too. Do not blaspheme him even once you have been saved. And now, Fernand, tell her what it is that you have to say."

"It's not much," Fernand said, as he crushed out the cigarette he had used to produce those perfect smoke rings while the priest was giving us his little speech. "It's not much. We are going to travel by night, on foot. We will not be taking the usual paths. I will move along with you on skis - with you, though out in front. You are only to walk in the grooves that the skis leave in the snow. You are to stand still or crouch down and wait if I leave you behind for a moment in order to scout out the route, and you are to walk in single file, never side by side, and follow where I lead once I return. You are not to speak at all, not one single word. Should I choose to whisper something to you, then you may respond likewise in a whisper. I will not whisper a thing if the moment is not right for you to respond. By day you will rest in the granaries that will be put at your disposal. Though it will not be anything like this place of kindness and hospitality. That's everything. I know the route, just as well as I knew the way from my own childhood bedroom to my mother's room. I will not tell you the route, but it is marked out on this piece of paper here." He spread a sheet of paper before us, where he had drawn with his fountain pen landmarks noted along a winding line while they had discussed things over the tablecloth.

The letters were so small that we could barely make them out, but the first location - Saint-Claude - was clearly visible. This name was writ large, as was the final destination, writ large as well - La Cure, Switzerland. He folded up the sheet of paper, placed it in the hand of the priest and said, "That's everything. All that I can tell you is that you will be crossing the border at La Cure. If you get lost in the snows you must remember this name - La Cure. We will manage to get whatever hurried rest we can at the various stops along the way. Each spot is planned, each spot is ready and waiting for you. It is all very precise - that is the foundation of all the secrets of our trade. You need not know all, in the event that you are caught and forced to sing, as it were, all that you know, for then the Teuton Boches would destroy this route along with anyone expecting your arrival along the way. These good gentlemen know all, as they have to. God is watching over us from on high, while these men, led by our priest, this man of God, are watching over us down here. This is the most fitting arrangement as far as God is concerned, and in the eyes of man as well - if one may still express something of a theological desire these days. Forgive me, Madame, not for my meaning but for my choice of words, 'theological', that is.

"Though once we are on the topic of theology, let me also mention that you must settle your bill with them now. You have no direct connection to me, Madame. You must settle with them, and they in turn will settle with me. That is the arrangement. It is easier that way for everyone. At nightfall Phillip will bring you to the spot from which we will be setting out." He got up, shook my hand and the hands of the boys, called to Madeleine, kissed her on her cheeks and bid farewell to the priest and Phillip and the farm owner and then left the same way that he had come.

Phillip was the one who estimated the value of the diamonds that I had left with me. I suppose that he had learned the trade from his father. He examined all the stones, carefully folded the white envelope in which they had been resting all this ti-me, took it in his hand and said to the priest, "May I have a word with you?" The two of them got up and stepped off into one of the corners of the room and exchanged a few words between them. When they came back to the table the priest said, "You will not have much left, Madame

Mayer. I do not want to tell you the numerical value that we have estimated for the diamonds that you have with you, nor what this entire journey is going to cost until it reaches its happy end. You will no longer be needing the block of soap, Madame Mayer. It has done its job to the best of its abilities. Leave it here now. It will not be used. I will look after it for as long as need be. I will not even reconnect the two halves. If I should be left some small spot of my own on this fair earth I will place the two halves on a little wooden platter, made from the wood of the area, Madame Mayer, and set it down on one of the shelves in my library - not among my medical books, though, no, no. And should anyone ever ask me the why and the wherefore of this item, I shall simply tell them that during this war, this foulest of all wars, even a forgotten block of soap managed to play an unforgettable role."

Phillip and the owner of the farm eyed him as he spoke and he returned their gaze. He seemed to nod in their direction with his eyelids. Out of the corner of my eye I saw Phillip slip the envelope into the pocket of the shirt that he was wearing under-neath his thick woollen sweater. He came over to me, shook my hand, sat down and said, "I could use a drink." The owner of the farm brought over some wine and a thick ceramic bowl. He poured out the glass-es, including one for me. Before we drank, the priest placed the two halves of my block of soap in the bowl, waved his glass in one hand, as he held Erwin's shoulders with his other hand, and Erwin held mine, and I, in turn, held Jackie's, while Jackie did not place his hand on anyone's shoulders, though Phillip and the owner of the farm each held the other's shoulders, as the priest intoned, "May God bless you all," and the farm owner added, "safe travels," and even Madeleine joined in and quickly poured herself a glass that almost overflowed as she said, in a fairly joyful voice, "safe travels." And so we stood there, for-ming a small circle in that little wooden room of our hidden tower, and we each sipped from our cups, even the three of us, Erwin, Jackie, and I, as the two boys asked for the very slightest touch of wine themselves, and not one of us spoke so much as a single word, we did not make a sound. It was truly a sight to behold.

We were told to get some rest in the afternoon. The boys rested on their single bed, back to back, and did not say a word, though I could tell that they were wide awake and already anticipating night-fall. Through my fluttering eyelids I could see Madeleine come in on tiptoe, checking on the boys to see if they were sleeping, and then coming over to me to see if I had fallen asleep as well, and then gently setting about packing up three backpacks - two rather large ones and one considerably larger one - taking care not to wake us up, God forbid. When she accidentally knocked two cans of food to-gether, making a sharp sound, she immediately froze and checked to see if any of our gentle sleep had been disturbed and then continued with her preparations. I saw her wrapping three large, round loaves of bread in brown paper, which she could not keep from rustling as she folded and fastened it in place. Had we actually been sleep-ing we would have woken up, but given the fact that we were not, in fact, sleeping, the rustling sounds could not actually awaken us, much to the concerned, cautious Madeleine's delight. I did not know how the children would manage under the weight of the knapsacks through the long and difficult journey, nor how I, for that matter - given my rather particular condition and somewhat diminished strength - would manage the one that was being prepared for me. I told myself that the journey could not actually be all that long if the knapsacks were to be so heavy, but then I immediately retorted that it precisely could not be a brief journey if our saviors were busy preparing such full knapsacks for us to carry. My thoughts revolved entirely around these knapsacks that were being packed up before my supposedly closed eyes.

Suddenly, to my embarrassment, I found myself entertaining the question of whether Fernand - who had told us that he would be on skis ahead of us, marking out the route for us - would be carrying his own provisions on his back, or whether we would ac-tually be carrying his provisions too in our own sacks on his behalf. The purpose would be to ensure that he would remain light on his feet precisely for our benefit, but if some mishap should happen, he would then be able to escape while we would be crushed on the spot. I immediately told myself that this was not possible. No man in his right mind - not even a smuggler in a time of war - would ease his own burden in order to load it onto the backs of a pregnant woman and her small children, but for some reason I also immediately recalled what the priest had said to us, "If you only knew his name, you would ask yourself how such a well-known individual managed to become a smuggler." Could it be that although I had failed to recognize him - and I was sure that I had not - I nevertheless knew just what he was like? I was ashamed. I was confused and would only have become even more confused if I continued trying to judge and justify, judging and justifying this 'guy' of ours, the riddle of whose 'true identity' so occupied me, despite the fact that common sense dictated that it really did not matter anymore at that point. If I had allowed my thoughts to continue I would have maintained - and then immediately denied - that he was some nobleman who had gone bankrupt, or a gypsy fiddler who had run off on his own into the arms of the French bohemian scene, or even some Jew who had emigrated from the *Cheder*, the religious day school, to the public high schools, and from the public high schools on to joining the communists, and the communists had then led him to the salons of rich, bored, high-society ladies, and from there he had fallen in with helpless people like me who had no other option. And so I suddenly got up from my bed in order to put an end to all these rambling assumptions and approximations, and I said, as though in complete surprise, "Madeleine, what are you doing here? Please don't tell me that you're going to all this trouble for us."

"It's no trouble," Madeleine joyfully replied, and she immediately put her finger to her lips, as though to stifle her own voice in order not to wake the boys, who could restrain themselves no longer and raised their heads in unison from the flat bed where they were lying. "It's a good thing you've woken up. You were sleeping like logs. Wonderful. You will be setting out in about another half hour. I was just about to wake you up. How did you know to wake up all by yourselves? Terrific. Get up. Go to the toilette, dress very, very warmly, and then take your knapsacks that have already been packed up by some kind fairy who had no idea just what to fill them with. Seal the packs and off you go. Safe travels, and, of course, take care - and that's it!"

We made our final preparations when it was already dark. Madeleine, who was with us the entire time, lit a single lantern by whose light we got dressed in our warmest clothing. She helped us get the knapsacks on our backs, then picked up the lantern in her hand and stepped before us as we followed her down the wooden steps with added caution. We passed among the cows, though all we saw was the bobbing bit of light from the lantern dancing before us, reflected in their big, black eyes. Madeleine opened the large wooden door. Phillip was standing by the car, whose engine was already rumbling in the darkness. He helped us remove the knapsacks from our backs and placed them inside the vehicle - two packs in the front seat by the driver and one in the back. Madeleine, in her light clothing, was trembling from the cold, as she kissed me and the boys goodbye and then ran back inside the barn, as Phillip got in the car and waited for the three of us to get settled in the narrow space left along the back seat.

We headed out in complete silence. After a few moments I mentioned to Phillip that we had not said goodbye to the priest. Erwin translated for me. "You already said goodbye," Phillip responded. "We drank and all bid each other farewell. You already said goodbye to me too, but I still have to take you to your meeting. But not the priest. He is a good man, this priest of ours. You were lucky to have met him. You are perhaps his final charges. He is insane. He knows that fortune is not some sort of bottomless well, and that even a man like him can not rely endlessly on God. But that's the way he is and there is no changing him, and he will continue to be like that. He will either put an end to the war or the war will put an end to him." "And you?" I asked. "I am a different story." "And 'the guy', our smuggler?" Phillip was silent for a moment and then said, "'The guy' is yet another story, another story altogether."

We drove along through absolute darkness. The vapor of our breath clung to the car windows, as the vehicle rode on with its headlights off. If not for the rolling sound of the engine, I could have imagined that we were gliding along silently in the darkness and that the entire field of snow lay spread out before us, as the pitch-black forests marked out a path for us straight on through. After about a half an hour the greenish light of a lantern flickered before us and signalled us to stop. We pulled up by the side of a small wooden cabin. Fernand, a huge black shadow, was waiting for us to get out. Phillip did not turn the engine off. He ably assisted us to get the knapsacks onto our backs once more, rubbed his hands together in order to keep them warm, and said, "It'll all work out," and then he left. The sound of his car engine, that suddenly sounded like the voice of a loved one, died away in the darkness.

Fernand led us inside the cabin and set the lantern in a place where the light it gave now shone up from the floor. We were all illuminated from the ground up and so seemed much taller than we were actually used to being. Fernand, of course, towered over the rest of us. He was holding a pair of skis that were resting on his shoulder, and a dark woollen cap came down to his eyes. His ski outfit was also dark and consisted of a jacket, pants, and heavy boots. A small knapsack was pressed close to his back where it hung from his shoulders, and there was not a single trace of the man that we had met just a few hours earlier.

"I want to know if everything is essentially clear to you," he said, though he did not wait for a response as he added, "I know exactly where we are headed. The snow does not know a thing, but I do, and so do you, precisely. Even if it seems to you at certain points that we are taking our time along the way, we will get to where we are going quicker than you can possibly imagine. It will not be an easy night, but you are hardy travellers. Things will get harder tomorrow night, and then they will get even harder the night after that. Nothing will be easy until we get to where we are going. Not for you, Madame, and not for you, my young men, but we will manage. If we should fall along the way that would be much worse. I have faith. Do you? This is an important point. Everything depends on this. You have faith, I know you do. You have no other choice. Besides that, luck is on your side. This winter is milder than any other that we have known in the region for years. That means that it is beastly cold, but it could have been worse. That's both good and bad. It's good because it's a little like a discount in a store that is still pretty expensive. And it's bad because the scoundrels can roam the area more freely in search of clients, as it were. But I will be here with you, the entire time. They won't get to you. Have faith."

He attached the skis to his feet, took the lantern in his hands, switched the light to green, turned it on and off a time or two and then said, "This will be our sign. If it blinks once, that means I am moving off. Three times means I am coming closer. Four or five in rapid succession mean danger, hide if possible, and if you can't, then don't make a move. You are not to run. There is no such thing as an escape route in the snows and forests of the Jura. Now everything should be clear to you. Remember the green light. That is your color. Any other light - and there will often be others - is not meant for you, and generally not for me either, but I know how to read the other lights - who is signalling whom and for what - and sometimes the messages are even meant for me. Green is your color. If we need to communicate, it's green." He emerged from the cabin like a bird limping along on open wings, and we followed heavily after. The cabin door closed behind us. He skied on ahead of us at a slow, measured pace, and we walked along, with Erwin up front, followed by Jackie, and then me, following one of the two grooves that his skis left in the deep, soft snow that carpeted the mountains.

My dear Moritz, I can not possibly tell you all that we went through during the long trip to La Cure. I remember everything but I no longer recall just how to remember all that I remember. Time travelled with us but we seemed to be walking along on some endless journey while time stood endlessly still. I know that these lines are somewhat complicated, and that they perhaps do not manage to express anything more than a series of disjointed, senseless words possibly can. But that is how things went. The night only came to an end at dawn. Seemingly available woodcutters' cabins were our accommodations during the day, which only came to an end once the stars came out. It was in there that we ate whatever we ate, and Fernand would eat whatever he ate alongside us. There were beds and a closet and folded blankets in the cabins, there was a cold, silent, black iron stove that we could not light for fear that the rising smoke might attract the armed and the curious. The dread of the cold was even worse than the cold itself. I was afraid to let the children remove their boots for fear that they would not be able to get them back on again. And even though they were meant to be waterproof, little bits of frozen snow managed to work their way inside and immediately melt there into their socks that the interminable progress on foot fairly tore to shreds. I tried to take my own off, but

my feet refused to emerge from the boots. They were so swollen that
if I had even managed to get them out of the boots I would never
have managed to get them back on once more. So I gave up. I had a
tough time retying the laces on those foul boots that I had purchased
when we were still in Marseille and which were, in fact, not at all
suitable to this journey through the snow-filled mountains. I did not
want the same thing to hap-pen to the children. Jackie did not say a
thing, but he was constantly stamping his feet, both in order to keep
them warm, and in order to communicate to me - that I really ought
to have taken a path that would allow a young boy to remove his
waterlogged boots. The three of us huddled together as we covered
ourselves with the blankets, fully clothed and with our boots still on,
wide awake, though unsure which one of us had actually fallen off
to sleep, or was sleeping and still so unsure if we were, in fact, still
awake. And despite the windows that were firmly sealed in order
to turn the day inside these cabins into night, I can not be sure that
when night fell, just before we set out on our way once again, we
had actually managed to sleep at all.

I do not know if Fernand slept, or where, for that matter. Perhaps he disappeared to some neighboring village, to a friendly inn
he knew, or the house of some woman who was the wife of one of
those husbands that had failed to come back home. Who knows?
The children wondered the same thing, and Erwin asked in a whisper if I knew for sure that Fernand was there with us inside the
cabin. I told him that it would seem that Fernand had some hidden
little corner of his own, but since he himself did not have to fear the
light of day all that much, he must have headed out to check if the
route was clear and to pass on messages to our benefactor the priest
that everything was going as planned. The children believed me.
And I, for my own part, I must admit, I found that I too believed the
things that I told them. In any case, when night fell, Fernand was
there, refreshed, and full of energy, and completely alert, and I am
sure that his boots in those skis of his were dry.

We barely spoke with Fernand at all. In reality , we were hardly ever together. When he was marking out the path, he would ski
along at a distance of about twenty to thirty yards in front of us, a
distant shadow in the night that we could barely make out, and it

was impossible to say a word to him at that point. From time to time he would increase the distance between us considerably, though then he would return, after just a few moments, or sometimes even fifteen minutes, a half hour, an hour, or even more. All that time we would not even see the blinking green lights of his lantern, but we would walk on without stopping up to the point marked out in the snow by his skis, and then we would wait where they ended for him to return, when we did not know which way to proceed. In some places the snow was hard and almost frozen and it hurt our feet to walk, like we were moving along the face of a huge rocky boulder, though other times you could tell that it was a mild winter by the softness of the snow, as we sank down past our ankles. Progress was difficult and exhausting and slow, and we would find ourselves breathing hard after only a few steps, stopping for a moment, completely worn out then gather more strength, and then setting out once more in single file in the direction of a destination that seemed to be always further off and almost desperately out of reach.

Fernand did not offer us any words of encouragement. Whatever he had to say he would tell us inside the log cabin from where we would set out each night. As the priest had said, he was indeed a professional. He did not buck us up, he did not offer words of support, and he did not try to soothe our nerves. He did not show any traits that could possibly detract from the figure he cut of a man who was an expert in his field. He was not taking me across the border as some sort of personal favor to me, or Erwin, or Jackie. We could have easily been a completely different group of people. He would have treated them the very same way that he treated us, since they, like us, would have been no more than a sort of collection of living, breathing objects, that had no idea how to get by themselves from that place in which they had no future, to the border on whose other side they did, perhaps, have a future, yet he knew how to get there, though we, and anyone else like us, did not.

The worst was the third evening. We had been walking along for about an hour when Fernand suddenly skied over to and whisper to me, "We must go back. There is no danger, but we must go back." We did not retrace our steps. At night - and perhaps not solely at night, for that matter - a person walking along through the forests and snow in the mountains has no idea where he or she is headed unless they have someone like Fernand to lead the way. There are no signposts that such a person could possibly recognize, no marker that they might remember, even if they had left one along the way as they went. The entire world turns into one vast no-man's land. It was only once we got back to the cabin that we had left two or three hours earlier that Fernand told us that he had noticed a sign, which I had not picked up on, that indicated to him in accordance with a prearranged system that the route was blocked that night by what could only have been a squadron of border patrol guards. There is nothing to be done in such an unexpected situation but to head back to a spot where one is relatively safe. "Tonight you will sleep at night. You may have difficulty tomorrow, because all day we will not be able to leave here until night falls. But we already discussed this, isn't that right? and we said that if we fall along the way it would be even worse. I am here with you. The entire time. If not the entire time, then most of the time, at least. Now not another word, not even a whisper. Everything is the same as it always is. Ah, yes, I forgot the main thing. I recommend that you not remove your boots. You will have to put them on once more and who knows if you will then be able to. It is perhaps a minor issue, I know. But it is better that you be aware of it, it's something you ought to know."

That entire day we did not leave the cabin. Even when night fell we remained inside and the whole next day as well. I am not really sure anymore when it comes to the whole aspect of passing time. I already said something to you about people walking along while time itself has come to a complete standstill. Now I am talking about things that happened while time kept moving right along but the people themselves had come to a standstill. It is all one and the same... perhaps. Either there is no one there to even keep time, or there is simply no time to be kept. But I did. How did I manage? I suddenly felt a slight pain in the middle of my back. It came on all of a sudden and passed almost as soon as I felt it and then came back a little while later. I was filled with a tremendous terror that I was in fact going into labor, though it was not yet actually time for me to give birth, as far as I could tell - as though the baby was alerting me that it was going to emerge somewhat ahead of schedule. What would I have done if I had indeed gone into labor? But the pangs I felt were not labor pains. I already knew what those were like, but it was enough for me to feel this other sort of pain for me to worry about going into labor. I denied its existence, but I was on constant alert, like a woman gripped by the fear that the pain would sooner or later return. And it did. It came back once, and then again, came back and then disappeared, then came back again, and that was how I kept track of time, that seemed to stand still like a river whose source has been sealed and whose mouth has been completely blocked up, and so I counted these bouts of pain in order to plot the length of the day as it stood stock still. From time to time I would lift my hand to my forehead in order to convince myself that I was not suffering from a fever as well. Erwin sensed the meaning of my gesture and gave me a questioning look. I gave him a sign to say that everything was going fine and took his hand, removed the woollen gloves that he had not taken off since the first night we had set out on our journey, and passed the cold palm of his hand over my forehead in order to get him to relax, for even though my forehead was no doubt warmer than the palm of his hand, he could certainly tell that I was not feverish. He checked the warmth of his own forehead, put his gloves back on, wrapped his arms around my waist and sat there embracing me, with his head on my shoulder, without moving a muscle. Jackie did the same, removing his glove, checking my forehead, then hugging me and placing his head on my other shoulder, and that was how we stayed for quite some time, the three of us completely motionless.

Fernand was barely with us. He sat off in the darkness, with one of his skis re-sting right nearby and holding the other in his hands, as he seemed to be using it to prop himself up. That entire day I seemed to drift back and forth, in and out of sleep. My eyelids felt heavy and would sink down over my eyes without my noticing it, until I would suddenly feel like I was about to actually fall asleep, and I was exhausted, almost completely lacking any volition or even the ability to desire any-thing whatsoever, and then I would open my eyes and look around in order to make sure that everything that had been there with us when my eyes had closed was still with us now that I had opened them once more. This too is sleep, or at least one type of sleep. Everything would seem the same as before, but Fernand would no longer be sitting in the same spot. He would disappear for quite a while, and then come back and sit down once more without saying a word, and then disappear again, only to come back once more.

At that point I had no doubts whatsoever. I do not know what he knew or did not know when it came to the goings-on outside the cabin, whether he had seen squadrons of border patrol guards out there or not. I did not know if someone had left him a sign to say that there was still a threat of danger in the area, or if there were no signs being left during daylight hours and so he had to wait for some new sign in the night. He may well have known what he knew for certain, or it may be that he simply had a knack for sensing the situation somehow, being an expert in taking the necessary precautions and judging which chances you could take and which were absolutely prohibitive. At any rate, I was hidden away, walled off with my children inside a freezing cabin because of some danger that I could not see, trying to protect myself from a pursuer whose whereabouts I was not aware of, concerned for this life of mine that might come to an end at any moment in the hands of an enemy for whom the entire countryside was one big ambush, and wherever I tried to hide I was at once a survivor and a sacrifice. This Fernand of ours could not possibly understand that a woman, a mother with her small children, gradually begins to lose her mind when all she can do to fight for her life is to sit still and do nothing at all, and all the demands she makes of herself regarding an awareness of the location of the evil that will soon swoop down on her is a sort of hopeless set of demands to begin with. But there was no reason for Fernand to have understood. All he had to do was get us across the bridge. That's all. His whole life began and ended on that bridge and that bridge alone. How had the priest referred to him? - 'One of ours'. But he was never more than just one man, in body and soul.

What did 'one of ours' mean? Were they some cabal of volunteers plucked from among the righteous gentiles? Were they a group of Maquis resistance fighters? Were they any sort of resistance, some sort of underground - be it the communist reds, the black catholic communists, or patriots of any stripe or faith, so long as hatred of the Germans was the deepest belief they shared and the brightest color in their ideological banner? Fernand might well have been a man who was prepared to die for his country, if he even had a homeland, or for his comrades, if he truly felt that he had any, or for his beliefs, if he had any of those, for that matter. Did he have a wife, children, any borders whatsoever, aside from the border between neutral Switzerland and occupied France? Had the priest entrusted our souls to a man like that? And if that was the case, then who was the priest really? Or perhaps that was precisely it, he had entrusted our souls to a man just like that, only a man like that would do, a man who owes nothing to anyone other than his profession itself, who is faithful to nothing more than his own expertise, and is willing to go above and beyond his calling today in order to be chosen once more for the task tomorrow. Then again, perhaps this priest of ours - who was truly a man of God, as I believe with all my heart - knew full well that the only ethics left consisted in a devout profession-alism, and any other form of ethics could be nothing more than a series of good intentions, at best, and anyone who trusts people with their good intentions had better add quite a healthy dose of those prayers that only the priests themselves know if they work or not.

Fernand invaded my mind. He assumed such outsize propor-tions in my thoughts that there was no room left for me to consider anything or anyone else. I thought to myself that if I were to go mad and then recover - aided by the doctors or the very heavens themselves, I could fully attest and claim that the moment at which I succumbed to this invasion marked the beginning of the onset of my malady. His presence grew when he returned from one of his periodic disappearances, saying, "From now on you are to call me Ferdinand - not Fernand, but Ferdinand."

"That's almost the same," Jackie said. "We're going to forget - we'll get confused and forget."

"You'll just forget 'Fernand' and you won't get confused," said the man. "There is no Fernand, there never was a Fernand, you never met anyone named Fernand. It's Ferdinand to you. Is that clear?"

It was all very clear. This man did not even have a name of his own that I knew of, and he was neither Fernand nor Ferdinand, other than for the sole purpose of his particular line of work. To-day he was Ferdinand, yesterday he had been Fernand, and the day before that perhaps he had been Henri, and then Michel, and even Michael - why not? - even Mechel, for that matter, or Patrous, or Mustafa Ali. He was all those men and he was not a single one of them at the same time. I was afraid that I was already beginning to grow delirious from the fever, but I did not even have a fever. What really bothered me more and more at this point was the fact that it was impossible to explain this adamant insistence on a sudden name change as anything other than a sign that he had begun to think we might get caught and would then be interrogated and asked for his name, while he, at the moment that we would be caught and interro-gated - where would he be at that point? Why did we, the children and I, why did we need even to know the name of a man who barely talked to us at all, other than in the event that we would be asked for that very name - but who was really going to ask us that? Some wolf in the forest? He went over and sat down once more in his corner in the dark, and I found myself murmuring 'Ferdinand, Ferdinand', in near silence, afraid that I might slip and inadvertently say 'Fer-nand' when the order came down, as though my very life hung in the balance and depended on this possible mistake. I am sure that the children were murmuring away just like me.

All my strength gradually slipped away. The total lack of activ-ity, paralyzed like that inside the dark cabin day and night, and the scanty provisions which the cold perhaps prevented from going bad but could not keep from growing stale, began to take a toll on me that seemed to constantly increase and even felt to me like it sur-passed the toll the long walks in the snow were taking. When you are walking along, the difficult part is getting where you are going. But when you are just sitting around waiting it is difficult just trying to be. The day will come - if it indeed ever does - when I will wonder how the children got through those endless hours, and how they managed to accept that verdict without the slightest complaint or objection. How did they actually know to accept the seeming sense-lessness of our flight as we ran from our pursuers, as we were con-stantly forced to swear that there was someone out the-re chasing after us, even though we had never actually caught sight of them at all? You can not really begin to imagine that God could actually be capable of preparing little children to stand the test that they in fact must face when it comes along, as they run for their lives.

When it comes to such a reckoning - the kind that you can only carry out once it is already completely impossible to ever change things - I hope that I will one day get the chance to work it out. And they will all have their day of reckoning, from the concierge at Rue Aix-les-Bains in Marseille right down to Fernand-Ferdinand of Lamoura - every last man and woman who crossed our path in their black raincoats, in their priestly habits, in their uniforms, in their grey farmer's clothing - and they will all stand there where the ghosts stand when everything is reckoned up in the world to come, that world that only exists so as to remind us of this world down here. And I will ask them my questions then - not as the submissive escapee that I am today - and I will interrogate them - not as the broken soul that I am now - and I will get to the bottom of whether or not they know who in fact created these children of war who knew how to survive in the face of all these tests that they were put to during the days of dire dread, and I will tell them all that if they do indeed know, then to hell with them! I have a lot to reckon with, there are many reckonings that I have to address, but that particular reckoning that I owe myself, and that you too, Moritz, owe both God and man when it comes to our children - that particular reckoning I do not quite know how to address... perhaps because it is impossible to actually conceive such a reckoning after all. As you can see, I was angry, you can no doubt tell that I was angry from the way that I am writing here, but I swear that at that moment I did not even have the strength to actually get angry and all that I had left in me was only enough to wish to survive, and then maybe one day I would get angry if I managed to even get that far.

I do not know how much time actually passed, whether a day and a night, or two days and two nights, for that matter, but at some point Fernand-Ferdinand returned for the umpteenth time and suddenly said, "The route is clear - quickly now!" And a few moments later we were on our way. It seemed to me like we were headed up a mountainside whose summit reached the very heavens and that I was too weak to reach, and I thought it was impossible that the children themselves had any strength left to keep climbing upwards through the snow, on and on. Fernand-Ferdinand's shadow did not stop moving for an instant, as he skied along at his measured pace out in front of us. The man did not even slow down when we began to lag behind. I suppose he did not even turn his head to see if we were following along behind him - why should he have turned around, after all? he was anyway too far ahead to be able to see us in the night. But at the point when he had already disappeared from view and we were left wondering whether to stand still and wait so as not to get lost in the snows if we continued plodding along, he suddenly appeared like a shot on his skis, stopped short and said, "That won't do, Madame, it would be a real shame if you were to lose track of me when we are almost at our journey's end. You may as well not even take the first step if you are going to give up before you manage to take the last one. God no. We are not there yet, but we are rather close. Tell me you can make it and we will continue. If you can't make it, don't bother telling me. You anyway have no choice."

All this was said in a rapid whisper that did not actually expect any response, but I whispered back all the same, since not whispering at that point was entirely out of the question. "I might tell you I can't make it," I said, "but I will press on even though I can't make it. I believe my boots are completely torn. Can you take a look and tell me what to do?" I leaned on Erwin's shoulder and raised one of my legs in the air and said to him, "Please, sir, I know you can't see a thing, but just touch the sole of my boot."

He bent down in my direction, leaning his left arm on the ski pole and feeling with his right hand, from which he did not remove his large glove, checking the condition of the boot on my slightly raised foot, which he illuminated with his green lantern as he said, "Madame, the sole of your boots is indeed torn. You are walking along bare-foot in the snow in your boots."

He straightened up, leaned forward on both poles with his head to one side, and in a series of rapid gestures that I could not even follow he freed his boots from the skis, stuck the poles in the snow, pulled off his gloves and then his coat, removed the woollen sweater he had on underneath, then took off his shirt and stood there

bare-chested for a moment so brief that I did not even get a chance
to see him tremble in the cold, as he quickly put his clothes back on,
except for the shirt, which he tore to shreds with both hands. Using
a pocketknife that he pulled from one of his pockets he turned the
shreds into orderly strips of fabric, then got down on one knee as
he sort of propped himself on his other leg. "Lean on the children's
shoulders, Madame," he said. "Take care not to slip. Give me your
right foot. Put it in my lap, like that, step down if you have to, you
won't cause me any pain. Silence now." He took the lantern in his
mouth and lit up my shoes with the light's green glow, as he wrapped
each one with the strips of fabric from his shirt, wrapping and fas-
tening and knot-ting away with strip after strip of fabric, first one
shoe and then the other. I could feel the sole of the boot clinging
more firmly now to my soggy, frozen feet. I did not know how far I
would get before the bandages that were now keeping the soles of
my boots attached would also betray me and give way.

At this point the border just had to finally stop retreating ever
further beyond the spot that it was even humanly possible to reach.
If God Himself had not decreed that the border must stop retreating
then I was certain that 'our guy' had instead.

The lantern went out. I stood on my own two feet. Quite a number of feet have been bandaged in the world by now. But who ever
bandaged the boots themselves? Fernand-Fedinand did not say another word. He did not ask me to check if the bandages worked, and
he did not wait for me to thank him. He slipped his boots back in-to
the skis and immediately shot off once more, as we began walking
along behind him again in our single file, and I no longer thought of
my boots or their soles, but thought only of God sitting in judgement
on this war, and over against an entire array of accusatory witnesses
there suddenly appears a single witness in defense, but for each defense witness that shows up another accusatory witness immediately
comes along to challenge him, and God is unable to issue any true
verdict when the earth is burning down below, neither on behalf of
the righteous nor the wicked. And if God Himself can not issue a
verdict then how can I? - but all the same I go right on accusing and
defending, and committing a crime when I commit myself to love,
because I do not know how to wait for that moment when I will have

the right to hate, and so I hate, because I am not prepared to wait for that moment when it will become clear to me that, in fact, I really ought to have loved.

I could not forgive this Fernand-Ferdinand, whose heart had revealed itself in one single moment to be an actual giant of a heart, since before and after it beat away incessantly as though it were nothing more than the most minuscule, unfeeling heart that had ever been created.

The strips of fabric wound around my boots began to tear. I could feel it. But I did not care. My back hurt more than I could bear, but I bore the pain all the same, and I did not care that it hurt so badly. I was on the verge of completely giving in to an exhaustion that seemed to be increasing to the point of fairly overflowing its banks, but I carried on and paid no mind to all this either. For the children - who walked along beside me, along with the unborn infant stirring inside me and on the verge of emerging into the light of this awful world in which we were living - were more vital than any of these concerns which were really of absolutely no importance to me whatsoever at that point; and so, like a climber whose hands are torn to pieces as they try to hold on tight to a boulder dangling out over the abyss, I clung to my dwindling life force, step after step after step, and as long as my breath held out and stirred the spirit inside me, my soul refused to cede.

And then, seemingly all of a sudden, we had reached the summit. A few lights twinkled off in the distance. In the absolute darkness that separated us from those lights it looked like they were floating off in the heavens. We all stood there together and stared at them. Perhaps that is how the sailors of a vessel tossed on the high seas and lost among the crashing, criss-crossing waves, look when they see the lights of the dock, as they rise like a miracle through the fog and mist. Fernand-Ferdinand said in a whisper: "La Cure." Erwin repeated what he had heard and said, "La Cure." Then Jackie said it too, and I wanted to say it as well, but the tears choked my voice in my throat and I could not make a sound.

"There is a hotel in La Cure, on the hillside," Fernand-Ferdinand whispered, placing added emphasis on each word as he seemed to slice them apart with exacting precision. "When you enter the lobby you are in France. Then you go up the stairs and out the other side and you are in Switzerland. One building - two countries. You are not going to enter that way or exit that way, because in there they will be waiting for you with rather open arms. The last light on the left is the one meant for you. It is a light hung from a fence that runs through the heart of a narrow, old road, half of which is French and the other half of which is Swiss, and the fence is planted up against the last isolated little house on the Swiss side of the border. But 100-200 yards further on, at a spot beyond the reach of the light, there is a breach in the fence. Is all that clear?" None of it was all that clear, but that did not bother me to the point of arousing any real fear. It was all those precise descriptions that actually had me terrified.

"It's not all that clear, but that doesn't really matter. After all, we'll just stay close and all be together when we get there anyway."

He responded immediately, without allowing himself a moment to get lost in any explanations, or justifications, or mere manners. "We're already there, Madame. We've gotten as far as I promised myself that I would go. It's better if we got every-thing out in the open. From here on you're on your own, Madame, and may God help you." And even before his whisper had died away he simply disappeared and was swallowed up by the snows, skis and all.

The three of us stood there all alone, now further away than ever from the blinking light that shone atop that last house across the snows that showed no sign or set path and seemed filled only with a dread as wide as the entire world itself. I could barely breathe. But it was not that sense of dread that was grabbing me by the throat. It was more the affront and the despair that were fairly choking me to death. I had been betrayed.

We walked along by ourselves in the direction of that last light. Although we were rather weak at this point, we walked on, as far as I can recall, making even quicker progress than we had the entire rest of the way. But where would the patrols be out waiting for us if not lurking in ambush right by the actual border itself? The last bit of caution we had left to us as we faced down this final trap was pre-cisely to hurry, to hurry as fast as we could, which might mean that we would slip and fall a little more, but we would then get up right away and move along without stopping a moment to rest, though after a little while it seemed to our amazement that that last light we were heading for was actually deceiving us. We were heading towards it, but it seemed to actually be moving away from us. First it seemed to be getting closer on the right, drawing near the lights of La Cure, but a moment later it actually seemed to be getting further off to the left. That was impossible, of course, it went against all our powers of comprehension, and so we continued walking forward. But now there was no mistaking what was happening. We were not getting any closer to the light - it was retreating further and further into the distance. We stopped in our tracks. We knew that in another few moments the entire town of La Cure would disappear into the snows and we would no longer know where to find it, and we had no idea where we had gone wrong nor who would be the first to get us - the border patrol guards' German shepherds, or the cold that our exhausted bodies could simply no longer repel.

"This isn't going to work, Ma," Erwin whispered to me. "If we head for the light, we'll never get there. We have to head for whatever stands between us and the light. There are a few isolated trees in the snow, there's always some barn somewhere, or a lone pole. We'll go from here to the tree, then from the tree to the barn, from the barn to the pole, and from the pole to the light."

"All I see is the light. I don't see a tree, or a barn, or a pole. I can't see anything at all," Jackie said, shaking from the cold. I also could not make out anything in the dense darkness that blanketed the snows. It was clear to me that Erwin had simply based what he had said on conjecture.

"Where do you see a tree, or a barn, or a pole? Erwin, if you see any of these things, I certainly don't." "I don't see anything either," Erwin said. "But it's out there. I'm telling you to wait, Ma. Dawn is going to break soon. We'll start to see things and then we'll head in a straight line for the tree and when we get to the tree we'll be able to see where to go next. We won't just be walking around and around in circles. We're not that far off, Ma."

Suddenly I felt like everything was fine. The boy sort of took my hand and just led me along. He was hardier than me and was asking me to trust him. But I couldn't. The first light of day might still be further off than he hoped, but it was more than that - dawn might well light our way a little bit, but it would also light us up and make it impossible for us not to be exposed at that point. We had to move.

"I think I see a tree. That's your first tree, then. I can see it over there like this huge shadow out in front of us. First let's head for that tree. At that point perhaps we will spot another tree. Maybe we'll even see the barn, or a granary, or the profile of some cabin forming a straight line with that last light of La Cure. We can't just stand around here like this, Erwin. We have to move."

"We can't just stand around, Erwin, we have to move," Jackie leaned in to Erwin's face, whispering into his brother's ear like an echo of what I had already said. And so we went. La Cure now seemed to be getting closer, at any rate. That last light also no longer seemed to be getting further away. At this point we were not merely close, we were truly right there. There was complete silence. It seemed like if there actually were any other living beings in the world they had all gone away and left us completely by ourselves. There was no sound of a rooster crowing, no dog barking, no owl off hooting in the distance. At this point the last light was already behind us. We kept on. I suddenly felt some fresh pain in my feet. They were no longer sinking in the snow that had been afflicting my feet with such hellish torture - and to which I was already accustomed at this point - but they were now striking some harder, rougher surface, something firm and crystalline. We had hit the road that was illuminated by the last few pallid rays of that final light.

Suddenly, like the ghost of some gargantuan green demon that had risen from the very *tohu-bohu* of the universe, a giant in a black German helmet stood before me, the collar of his heavy coat turned up to his cheeks and a rifle over his shoulder. I could recognize figures like him from both near and far, but the specimen shooting forth the hot breath of his mouth and nostrils like some foul vapor that filled my eyes was a completely foreign sight to me. I sank into the snow. Even you, my dear Moritz, if you had been there, would perhaps have allowed yourself to say that what I did was faint. I do not rightly know. All that I do know is that my eyes went black, and when the light came back on I saw myself standing there, supported by the huge palms of that soldier, as my breath - my very life breath, I might say - was virtually cut off by the very sight of him, and I saw Erwin leaning over me and I could hear him saying, in a voice that contained an intense sense of urgency, "He's Swiss, Ma, look at the buttons on his coat. It's a cross, Ma, not a swastika, it's a Swiss cross. We made it, Ma. Ma, we're saved." His voice came to me as though from beyond some frozen fog. I am writing what his words were because he later told me what he said, but at that particular moment I had no idea at all what he was saying. I had no wind left in me. I was standing there at the final stop on my journey from Marseille to La Cure, and all the miracles that had happened to me along the endless way had now come to naught in the hands of this huge Centurion as he toyed with me the way that the godless cat toys ad nauseam with a mouse before tearing it to pieces, just a moment before the desperate, hopeless escapee actually believed in all her foolishness that, in the end, she had actually managed to successfully employ every ounce of her cunning to survive and break free.

Two more soldiers came over and stood there facing us along the road. The fence did not stretch across the entire length of the road. It ran right up to a few yards to our right, and ended on the other side another few yards off to our left, and in the middle was the breach. But the soldiers who had come over - both that giant of mine, and the other two soldiers who had then joined him - would not cross the line where the fence, by right, ought to have been.

Life and death are locked in an eternal dance; the dance has its rules and they abide by them. At last I understood that we had fallen into the hands of soldiers on the side of life, and had we gotten lost along the road and wandered off just another step or two in the wrong direction, we would have fallen into the hands of soldiers on the side of death who would have then taken us to die, if we even had any strength left at that point to drag ourselves off to some hangman's noose, or perhaps they would have simply shot us on the spot if they saw that we did not have the strength to even make it that far. But here, even though the fence had been breached, the rules that had given rise to the fence to begin with had not been breached, and they were rules that were obeyed much more strictly than the commandment 'Thou shalt not kill.' That Centurion of mine no longer seemed a Centurion. With my hands still ensconced in their gloves I caressed the buttons of his coat, decorated as it was with that Swiss cross, and with whatever strength I had left I embraced him and said over and over again, *"Merci,"* while the German soldiers, who looked exactly like their Swiss counterparts, stood across from me and stared, and I swear that their eyes filled with rather human tears at the sight of a woman and her children - a woman who for all intents and purposes looked like she was about to go into labor - giving thanks like that, right across from them, for the very fact that she had been saved from their hands. There were about ten such soldiers there now, all fully armed. One of them was holding the leash of a dog that lay there in the snow right next to him. My own soldiers were three in number. Those ten Germans looked on as our little play unfolded. All they had to do was stretch out their hands in order to grab hold of us. But they did not. Those three soldiers of ours did not look at the Germans standing over across from them, but kept their eyes on us. The soldier that I had embraced delicately removed my arm from his waist and said, "You can not pass, Madame. The border." I did not understand what he was saying. I heard every single word. He was rather civil. He had uttered the five or six words that he had to say in a rather clear, mea-sured tone, softly, with evident restraint. But I did not understand what he was saying. He was speaking French, which I understood well enough, understood each and every word, but at the same time it was not French that he seemed to be speaking, or any other spo-ken human tongue for that matter. It was some sort of language that was not at all in use in this world of ours. There was no way that it could be. I believe that the Germans who stood there right nearby also heard every word he said and yet failed to understand his lan-guage either - yes, not even they understood. It would be impossible to use a language of this world, in a place like this, at a moment like this, after such a journey as we had undertaken, facing an opposing phalanx of soldiers with their dog lying there in the snow, as the dawn rose over the mountains, lighting up the evidence that human beings lived there among those peaks, in order to say, "You can not pass", and you certainly can not even begin to utter such a polite form of address as "Madame" in the midst of all that, and above all there is absolutely no place for the utterance of a term such as "The border" in this particular context. I had indeed crossed the border, and if despite this fact I could not even take another step further without crossing that said border, then all the world is one big border for me, insofar as wherever I stand I will always find myself on the death-dealing side of the border in question. These rules are not written down anywhere in any of the volumes of this world. "I do not understand, I do not understand," I said, in my halting French, and I grabbed hold of my soldier's coat once more, as the latter once more removed my hand, and said again those words that it was simply impossible for me to grasp, and pointed with his finger to indicate the direction I had to take. I looked where he pointed and saw the row of German soldiers standing there seemingly waiting right across from us with that dog of theirs, and I looked back at this soldier of mine, and this time I said, "You don't understand, you don't understand."

One of the other two Swiss soldiers came over to me and said, "Come with us, Madame. This does not mean that you are going to cross the border, it just means that we must discuss all this in an orderly fashion. It is simply unpleasant for us to have to degrade ourselves like this before that group over there," as he pointed in the direction of the German soldiers who seemed to have heard every word, and I saw - I am certain of this - their lips curl into smiles underneath their dark helmets. I gave Erwin a questioning look, as though asking him to translate, since I was not sure that I had indeed understood the entirety of that rather long statement which this civil, considerably troubled soldier of ours had uttered. We walked along for a minute or two until we came to a relatively small building. The soldiers went in first, and we followed them inside and then stood there, waiting. Two of the soldiers sat down, while the third stood by the door, surveying the border that was in such close proximity. A large, blackening kettle stood on the stovetop, letting off steam, while a wood fire burned below in the oven. It was rather warm in this little cabin. The particularly courteous soldier spoke up immediately as he said, "This is all rather unpleasant, Madame," and Erwin translated right away, without waiting for me to ask him to do so. "I assume that you have come on foot quite a long distance, along with the children, of course, though they simply accompanied you because you ordered them to do so. With all due respect, Madame, you can not very well expect some sort of reward for all these efforts of yours. You should have been very well aware before you ever set out on your way that the government of the Swiss Confederation simply can not allow you to cross the Swiss border, certainly not in this illegal fashion, at any rate. The three of us, Madame, are merely three ordinary citizens in uniform, but we are the law around here, and the law can not do any more than to issue a completely self-evident sentence, namely, that you must return from whence you came. This is final. It would be better if you understood this here and now while we are speaking with one another as completely civilized individuals. By right, in accordance with our orders, we ought to have prohibited you from taking even a single step into Swiss territory, but we thought it rather indecent from a human standpoint to force you to face the ineluctable reality that awaited you out there to the joy of those scoundrels standing around expectantly…"

At that point, Erwin suddenly stopped translating and began speaking himself. Not a soul in the world ever heard a child speak the way that he spoke at that moment. When they tried to silence him he raised his voice almost to a shout, though he immediately returned to a somewhat softer tone, that both shocked and amazed the soldiers, who had certainly never faced anyone like Erwin before in their lives. What did he say to them? I understood a bit of it, in fact I understood the majority of what he said, and what I did not understand I could pretty much guess at, for it was not just his mouth that did the talking, but his entire being was speaking, his face, his voice, his breath, his hands, his fists even, at times, the fingers with which he indicated his brother and me and the expanse of forests and snow that had seemed hermetically sealed in our faces, and whatever I could not make out or understand, you yourself certainly can, and if you had been there to see the faces of those soldiers as they listened, awestruck - yes, awestruck indeed - then you would have managed to understand even those things that you never would have thought possible to begin with. He tortured those soldiers, he stormed, he threatened, he fought for my very soul, and the soul of his brother, and his own soul for that matter, but mainly he fought for me, for my soul, and I heard him screaming that he demanded they bring a doctor. And suddenly he rushed over to the door where the third soldier was standing, as the latter seemed to retreat before him, and he slammed the door shut and stood there blocking the way with his little back, his two arms spread wide to either side, standing there as though fairly crucified and screaming, "Doctor! This woman, my mother, is going to die if you do not bring a doctor here at once." The soldiers were terrified. One of them said to the other that he would go and rouse the military doctor who was still fast asleep at that moment off in the village. He spoke German, since he rather innocently assumed that we certainly did not understand that language, as he said to his colleague, "I don't want her to suddenly give birth here or go and die on us, or anything like that. We did what we had to do, this wicked Confederation can't ask anything more of us than it already has." "Wicked," his colleague repeated this particular word. "I would not use the word 'wicked.' But we must get a doctor. She looks awful. Let the doctor decide. Why should I? Why should you? Are we the Confederation - wicked or otherwise - are we the ones responsible? I am going to go get the doctor."

And he left. Erwin exhaled heavily. He had no words left in his lungs. Jackie went over to him, put his arm around his shoulders, hugged him close and stood the-re next to him, and he suddenly began breathing in rhythm with his brother, and as Erwin gradually calmed down, Jackie calmed down as well. I looked over at these two brothers, so different from one another and so united at the same time, each one of them so very much a soul unto itself, and yet constituting one huge joint soul at the same time. I wanted to feel so very intensely, unbelievably happy, but I sensed that I simply was incapable of it at that moment, since I found myself simultaneously pitying them, and I was terrified that this cruel morning had led me into the horrible sin of pity, a sin for which there can be no atonement.

They now allowed us to sit down. The particular soldier who, for some reason, I seemed to refer to in my mind as 'my soldier', offered us something warm to drink. He poured the water into two aluminium cups - there were only those two cups in the entire cabin. "Drink, Madame," he said. "I think you need it. The boys can take turns drinking from the only other cup I have left. Sometimes the tastiest thing in the world is the army tea rivalled only by sewer water itself. Forgive me. I'm sure I haven't said the nicest thing I could have offered about the tea you are about to drink. But we're among soldiers, you understand? This young man," and he pointed at Erwin, "is a real man, like any other soldier. He is a warrior. He understands. He will forgive me." I suppose this was an attempt at humor, but even such a gentle form of humor seemed rather tasteless to me. The man turned my stomach. All of Switzerland depended on this man. He was Switzerland itself, Swiss law, the fence at the Swiss border, the only one responsible for deciding who would get to live in Switzerland, the hangman for all the women and children to whom he would forbid entry as he sent them back into the hands of their pursuers, without even considering the fact that this was indeed what he was doing. He was simply following orders, orders without any real content. The order itself was all the content that existed, not the woman who was being sent along with her children back across the border to die in the hands of acknowledged murderers. But he had not been outfitted with that uniform of his in order to provide any specific opinions regarding any particular woman, even if that woman had gotten entangled along with her children in the sterile net of the law and its legalese. He was nice, considerate, well-mannered, made an effort to please - a simple man, a courteous, civil man. Which only made him all the more loathsome, much more so than if he had been some raging bull in the arena. His encounter with the law was no more than a minor accident, such as all young men seem to eventually go through, particularly during wartime, and even if it involves a certain amount of unpleasantness, it does not really cause any serious injuries, nor does it truly leave any lasting scars. The boys did not touch their tea as they waited for me to drink first. I did not want to drink myself but the soldier urged me on.

"The doctor will not forgive me if you have not had a drink," he said. "How long have you been on the road? Since midnight? Since nightfall? Either way, it has been quite some time. The road was difficult, one can tell just by looking at you. It is important that you drink something. Please, Madame, drink." I took a single sip. Erwin immediately took a sip as well and passed the cup to Jackie, who refused it.

"I'm not thirsty," he said. "I haven't been walking all night long. It's been several nights already. I don't need a drink anymore. I'm used to it by now."

None of us drank anymore, not even Erwin or me, at which point 'my soldier' said to me, "I must apologize. There is no way that I could have made you tea, since I have none. The water is all that I could offer. You see, Madame, not everything is all that tasty here in Switzerland." He looked at me somewhat expectantly, as though hoping to catch some muscle in my face as it relaxed in recognition of this second forced attempt at using humor to somehow ease the bitterness of waiting like that in the holding cabin.

"May I remove my boots?" I asked.

"I noted your footwear, Madame. It doesn't look good, doesn't look good at all. I agree. I understand that you must want to remove those boots. But if you're asking my advice, I would not touch them at the moment. The doctor will be here any minute now. We are awaiting his verdict. If you remove your boots, it will be difficult to get them back on, and then how will you manage, if you have no choice and must go back once more." He pointed in the direction of France. "How will you make it there, Madame?"

The doctor indeed showed up as the soldier was uttering these last words, and it seemed to me that he had even managed to over-hear them. He was a soldier in uniform himself, with a helmet on his head, a rather short man with rapid movements.

"What happened," he said, as he removed his coat and placed his helmet on the table at which we were sitting. "I am the replace-ment for Doctor..." and he mentioned the name of the man that he was replacing. "I just arrived yesterday. Are you sure that if you had called on him he would have come? I have no real prior expe-rience. I am not familiar with the protocol. The other soldier ex-plained what the matter was on our way over here. And so I came. But I am warning you, if according to the established protocol this is none of my concern, then I am not going to get involved. What is the protocol in such a situation? Who is the senior officer on duty here? You?"

"Yes, me," 'my soldier' replied.

"Tell me, then," said the doctor, but he was actually more in-terested in what he himself was saying in his rapid-fire speech than what any of the soldiers might actually respond, as he stepped over to me as he spoke and began checking my pulse, taking hold of my wrist, and then shining a little flashlight into my eyes, as he looked in-to them and said, "Pardon me, Madame, but in this heavy coat of yours I can not properly examine you."

The soldiers turned around as though I were about to get un-dressed and the doctor stood facing me, with both hands on his hips, as he stared at me, once I had gotten out of my heavy coat, like a master looking at a slavegirl about to be sold - at least that was the association that crossed my mind at the time - and he said, "When, then?" He immediately sensed that I had not understood his ques-tion and so he expanded it somewhat, saying, "When is the baby going to arrive? You must have some idea. Of course you do. But you don't know." He turned to look at that senior officer of mine and asked, "What do you basically want from me?" Then he turned back to look at me and listened to what the soldier said to him without actually looking in his direction.

The soldier ignored what essentially looked like an insult to his position as he spoke. "This woman, there is no question about it, must go back. In her case this is clear. She is not a single individ-ual. She constitutes a group of three. There can be no question in the matter. Why is she here? Because we wanted to avoid a scandal in the eyes of the Germans standing on the other side of the road. So we brought her here. I hope that in so doing we did not violate our orders. Now we are facing an internal scandal. She would not move, and the boy there demanded a doctor. In accordance with established protocol, all this is acceptable. But we must send her back regardless."

"So why bring a doctor?" the doctor quickly asked, without re-ally looking for a reply, though the soldier said, all the same, "I don't know. You asked about protocol. That is the established protocol." He was somewhat embarrassed as he pronounced those last words, but the doctor did not give him the chance to get caught up in his shame as he quickly responded, saying, "Nonsense! Either you call a doctor or you follow the protocol. This woman will only be sent back over my dead body. Do you not see - what, are you blind or something? Have they poisoned your mind? This woman will die in your arms before she ever reaches the fence, both she and her un-born child will surely perish. If you send her back you will be walking a live woman out of this cabin only to toss a dead carcass onto the other side of the border. This is Switzerland, my good man, and it is not at all a Swiss thing to do what you are about to do. You are the commanding officer. But you are a Swiss officer. You have no such right. This woman does not come under your jurisdiction. She belongs in a hospital." That soldier of mine was not taken aback.

"Yes I do," he said. "I have the right and I have the necessary authority. That is the law. *Das Boot ist voll*, the rescue boat is full, didn't you hear? I suppose you did not. But I did. And I have been appointed to see to it that not another single soul shall board this full boat of ours, because one more person too many might well sink us all."

The doctor demonstrated a complete disregard for these last words, as he did not even respond and instead said to me, "Sit down, Madame. Slowly take off your boots. I will help you. They brought me here for this express purpose. You understand? Even if it causes you great pain, and I know well that it will, you must remove your boots." I sat down. Erwin and Jackie came over to help. The doctor stopped them. "Not you two," he said. "This calls for a doctor." My boots came off. He very carefully removed my socks as well, the state of which I can not, and perhaps very well should not describe, altogether. My bare feet were now revealed to me and I sat there staring at them. I should have been quite frightened by the sight, but I was not. They looked so bad that no one could ever possibly have imagined how they really ought to look. But I knew and I was already over my disgust at the sight of them even before I had truly taken a look at what could not really have looked otherwise, to be honest. The doctor took my ankles in his hand and carefully examined my toes, my heels, my ankles, and all the while he did not make a sound, but that soldier of mine suddenly said, "Please sign here." "I'll sign, you fool," the doctor said, without raising his head. "I'll sign for her, and for her children, and for you too, and your friends there, in case you haven't understood. One signature will do for the whole lot of you, just call me an ambulance and get lost, all of you. Take a form and write the following: La Cure, Sunday, March 14, 1943, Madame - what is the lady's name?" "I have no idea," said that soldier of mine. "What, you haven't checked her papers, checked to see if she even has any documentation? You didn't even ask her her name? You were all set to send back someone whose identity you didn't even know? What do you think this is here, a case of some wayward cattle that mistakenly crossed the border and must be returned to its own proper pasture? Have you lost your mind? What is your name, Madame?" I whispered with what little strength I had left, "Rosalia Mayer." And then, it was as though some thick curtain had come down out of nowhere and cut me off from the entire rest of the world, and I no longer re-member a thing, the way that a dead man no longer remembers what he once was or had, until the resurrection of the dead comes along to restore him to life as well.

I only came back around once I was in the hospital in Lausanne. I do not know how I got there. Even once I had opened my eyes I could not rightly tell if I was hallucinating that I was awake, or if I was not, in fact, hallucinating but was indeed truly awake and embarrassed by the fact that I had gotten caught up in some sort of riddle I simply could not resolve. I could not really see myself in that place and the place did not at all seem to be made for me, and though I knew that I was in a room in a hospital I was not actually entirely sure that it was really me lying there, until two male orderlies dressed in white came into the room and tapped me on the shoulder and said my name, as they told me that I was being transferred to the detention center. I mumbled a thank you, though I do not quite know for what, certainly not for the way that they had treated me since my arrival, since I had no idea what had gone on and no recall of that time whatsoever, and I was not thanking them for sending me wherever it was that I was headed, for just as I was completely uncertain whether I was really where I was. I also had no concept at all of where I was headed, since the name of the place that they had mentioned meant nothing to me whatsoever. I was unsure if the orderlies who were standing over me had come from some region of this world with which I was not familiar, or if they were not, in fact, from some other dimension altogether in which I had now arrived, all of which faded with the arrival of a female nurse who brought me my clothing and helped me get dressed, and the broken conversation that she conducted with me about all sorts of minor points of the procedures for release gradually restored me to my full senses.

She brought me back around to reality in a rather graceful, charming fashion, amused as she was by the fact that I was not aware of what every person knew, and she was rather happy to fill in the gaps with a natural ease. However, aside from the fact that, from what she told me, I was now in Lausanne, and had been in a rather worrisome condition over the course of two days and had only now come around to full strength after about the fourth or fifth day, there was little else that she could tell me.

The clearer my mind got the more it seemed like I was in fact losing it. Where were the children? I had no idea. The nurse seemed to have no knowledge whatsoever of the fact that I already had two children. All she knew how to do was repeat the fact that just as I had received the most attentive care possible, somebody must be taking care of my children as well in the most wonderful manner available. "What do you mean by 'taking care'? Who is 'taking care' of the children?" My questions probed with an impatience that bordered on hostility. The nurse responded pleasantly that it was not her responsibility to know the answer, and that I would certainly be told all that I needed to know once I was transferred to the detention center. Suddenly those words came together for me and at last assumed their true sense.

"I am being released to a detention center? Doesn't that seem a little strange to you - 'released', to a 'detention center'?" "I must admit it does," the nurse said to me. "But you must expect all sorts of strange things when your life itself is rather strange."

She could not possibly have meant what she said in the manner that I was drawn to interpret her words, as I said, "Strange? My life is strange? Is it because my life is strange that I do not know where my children are? Is it because my life is strange that I am being released to a jailhouse? Do you know where my children are?"

"No, on my life I don't." She suddenly felt guilty over the fact that she did not know.

"Do you know where they are?"

"No. They do not tell me such things. I'm just a nurse." Now she was defending herself. I once again experienced something that had happened to me quite a few times already in the past. The sweetest people, those most innocent of any evil intentions, would suddenly turn into my direst enemies if they simply did not know, or could not possibly know, how to soothe my concerns over the fate of our children. Our children were the one and only test, the first and last litmus test, as it were, of what was absolutely good and what was absolutely evil, without any further justifications, without any explanations, ulterior motives, or mitigating window-dressing. All those people who had any contact whatsoever with our children - be it in deed, word, knowledge, or lack of knowledge of their whereabouts and well-being - had to live with the results of this unique test which determined whether they were for us or against us. The question of whether they were right, or if they had made some mi-stake, or had even deliberately done wrong, for that matter, could not even begin to be posed, because such a question did not even exist to begin with, nor did it surface in the final analysis, for it completely lacked any relevance to either side of the considerations.

This simple, innocent soul of a nurse therefore had to suffer all of my collective anger which washed over her without her knowing why or wherefore. I rebuked her. I screamed at her. I could not forgive her, not merely for the fact that she did not know what had become of my children, but even for what she herself had, as it were, done to them, without being aware myself of just what it was that she had done, though it seemed that she was doing it to me right there and then. I could not take another single life-sustaining breath without unleashing a string of relentless blows against some sort of sacrifice that had to pay for the fact that my children - for whom I had crossed an ocean crawling with pitch-black eels, in order to convey them with every remaining ounce of strength in my body and soul to the last safe shore left in the world - these children had now disappeared on me and I had no idea where they were now that we had all landed at last - all of us saved, if somewhat scarred, but alive, at last - along that longed-for shore.

And so she took off. She ran out of the room crying loudly, leaving me standing there partly dressed and crying myself, shedding a stream of tears that rose into a veritable wail. A moment later a statuesque woman entered, with her greying hair carefully gathered at the neck and a well-starched, candid white crown pinned to her head. A white gown hung down to about the middle of her red skirt. Her slender legs, to which a pair of white socks clung closely, ended in a pair of light-colored shoes with a modest heel. She was accompanied by an orderly, and that nurse of mine stood behind the two of them, dabbing her cheeks and nose with a handkerchief.

"I got dressed up before coming to speak with you, Madame. They tell me that you speak German. I will wait for you to finish and therefore speak German with you, as well. I assume that you no longer require the assistance of a nurse. They have told me that your strength has rather fully returned. I am waiting." Somewhat chastened, I finished getting dressed by myself, placed whatever I did not need anymore on the bed and then stood there facing those three figures who seemed to me like some panel of judges, presided over by a rather severe chief justice, as I awaited their verdict.

"Madame," the woman began, firm and motionless in that clothing of hers that seemed to rest along her body, as I suddenly noticed, the way that the fabric of a flag rests on a statue properly placed on its pedestal. There is no exaggerating the severity with which I must view your recent behavior. The nurse in whose care you find yourself is known for her reliability, fitting manners, and absolute fidelity to the team and this hospital of ours where she completed her studies and in which she is currently employed. You have humiliated her, Madame. In this, our country we learned a long time ago that no citizen has the right to humiliate his or her neighbor, certainly not over some wrong for which the latter is not even responsible. And what is valid for every law-abiding citizen is certainly valid all the more so for anyone requesting to benefit from the hospitality of our community, without having ever received a formal invitation to enter our community. You, Madame, have thus committed a two-fold crime. You have rather crassly wounded a young woman who might, God forbid, learn from this painful experience that her choice of a profession whose sole purpose is to serve humanity can nevertheless be a rather thankless endeavor. This is a terrible thing. You will never know the dedication she showed in caring for you. But that is not all, and we need not address that fact any further since it was, after all, her duty. In addition, you have committed an ethical crime. Your behavior demonstrates that this country's hospitality does not obligate you in any way whatsoever. That is rather disturbing. No, do not interrupt me. I am the one speaking now. We have got-ten you back on your feet. We took care of you, not your children. We did not expect you to thank us for what we did on your behalf in the fulfilment of our duty, but we certainly did not expect you to blame us for what the Confederation did on behalf of your children in the fulfilment of its own ethical obligations. That was never our concern, and it is not now our concern, and it will never be our concern in the future, either. I am sure that you can be extremely thankful for the way that your children are being taken care of. They are in the best hands possible, not only under the current circumstances but at any time altogether. Either I know or I don't know, but either way I can not tell you anything on that score, as it is not my responsibility.

"I wanted to inform you that I am releasing you to the detention center without a written note. I am willing to forgive you because the nurse that you attacked has also forgiven you. She told me as much of her own absolute free will. Either I know or I don't know what you went through before finding your way to us, and so I can certainly take into account the fact that a woman like you might well get rather worked up at a moment when her self-control fails her. It seems that you will be coming back to see us once more in just a few days. To another department, of course. I wish you all the best. No, there is no need for you to respond. I came here simply to tell you what was absolutely indispensable, not in order to listen to anything that you might have to say. It is better this way, trust me. Anything you might say could only make things worse. They have come to get you now. Go in peace." She handed me a bag. "These are your documents. Hand them over to the police officers, either here or there, it is no concern of mine. You have your medical certificates with you as well, of course. They are private and confidential. We have included them as a formal attestation."

Two young men stood in the doorway, still wearing their coats, and seemed to be waiting for me. The nurse quickly gathered up all the things that belonged to me and placed them in a bag. I took it from her and moved with my head down in the direction of the police officers, accompanied by the orderly and the nurse. The lady stood still where she was. Before leaving the room I stopped, took the hand of the young nurse in mine and held it for a rather long moment. She did not remove her palm from mine. I looked into her eyes, and she looked back into mine, as though staring through her tears into my own.

A doctor examined me before assigning me to a bed. He looked over the medical certificates that lay on the table for quite some time, reading and looking up at me occasionally, , as though trying to corroborate what was written down through his own impressions. He did not say a single word to me, and even when he checked my heartbeat he did so after silently indicating that I ought to undo the top buttons on my blouse, saying nothing to me whatsoever, for better or worse, not a single question or statement, nothing at all, until he finally gathered up all the papers, wrote whatever he wrote on top, and returned them to their folder, painstakingly arranged and straightened in place. He closed the folder, whose binding bore my name, as I noticed, along with a number that I, at first, could not manage to make out, but after making a concerted effort that suddenly seemed of particular importance to me, I recognized as N 9320. Clearly satisfied with the work he had done, he patted the folder with his hand, and rose from his chair, thus indicating that my time in his office was up. I too got up and cast a vague, parting, glance at my file, which he was still tapping with his hand and from which it appeared that my name had now become N 9320. I left the room a complete stranger, just as I had entered it, someone to whom no greeting is offered on arrival and no words of farewell as she departs, because that is simply the fate to which all strangers are condemned.

The door closed behind me. I stood in the hallway next to a single bench. I sat down without knowing if I was waiting for anyone or anything at all for that matter. A few moments later a policeman came out and led me along to the far end of the hall-way, where he opened a door before me, as he said, "The refugee Madame Mayer." A man in uniform sat there behind a large desk. He got up, came over to the door and put out his hand to me, saying, "Captain Galopin, in charge of the Orphans' Camp." I very specifically remember the name of both the captain and the detention center, because the way that he got up from his chair and gave me his hand, and the tone of voice that this rather powerful man adopted in introducing himself to this rather shabby woman somewhat surprised me, to the point that I feared for a moment that they were laying a trap for me. He took me over to a chair, asked me to have a seat, then went back behind his desk, sat down as well and said, "I am glad to see you. You look completely different than the way you did when I first saw you." I did not understand a word of what he said.

"You already saw me, sir? I have never laid eyes on you in my life." He smiled.

"You've seen me, of course you've seen me. I am surprised that you do not re-member. I came personally to the hospital to which the doctor from La Cure brought you specifically in order to receive you in this camp of ours. We had a little talk there, not a long one, by any means, but we did speak. You filled out questionnaires. You signed. You were admitted to the hospital from here - that is, officially, you were admitted from here."

"I don't understand," I replied. "Where are my children?"

"Of course," he responded. "I was convinced that that would be your first question. As the commanding officer I have a personal obligation to tell you the whole story, Madame. It is, after all, your story."

There was nothing artificial whatsoever in the way this rather pleasant man held himself or addressed me. He treated me like a human being. He talked to me, looked into my eyes. His hands barely moved, but his features were complete accomplices in the simple, smooth flow of his speech as he stuck to the facts without wandering off to those regions where apologies and explanations seem to burst forth of their own accord. I listened, without stopping him to ask or clarify anything at all - it was all entirely understandable in its simplicity.

"Let us begin with what is most important to you, Madame Mayer. The children," and he looked at a document in the file that lay open before him, "Erwin, October, 1934, and Jack, April, 1936. Is that right? A young pair of boys. Rather impressive. By law, Madame Mayer, they are being detained here in Switzerland just as you are being detained. But they are not prisoners. They are children. In accordance with the laws of God that are valid even during the days of this rather troubling war, they have the right to live as free children, to attend school, to receive food and clothing, medical care, everything, in short, other than the right to leave the place to which the authorities have sent them. As illegal refugees they are obligated to pay for every-thing that I have listed. I am sorry to say that there is no difference between them and independent adults who are also required to pay for their stay among us. But they do not have the means with which to pay. In accordance with the agreement that we have made with the Jewish community here in Switzerland, the Swiss Jews pay for every illegal Israelite refugee until the circumstances will allow for them to be returned to their homeland. The story of Erwin and Jack made quite an impression on a rather well-to-do family by the name of Gideon, originally from the villages of Endingen and Lengnau, and they took it upon themselves to take your children in and hand them over to the care of a woman about whom we have heard only excellent things, a woman by the name of Frieda Gantert, a longtime resident and God-fearing member of the community of Eglisau, by the banks of the Rhine along the border with Germany, rather far from here, unfortunately, on the other side of Switzerland. They are in the best hands possible. Father Voget, a holy man, believe me, well known as a pastor to all refugees, called me personally - he is apparently a good friend and fer-vent admirer of Madame Gantert - and he gave me his word that the children will receive an education that will not make them forget the fact that they are Israelites, without anyone actually specifically reminding them of this fact, of course, and that he, fur-thermore - this straight arrow of a man - guaranteed that they would receive much more than fate had actually ever had in store for them. They are already there, Ma-dame Mayer. To my regret, we could not wait until you would have the chance to say goodbye to them, as I am sure you would have preferred. On the other hand, perhaps it is bet-ter this way. Such a separation might have been too much to take. It is not certain that either you or the kids could very well have handled it, particularly after all that the three of you have been through to-gether. Now, all that remains are the facts. We can all handle the facts. You are well aware of this fact, Madame Mayer. Even your children, young as they are, have matured rather quickly to the point that they, too, are aware of this fact."

I considered him carefully for some time. I wanted to be sure that there was not the slightest hint of irony in the difficult things that he had told me, but I could not quell my own sense of irony, as I said, "You are rather well organized here in Switzer-land, Captain, sir. Nothing catches you by surprise. I am sure that this fact has earned you quite a fair share of admirers. But me? All I want to know is when I am going to see my children." He intuited what I had not actually mentioned, and said, "There is no way that you could bring your children up by yourself while you are in prison, Madame Mayer. You are under arrest. You must understand everything that this implies." I swallowed hard and gathered all my strength in order to say, in a soft, controlled tone, "I already understand everything that this implies, Captain. What mother would not understand everything once they have taken her children from her without notifying her, without asking her, without consulting her, without waiting even the 24 or 48 hours that always pass rather quickly in order to consult her, ask her to understand, to give her authorization, or to ask the children to understand and obtain their own authorization? You wonder whether I have already understood all that is implied by the fact that I am a prisoner? When will I be allowed to go see my children? When will they be allowed to come visit me here? Switzerland has saved all three of us. This rather well-organized country could not come up with any better solution than separating a mother from her children?"

He was clearly saddened. He did not resent the things that I had said. Neither did he defend the things that had already been done. This man did not see me as a criminal, but he was beholden to the facts like a lover, and the fact was that I was a criminal; the fact was that I was subject to the law which required that I be detained as a prisoner; the fact was that the children were already no longer here with me; and the fact was that neither he, nor I, nor his commanding officers, nor the entire country as a whole, with all of its governors and parliament members, could change the facts from what they were. It was painful for him that I was in pain. But this too was a fact. The sorrow that was clearly visible in his face was also a fact. Life, as far as he was concerned, was a series of facts that could only be understood by learning to live alongside them with due reverence. And that was what happened to me. I was not allowed to travel and the children could not come to me. I could submit my requests and the proper authorities would take them up. Not in Geneva, but in the capital city, Bern. I had committed a federal crime. It was not merely a cantonal crime. This too was another fact that I had to understand, with all that it implied. In any event, I first had to give birth, and that could well take place any day now, in accordance with the prognostications of the doctors. No one was going to take up my requests before I gave birth and it was determined where and how I was going to raise my baby. I was exhausted and I told him so. He told me that he understood, but that he had to offer me regards from the doctor who had brought me to the hospital from La Cure. "He is an interesting man. Swiss and stubborn. The kind of Swiss that I love. He was ordered to bring you here. But he brought you to the hospital and then brought us there. One must follow the protocol, but the protocol must sometimes be tailored to fit what truly matters. We gave in and accepted you at the hospital. He would not allow us to demand that you fill out our questionnaires. But we were already there and at that point he had to give in to us. Here is what you wrote, Madame Mayer." He pulled out a page or two from his file and showed them to me. My handwriting looked like that of a drunken person. In answer to the question of where I had come from I had written Marseille, with a number of spelling mistakes, and then I had crossed it out and written it again, with a new series of mistakes, then I wrote that I was Hungarian, then on another line I wrote that I was Belgian, but lacked official citizenship in the country, then I had crossed that out and written that I was Romanian because you were Romanian. I wrote that I was born in 1970, not 1907. I looked over this document and could not believe that I had been in any condition to fill it out.

"I do not remember writing all this."

"I believe you," said the Captain. "The doctor warned us that you might well state that you were a Habsburg princess, or the wife of William Tell, because if you were even able to function altogether at that point, it was only as some sort of an automaton. But we were responsible for the protocol, not the doctor. You had to sign in order to be admitted to the hospital. At that point you were not even able to function anymore as an automaton. We agreed that the doctor would sign on your behalf, as your legal guardian, as it were. That would then be valid for your initial general admission and for your eventual transfer to the maternity ward. The doctor was not sure where you would be taken first. I do not even know the name of this extremely kind man. He simply disappeared. He asked me to tell you that as long as he lived he took care not to be called upon to do any particularly good deed. Because of you, such an opportunity finally came his way. Very nice. There, I have conveyed the message, now go rest. You have earned it."

"I want you to give me the address where my children are. I want to write to them."

"Of course," he said, turning pale. "I apologize, with all my heart I must apologize. They have already written you. That is to say, before leaving here they left a letter for you. How could I forget? That is unforgivable. If it were here in your file, I would not have forgotten. But I put it in one of my drawers. Here it is. Go to your room, read it there, there is no reason that you have to read it here in my presence. That would be rather embarrassing. And I will ask them to bring you the address. A thousand par-dons, Madame Mayer, I hope that you can forgive me. Who knows when I will manage to forgive myself."

The majority of my time during the few days that I spent in the detention center was taken up with filling out further forms, and in hearings before various police officers, interrogations, and the provision of precise testimony concerning all that I had been through, sitting with one officer to discuss everything that I had been through from the time I was born until I had illegally entered Belgium, then sitting with a second officer to discuss our life in Antwerp, then a third officer with whom I had to discuss our escape and existence in occupied France, and finally a pair of officers with whom I had to discuss the whole journey that the children and I had undertaken until we had stolen across the border into Switzerland. For each stage along the way, our discussions were written up formally using a large typewriter, and I had to sign each of these documents, and other than writing a long letter in German to Madame Frieda Gantert - thanking her for what she was doing on behalf of our children and asking her to translate all that I had written for the boys, who did not speak any German - I did not actually do a thing. I did not think of anything at all, I did not recall anything at all, I simply was and I waited - perhaps I was not even waiting in the ordinary sense of the word - for the moment when I would go into labor and they would take me to the hospital to give birth. But before that ever happened they transferred me to a camp that they called Le Rosier, and the Captain in all his glory came to personally say goodbye to me, telling me that I had complied with the entire protocol and was now being transferred to the camp. I did not ask him what the difference was between the detention center and the camp because the distinction was of absolutely no importance to me altogether. I was being transferred because they had to transfer me and that was that. The Captain took both my hands in his palm and said to me, "Madame Mayer, you are a brave woman. The baby to which you are going to give birth, whether a boy or a girl, is going to be a Swiss child that will make all of us rather proud. Before you go I want you to know that I managed to get through on the phone to Father Veget and he promised me that he would personally go and visit your children in Eglisau. Just a short while ago he got back to me and told me that he had been to see them. The children are well. They asked how you are doing. They know that you are on the verge of giving them a little baby brother or sister and pray that they will get to see you embracing this newborn child very soon. The pastor said that Madame Gantert told him that the world has blessed her with two children unlike any others anywhere in the land, and that she offers up a little prayer for your well-being every night before she gets in bed. Isn't that all rather fine? You are crying, Madame Mayer. Don't say a word. There is really no need at this point."

That was March 29th. Two days later, shortly before dawn, on Wednesday, March 31, fourteen days after my journey and the journey of that unborn child in my womb had ended, I was taken to the hospital to bring that little boy of ours - yours and mine, dear Moritz - into the world, in Lausanne.

I only vaguely recall giving birth. They may well have drugged me up a bit, since they did not trust that I was healthy enough or fit enough to face the task without some assistance. I did not pass out. I was a distant party to the labor pains that continued to increase in strength and frequency. It seemed to me like I was hearing the voice of some other woman struggling through her labor and that I was lying there like a dead woman unable to offer her any help. A mass of faces leaned over me, from the right, from the left, side by side, a vast wide-eyed circle of faces, all wearing masks, beneath the blinding light, while I - and this, at least, I clearly recall - suddenly sat straight up and raised my head to see which one of these faces held my newborn child in the air by its ankles, and I heard a deep voice that seemed to rise from the very depths of some distant well, saying, "Toi, toi, a baby boy", and all around, other voices echoed, "Toi, toi, a baby boy", and I sank back down and closed my eyes and saw you leaning over me and smiling and caressing my sweat-soaked head, repeating this silly little phrase yourself - but how could that be, how could it be that even you, in that distant voice of yours, were saying, "Toi, toi, a baby boy"?

They only brought the child to me in the morning - a son, my son - freshly washed, his two hands balled up into little fists. I opened those fists with extreme caution and counted his little fingers, like any other new mother in the world, straightening them out one by one, and the transparent, fairly pinkish fingernails were a source of wonder to me, as I kissed each one of them and then placed him at my breast, as the nurse who was standing by the bed asked politely, "Do you think you can?" But I did not respond, as my child relaxed there on top of me in my arms like a minor miracle. There was simply nothing like him in the world. The nurse by my bedside, who was keeping an eye on every movement of mine, said in a voice that was rather saturated with real amazement, "What a beautiful, sweet baby your little Yvan Pierre is." I smiled happily in my own amazement, but then suddenly felt like I was being strangled, as I realized that she had just called my little boy 'Yvan Pierre', and I said, "My boy's name is not Yvan Pierre, Madame." I held the infant up at a distance and examined him with the eyes of a mother who sees all. It was indeed my child, but the name was not his name.

The nurse was fearfully confused but managed to say, "Yvan Pierre Mayer is your son, Madame, no one simply gives the children their names. It is written right here, Madame. Is the family name not Mayer?"

"Mayer is the family name," I said as I nodded, and she then replied in a somewhat victorious tone, "If so, then Yvan Pierre is also part of his name. It is written right here, Madame, as I already told you. No one else came up with it. Can it be that you truly don't remember? You don't remember registering his name?"

I did not recall registering anything at all. I was not at all aware that they had already registered my son's name. I was living inside some sort of method that moved along without me, moved rather efficiently, at that, moved mercilessly, grinding me to bits in its wheels - at least that was how I felt at that moment - and my son's name - that son who could not be anything but entirely yours and mine - had also been ground out and emerged as Yvan Pierre when it was spat from the other end of that masterfully methodic machine - a strange-sounding, foreign name, a name so weird that it had never even vaguely crossed my mind even as an option, and I could not manage to recognize that name as his, except that now here was this nurse telling me that it was indeed my son's name. I did not get angry with this nurse - who I could tell, despite the rather confident tone with which she said what she said, was clearly frightfully confused - either because of the fact that when an age-old method begins to collapse there is a serious threat of a real riot, or because of the fact that there is no wisdom in the world that prescribes the manner in which one ought to treat a woman who chooses to part ways with such a method; though then again, perhaps I did not get angry with her because I still remembered what had happened to me the last time I got angry at a nurse just a few days earlier.

"Look," I said to her, "there's no question that a grave mistake has been made here. I want you to show me the registration. I never registered my son's name. Who registered him?"

She was now extremely embarrassed. "This never happened to me before, Madame. All that I know is that when they placed the baby in my care his name came with him. I am not responsible for any mistake, Madame. After I bring little Baby Mayer - forgive me if I refer to him like that - back to his crib in the room with the other newborns, I will go and see if I can get them to clarify this entire situation."

I could not wait. "Go now." Nothing had prepared her for this departure from standard procedure. "I will, Madame, but I must bring the baby back to his crib first."

"The baby stays here with me. Nobody is taking my baby from me until it's clear to me just what sort of world I've ended up in." I was firmer than her.

She begged me, "Madame..."

I looked at my son as he lay in my arms and lustily nursed the milk from my breast, and without lifting my eyes I said, in a voice that verged on a scream, "Go now!"

"It is not allowed, Madame, I am not allowed to leave the child with you without any oversight," she said in a voice dripping with supplication. I did not look at her. I paid no mind to what she said, as I raised my voice even more and said, "Go, or I will get up myself and walk all over this entire hospital."

She could not take it anymore and ran out of the room, casting a rather reproachful glance over her shoulder for a moment in my direction, and the five other women in the room with me, to whom I paid no attention at all, began whispering their shock and amazement to one another from bed to bed, while my boy and I sat in the middle of it, all by ourselves, as though nothing else existed in the entire world but us.

Our son's name was like some sort of guarantee we had pledged to one another. From the day we had found out together for certain that our love was going to bring another child into the world we had begun to discuss possible names. I do not know if you remember everything you ever said - how could you? - but I also do not know what you have forgotten. I, for one, remember everything. You told me that if our baby had not already begun to make his way into the world, then you were of the opinion that if God exists He ought to really hold all new children back in heaven until this awful war had ended, for it was a sin to send children who were not responsible for the destruction of the world to go and live among the ruins. Though then again, you said, perhaps the opposite was true, and it was precisely because there was a God in heaven that He was rushing all the waiting babies up there into the world at once, to try and at least save hope itself from the jaws of all those predatory wolves. I told you that you were waxing philosophical and that one ought not to philosophize with a pregnant woman, one has to stick to the facts, such as - if I am carrying a baby girl inside me then we will call her Esther, after my departed mother, God rest her soul, and if I am carrying a baby boy in my womb then we will call him David, because that was what my father - may he live to a ripe old age - had made me swear in the letter in which he told me that his brother, my uncle David Martin Winkler, had passed away. You tried to make fun of me a bit and said that I had some rather strange notions when it came to the facts, since I myself was saying - 'if it's a boy', and 'if it's a girl', 'if this', and 'if that', and the facts are that these propositions posed certain contradictions in and of themselves.

"No they don't," I replied. "The fact that I am carrying a child is a fact, even if we don't rightly know just what it will be, and whether we will be welcoming a little boy in-to the world or a little girl, that little boy already has a name - that is a fact - and we will refer to him by that name in our hearts until the time when he comes out; and that little girl also already has a name - and that too is a fact - and you and I, and only you and I, will already begin calling her by that name in our hearts, from this point on." You hugged me close and said, "If that's the case then the boy will be called David - if we are to have a boy - and the girl - if it is a girl - will be called Esther. Let God decide for us which soul shall live on in the name."

"God has already decided, Moritz," I said to you, and you immediately responded, "If so, then you have managed to do Him one better, for He only chose one soul, but you have chosen two." I will never forget that talk. Throughout the long days when you were already no longer by my side and I had to carry my child inside me up to this point all by myself, I did not stop carrying those two names around in my heart - David and Esther, Esther and David - and I waited for God to reveal to me which of the two names He had chosen, on that day that my soul longed for so very much. So now, you see, 'Yvan Pierre' was not just some sort of mistake or mix-up. 'Yvan Pier-re' was outright theft.

The nurse came back. She exhaled deeply and said, "The lady in charge is on her way. She asked me to bring you to the room next door. She will wait for you there. According to her, it seems the matter is a rather private affair. Is that okay with you? You are not really allowed to get out of bed yet, but this is rather important. An orderly - there he is already - will help me get you into a wheelchair." They brought me, with my baby in my arms, into the room next door. I was not surprised to find that the lady in charge who was waiting for me there holding a bundle of documents was already well-known to me from my previous encounter with her in the general admissions ward. She had the same air of authority, the same overall appearance as before, the very same outfit.

"I told you, Madame Mayer, that you would be back, but I did not know that we would be seeing one another again. Let me first tell you that they told me that you gave birth to your son like a real heroine. I had no doubts on that score. You came to us a heroine and you gave birth here a heroine. This will not be forgotten. I wish you and your baby well. You were admitted by our department. Here is your file in my hand. I understand that you were shocked when the nurse called your son by his name. What else could she call him, though? That is his name, Madame. There is no mistake whatsoever. Here, I have brought the documents, have a look at them." She handed me a form but I refused to even look at it. She put the paper back in the bundle that she had in her hands and continued, "You were brought here to us barely conscious. As far as we are concerned you were, in fact, unconscious. When we asked you to sign the papers you were not able to do so. The military doctor, who took such good care of you throughout the long and winding road from La Cure, authorized it, and when he recommended, or we recommended, that he sign as your legal guardian, you authorized him to do so, both with a wisp of your voice and a nod of the head, and he duly signed. The signature was critical. In your case it was of the utmost importance. The doctor was of the opinion that you were going to probably need to undergo a caesarian birth, and he stipulated in writing that whatever might happen - and there were quite a number of possibilities - if the baby should turn out to be a boy his name would be Yvan Pierre. You appointed him, Madame Mayer. He signed in your name, and made his notes in your name, you authorized the whole thing, including everything he wrote down, it is all legally binding, Madame Mayer, even if you do not recall a thing. He did not leave any instructions in the event that the baby should turn out to be a girl. But that does not matter. You had a boy."

Everything was so very clear, so legally binding, so well-organized. I could not possibly have any objections. But I tried all the same. "I never authorized that man to give my child a name. He had no right. Legal guardians are not responsible for naming babies. Perhaps I was barely conscious, perhaps I was entirely unconscious, but now I have all my wits about me. When you sent me to the jailhouse I was fully conscious, and when I came back here I was likewise fully conscious. At that point I no longer had any need for a legal guardian. Why were you in such a rush? The name that was given to my baby is completely mistaken, from every point of view, any way you look at it, even the way you all seem to look at it, even from the point of view of the well-ordered world that seems so important to all of you. I am asking you to change the name. Nothing could be clearer or more self-evident than that."

Not a single muscle moved in the face of the woman who stood before me. "That is impossible at this point, Madame Mayer. It has already been registered. The name has already been sent to Bern. Of course, you can file a legal complaint. I do not recall such a thing ever happening before, and so I do not have any experience with the filing of such complaints, but I am sure that you still have the right to file such a complaint, just like any other individual - even if you are a refugee. But the way things stand right now, the child that you gave birth to - a wonderful, healthy child, that should be nothing but a source of considerable joy to you - this child's name is Yvan Pierre Mayer. It is a rather pretty name, Madame." And she left the room. I was left sitting there in my wheelchair. The nurse gently took the baby from me and brought him to his crib. The orderly asked to wheel me back into my room. "Give me a minute," I told him, and he walked out. I sat there staring straight ahead at nothing at all, my eyes dry, and my lips pursed and sealed in the face of all the words I knew, since not a single one of them seemed capable of expressing anything of any real significance anymore.

All the other women lying in their beds in my room were graced with visitors during the hours set aside for such. But not me. This mere fact was enough to form a sort of unseen partition between us, for despite the fact that women who have just recently given birth in the hospital all seem rather similar to one another, the fact is that I was somehow different. However, two or three days later I was notified to my complete surprise that I had a number of important visitors, who were waiting for me in a special room reserved for guests of the hospital. A trainee nurse helped me get washed up, combed my hair, gave me a robe and accompanied me to receive my visitors who were, in fact, rather important in the eyes of the hospital staff.

I entered the room and three people - two men and a woman - got up from their seats and offered me their congratulations, as one of them said to me, "*Mazal Tov,* Madame Mayer - French? German? Yiddish?"

"German," I said. "Thank you."

I did not know if they were Jews and that that was why they had said *Mazal Tov,* or if they were not in fact Jews but wanted to somehow communicate to me in what they considered to be the language of the Jews that they were happy to be there visiting with me. All that I had learned in the course of the few days that I had spent so far in Switzerland was that it was a country where everything was very official, and so even these visitors - once they had come to see me - were official guests, and three in number, as befitting an official delegation, and so even their words of congratulations had to be official and so their *Mazal Tov,* for that matter, was merely a formality, and it was all the same whether it was officially Jewish or not. The features of the man's face, along with those of the other two visitors who had come with him, were duly pleasant and smiling, and I had no idea whether they reflected a sense of satisfaction at the fulfilment of *Bikur Cholim,* the commandment to visit an invalid - in turn causing these visitors to feel good about themselves for having done so - or if they were in fact truly happy to see a healthy mother who had only recently given birth to a brand-new baby boy after the troubles and hardships of a journey they had perhaps heard a little something about. I was reserved and cautious and waited for the three of them to say something.

"My name is Mr. Dreyfus," the seeming spokesman said. "I am the president of the Jewish community in Lausanne. This lady here and my brother are members of the community's board of directors. How are you feeling, Madame Mayer?" I replied, in rather clipped fashion, that I felt fine. The man was extremely polite. Everything that he said was accompanied by the nodding agreement of the other two visitors, who had not yet uttered a single word themselves. The protocol, he explained to me precisely and patiently, is that the authorities immediately notify the Jewish community organizations in Switzerland when an illegal Jewish refugee has been taken in, and these organizations, in turn, in accordance with an agreement that was reached on the very eve of the war, guarantee the maintenance and related expenses of said Jewish refugee, who is considered a prisoner by virtue of the crime of having illegally entered the country - a status that remains until the refugee's stay in the Confederation comes to an end.

"We thank God," said Mr. Dreyfus, "that during these awful times when God has hidden His face from our fellow brethren among the Children of Israel, and they are being hunted down throughout the confines of the countries at war, we - who, thank God, live in the relative security of a country that has been spared this world's war - have been called upon to do what little we can on behalf of our people." He stopped for a moment, perhaps in order to add a certain resonance to these words of his and let them truly sink in - words that seemed to me to have been rather well-prepared in advance and were now sort of being read forth from some written scroll. I remained silent, as he continued. "Please look upon this community of ours in Lausanne as a personal pillar of support, and do not hesitate at all to turn to us for anything that you might need. Of course, the overall responsibility has been assumed by the National Union of Jewish Communities. They are the ones who took care of your children and found an excellent arrangement for them, in complete accordance with the evident requirements, of course, of two young Jewish boys. The government of Switzerland does not make even the slightest move without first consulting the Union. We are here as their representatives, as it were. We have rather excellent news concerning your children, and we have already approached the authorities on your behalf to request that they speed up the process of authorizing a visit between you. That is no easy matter, as you know, they are where they are by law, and you are he-re by law, and they are not allowed to leave their location without official consent, and you, likewise, can not leave your own location without authorization. This is all rather unpleasant, but let us admit rather frankly that this is a price that anyone in their right mind would be more than willing to pay in order to be saved from hell."

Here he stopped once more for a moment. I once again limited myself to saying, "Thank you," and waited for him to continue. This time it was his brother who spoke, in almost the identical voice, and certainly with the identical tone. "The doctors have told us that the baby is a healthy boy, thank God, and I am sure that you would like to ask us about the matter of a *Bris*, a circumcision ceremony. You did not ask anyone at the hospital, as we already know. If you had, they would have approached us about the matter. But you did not ask and no one has approached us, yet we see ourselves as obligated to help out in that regard in any event. We told ourselves that you may well be bothered on that score but not know what it is permissible for you to request. And so we came to you of our own accord, and here we are. We are the Jewish community. You can ask us anything you want. Would you like to have a *Bris* for your son?" He waited for my response. I had never in my life imagined that there were any Jewish mothers anywhere who did not see the Bris as a sort of ex-tension of giving birth to a boy, but I understood from the tone of his question that the leaders of the community in Lausanne were afraid that such women did indeed exist these days, and that the hidden face of the Lord to which Mr. Dreyfus had referred was a two-way street, and so the community had to take care not to be blamed for trying to force itself on women such as myself. He had no idea just how bothered I was about the idea of having a *Bris* and that, until now, I indeed had had no idea who to turn to in that regard. The *Bris*, as far as I was concerned, was the only possible corrective that I might apply to 'Yvan Pierre', for I knew that I was never going to file a complaint with any of the authorities anywhere, if only because I was sure that there was no office that would even agree to receive my complaint. It may well be that the-re is a law that decides who is allowed to give a name to a child that is not their own, but there is also a law that determines just who is an illegal refugee. I did not think of the *Bris* as the covenant of our forefather Abraham, nor did I think of the *Bris* as a sort of oath taken by the mother that the fruit of her loins was a Jew. I thought of the *Bris* solely in terms of a covenant between me and my son, an oath that I owed him the name David, and that I was obligated - in this world that is threatening to turn all of us into a veritable fleet of unmoored canoes, set of from the pier and set adrift on a sea with no shore in sight - obligated to bind him by this name to me, and to you, and to his forefathers and distant ancestors. Only the ritual of the *Bris* could give my son his name back, that name that he had had even before he was born, and which had been stolen away from him when they signed for the theft and sealed it with the seal of their Confederation. It is a big word, that - 'Confederation' - a rather big word.

Now I could talk. "How can I thank you for the fact that you have come on behalf of my son's *Bris*. God only knows that I can not fully be considered to have brought him into the world until he has his *Bris*, until he duly enters into that covenant, in accordance with the custom of our forefathers. I did not make any inquiries. I was afraid that they would tell me that I only had the right to receive the services of a doctor, and I had no idea how to explain to them what a *Bris* is, and how to ask them exactly if there is a Mohel, a ritual circumciser, in Lausanne, and whether the authorities would allow me to call on him, and if they did, then who would pay, and if they would say no to the *Bris* but yes to letting a doctor perform it, then would I be allowed - or, what's more, would I even be able to say that I do not want the doctor to do it, or would I be forced to accept their decision for lack of a better choice and simply preferring to have a doctor do it than not to have it done at all."

The woman looked at me, as though monitoring every movemy lips made, placed her hand on my arm and said, "You are feeling emotional, Madame Mayer. But know that you are not alone in the world. There will be a Bris. There will be a proper Mohel. There will be a *Minyan*, a quorum of men, and there will be a Sandak, a godfather. Mr. Dreyfus, the president of our community, will serve as the Sandak, which is to say that the entire community of Lausanne will be your son's godfather, Madame Mayer. It is a great honor that you are doing the community. One might even call it an act of kindness. So many hopes are riding on the *Bris* of your son. I could not possibly explain it, but I can tell you that this is, at least, the way that I feel. We have a rather good relationship with the hospital and with the authorities - isn't that so, Mr. Dreyfus? - I might even say that we have an extremely good relationship with them. We will have the *Bris* here. They will provide us with a small but rather suitable hall. There will be invited guests - the Rabbi, the *Chazan*, the cantor, the leaders of the congregation, and Captain Galopin - I don't know if you remember him - who asked us to invite him as well. He specifically requested it. Personally. I went to see him at his request. I hope that you will have no objections. I think it is actually rather touching."

I could not hold back and asked her, "Did you also invite the doctor?"

Mr. Dreyfus, the president of the community, immediately responded, saying, "That is just not done. I do not even know if the
doctor in charge of the delivery was a man or a woman - though
perhaps you were referring to the military doctor, who, as far as we
were told, essentially saved your life? Perhaps we really ought to
have invited him..." And he turned to the other two and asked them,
"What do you both think?"

The woman immediately responded, "I already thought of that.
But I told myself that it would simply put him in an embarrassing
position. After all, I do not know to what extent he would like to
publicize the fact that he was the one who decided personally to
break the law. Praise the Lord that there are people like him, but
there are those who would say that in these days when we all live
under a constant threat to our homeland, one must first and foremost remember that one is Swiss - being a hu-manist is all too easy.
Though there are those who would say just the opposite. Such as
Captain Galopin, for example. This military doctor did his part. He
is cer-tainly proud of the fact that he did. I was told that he requested that the child be cal-led Yvan Pierre - which is either his name, or
his father's name, I am not sure on that score, some people have the
first custom, whereas others observe the second - as a sort of tribute
to the finest deed he ever did in his entire life, that much I am certain
of. At least I heard that that is what he told someone, though I can
not quite recall who that was."

President Dreyfus, who clearly knew nothing of all this, said,
"I think we will just let that one go, unless you absolutely want the
doctor who saved you to be invited. If that is your wish, then we
will certainly do our best to locate him. What do you say, Madame
Mayer?"

I had tears in my eyes. "You have already done much more than
a woman like me could have possibly expected of you," I said. I felt
a tear begin to roll down my cheek, as I added, "Thank you," though
I could not manage anything more than that.

The woman wiped away my tear with her own handkerchief and
said, "You are crying, Madame Mayer. I completely understand you.
I know precisely why you are crying."

I got up. I could not remain seated any longer. She so very much did not know why I was crying.

Mr. Dreyfus clearly felt as though his work was not yet finished and so he said, as though rising to take his leave of me himself, "Your son's name - Yvan Pierre, if I have heard correctly - is his secular name. His Jewish name will of course be confer-red at the *Bris*, and that is how he will be registered with our community. Have you already thought of a name, Madame Mayer? There is no rush, although we do prefer to have everything prepared in advance, though of course you will not actually be causing any real delay if you wait until the *Bris* itself to communicate the name to the Mohel. Have you already thought of a name?" I shook my head and said, "I will do some more thinking, Mr. Dreyfus, with your permission I will do some more thinking."

The woman said, "Of course, of course, I understand how complicated that can be, Madame Mayer. We have all the time in the world."

There was a *Bris*, Moritz. Your son's name is David. David ben, son of, Moshe Leib. There was a *Minyan*. There was more than a Minyan. Even Galopin came. But you were not there. Erwin was not there. Jackie was not there. My father was not there. Your father and mother were not there. Your brother was not there. Your sister was not there. My brothers and sister were not there. Andor was not there. The Schecks were not there. The Baums were not there. The Renicks were not there. None of them could make it. I was all alone, Moritz, alone with my son David. But do you know who was there? The concierge from Marseille, and the officers who had interrogated us on the train, and the policeman from Annemasse, and the nuns, the nuns were there too, and the innkeeper and his wife and their son Phillip, and the neighbor from Saint-Claude, with his wife and his bicycle, and the security guard from the maternity ward at the hospital there, and the border patrol guards at La Cure.

All these people were there, along with every single man and woman that had crossed my path from the day you left, headed I know not where, until the day that I completed my journey - along with the ultimate salvation of our sons, Erwin and Jackie - that day that our new son David had his *Bris* and entered into the covenant.

I saw them all. But I did not see Fernand-Ferdinand. He was not there. He had disappeared into the snows and never found his way back to me. I also did not see the military doctor, though I truly wanted to. I owe him so very much. But he was not there. Perhaps he was embarrassed. Who knows. Perhaps there was another woman to be saved at the border. Another baby on the way. Another Yvan Pierre - God only knows. And the last one of them all - he was late, for some reason he came late - the priest was there too. I saw him in his habit, smiling at everyone, and I heard him saying, 'I am Doctor Albert DuPont', and I wanted to ask him where he had come from, and where he had disappeared to, but he was already gone. And then everyone else was gone too - the *Minyan*, the *Mohel*, the *Chazan*, the Rabbi, the *Sandak*, Mr. Dreyfus, along with his brother, and that woman who had taken such pity on me - they were all gone, gone wherever it was that they went, and I was left all alone, holding our son David in my arms.

I am writing these last lines after they already released me from the Le Rosier Camp, and transferred me and our newborn son to a boarding house, or at least what had once been a boarding house and has now been officially designated as a holding center for illegal refugees such as myself. The living conditions are not all that bad. I have a room, and there is a wooden crib in the room for the baby, and David, the sweet child that he is, sleeps just like a prince in that crib of his. I have said that these will be my final lines because I am incapable of writing anymore. From this point on - and I do not know how long that will be - weeks, months, years, who knows? - nothing else whatsoever will occur. In this land of the lakes time itself will turn into a lake, a lake from whose look it will be impossible to tell if it still recalls or has in fact forgotten all the foaming, wild fury of the rivers that rushed down the rocky slopes to gather in its depths and form that very lake itself.

What could I say of the time that stands still after all that I wrote of the time that rushed past? Not a word. I will be a prisoner. I will live my life. Not a soul will threaten my existence. I have a place to rest my head. I will have what to eat. That will have to suffice. The children are attending a school for the first time in their lives, and they will certainly continue to attend that school properly. They wrote to me once more. They told me that they were doing fine. They have been granted permission to come visit me. They will be here in May. Madame Frieda Gantert also wrote me. She is a wonderful woman. She will take the train with the boys from their distant village to come see me, and she will stay two days with them here and then take them back with her to Eglisau. I am sure it will all happen again. I will get to see them, they will get to see me. But we will not quite have what we once did until the war finally ends and we are deported, and you, wherever you are, will make it out alive - I still swear you will - and be free, and you and I will once again set off on our respective journeys - each one searching for the other - and then, too, there will be nothing for me to write. For why would I write - if we find each other, then there will be no need to write, and if we do not find each other, then whom would I be writing to, and so everything that I have written up to this point is complete and has now come to an end.

I am a woman in custody. Madame Winistorfer - whose official title is 'Boarding House Manager' - is responsible for me. Everything is very well-organized here, even the titles. This woman receives her salary from the government, and she is re-quired to treat all those who are ordered to live at her place to the best possible service available, without getting too close to any of her charges. But you can relax. She is not all that strict about observing these rules. Just a day or two after I got here she began visiting my room and telling me all about her troubles and her concerns, and, when it would be time to leave me, she would remind me not to tell a soul about the fact that we had begun talking to one another the way that friends talk, and under no circumstances was I to repeat to anyone the actual content of our conversations. In any event, I am including her name and our address here, Avenue de Riant-Mont 6-8, Lausanne. I am placing everything in a large envelope with our names on it, and it is ready at any moment. On the day that I will finally have heard from someone, man or woman, that they have seen you, or from the Red Cross, to whom I have already turned with Madame's help - when that minor miracle will finally take place, and I will know where you are, where you are located, what your address is, then I will seal the envelope and send you everything. And I will not at all be afraid that the envelope will get lost on the way, or that someone might open it up and confiscate the things that I have written, or erase the sections that your captors might think it better if you did not know. And when that happens, then you will know where to find me, or at least where to start looking for me, in the event that life has already taken me on to further places that I can not even imagine, but which can anyway be reached by star-ting out from that rather well-known point of departure. And maybe I will write once more.

Perhaps the war is not yet over. Perhaps in this world that we have gotten caught up in there is no such thing as time that stands still like a completely peaceful lake, for even such a lake is surrounded by manmade cities, towns, and villages, and even though on the surface of things it all seems calm and perfectly quiet, there are creatures lurking all around, and they whip time itself into a frenzy, forcing it to dash headlong back into the storm, into all that can not be avoided. That is what these creatures do, in their folly, everywhere, always. There is no street or alleyway or single solitary location anywhere in the world that is filled with men and women and still capable - and if capable, then willing, for that matter - to close its doors to that madness that is always waiting there in the doorway like evil itself.

And if that will be the case, then I will write once more. From the eye of the storm. For if I do not write then I myself will not be able to believe that what I remember could actually ever have truly happened, and is not rather a mere product of my own imagination.

AFTERWORD

With the birth of my baby brother David - Yvan Pierre - my mother, may she rest in peace, put down her pen, and did not write another single word to my father, Moritz Mayer. I do not know, and have no way of ever knowing, if she did so because she had independently come to the conclusion that ltters which can no longer reach their intended destination ought not to even be written to begin with, or perhaps because once she had been saved and given birth to her baby boy - both of which rather verged on the miraculous - her life had assumed much more minor dimensions and no longer seemed worthy in her eyes of being documented.

But the journey was not yet over. This single, solitary woman was from this point on a prisoner for all intents and purposes in one of the boarding houses that the Swiss had set up in order to absorb all those who illegally crossed the border. David - and I will refer to him solely by that name from this point on - was there with her. She provided for herself and little David - including the expenses related to their stay under house arrest - out of the barely sufficient pittance allotted to her by the government of the Confederation, along with an additional subsidy provided by the Organization of Jewish Communities, who had assumed the responsibility, before the appropriate authorities, to cover the expenses incurred by every Jew who entered Switzerland illegally.

Meanwhile, the two of us - my brother Yakov (Jackie), and

myself (Erwin) - were transferred to a little village in Eglisau, along the banks of the Rhine, and were placed in the care of Fraulein Frieda - a devout Christian woman, who, in her youth, had studied theology at an English university, and provided us with an exacting education based on proper manners and behavior, a love of labor, respect for all creatures, and complete fidelity to our Jewish heritage. A philanthropist by the name of Gideon paid her salary as required by the government.

The separation from our mother was difficult for both her and us, though I do not recall ever hearing my mother lament the bitter blows that fate had dealt her, nor did she ever cry in my presence over the loss of my father, nor did we feel like orphans in Eglisau. Years later, when I returned to Eglisau as the Israeli Ambassador to Switzerland, at a reception in which the entire village participated, they hung a huge sign that read:

Das Flüchtlingskind ist wieder da - 'The refugee child has returned.'

We had indeed been refugee children, and as such, we were a part of the Swiss war scene. During that same visit I met up once more with the teacher who had since become an old man, and used to teach a wide range of boys of varying ages in a single classroom at the school. He had kept a copy of a certificate that I had been awarded, on which was written 'Bravo Erwin!,' and it was signed 'Heinrich Himmler,' which was his name.

After about a year in the village, the authorities had decided that we were to join our mother in Lausanne, where she had in the meantime been transferred from the boarding house to an apartment for prisoners. But we could not stay with her. She had no means of providing for us and so we were transferred to all sorts of institutions that had been established on behalf of refugee children in the abandoned hotels that once hosted tourists in that mountainous region. My mother was not even able to continue providing for David out of her meager subsidies. There was a priest, who excelled at providing humanitarian aid for refugees, who turned to a devout Christian woman and asked her to take David into her care. The child called her 'Mutti', while he referred to our mother - who visited him once a week - as 'Mammi.' To this day, David and Mutti's older daughter, Franny - whom I located by chance over fifty years after we had left Switzerland - still refer to one another as brother and sister.

The war ended in May, 1945, and in March, 1946 we made *Aliyah* to the Promised Land. By that point the fate of the majority of survivors was known, but the fate of the majority of those who had perished remained unknown. The news that my fa-ther had died in Auschwitz was a palpable reality, but there was no real concrete proof. In July or August of 1945 the Swiss had already sent us deportation orders. One bureaucratic arm ordered us deported to Belgium, for that was the home that we had left when we first began to run for our lives at the beginning of the war, while another arm of the law ordered us to be deported to Romania, because that was the country in which my father, God rest his soul, had citizenship, or to Hungary, the country where my mother, who now rests in heaven, was born.

All the people that my parents had known in Belgium before the war had perished. My grandfather and grandmother in Romania, along with all their children and relatives, perished. My grandparents in Hungary, along with all the members of their family, were wiped out in Auschwitz. There was no place for us to be deported to. One of the members of the Zionist movement among the refugees in Switzerland showed me an album one day containing pictures of white houses, with a sign hanging from one of them that said, 'Shoemaker', in Hebrew, and a palm tree at the end of the street.

The Hebrew letters, which I did not yet know how to read, made off with my heart. My mother said that if we did not have any place to go back to then we would go somewhere where it would be possible to make a new beginning. Yakov and I received certificates under the guise of pioneer settlers, while my mother, along with David, hoodwinked the Swiss authorities and joined us in traveling to Marseille, where we boarded the ship known as the 'Champollion', which was carrying a few hundred legal immigrants along with a few thousand illegal stowaways who had boarded the ship with the help of members of the *Hagana,* dressed in Jewish Brigade uniforms. My mother and David were among the stowaways. On the high seas the members of the *Hagana* tore up the certificates that only a few of the passengers had and the entire ship thus became one big boatload of illegal refugees that was captured by the British, and all the passengers were transferred to the Atlit Detainee Camp.

The trucks and buses that were to take us from the port to the detainee camp were filled with the passengers from the boat, while on either side of the road, just beyond the fences, stood thousands of people already living in the country who would come to Haifa whenever the word went out that another ship of refugees had arrived. They were all shouting names in the hope that one of their relatives might answer them after having been saved from the conflagration that had consumed Europe. That was where we suddenly heard a woman's voice shouting 'Winkler' over and over again - my mother's maiden name. It was her sister Olga, whom my mother had described in her letter to my father. So it turned out that we had a relative in the Promised Land.

My brother Yakov was accepted into one of the institutions for Youth Immigration, while my mother, little David, and I went to live with Olga in Bnei Brak, in the single rented room where she lived with her husband - who had returned from captivity - along with their eldest son, Dov. My mother found work as a seamstress in the 'Ora' Youth Center in Bnei Brak. Meanwhile, I spent the summer a barefoot vagabond. There was no room for me in the house, and out in the street I did not yet speak the language. I spent long days visiting my brother at the institution where he lived in Ra'anana, but there was not really any place for me there either.

Before the start of the 1946-47 academic year, my mother reached an agreement with the Center where she worked whereby they would take me in if I paid for the cost of my maintenance. She found me work with a carpenter who made children's toys, and I worked four hours a day in his shop. Some time later I was hired as an assistant counselor at 'Ora', and later I became a full counselor myself. I enrolled at the 'Zeitlin' School in Tel Aviv, and I used to do my homework every day aboard the No. 54 bus.

In 1949 my mother's religious-legal status as an *Agunah*, an abandoned wife, was resolved. We were informed that my father Moritz Mayer had been sent to Auschwitz from Drancy in September, 1943, as part of Transport 59. We were told that only seventeen of the more than a thousand people included in that Transport were not put to death the very day that they arrived. Someone passed on the information that my father had been among those 17 who were spared, and that he was last seen in 1944. At that point we no longer know what happened to him, and there is no one in the world who knows the day he died or where his body found its final resting place. Some time later my mother got remarried to one Yitzchak Yisroel, a first cousin of my father's who had lost his first wife and all five of his children in Auschwitz. The day that she remarried I took it upon myself to say *Kaddish*, the mourner's prayer, for my father on Yom Kippur. I refused to accept the Tenth of the Hebrew month of Teves - which was recognized as the official day for the recital of an annual inclusive *Kaddish* - as my own day of remembrance. My father had died alone. Yom Kippur became the day on which I commemorated his aloneness. I did not consult with either Yakov or David when it came to this. I did not even talk to my mother about it.

The person that my mother married was a God-fearing man who was strict in his observance of all the religious commandments, both major and minor. He treated my mother's grandchildren in a paternal, loving fashion. They all called him 'Grandpa'. He and my mother opened a small grocery store in Netanya, where they worked quite hard for many years. I was no longer living at home, I had moved to Jerusalem, where I worked as a counselor at the Children's Home in Motza while attending the Hebrew University at the Terra Santa building, along with being an active member of the 'Yavneh' Student Union, led by Yehuda Blum, Ephraim Halevy, Gavriel Cohen, Simcha Rakover, and myself. I barely earned enough to get by. When I would come for a visit, my mother, may she rest in peace, had the habit of slipping me a few liras, making sure that her husband did not notice. When I tried to refuse the money the first time, she burst into tears and said, "You won't even let me do this...?" and I never turned her down again.

Yakov could not quite adjust to the 'Aliyah' institute to which he had been transferred. He did not want to study. So he left, returned to our mother's place in Netanya, and began working as an apprentice to a diamond dealer. Some time later, he enlisted in the army and joined the theater troupe for the Northern Region, with whom he performed as a supporting actor in the play, 'Moishe Ventilator', alongside Yaakov Bodo. The lifestyle of the troupe, including long trips to distant locations to perform on Friday night - at a time when Sabbath observance was not all that strict in the army ranks in Israel - depressed my brother. He left the troupe and joined a 'Geulim' cell on the religious kibbutz Tirat Zvi.

After completing his military service, Yakov decided to dedicate himself to completing what he had dropped in a sort of secretive bitterness - his education. He did not have a high school certificate. He was hired as a counselor at the Children's Home in Motza, where I had worked as a counselor myself, and where my future wife had also worked as a counselor, and where our youngest brother David was a student. Yakov diligently dedicated himself to his studies day and night. It was there that he met Mika Arzi, whom he eventually married. It was not long before they brought two children - a son and a daughter - into the world. Yakov was accepted at the Hebrew University and became one of the top students in the Philosophy Department. He earned his living teaching in Ein Kerem and at a high school right near the university, and was known for being a rather creative instructor. He soon began teaching at the university level as well, in Beer Sheva. During the Six Day War, his study companion from university days, Major General Tal, chose to recruit him for the unit run by Uri Ben Ari. He was in the first tank that broke through at Givat HaMivtar into Jerusalem and was killed by what is referred to these days as 'friendly fire.' He left behind his wife Mika, who never remarried, his son Moshe - now Dr. Moshe Mayer - and his daughter Chani.

Our mother never recovered from the loss which fundamentally shook what remained of her faith in justice and its concomitant kindness. She began to fade in the year 1967. Her relatives interpreted the change in her condition as a neurotic form of sorrow. But I knew what it was. Her soul was slowly leaving and it was simply too much to bear.

David, the boy who was born into this world already orphaned of his father, was a young soldier when those bullets took his brother away from him as well. He grew up in our mother's home and never once referred to his biological father, but he never stopped digging for an instant to try and locate any possible scrap of information concerning him. I, for my part, had a rather clear memory of my father, but I do not recall David ever asking me anything about him - not what he looked like, nor what his voice sounded like, nor how he carried himself, nor what his life was like, nor how he died. He searched for the information all by himself. When Yakov, whom he knew and loved, fell in battle, he mourned him as though he was mourning a father. He studied economics at the university, married Carmela Friedman, and fathered four sons. He named his eldest son Yakov.

I never knew how to tell my own story. I never really spent time in what could be considered the family home, other then the period until the age of six at our apartment in Belgium. I have worked to support myself since the age of twelve. I quickly picked up the Hebrew language. From the time of my earliest adolescence I already began writing poems and plays for children and young adults in Hebrew, but my greatest love was and remains education. I have had the luck to work as a counselor, a teacher, an administrator, and to serve as the head of the Yemin Orde Youth Village for eighteen years, in addition to serving as the Head of the Department of International Torah Education and as a member of the Administrative

Board of the Jewish Agency, along with lecturing regularly and giving classes in Jewish Ethics until this very day. My great love for the
language and education has been amplified by a deep involvement
in social matters. I was and remain a dedicated follower of Pluralis-
tic Judaism, which draws its nourishment from the age-old sources
while incorporating a healthy dose of the many thousands of other
flavors that fill the world.

I spent many years working as an emissary around the world,
both as an educator and a diplomat, sometimes even working un-
dercover. The field of education afforded me the opportunity to do
some of the most meaningful work possible. Representing Israel as
the Ambassador to Belgium - from which I had escaped during the
war - and serving as the Ambassador to Switzerland where I had
been a refugee at a time when the State of Israel did not even yet
exist, brought me the greatest possible honor that little Erwin could
ever have earned.

I love my life in every single sense of the word. My wife Riv-
ka, née Gormezno - a painter and teacher - and I were married at
Kibbutz Shluchot in the Beit Shean Valley, in 1957. We are the
proud parents of three daughters. The eldest, Esther, named after
my mother's mother, is an author and painter. My second daughter,
Efrat, is an actress and educator and bears the name of my wife's
mother. My youngest daughter, Dr. Chayele Mayer, bears the name
of my father's mother. They all love Yiddish, as well as Ladino, and
they all inhabit worlds that no longer exist, breathing new life into
lost souls from whom we were sadly separated.

More than any child might fairly admit, I humbly acknowledge
that from the time I was a little boy I was rather intimately familiar
with the private conversation my mother carried on with life itself. I
am well aware that she told herself that though the rough waters of
the world had risen against us to drag us off into the deep, she had
emerged battered but victorious.

Her sister Manya, who stole across the border into Switzerland before her, tossing her infant child over the barbed wire fence,

was left with a child who suffered from considerable brain damage, which the medical establishment never managed to repair. Olga, her youngest sister, who was widowed as a young woman, lost one son, Moti, in the War of Attrition, and lost her second son to a fatal illness. She herself died while my mother was still alive. The cursed war continued to chase down the survivors even as far as the Promised Land. But my mother now looked happily on those two boys of hers who had traipsed alongside her through the snows, along with her last child, David, whom she had carried with her to the one place where it was still possible to bring a baby into the world in those days. We put down roots in the Promised Land. It was not all white houses and the lettering here was not always clear, but her sons turned this land into her own homeland. I do not know what prayers she offered up when she did pray. But I do know that she offered up a prayer of thanksgiving for the victory that had not come without its share of bitter poison.

In 1967 her world was completely destroyed. My brother Yakov fell in battle. It was then that my mother truly died, though she died once more, one final time, on the eve of Sukkot, in 1975. I was in London at the time. I was given the bitter news on my way to the synagogue for Sukkot prayers. I missed the funeral. My brother Yakov was buried in Jerusalem during the Six Day War before the family even knew that he had died. I missed his funeral as well. Though I missed my father's too.

But I have written out the letter that my mother wrote my father, and I can hear the soft murmur of their lips still moving in their graves.

Yitzchak Mayer
October 2010